MW01600270

Dear Kathleen,
   An importa
that the moral
are strongly influenced by the beliefs, words,
and actions of the friends one makes. We
both are blessed to share Jim Glessner as

BORDER OF LILIES

a friend with whom we can reflect about
the serious and ## AND laugh at the
humorous circumstances of our lives. May
we continue ## MAPLES to do so in
health, happiness, peace, and prosperity.
                    All the best,
                    J. Barry

JOSEPH BARRY GURDIN

Joseph Barry Gurdin

PublishAmerica
Baltimore

First printing

ISBN: 1-4137-4914-3
PUBLISHED BY PUBLISHAMERICA, LLLP
www.publishamerica.com
Baltimore

Printed in the United States of America

*To my wife, Rita Jeruchimowicz Jeremy,
and our son, Boaz Nathaniel Gurdin,
whose love and support made telling
this story possible.
And to the attentive ears, keen minds, and
aesthetic sensibilities of the scholars of the
Canadian Studies Program of
The University of California, Berkeley,
who provided me with a welcoming forum
to air some of the contents of this book.*

CHAPTER 1

"You know, I could graduate in March, and I've been accepted into graduate school in anthropology, and I'd like to go, but if you tell me 'You're going to be drafted,' 'We're not going to allow you the normal four year deferment,' then, I'll simply choose not to file the computer card that will make me graduate, and, instead, will complete my pre-med requirements."

In her late fifties, the short, thin, plainly-dressed woman with horn-rimmed glasses replied, "Well, Mr. Green, we can't really say exactly what this new executive order means or how it's going to be enforced. On the surface, I'd say you're taking your chances if you graduate in advance and continue in graduate school. On the other hand, the way things are in Vietnam, you never know; it might be a very short-lived thing."

"Well, if you were me," Henry asked with scrunching eyes, "what'd you do in my shoes?"

"Sir, I really can't say. It's your decision to make."

Henry never liked to gamble with bureaucracies. Given his totally insecure childhood—father dead at two, mother continually ill, his being shifted from one household or school to another, about the only thing he had come to count on outside of himself were his meager Social Security checks which would keep on coming until the end of his twenty-first year as long as he stayed in school. And he had had to threaten his mother's sister's husband with a court case to get these. Until he was almost nineteen, his southern uncle—never his legal guardian—had taken these checks and passed them on to his mother, while proclaiming to her and the world that he was giving her this money out of his own pocket. It was only in Henry's first year in university where he had made friends with a lawyer and philosopher that he had learned that he was entitled to these funds. On investigation at his local Social Security Office, he had learned that this money was being sent to his wealthy uncle.

On April 4, 1968, just after his graduation, a white southerner, James Earl Ray, assassinated Martin Luther King, Jr., in Memphis, Tennessee, and Henry attended memorial services for Dr. King at an Episcopal Church just off campus in Los Angeles. One of his great heroes had been killed. For Henry, Martin Luther King Jr. was fighting for the rights of all Americans, and he sensed that his work had greatly advanced the cause of equality and justice. But Henry had watched these events more from the outside. His family were southern Reform Jews, but very intermarried; his sister had converted to her husband's Catholic faith when she had married just after high school, and he had been raised by his father's brother's wife, who was from a family of rural Methodists.

Indeed, in high school, he had been required to attend the local Methodist church and had neither been Bar Mitzvahed nor confirmed into the religion of his ancestors. Inspired by democratic socialist, non-observant Jews from New York who had worked in the Jewish Community Center where he had been a junior counselor one summer, he began to read and identify with the Bund and the Jewish Labor Movement. This philosophy made sense to him. His was the only Jewish family under the poverty line in his town, and his wealthy relatives never helped them out of this rut despite strong family values and rather conservative views about state aid. When he had worked for the Job Corps, he felt brotherhood with the other poor young men with whom he had worked, although his idealism had been hurt when he had lived through a racial brawl that had broken out on his crew. He had taken a sanguine attitude that he had a job to lose, had run to the nearby home and had called the police before the local news got word of it. It had been quickly stopped, and that had been that, no mention of it in the media. Of course, only the black teenagers involved in the fight were arrested and charged with profanity by the local white police—*iustitia americana.*

Henry felt good about himself but very unsure about "the times." He had managed to finish his B.A. in a little over two and a half years from the University of California while working twenty hours a week in a variety of odd jobs—dishwashing, serving in the line of a cafeteria, construction, researching and designing signs for a zoo, clearing parks and urban trenches for President Johnson's Job Corps, babysitting, working nights at the Crazy Burger and a fifteen-hour-a-week regular job at the UC Library. Still, he knew he could not have afforded UCLA without receiving his father's survivors' benefits from the Social Security Administration. By that time he had sensed that he had discovered his life's work, anthropology, and had learned where many of his talents and weaknesses lay. With attractive and intelligent women, he had been successful and his need for their bodily warmth had been fulfilled when his tight schedule permitted. Despite this luck, he was on edge. In December 1967, President Johnson had eliminated graduate deferments.

Ten days after he had entered the M.A. program in anthropology, Henry received notice to report for his physical at the downtown induction center on Broadway in Los Angeles toward the end of his quarter. Meanwhile, he tried the old exemption from President Lincoln's day. He was the only surviving son of a destitute mother. Despite the military lurking in the background, his first quarter in grad school was an intellectual and spiritual high. The courses, profs, fellow students and his grades at UCLA were bright. He especially liked Paleolithic Archeology of the Old World.

Four fellows shared a bachelor flat just off campus—$140.00 a month. With two beds that converted to couches, they rotated places every month. Two guys slept in sleeping bags on the floor. Nobody seemed to mind. What a medley! Juan, from the Chicano barrio, taught the others the basics of Mexican cooking. Ivan, a handsome Russian gentile, had quiet intense looks. Yerger, a tall sandy blond California WASP—whose slightly browned skin was like cream kissed by the sun—studied Japanese culture. Yerger was pursued by a jovial Mexican-American from Fresno. Rarely, Yerger and Juanita feasted on brownies baked with marijuana, but their munchies and giggles, derivative of these drugs, so shocked Juan, he wanted to move out at this news. Ivan told Henry, who, while relishing the spice of the story, was tortured about whether or not to tell Marlene, his fun-filled co-worker who had fallen in love with Yerger. All of her roommates with whom Henry decided to discuss the matter without Marlene's knowledge shouted at him, "No, don't!" Henry followed their advice.

CHAPTER 2

Henry thought he would fail the physical examination for the army, but when he saw the other wrecks at the Broadway induction center, he moaned to himself, "Oh, no!" So, completing the forms on subversive organizations, he filled out "yes," to the question that he had attended a meeting of a few left-socialist organizations. He really didn't know what they were but thought that the government had no business throwing suspicion on anyone's patriotism for having been present at a meeting of any of those organizations, all of which sounded like turn-of-the century immigrant leftist groups that probably had a handful of members left in retirement homes. However, when the office dealing with subversive activities called him in to ask why he had attended the meeting of the Circle of Laborers, he said that it had been for a term paper for a sociology course on immigrant political associations. Why hadn't he gone through with this story? He didn't know. Events just seemed to keep going.

Just to make sure that contemplating about going to Canada was a product of normal thinking while taking advantage of a free professional service, Henry set up an appointment with UCLA's psychiatric services to talk it over with a doctor. Henry had been nervous taking off this time from his job at the library but it was important. The receptionist led him to a plain off-white room, lighted in a soft indirect light and a comfortable leather cushion chair in front of a wooden, modern Scandinavian desk. Henry dropped down in the comfy motherly seat and took out a copy of Thoreau's *Civil Disobedience*.

Walking in about five minutes late, Dr. Adler matched the role of a classical shrink. He was a white-haired Jewish man in his early sixties who spoke with a notable Viennese accent.

"My name is Max Adler. You're Henry Green?"

"Yes, sir," the "sir" an embarrassed relic of Henry's southern upbringing unwittingly creeping out at the wrong time.

"What can I do for you?"

"Dr. Adler, I want to talk over with you my thoughts about resisting the draft by going to Canada."

"Yes, what's on your mind?"

Henry summed up his life history in about ten minutes, and then Dr. Adler inquired. "Well, what does all this have to do with what's bothering you about the war?"

"Is it normal, Doctor, or is something bad or evil or sick motivating me?"

"Henry, these are hard times for young men. I myself had to face a tough decision about whether or not to stay in Austria and fight. I was an activist in the left wing of the Social Democratic Party before the Anschluss, and then it was all over. We didn't know what had hit us. The opposition collapsed in no time, and my family and I were lucky enough to get out in time. I don't think anything so dramatic is happening in America. The good old USA has a long history of democracy, but the opposition to the war is still a minority at this time. We can change that."

"Does that mean you're against the war?"

"Yes, I am. Why do you feel that there could be something abnormal motivating your decision?"

"I don't really think that there's anything wrong with it, but I wanted a professional opinion."

Years later Henry would think that he should not have consulted a good psychiatrist but a good lawyer. In retrospect, this psychiatrist had been asked about matters of the mind. Why should he have judged this case to be one more appropriately the domain of law?

"If it will make you feel any better, I think you're doing the right thing morally and psychically. It is not a question of unclear thinking or confused emotions in your case."

"Thanks, Doctor."

"I wish you a lot of good luck!"

"Thanks again. I'll need it."

11

CHAPTER 3

About 5 A.M. on the morning of June 5, 1968, Carlos, who lived a few buildings up on Landfair Avenue, came running down the hill to his buddy Juan's apartment.

"Hey, you guys, get up, something horrible has happened. Robert Kennedy was shot last night at the Ambassador Hotel!" Carlos shouted at the top of his lungs, almost beside himself.

"What? What's going on?"

"Kennedy has been what?"

"Is he alive?"

"They aren't sure. I was up studying and one radio station reports one thing and another something contradictory." There was a general groan in the room, a feeling that there was something they must do, yet life had to go on, too. They all had tiring jobs, and they would be exhausted if they stayed up.

"Do you think there's some kind of right wing coup going on?"

Ivan yawned, "Look, guys, it's terrible, but I'm sure the government has things in hand. Let's all go back to sleep and get up at our usual 7:00-7:30 time, and they'll know more by the morning."

Juan looked sleepy but concerned. "Thanks for telling us, Carlos. Keep us posted. Why don't you come over for breakfast and tell us what's happened?"

Robert F. Kennedy was assassinated. Another of Henry's heroes was dead. The acceptance letter from The University of Toronto lay on his desk, alongside an "in" Navy recruiting joke that had scared the hell out of him. It began, "You don't have to go to Canada."

That weekend Henry was invited to his rich uncle's in Beverly Hills and began conversing with his uncle's even richer friend.

Henry looked down at his feet unsure of himself. "Tony, I don't like conspiracy theories, but I am beginning to believe the stories on campus that the assassination was organized by primarily Texas oilmen who want to drill off the shores of Vietnam, and who, therefore, want the war escalated."

"Henry, personally, I think that's a lot of crap, but I know if I believed it, I wouldn't fight there."

Listening to the conversation behind him, his Uncle Bernard cut in. "Henry, it has to be your decision."

Henry felt uncomfortable. He wondered, *Were all these people sincere?* His uncle just gave him the nicest gift he had ever received in his whole life, a month's Eurail Pass for Europe. This unexpected surprise was a way his uncle had to say, "Thanks for being independent; congratulations on your hard work." Henry did not wonder whether he could expect any real monetary aid. He had never received anything but warm hospitality and this gift and perhaps some contributions to his upkeep as a child. About that, he could never be sure because all his relatives contradicted one another about who had "helped out," and yet none ever presented him with any concrete evidence. The only thing he could document was having his Social Security money illegally diverted from him by a wealthy southern uncle. But he concentrated on what he felt to be a caring for him—the feeling was most important. Henry was proud he had made it on his own. He liked the feeling of independence. After selling all his possessions he had managed to save $120 for three months in Europe and $700 for Canada.

"Uncle Bernard, I am thinking of going to Canada. I'm not a pacifist. I'm not a conscientious objector. I would have been one of the firsts to volunteer to fight in the Second World War. I would fight in a war I felt to be just. The War in Vietnam is wrong. Had America not attempted to assume the role of the French colonialists, Ho Chi Minh would have been our friend. OSS officers—remember our spies before the CIA came into being—stressed he had helped America during the Second World War. He wrote President Truman to persuade him to recognize Vietnam's independence. Instead, we allied ourselves with the most corrupt elements of Vietnam and are making a last dash attempt to create a phony republic after dealing with dictators there all along. I won't fight for the rights of a few landowners and the military to maintain their privileges. 500,000 people are estimated to be in jail in miserable conditions," Henry uttered in his usual soft factual way while feeling very angry inside.

"It's not a good situation. We shouldn't get tied down in a land war in Asia. Our best military men warned us against that...Well, whatever, we're not going to solve the problems of the world; let's go out to the pool," graciously interrupted Bernard, a former major during the Second World War. He was trying to soothe the anti-Communist feelings of his younger neighbor-friend who had served in Korea and his brother's son who had had a hard life.

CHAPTER 4

The next day the interview at the Canadian Consulate in L.A. went well. The consular officer was a French Canadian in his thirties. Wearing a trimly-fitted, blue pin-stripped suit, he looked at his letter of acceptance from The University of Toronto rather thoroughly. The official was impressed with Henry's bilingualism and educational background. Henry was sure that he would get the landed-immigrant status.

The student flight left from New York, so Henry planned to fly to Detroit and hitchhike to Toronto to check it out before settling down there. The stand-by flight was alarming. A drunken man in the seat on the same aisle across him had tried to rape the woman passenger next to him. It had taken Henry and several flight attendants to stop the violence.

On arrival in Detroit, Henry sensed that this city must be marked by America's worst problems, not the least of which were obviously tied to the country's addiction to the high-powered, gasoline-driven automobile, of which this city and Los Angeles represented the epitome of production and consumption. But the cheerful, brotherly hope that everyone could become a star in L.A. contrasted with the nasty, racist slurs of one group towards another in Motown, which could be overheard in every conversation. The ultimate optimist, Henry passed off all the talk of danger and crime as just another prejudice and had a nice stroll around the downtown area. Still there was something heavy and foreboding about the mood of the town. It left him tired. He walked through the tunnel to Canada. Once the officials checked his passport and money, there was no problem of crossing the border.

Besides the cleanliness and orderliness of Ontario, the first thing that struck Henry about his proposed new home was the seriousness of the young people who gave him rides. They all held down such conventional jobs at such a young age. They looked older and asked questions stable family

15

people tended to ask in the States. These were just first impressions and he refused to pay these notions any heed. This was just going to be a brief visit.

Toronto was the first north central or northeastern North American city Henry had visited since his childhood. It was cold and rainy and the buildings looked old. The only place where he could afford to stay was a fraternity that let out its rooms in the summers to visitors. An Irish lad with whom he shared a room appeared to be on a road to ill health—he was an excessive drinker of spirits and two-pack-a-day cigarette smoker. Henry never really cared for either of these habits, and he had never been able to be very empathetic with alcoholics. Not that he didn't want to be, but there was something about their bodily tension and hostility that put them at such a different vibratory levels from his own. *Oh, it's only a few days*, he thought. It rained and was dark nearly the whole time Henry was in Toronto. Nigel, the Irish fellow kept saying, "They call it Hogtown, ya' know." Frankly, at first glance, the city was a real downer compared to L.A. Henry did not want to bank too much on first impressions. They were deceiving. Yet he was depressed about the prospects of moving there.

CHAPTER 5

Twelve bucks student fare to New York by air; that's not bad! Henry thought while quickly throwing his greenbacks on the counter. Seated next to him on the flight was a very old and short generic grandmother from London, England.

"This was my first time in Canada since my daughter moved here twenty years ago," confided Mrs. Jones. "Could I offer you a brandy?"

"Well, I rarely drink, but why not?" Henry found this offer delightfully strange. He liked to think of himself as a bit eccentric, but here he was, a full-grown prude, appearing to be a cheapskate, letting himself be treated by a "sweet-little-old-lady" to a drink for which he really did not care.

"Why not?" he repeated clearing his throat. "How did it go?" inquired Henry, suddenly realizing that he could reciprocate with some free family therapy.

"My daughter, Jane, and her husband, Peter, are very hard-working people. They're quite religious too—something I can't say I provided in my own home. They've worked twenty years to buy a quite attractive home in one of the new suburbs. My grandchildren, Carol and John, are well-scrubbed and good students. But the whole lot of them are a bit on the cool side—you know what I mean? I know you Americans think of us English as cold and austere, class conscious and all that, but underneath it all, there's warmth and concern and a sense of fairness.

"My husband and I worked ourselves all our lives—he as a contractor and I as a teacher. We both came from working-class backgrounds and have participated in the Labor Party over the years. To be honest, I think Carol and John have lost the sense of social justice that pervaded my own home. Maybe that's why they've gone to the opposite extreme. Maybe Carol felt insecure and dirtied. They've disciplined their children as though they were born with the worst of original sin. You know, I've always thought that children were born good. They're innocent; and that's affected the way I've dealt with people. Toronto was a bit stuffy, didn't you think? It reminded me of a provincial city."

"Family life is complicated, isn't it, Mrs. Jones? It seems so unpredictable and confusing at times." Henry answered with a touch of sadness in his voice. Below them, the outskirts of New York began to appear.

"I'm glad I went, anyway!"

"Thank you ever so much for the drink and company!" Henry smiled with a light-headedness and fuzzy tingling sensation throughout his body.

CHAPTER 6

As soon as he landed, Henry rushed over to confirm his charter flight to London. It was leaving in four hours, just enough time to walk around the airport, write a few letters, make a few calls, and take a walk outside. The charter he had booked at UCLA was jammed-packed. He liked it that way. The airplane looked just like any other, maybe the inside not as perfectly antiseptic as on a regular flight. His seat was next to Blake Nichols from the University of California, Berkeley. After an initial introduction, they read for about an hour. Henry struck up the conversation, "So, what's it like at Berkeley? I want to do my Ph.D. there; in fact, I wouldn't mind finishing my M.A. there if it weren't for my old girlfriend I just broke up with."

Blake, feigning disinterest, and a bit of intellectual disdain, probed, "Oh, you mean 'Cal?' What's your ex-girlfriend's name?"

Always loving the encounter with a stranger, but never letting his defenses completely down, Henry responded, "Lisa Berger."

All of a sudden, the overtly frozen Blake lunged forward hitting his head on the seat in front of his own.

"Incredible. Man, is this strange, weird! I know you won't believe me, but I just broke up with her, too. We just met after she transferred to Berkeley."

They took a good look at each other. Indeed, they looked quite a bit alike. They were both six feet tall, had very wavy dark hair, possibly covering curls that they dared not yet grow out in the current Afro-fashion. They both looked quite straight and simply dressed in jeans and a plaid cotton shirt. Blake looked more debonair. Henry's black plastic glasses seemed incongruous with his looser body posture. Blake carried himself like a general.

His heart beating faster than expected or wanted, Henry asked, "What happened?"—not knowing if he was asking about Blake's or his own relationship with Lisa or what Lisa had done the last quarter at Berkeley.

"Little Miss Twiggy has become a big star on *The Daily Californian*."

"How does she fit in there? I thought they're really committed to social change. Lisa can't commit herself to anything or anyone," Henry commented, still irked at Lisa's hopping off to Berkeley.

"I guess that's what it takes to be a good journalist, though. You can seem to side with the people you're writing about. At least you maintain enough distance that you come out with some nice concise statement of the happening, shaping the story in your own manner."

"Congrats to Lisa for making it," toasted Henry with a make-believe mug in his hand.

With puckered lips, Blake responded, "Yes, she deserves it. But I wonder if she'll ever make it with anyone in the other sense of make, if you know what I mean?"

"She's so flighty. Take drugs, for example. This is between you and me. I don't like drugs; I've cringed at getting shots from the time I was a baby to this day. I've always hated pills. Smoking is an irritant. I've never been attracted to Timothy Leary's philosophy, and the drug culture of rock leaves me cold. But I'm a very tolerant person. If that's their thing, they want to do it, fine, as long as they're not hurting anybody else. But with Lisa, she'll try anything just to be in and ahead of the crowd—maybe I should exclude coitus from the latter statement." Oops, Henry had not meant to utter the last declaration, but it slipped out anyway.

Rapping his knuckles on the armrest, Blake emphasized, "You can say that again. She's the tightest cunt I've met since I've been in college. Not that she has any moral scruples against it. She sounds like she would sleep with anyone she found attractive. Then she tightens up and gets into her workaholic routine."

Getting back to his pet-peeve about this ex-girlfriend, Henry added, "Yes, but she finds time to smoke grass and hash, although she really doesn't like them. She always gets sick the next day."

"Perhaps she's ashamed of her small breasts. I don't see why. I think they're rather cute. But she seems to have a complex about them. I've never really gone in for big boobs myself. If they accompany a nice person, fine, but I don't seek them out," Blake noted, scratching his head.

"I think her best relationship is with Susan. Susan came up with her Iranian boyfriend from L.A. several times."

Blake interrupted, "Aren't they a great couple?"

"Yeah, Susan's so warm and Darius could laugh his way into anyone's good graces. He always imitates Susan's mom. 'What is a nice Jewish girl like my daughter going out with a Muslim boy like him?'"

"You know, Susan and Lisa were room-mates at UCLA. They hung out with a weird, mixed group. They liked the movie-acting crowd from L.A. and immigrant men from poor countries."

"I guess Lisa liked me because she felt sorry for me like her poor immigrant, serious student types. Yet she never understood why I remained so close to my rich relatives who never helped me out. She even suspected I was lying about that."

"That sounds like her; she never trusted anyone, not even herself that much. I guess it has something to do with her parents getting married and divorced from one another four times. Crazy. Not exactly an atmosphere conducive to feelings of trust," grumbled Blake.

"You can say that again."

"She was fun in bed. She would tease and tease and tease, but would never go all the way. Funny. Totally open, soft, somehow relaxed up to a point and then she'd put down the stop sign like there was a major accident on the freeway."

Slightly changing the subject, Henry confided, "I am going out with someone else now. She's not all that good looking; maybe she's plain but tries hard. Why am I talking this way? Probably because she's so down on herself. Anyway, we have a lot of common interests in anthropology. But I'm afraid she would like it to be more serious than I want it. We disagree about the kind of family we'd like to have, too. I'd sort of like to adopt an interracial family: have a black kid, an Asian kid, and a European kid. Something like that. That gets her very upset. I don't know why. She can't really put her finger on it, either. I think she really wants a MRS. degree in the worst way. She lost her dad just a few years ago, and she's very close to her mom. She still lives at home. She's used to a very upper-middle class sort of life, and I don't know if I will ever be able to provide or want to provide that kind of life. Anyway, we enjoy talking about the Olduvai Gorge."

"Me, I'm not going with anyone at the moment, just having a good time, I'd say. Where are you staying in London?"

"The cheapest place I can find," smirked Henry.

"Sounds great. Mind if I join you?"

"Not at all."

CHAPTER 7

The plane was landing in Prestwick, Scotland—their first time in the Old World. Sweeping down over the rolling verdant hills, the landing was safe, smooth, and swift. They both were shaken by the freshness of the air. Inhaling deeply, Henry felt high. Blake just looked at him, awed by the surrounding hills, and laughed.

"Groovy," was the only comment that the usually articulate Blake could get out.

"Yeah, this must be a shock to my lungs so accustomed to all the putrid particulates in LA's atmosphere," replied Henry. "It feels so good you can taste it. It's so refreshing."

Blake confided, "You know, right before I left California, I took a camping trip with my best buddy, high up in the Sierras. But there's something extra special about this. It's pristine."

A few other young men walked up behind them. "You're going to London, too?"

"Uh huh."

"The bus is on the other side of the customs' official. Hey, men, watch out, this Scottish guy on the plane told us that Glasgow is an ugly, dangerous city. Guys like to get in knife fights and things like that."

"Oh, we're going directly to London."

The group of the five of them boarded the bus taking them to the connecting flight at another airport.

Suddenly the pristine air smell was filled with diesel fuel, an odor that was new to all five of the new company who took seats near one another on the bus. Having taken the aisle seat next to him, Blake turned to Henry, "You know, I mentioned to you that my best friend and I took a camping trip in the high Sierras just before I left. Something very scary happened. I really haven't told anyone about it since I am a rational person and don't really

22

believe it myself. Each of us had his own good sleeping bag but no tent. The dome of heaven was our only cover. I wasn't sleeping well, so I gazed at all the stars. We were so high up—9,000 feet above sea level—when all of a sudden one of the things I thought was a star started looking like an airplane at first, then kept growing in size. In a few minutes there was a large glowing white-beige sphere hovering in the forest just about 100 feet away from where we were camped. I wanted to stir my buddy who was sound asleep, but I couldn't get a word out of my mouth or move my body. The sphere kept hovering there and seemed to settle on the treetops. Finally I got my leg gently around to Jamie, who was irritated at being awakened from a deep sleep. But he opened his eyes wide enough to get a glimpse of the same thing I saw and was also frozen shit-stiffless. We both were thinking, well, if it takes us into outerspace as specimens of earthlings, I hope we won't have to endure the same sort of torture we do to lower level living orders on our planet. It was as if our bodies were coordinated out of fright, so we just shut our eyes as tightly as we could, as though we were little boys trying to avoid a bad dream. Somehow we fell asleep. When we woke up the next morning, we tried to discuss what we had witnessed. The sphere had left by then. Jamie wondered, 'Should we report it as a UFO?' I never believed in UFOs but was quickly beginning to reevaluate my former assumption. Two close friends had seen empirical evidence to the contrary. I questioned Jamie, 'Do you think by happenstance we came upon some secret military test area?' Jamie reminded me that it wasn't posted or anything like that. We both were angry and embarrassed at ourselves for being so chicken, but that was honestly our reaction," shivered Blake, remembering the bizarre phenomenon.

Turning to more pressing matters, Henry inquired of Blake, "What do you think about the war in Vietnam?"

"I'm against it. I've been to demonstrations against it. I've leafleted against it. I've written my local newspapers, representatives, senators, you name it, against this fuckin' stupidity."

"How could a domestic liberal like Johnson escalate the war so much?"

"It's the same old line; he doesn't want to appear soft on communism or he'll lose the support among Democratic conservatives and moderates whom he needs to push his programs through Congress. Maybe he really believes in the Domino Theory, too. "

All this sounded logical, but Henry was always more interested in the effect of public events on private lives. "Blake, what are you going to do personally?"

"I'm a conscientious objector. I guess I'll end up doing a stint in a hospital or something like that. I'm lucky to have a dad and a mom who believe in what I'm doing and will pay for a good lawyer to make sure I don't make any mistakes, but to be honest with you, I'm not going to apologize to anyone for being fortunate. In front of evil in the world, you have to survive as honestly as you can, given your circumstances. And as long as we have our democracy, I can at least protest against what I believe to be a wrong action."

"Blake, do you think I'm crazy for wanting to leave the country if I'm drafted? I want to make some strong statement that will have an impact. I'm not a conscientious objector; I would have fought in the Second World War. I would fight in any war that I believe to be just, but Vietnam is not a just war."

"What war is, Henry?"

"A war to protect your country from invasion by an aggressive enemy and a war to protect an ally invaded by a fascist, racist dictatorship are just wars. Face it, my people would have been destroyed along with parliamentary democracy in the last great war if someone had not stood up to Hitler."

Blake said gently, "Gandhi told the Jews of Europe to use passive resistance against the Nazis."

Henry disagreed. "Had they done that there wouldn't have even been the Warsaw uprising and the Partisans."

As if to add a touch of distanced sympathy, Blake rejoined, "Henry, my grandmother on my mother's side was a Jewess."

Perturbed, Henry retorted, "Well, some European peasant or crusader probably raped some ancestor of mine. I hope you realize that had it been discovered in the Third Reich that you had such a close Jewish ancestor that you'd have been marked for discrimination at the least and, depending on bureaucratic whim, extermination, too."

Eyes turned to the foggy valleys and green hills; Blake responded softly, "No, I didn't know that. But I'm still strongly inclined to the messages of the eastern religions. I'm reading a lot of Alan Watts now. The western faiths are too wrapped up with ego. Such concern produces violence. He who doesn't believe what you believe gets uprooted, persecuted, destroyed, or attacked. Just look at history."

"It also produces a sense of justice, equality, individuality, and hope."

In their different ways, both boys-soon-to-become-men argued in very intellectual, heady ways. Despite their differences, they liked one another.

CHAPTER 8

Blake felt very secure when they boarded the short flight to London. The cabin of the airplane was spotless and the little white curtains beside each window seemed to have just been ironed by his own tidy housekeeper. He felt silent near the land below from which many of his forefathers had come. The only comment he made to Henry the whole flight was, "Do you think we can see Hadrian's wall from this altitude?" Henry respected his new companion's need for solitude. Much was on his mind.

"Should I go to jail like Thoreau? Things have changed in American jails since Thoreau. He and I would be raped or killed in one of the American prisons today. They don't separate political prisoners from common criminals. Just think what happened to Wilhelm Reich in the 1950s, and knowing my relatives, they'd just let me rot there."

Three young men pricked their ears to Blake's and Henry's conversation. At one level of perception, at what felt like the top of their eyes and ears, both Blake and Henry were irritated at other guys' eavesdropping on them, but maybe these fellows were just trying to politely butt in. After all, this comic trio, reminding Blake of Chekhov's *Fat and Thin*, with a mesomorph in-between, had helped them find their bus. The curt jerky halt of the plane went along with the overwhelming excitement of all the other passengers. One could sense in the air of the maiden flight of these New World youngsters their excitement. Many of them were digging down to the real relics of their ancestors or studies: London, England, the United Kingdom. Tony Jones, the middle-sized companion, usually squeezed in between his obese buddy, Jim Turner, and his slim, bean of a friend, Roger Smith. This tall, thin fellow almost shouted, "Hey, guys, can't you just feel the vibes? Man, you can just groove upon everybody's thrill. Wow."

Bursting with equal enthusiasm, Jim squealed in a close second, "Just dig it! I mean, just dig it."

Their more reflective wise man, Roger, waited a few minutes, squinted his small eyes behind his "granny" glasses, patted the stomach of Jim's nearly two hundred and fifty pounded, five-foot-six frame. Meanwhile, in his typical "downer" view, Jim weighed the bad as well as the good aspects of the scene at hand and reminded everyone, "Don't forget we have to find a decent place." Finding Blake's and Henry's conversation worth following, Jim wanted to enlist them for the search. Secretly, Jim dreaded the long walks that this trip was going to entail. Jim hoped that by recruiting Henry and Blake into his group, the level of culture would be elevated so as to spend most of the time in the British Museum. Yet, he knew that Tony's and Roger's greater first-time curiosity would push him to walk around crazily. Roger inquired of Blake, "What are your plans?"

Interrupting his heavy dialogue with Henry, Blake answered, "After Henry and I find a place to stay, we're planning to see as much of everything that we can squeeze into the three days we've allotted for our visit."

"Three days to see Merry Old England. What a travesty!" Roger almost whined. *Nevertheless*, he thought, *maybe we can save money in this expensive place by combining our resources with theirs.*

"That's all we can afford in time and money. We're both more interested in the continent."

"Let's go to Victoria Station and start hunting around there."

"Sounds fine to us. Our $5 a day guide says it's a reasonable place to look." Blake nodded at Roger, looking quickly over at Henry to see if it was O.K.

The rush at the airport and the bus ride into the city under a light drizzle added to their stereotypes of the city. Being dropped off at Victoria Station opened them into a living history book, a spy thriller, and a rush into an exciting past. From the other side of the crisscross metal of the high roof enclosure, a scruffy man in his fifties approached the boys. Despite his wrinkled suit, he exuded an aura of trust through the grays, browns, and greens of his ever-enduring tweed, which encased the low tones of his deep but perky voice. "Heh, lads, are you looking for a bed and breakfast that is nice and affordable?"

"What do you mean by 'bed and breakfast?'"

"You Yanks don't know what a 'bed and breakfast' is? Well, mates, it's a place where you can get lodging with a free breakfast thrown in to boot in the morning. I charge only a modest fee to find you one where all of you can stay together."

The young men, forming a sort of football huddle, contemplated the prospects. "Well, that's about twenty-four bucks divided by five; that's less than five dollars a night, with one meal, too. Not bad. Let's take it."

"Yeah."

"Uh huh."

"Yep."

None of these loyal Californians had for one minute any doubt that this old World War II veteran was anything but a reliable finder of housing. Within about twenty minutes, John, the bed and breakfast finder, had returned with good news. "Mates, I have a nice little place for you just a few minutes walk from the station here." Loaded with shiny blue-nylon backpacks, cameras, bags, and a few suitcases, they followed their senior.

On arrival at a row house, John introduced them to Mrs. James who led them up through a narrow staircase to a converted attic papered with a violet design. There were six cot-sized beds of curved iron metal, fluffed up around their irregular surfaces, on top of which were quilts of faded flowers. All looked somewhat clean, even if smelling a sniff of sweat and of flesh, fed on food not-their-own. At least that's what Henry was thinking—remembering the proper admonition anthropologists addressed against the southern racists' ignorant remarks about Negroes. To immigrant Chinese Americans, Caucasians smelled foul, but not to assimilated Chinese Americans; his teacher had emphasized it was basically a matter of the difference of food consumed by these different groups. Maybe it was true of the English to American noses as well, he was wondering. More likely it was just people of many nationalities with a limited housing budget. They dumped their packs and bundles on their beds, paid Mrs. James, and set out to see the town. On their way by foot to Westminster Abbey, Henry saw a French-looking fellow about his same age. The guy had a forlorn expression of protruding puckered lips and squinted downward-turned eyes. What an opportunity, before they arrived on the continent, to see if his French worked and to cheer up someone, too.

"Bonjour, comment ça va? Je m'appelle Henri et je viens d'arriver des États-Unis avec quelques copains."

"Your French is not bad. My name is Pierre Moreau, and I am from Nancy. I am looking for lodging, but I cannot find a place." Pierre spoke in a heavily-accented English.

"Ne t'ennuies pas. Je demanderai à mes amis si tu peus partager notre pension avec nous."

"Heh, guys, I just met this fellow from France who's looking for a room but can't find anything. Can he share with us?" Henry asked.

Everyone seemed to agree except for heavy Jim, who grumbled to Tony, "If he keeps picking up every kid in London, there's not going to be room for us." Jim took Henry over to the side, "Look, there are enough of us now. This is the last one we're gonna allow. You dig!"

"Sure, I understand. Pierre'll be the last."

Turning down Vauxhall Bridge Road to the River Thames, Henry whispered to Blake, "I'd like to get away from Jim, Tony, and Roger for the afternoon. Jim can be such a bore; he's always on edge, afraid to try anything, and, besides, he's so lazy that by mid-afternoon, he's going to be so tuckered out that he'll do nothing but sit in a pub."

"You're right"

"Is it O.K. if we ask Pierre to join us?"

"Sure."

Just as they swung around to the left on Grosvenor Road, Henry asked Pierre in French, "Come with Blake and me. We're really going to do a lot of walking. We want to see as much of the city as we can while we are here. The others don't like to walk as much as we do, and they'll probably sit a good part of the afternoon after seeing the Parliament."

"*Ça me ferait plaisir de vous accompagner*. It would be great." Pierre smiled, lighting up his unfiltered Gaulois, while still keeping up with these two athletic Californians.

By four that afternoon they had managed to take in the Houses of Parliament and Buckingham Palace. Blake looked exhilarated, almost in a religious trance. Regarding his map and wanting to begin their concentrated tour, he took the initiative. "Would you two like to see Hyde Park and Kensington Garden?"

"Sounds fine with me."

"Me too," said Pierre.

By four thirty they found a bench to sit down and looked out at the lush green and the many relaxed tourists. Blake thought, *How lovely!*

"There is something refreshing about it, I must admit," Pierre commented in English with a strong French accent. "It's austere, the architecture, I mean. This park is beautiful," Pierre exhaled in a cloud of bluish white smoke that seemed to continue to bellow forth from his nostrils and mouth. "What is happening in your country now? The beacon of liberty seems to be very angry at herself and the world."

"You can say that again," replied Blake.

Philosophizing, Henry offered an explanation, "It's a whole generation mesmerized and propagandized by the boob-tube."

"What does that mean 'boob-tube'?'" Pierre wondered.

"Oh, sorry, it's slang for 'television.' But boob is also slang for a woman's breast," Blake gleefully informed him.

"Oh, it's more than that," interjected Henry, who was still entranced and felt very much part of the nature around him." It's similar to the mentality in your country when you began to lose the colonies. The collective mind is filled with racism, xenophobia, anti-intellectualism. It's a pride bounding in faith in technology while Americans pour napalm on innocent women and children in Vietnam and murder their black and liberal leaders at home. In the army they teach them to kill what they call 'gooks.' That's their slang for people with epicanthic folds in their eyes. In the richest land in the world millions live in destitute poverty."

Blake looked at Pierre seriously. "But Henry and I disagree about how to fight it, in a way. I'm a pacifist; I'm going to be a conscientious objector. Henry's trying to figure out this summer exactly what he's going to do."

Pierre just stared at both of them, continuing to inhale deeply on his Gaulois. The sharp smoke irritated Henry, although the effect contributed to Pierre's mysterious intensity.

"I don't know, I don't know, I don't know, I don't know. America is good, too. We've made a lot of progress in almost 200 years, but how do you fight a society when it goes mad? America has been good to my people, even if not to my immediate family; that's why my rich relatives are so mealy-mouthed about everything. 'Shut up and obey authority.' That's why they ended up with everything, and we ended up with nothing. They didn't even go out of their way to help our own people in Europe during the period before the Second World War. Economically, the middle ground is slipping and, as usual, when those things occur, a foreign enemy is sought—the ever-present Communist menace is conveniently brought up to whip up hysteria. It turns out that Ho Chi Minh used to work for the OSS—the predecessor of the CIA—and that our own agents felt he was more of a nationalist than a Communist. Well, this time, it's not working as well as it used to. People are too smart to fall for such a trick this time around!"

Blake interrupted, "Let's get a bite before it gets too late. Or maybe we should meet the others back at the pad before we go out again."

Pierre yawned, "Well, I'd like a good coffee, but I understand the English do not know how to make one. How about Piccadilly Circus this evening?"

29

"Fine with me. Let's go even if the others don't want to tag along."

They walked fast back to their room picking up a few pieces of fruit and a bread on the way. Pierre went through with his plan for a coffee on the way back only to spit out the first mouthful, which was not potable. Blake was anxious to try the jar of Bovril on the fresh bread they got. At least the rectangular crust appeared thick enough to contain some nutrition. In Blake's reading on nutrition he had learned that this dark brown paste was full of brewer's yeast and had a slightly meaty flavor if spread quite thin. Evidently it had been used during World War II as a source of low cost, high value food. Henry bought a large bottle of milk and a head of lettuce, and Pierre had some Swiss chocolate in his pack, which he contributed to this feast.

Roger and Jim were sprawled out on their cots when Blake, Henry, and Pierre returned. Just before they entered, Blake overheard Jim say to Roger, "I hope the Froggie doesn't smell up our flat with his putrid smelling weeds." Before Roger had time to answer, Jim followed, "And, it's not good for my heart."

This time Roger put in his two bits, "And we told the landlady we're non-smokers." As they were turning the key, Blake was hoping that Pierre had not understood their conversation.

Henry had the suspicion that Pierre did not, for he spoke better that he understood spoken English. Anyway, he took the initiative, "Pierre, you're not supposed to smoke in the room. The landlady said it's against the rules, and we told her that we don't smoke." Pierre mournfully looked at his blue thick pack in his leather coat pocket.

"*C'est la vie*," Pierre said openly, thinking to himself that he had always heard his fellow Frenchmen reproach the Anglo-Saxons for such restraint and prudishness.

Back in their room, as predicted, Jim was sacked out, stomach down on the musty quilt. Roger and Tony were silently playing a game of chess on a portable magnetic set.

"Hi, fellas."

Henry's acknowledgment was responded to with a low grunt, "Uh huh."

"We're going to grab a bite and see Piccadilly Circus. Want to come along?"

"Uh uh," bellowed negatively from their stomachs, enthralled in their game.

After about a twenty-minute catnap, the trio set out again. They passed a small restaurant with a dark brown wooden interior. On the menu posted in the window—which Pierre had instructed Henry and Blake always to read in Europe—there was kidney pie and bread pudding advertised for about a pound. This was above what Henry had budgeted for food, but he thought that it would be O.K. to follow the other two without ordering anything more than a tea. Blake and Pierre had read about kidney pie and bread pudding but had never really tried it before. In the individual booths, the plain brown chairs with leather-cushioned backs matched the low beige light reflected from bumpy yellow glass-shaded lamps. They ordered, and, being the earliest of the customers for dinner, were served within a half-hour. The steamy kidney pie smelled of meat and vegetables, but Pierre was quick to question, "Is it conserved, no?"

Henry corrected him obliquely, "You think it's from a can?"

Blake nodded "yes," but added, "still, the crust has a nice, light flaky texture, and the kidneys are plentiful and meaty in taste but different from anything I've ever had before. Here have a taste."

"No, it's not bad at all."

Pierre, picking up on the situation that Henry was short on cash offered some of his dessert, "Try it, it is thick and chewy and creamy, this bread pudding."

"I like it."

"Do you guys want any of my tea? I'm getting tired of drinking it."

Both Pierre and Blake took sips.

"Let's get going," Henry anxiously interjected, his culture-vulture part asserting itself.

"Asses in gear; go!" jumped Blake.

Not understanding the details, Pierre was, nevertheless, carried away by their enthusiasm.

On the way to Piccadilly Circus, they took the wrong lane down a side street. There was a small group of young men about their age whose skin was a sheetish pale. Two had very reddish pimples on their scrawny faces.

Blake whispered to Henry, "Do you think they're addicts?"

"Given the way they're standing with their rumps stuck inwards and their cocks forward, I'd say they're prostitutes advertising their wares."

All the traveling companions increased their pace. Pierre tried to show his disapproval and reassert his masculinity by saying nothing, lighting up, and inhaling deeply once again. He thought to himself, *Why do these Americans have to talk about everything, even that about which it is inappropriate to comment?*

When they reached the place, they sat down on the sidewalk, backs against the wall, and watched the lights and the excitement of the passers-by. Blake just smiled. "It's groovy! Yeah, man, very groovy."

CHAPTER 9

Being "groovy" expressed feeling one with the world because it is exciting and exhilarating. For some it meant that an object or place is literally "in" as in a groove, or fashionable. To others it signified that an individual's or small group's behavior is totally appropriate but done with style. For Henry, the word smacked of conformity, doing what the crowd expects. No matter how unlike him, during his years in California, it occasionally slipped from his lips as a key into the group to which he was seeking acceptance.

That day all six finished Mrs. Jones's rather stale crumpets and orange marmalade along with a cup of tea, only a spot above good ol' American Lipton's. Then they quickly dashed off to see the Tower of London.

It was not until they reached the four turrets of White Tower's Kentish ragstone and French Caen, constructed by William the Conqueror to lord over London, that the association of power sneaked into Henry's thoughts. Or maybe it had been the bright read coats and the high socks of the Yeoman Warders, capped in round black hats set off in symmetrical gold and black lines, and holding sharp staffs that brought to Henry's mind the association with his Aunts', Sue and Genevieve, and Uncle Mark's pompous authority. From these images, after hearing of Henry the VIII's murder of Anne Boleyn and his fifth wife, Catherine Howard, here Henry's imagination began to recall the less brutal, though painful, tribulations of his own sister.

He always contemplated his sister Diane's life in an apologetic way. She had had a life equally as rough as his own. In order to escape, why had she voluntarily locked herself into another prison? A decade older than Henry, Diane had been part of the conformist '50s. If you worked hard and didn't rock the boat, you got your little bungalow and two cars in the suburbs. For Diane, that was plenty to achieve in starting out from nothing. When they had been sent to live with Jake, his uncle, a furniture store salesman for the only

Jewish-owned furniture shop in their small southern town, Diane began to fight bitterly with Jake's second wife, Sue, who was a very attractive green-eyed redhead from a rather mainline Protestant farm family. When they took on Diane and Henry, after years of being married, they didn't think that they could have their own children. Sue was in her late twenties at the time and Diane was an early teenager who had the appearance of a young woman in her late teens. Henry remembered hiding under the metal frame of his aunt and uncle's bed while Sue chased Diane to beat her with her belt. Embarrassed at his childhood powerlessness and inaction, his wondering mind captured a lighter catastrophe. Henry chuckled recalling their worst fight when Diane threw out Aunt Sue's hominy and gravy, which she had mistaken for burned cereal. It suddenly struck him that this episode must have been a major thrust factor in Diane converting to Catholicism instead of to a Protestant denomination. Sue was a Protestant, so Diane couldn't stomach being anything like Sue.

Suddenly, Blake nudged Henry with his elbow. "Are you daydreaming or something? Beat from last night? You're missing the best part of the tour." The guide was explaining, "Shakespeare, recording tradition in *Richard III*, iii, and elsewhere, claimed that Julius Caesar had founded the tower. This assertion is supported by archeological evidence of Roman fortifications below the present site."

Henry replied to Blake, "Somehow this prison made me think about my sister's life. Am I associating with something or making a metaphor of her existence?"

"Ssh, tell me later; I'm interested in this story," whispered Blake curtly.

The guide continued, "From a historical point of view, the principal interest in the Tower derives from the prisoners who were put here. For example, Bishop Fisher and Sir Thomas More were confined to the Bell tower. The Roman Catholic prisoners of Elizabeth's time were put in the Salt tower and Broad Arrow Tower, and in 1671, Colonel Blood was housed in the Martin Tower after he nearly succeeded in carrying off the crown and regalia."

Wandering back to his own thoughts, Henry recalled how Diane used to iron her coarse Russian-Jewish hair that later began graying fast in her mid-twenties. Sue used to jab her about her 'horsehair' and Diane used to pretend to ignore her comments.

Henry went on to recall the incident when he had a bowel movement in the bathtub and Diane refused to clean it up. Aunt Sue once again started chasing

Diane with that thick leather strap. That was almost the last straw, until Diane finally tried to run away. It must have driven her to smoke so early, too—that with all the aunts, uncles, and parents smoking away like chimneys.

The night before Diane had been shipped off to St. Catherine's stood clearly in his mind. Aunt Sue had always liked military schools, but there were none that accepted girls. When Diane was at school, Aunt Sue had checked out the costs; they could afford it. Use the Social Security money and ask each of the rich aunts and uncles for $25 dollars a month. They could all write it off their taxes, anyway. That night contortions wrinkled the olive skin of thirteen-year old Diane's face. The wrenching and stretching of nerves between Sue and Diane filled the air of their little cottage with anxiety.

Uncle Jake's passive nature showed itself once again. He pulled out a cigar, let tiny Aunt Sue call all of Diane's relatives collect and, talking at their expense, besmirch Diane's character. He was able only to throw an occasional sympathetic glance to Diane when Sue wasn't looking. Diane had remained strong, yanking in everything to her insides.

The next day Diane was gone. Henry saw her only once or twice a year from then on throughout his grammar school and high school years. Life is strange, isn't it? Sue had worshipped Aunt Genevieve, one of Mother's sisters, who had married well in Atlanta. Aunt Genevieve was always courtly, always sought-after for her elegance and social graces. She carried herself like a queen in her small social set, entertaining the New York executives of her husband's national company, of which he was the regional president. She was a finely tuned woman, around five-foot six with the gray eyes of a cat but the disciplined body positions of a well-trained greyhound. Her slenderness had been maintained over the years more by smoking than by exercise. "Follow our advice and we'll get you married off to a handsome provider down here." Diane was pretty, so everyone fully expected that to be her *cursus vitae*. Except for rebelling when placed under the intolerable circumstances of Aunt Sue's imagined sexual rivalry for her weak husband, Diane had done only one thing out of line, and that was within the context of a proper southern belle's teen-age upbringing–she became intoxicated at a party. For this, Aunt Genevieve had made her polish all the brass doorknobs of her two-story home.

Blake jabbed Henry in the rib cage. "Hey, guy, what's with you? Listen to the guide!"

"There were executions both inside the Tower and on Tower Hill. Among those who perished here, whose names you will recall, are those of Henry

VIII's Queens, Anne Boleyn and Katharine Howard. Outside you will notice the Yeoman Warders of Her Majesty's Tower of London whom we call Beefeaters. They are dressed in Tutor costume."

"Gee, Blake, this is interesting. Something's bugging me. I can't figure it out."

"Well, the tour's over. Let's rush over to Westminster Abbey." The six traveling companions followed one another, but Blake and Henry walked a little ahead of the others.

"Let's stop by a store to pick up a few things for lunch and supper on the way there. Maybe we can have a picnic by the banks of the Thames?"

"Sounds fine with me."

Pierre rushed into a small bakery and bought a large un-sliced loaf of bread. Roger picked up a large chunk of a yellowish cheese, a bottle of milk, and a can of green peas. Jim found a nice looking tin of herring and relished trying the large bar of chocolate displayed behind the glass and wooden counter. Everything came to fewer than two quid, around five dollars. Jim quickly called out to Blake, Henry, and Tony, "We paid; so you'll each owe us about a buck, in English change preferably." Sitting down on a bench near the Thames, Roger, Henry, Jim, and Tony laughed at Blake and Pierre who put their feet upon a bench and laid their heads on a stony footstool they were using as pillows. Pierre yanked off just the right size of bread for each person. Jim dabbed on a piece of herring, and Roger took some green peas, while Tony peeled a carrot.

"This is one of the best meals I've had in England," Jim remarked seriously.

Pierre thought to himself, *It's probably because he was too cheap to spend any money on a decent meal. Good for him; maybe he'll lose some weight.*

They all ate leisurely, looked around, and said hardly a word.

Finding a bench, Blake took out his pocketknife to cut the cheese. "What in the hell was going on in your head in the Tower? You looked like a zombie most of the time."

"Oh, I kept having these flashbacks about my sister's life. I don't know why. I hardly ever think about her."

"Tell me about her."

"You can't imagine anyone so different from me. She was raised in such different circumstances at such a different period of time. She was placed in a really strict Catholic school in the south by a really rigid Protestant aunt of mine. That aunt used to stand in our backyard with a .22-caliber rifle and shoot at my best friend's family's compost pile proclaiming to the neighbors and the City Health Department that there were rats in it. But there were no rats indigenous to the region. You get the picture of how balanced my aunt was?

"My sister hated the school but because she's so sociable, she made a lot of friends. She met a guy in the neighboring Catholic boys' school who was going to become a priest, and they got married just after high school. He came from a poor farm family who made quite a bit of money when their land was bought up for suburban development. She converted in her senior year. It's funny; nobody in our family, except my mother, protested at her conversion, but they kept their distance after she went through with it–not that she was felt to be a traitor or an outcast, but just in the air you got the feeling that things were not as they should be. I get the feeling that a lot of awkwardness came as much or more from social class differences as much as from religious ones. Her in-laws and husband spoke a crude, mumbled, muffled dialect of southern English with a heavy twang. It always conveyed to me an attempt to be contrite and submissive as though conversation and analysis were signs of haughtiness before God. Someone once confided to me that the conversion was what her family sensed to be the block in communication. I don't really think so. My family was not intellectual at all. The only thing they were interested in was in gracious living, in making money, and being perceived as good people by their friends and community. They were scarcely observant and had little knowledge of Judaica and none of Hebrew or Yiddish language or literature. Two out of five of my father's family had married non-Jews, one a Protestant and one a Catholic, and their children had been raised as Christians, but they were more cultivated people, and I think that's what made the big difference. There was no block in words or feelings between these groups. There was something of peasants that characterized the family into which my sister had married. They were hardworking, religious folk though, and I think those qualities were respected, not disliked, by my aunts and uncles."

Blake had always prided himself on being a good listener, but ever since he took a class in communication, he had become fixated on styles of looking at people. Yes, Blake's eyes were cast downward and his ears seemed to tilt at a forty-five degree angle from the sound waves projected by Henry as they both walked forward with their heads turned toward one another. Blake's large eyes encasing a bluish-gray pupil cast into Henry's small dark brown beads only twice during this long monologue. Blake focused less on the whole of what had been said than on the flat, matter-of-fact tone with which Henry had spoken. As he heard Henry's story, Blake's torso curved as if to provide a warm basket in which to store these shared secrets. Perhaps, it was better not to reply until he had ruminated about the significance of it all.

CHAPTER 10

Walking in through the great west door, Roger opened his guidebook.

"Fellas, this place is the most famous church in the Commonwealth. Wow! In 1050, Edward the Confessor erected a new church here in cruciform with a central tower and two western ones. In 1245, Henry III started to rebuild the church east of the nave. The guidebook says this Collegiate Church of St. Peter in Westminster is a superb example of the Pointed Style."

Jim, gritting his teeth, his lips puckered inward forming his mouth into a line, bellowed, "I plead ignorance. What is a nave?"

"It's the main body of a church built in the form of a cross. It's the part between the side aisles," Roger declared to his friend who had a double major in business and engineering.

Though Jim might have not kept up with his English history, he was up on current events at a price he would permit himself—free. He had found four recent copies of London's *The Times* on the floor of a W.C. in the Parliament the previous day. As his traveling companions were in rapture with the beauty and history of Westminster, Jim sat down on a pew and skimmed over the news. The headline of Monday, June tenth, 1968, read, "U.S. Justice Department Chief Interviews King Case Man; James Earl Ray in London." On the front page there was a large picture of Mrs. Jacqueline Kennedy and her two children, Caroline and John, kneeling the day before at the grave of Senator Robert Kennedy in Arlington Cemetery. Jim's eyes moved heavily down below the center of the page, "American Election Moves Backstage." He glanced upward to the right. "Tito Stakes His Leadership on Solving Crisis." Shuffling the pages, he got stuck on page five. "In Saigon the War Continues. Vietcong Survivors Surrender."

Jim thought, *I'm not going to debate it with these ratty-lib types, but I'm going to enlist or let myself get drafted. They'll take anything on two legs at the moment. So, I'm really overweight. They're not going to take it all off. It runs in the family anyway. With my B.S. in engineering and business from UCLA, they're going to use my skills at some desk job the same way they did with Dad and Grandfather. Besides, the Commies are dirty bastards who'll turn that fuckin' hole into a pit.*

Jim went on to *The Times* of Tuesday, June 11, 1968, and read the front-page headlines: "Murder Warrant for Arrest of Ray Issued. Paris Riots After Student Drowns." He commented, "Boring!" Then he moved onto the next day's edition, "Cohn-Bendit in Britain for 24 Hours; Airport Police Break Up Demonstration." Peering over to *The Times* of the thirteenth, he looked at the front-page picture and read the caption, "Daniel Cohn-Bendit, the leader of the French students, giving the clenched fist salute at the BBC television Center yesterday, flanked by Tariq Ali, former President of the Oxford Union, and Dragona Stavijel of Yugoslavia. They are taking part in the programme, 'Students in Revolt,' on BBC 1 tonight." Jim laughed to himself, *At least you don't have to be a skinny runt with a squeaky, scratchy voice like Bob Dylan's to be famous here.*

Jim stretched out on the pew resting his thighs on the end of the bench and leaving a big gap between the mid-point of his back and his legs. He chuckled to himself, *Imagine that, a Jew, an Arab, and a Commie on the front page of the London paper trying to tell us White, Anglo-Saxon, Protestants how to run our countries. Not any of them can get their act together. No wonder you get some weirdo like that James Earl Ray blowing his cool and bumping off the Negroes' leader. When you put the average person under too much pressure, he cracks. It's like too much steam in a boiler.*

Jim felt comfortable here in Westminster, the starkness and the splendor which the centuries of English rule had bequeathed to her progeny along with order, law, and a passionate, yet disciplined debate. That is what democracy and godliness were all about. No, he no longer believed in God, but maybe it was good for the common people to have God to believe in. Jim was above all that. He was a rational engineer and businessman. He liked his small pleasures. He prided himself on doing quality work for himself, which others would buy at the right price. Such behavior led to a fairer world where everyone could enjoy at least a modicum of material comforts and a lot if they deserved it.

Jim had been totally turned off from his Episcopalian upbringing by his twelfth grade trigonometry teacher who was the most devout member of his high church. Mr. Smythe, mathematician and organist, lived with his elderly mother in a Tutor house decorated in regal velvet purple. Ugh. It made him sick just to think about it. This pretentious man was a methodical teacher who managed to cover up the smell of Johnny Walker Black scotch with his chain smoking of Pall Mall cigarettes, although Jim had to admit Smythe was popular with the members of the senior class who found him debonair, competent, and witty. Jim had been at the top of his trig class and visited the Smythe home as treasurer of his church youth group. He had been outraged when it had first been alleged that Mr. Smythe had been having an affair with Mr. Pickett, Jim's Latin teacher. Indeed, Mr. Pickett, a married man with a pregnant wife, had been "run out of town on a rail" when it had been discovered that he had been drugging the school's toughs with whom he would engage in fellatio. One of them became conscious during the act and had run in a rage to the headmaster.

By the morning, Mr. Pickett and his wife Jane left, never to be seen again. That's when the school had hired an Italian to finish off the year of Latin, suddenly requiring the students to switch from the Germanic to the ecclesiastical pronunciation. Even though Jim had never spoken about it to anyone, he had no doubts in his mind that Messrs. Pickett and Smythe were "carrying on"—to use the euphemism of his high school English teacher, Mr. Childs. When Jim had given his report on the church youth group finances to Mr. Smythe, his eighty-four-year-old mother served their guest tea, and Mr. Smythe retired to his "study." On two occasions, Jim had seen Mr. Pickett in an alley outside the Smythe home, shutting the back gate. The only exit was from Mr. Smythe's back stairwell, leading from his study. Noticing how disheveled Mr. Pickett's ordinarily immaculately-combed hair was, Jim thought, *How dishonest!* Moreover, he was still furious with Russell, one of his school's two "liberals" and a former friend of his who had dared suggest that it was his school's intolerance and bigotry that made the whole thing seem so sordid. At least Russell could have had the decency to keep his opinions to himself, but, "oh, no" he had made a big issue of it by lecturing to the other students and faculty in a holier-than-thou way, during his required turn to read the Bible in chapel. That had been the last straw! Jim had seen through the whole hypocrisy of it all. He had followed through with his required church attendance at high school. But that had been that! "Leave the church for the rabble and the mystics" became his new credo. Practical men like Jim should take charge of the world, of the day-to-day necessities that make things run well.

Since high school, this was the first time he had been in a church other than his cousin's wedding and his granduncle's funeral. Despite his agnosticism, everything felt good at this moment. Dad had shown him his pictures of his grand trip to Europe in the thirties just after he had finished Yale, and now Jim would have his pictures to show his kids—maybe not in the same grand style of hotels and big trunks on ocean liners the way his father had traveled. He would see the sights he should in this day of charters and Eurailpasses for the great middle class.

Glancing down at his guidebook and up at various nooks and crannies in the church, Roger approached Jim. Feeling totally exhilarated having plunged through time, having walked in the abbey where every British sovereign except Edward V and Edward VIII had been crowned since William the Conqueror, Roger tempered his enthusiasm before approaching his friend Jim, whose belief in their common religious heritage had cooled to the point of respectful tolerance.

"Jimmy, I think if I spent the rest of my visit in England in this church, I still couldn't begin to learn all there is to know about it."

Jim tightened his lips and upper chest and indicated his desire to get out of the abbey. "How much longer are the other guys going to be?"

"Oh, they're just behind me."

Pierre and Tony walked a step in front of Henry and Blake. Filled with the spirit of ecumenism, Pierre, a very liberal and not very observant Catholic, believed that he had just done something to bridge the gaps between Catholics and Protestants, between the English and the French, and to top it off, he was finding that he could communicate best with an American Jew. *Mon Dieu*! Blake was impressed, perhaps even awed, but felt foreign, "Well, Henry, I guess I am an American after all. It's beautiful; it's gorgeous; it's overwhelming; but I guess my spirituality is simpler. It's not so bound to a past of kings and queens, Wrens, Hawksmoor, James, Scotts, and Pearsons."

Henry was a Jew who had been compelled to attend a Protestant Church every Sunday and chapel every school-day morning for the four years of his prep school. None of his relatives had wanted him to live with them. So Henry maintained an academic curiosity shaken by an occasional spinal jolt as he walked down the aisles of the abbey. Noting Blake's reactions, Henry felt that it would be more appropriate if his traveling companion spoke first.

Taking the initiative to go, Blake whispered to the others, "You guys ready?" Everyone nodded and began to follow Blake's steps outside. It was already early afternoon. "I'd sort of like to just walk around the city and get a general impression. Tomorrow's our last day in London."

42

Pierre and Henry had the same thing in mind, and Roger knew that if he accepted, Jim would reluctantly follow suit. Roger looked at Jim with a "Sorry, buddy" expression, and then replied to Blake, "Sounds good to me, too."

Not wanting to appear disagreeable, Jim chirped in, "O.K. guys, but keep the pace at a rate a featherweight like me can follow." Everyone laughed and, for the first time, there was a feeling of some solidarity among all six.

CHAPTER II

The young men wound down Chancery Lane into New Oxford Street, turning right on Tottenham Court Road toward the British Museum and the University of London. They became as much engrossed in one another's conversations as the passing architecture, which they processed on a second track.

Tony peered at Blake and inquired, "Did you hear about the trial of Dr. Spock and Reverend Sloane Coffin on the radio last night?"

Blake replied directly, "Yeah, there were three more of them: Goodman, Raskin, and Ferber. They're brave men, but frankly I'm pessimistic about the outcome of the trial."

Not wanting to continue to stand out like a sore thumb, Jim reported, "I didn't follow that story, but I heard that General Westmoreland thinks we should concentrate on peace in Paris. He believes that we are fooling ourselves that we're going to win in battle—given the restraints that the Congress has placed on the war."

An avid reader of newspapers, not only of religion and philosophy, Blake retorted, "Westmoreland. Don't trust him any further than you could throw him. He's been constantly announcing that victory is only around the corner and the more troops the guy gets, the further away victory becomes. The reason is simple; in allying ourselves with the rich landowners and militarists throughout the Third World, our highest elected officials are working for the profit of multinational corporations and not for people like us. It sickens me that a host of hypocrites pretend that they're encouraging small scale enterprise abroad while in fact the U.S. government's military guarantees the policing for the largest corporations in the world who exploit cheap labor most everywhere. But I think the people from Asia understand that the world turns. Those who are on top today may be somewhere else on the wheel of existence in the next life. I guess I'm becoming syncretistic. Perhaps, I'm coming back to what Jesus said. 'Give unto Caesar that which is Caesar's and unto God that which is God's.'"

Jim responded indirectly, "Well, you know, the Vietcong and the North Vietnamese aren't exactly innocents. Did you hear the news that their rockets have been whining almost everyday over Saigon? It could wreck the negotiations in Paris."

Unable to hold in his chest the disgust he felt at Jim's whole attitude and conduct toward life, Henry answered, "It's war. It's either the fascistic militarists who support the large landowners or the leftist nationalists. Yes, I believe that they're more nationalists than communists, if we don't continue to drive them right into the Kremlin's hands. If only President Truman had listened to Ho Chi Minh's pleading letters to recognize Vietnam's independence, I believe that he could have brought him into our camp. Even the Vietnamese militarists can't get it together. Ky and Thieu are struggling for power. Ky quit as head of the defense."

Sensing that Henry had pushed Jim too far, particularly noting the hurt look of consternation on Roger's face, Tony sought to change the subject and interjected a bit of humor. "The last news I heard is that the Neanderthal men liked flowers. Maybe they were partisans of the California Youth Party?"

Everyone laughed. Henry feigned a smile and just thought to himself, *I should go join one of the sit-ins that are going on all over Britain today instead of being with this crowd of flakes and egotists. But here I am, being a nice American student, learning about London.*

The groupies turned right onto Tottenham Court Road. Walking toward the British Museum and the University of London, they purchased some food for a picnic lunch.

Trying to jab Henry by upsetting Pierre, Jim inquired, "Things are pretty hot in France at the moment, Pierre. Why have all the students and workers been striking since last spring?"

Picking up the supercilious tone in Jim's question, Pierre sensed his not-too-amicable meaning. "This is just a time when oppressed people all over the world are saying, 'We're fed up; that's it! We're not going to put up with it anymore!'"

Passing the British Museum, Roger asked if the others wanted to spend their afternoon there.

"I thought we'd agreed to get an overview of the city," Tony replied.

"I intend to spend at least a whole day there on my way back," Henry said.

"Let's just continue our original plan of a long walk getting a general overview," interjected Blake.

"How about having our picnic at the University of London?" added Jim.

"Sounds fine," was the general agreement.

After a short picnic in Russell Square, they quickly walked around the very urban university quarter and then hopped on the nearby underground train to Regent's Park. They took a brisk hike along the row paths of the old Regent's canal and then embarked again on the tube over to the other side of the river around the Banks to where the Globe Theater and Tabard Inn had been located in their day and age. Noticing that Jim looked tired, everyone thought it would be cordial to go back to their bed-and-breakfast early, as dusk was nearing.

Back at their room, Jim plopped down on his bed and turned on his transistor radio. "June the fourteenth, and now for the summary of the news: Henry Kissinger vows to oppose curbs on Berlin travel…The student leaders who appeared on BBC 1 last night assailed voting and claimed that elections do not bring needed social change…Cohn-Bendit, objected to being described as "leaders," preferring "megaphones, loudspeakers of the movements" to qualify himself, Tariq, and Stavijel…Jeremy Charles Tupper, the American, twenty-one years of age, who had admitted being a deserter, was turned over by a London magistrate yesterday to the military who escorted him to the U.S. Air Force Base at Ruislip…In the United States, Senator McCarthy reports a new mood on the war and claims that the American public would support a unilateral withdrawal from Vietnam; he asks for help for U.S. cities…."

Jim just yawned and fell asleep. Although tired, Tony was edgy with the muffled buzz of the radio in the background.

"Ya' know, Roger, it never seems to stop. It's as though events have gone beyond me. They happen so fast that you can't comprehend what's going on. You have to make such snap decisions that mean life and death to you and others."

"I hear what you're saying, Tony."

Stretched out on his belly with both arms over a pillow, Blake was writing a few post-cards:

London, England, 6/14/68

Dear Mom and Dad,

I walked all around London today with five new acquaintances. One is from California (met on the 'plane) and one is from France (met in London). It's a beautiful, interesting city. It's like walking in a history book. My favorite spot, The Houses of Parliament, is even more wonderfully late-Gothic than all the pictures I've ever seen of its buildings.

Love,
Blake

Not able to contain his curiosity about the paperback he had seen Henry reading the last two days, Pierre inquired, "What is the title of the book you are reading, Henry?"

"It's called *Report of the National Advisory Commission on Civil Disorders*. It's about the causes and solutions to the rioting in the USA last summer.

"What do you think of it?"

"I am learning a great deal from the book. The Commission's conclusions are an understatement. Listen, 'The destruction and the bitterness of racial disorder, the harsh polemics of black revolt and white repression have been seen and heard before in this country. It is time now to end the destruction and the violence, not only in the streets of the ghetto but in the lives of the people.'"

"Do you think that is just rhetoric?"

"Sure, but they also came up with a lot of concrete recommendations in many different areas which, if acted on, would really improve the lives of many people. They came out for several social democratic-like policies without calling them socialist. What bothers me is that they stop short of advocating and designing policies for several major things that would help all poor people in my country, namely socialized medicine and full employment; but they're right in pointing explicitly to the importance of overcoming racial discrimination *per se* and to putting forward concrete policies for accomplishing their goals in the areas of housing, police, education, and the like. I'm not speaking off the top of my hat; I've given quite a bit of time to tutoring black kids in the South and young offenders in Los Angeles."

Pierre responded, "It is an incredibly complex problem. That's probably why I am here in England for the first time this summer instead of on the committees at home. In my economics course I learned about a spiral of wages and prices that lead to inflation. So if the workers in France get higher wages, then prices are going to go up, and they'll be back where they started. But I am for *autogestion,* which we have been talking much about this spring."

"What is *autogestion*?"

"I don't know the English term for it. It means the workers manage things themselves."

"That sounds like a good idea."

"Oh, it is, and much has been written about it both in theory and practice."

Finishing off his last postcard, Blake wondered, "Do you guys want to go out for the evening?"

"Yeah, let's try a pub," was heard from most corners of the room.

The night passed fast. Finding a neighborhood pub in the vicinity, they entered the heavily smoked-filled room and ordered the frothy beer and cider. Two blond young women of medium height eyed Blake and Pierre. Pierre found their cockney English difficult to understand but amusing. They made one another understood so well that Pierre didn't go home with the others. Intimidated by the forwardness of the slightly taller woman, who began to pursue him, Blake became so fixated on her poor teeth, deplorable English, and absolutely dumb conversation that he could only think of not wanting to waste a precious minute in London. It would be just to brag that he had come to know intimately one of the natives.

On the morning of their last day in London, Henry wanted to see the National Gallery. Blake particularly took a liking to the collection of the Italian School from Margaritone d'Arezzo to Leonard de Vinci's *Modonna and Child with St. Anne and St. John the Baptist.* For Henry the Dutch collection was his favorite, and he stood glued to Rembrandt's *Woman Bathing in a Stream.* That afternoon Henry had hoped to take in Hampton Court Palace, but, because they had agreed to meet with the others at St. Paul's Cathedral, they took the tube over to Mansion House and Blackfriars on the Circle Line. This church was the one bit of architecture Jim and Tony had known anything about. To sound knowledgeable, Jim noted, "I'm a Sir Christopher Wren freak."

To up him, Tony asked, "Roger, do you care for its Renaissance style?"

Now more confident as a tourist, Tony bragged to Henry, "It was really worth getting over to Buckingham Palace by 11:30 A.M. to see the changing of the guard."

Relishing the taunt, Jim put in his two bits, "It seems as though your buddy Pierre hopped on the local lilypads last night, if you get my message?"

Tomorrow Henry would be leaving for the continent and Blake began to feel pulled between wanting to spend most of his vacation in England and spontaneously accompanying Henry to Belgium and France. Pulled between learning more about his roots and his budding friendship with Henry, he decided to compromise, *Why not take the train to Dover with Henry and then hitch to Canterbury and Hastings.*

CHAPTER 12

The next morning the arrangement of convenience between the young men terminated pleasantly but without remorse. To be sure, Blake and Henry would miss Pierre, who was going to spend the rest of the summer in England. But the personalities, values, and opinions of Roger, Tony, and Jim were so different from their own, Blake and Henry would remember them as acquaintances who had brought to life what the other half was thinking and doing. Pierre exchanged addresses with them at the train station.

On the train to the sea, Blake pulled out J. Duncan Spaeth's translation of the English classic, "The Seafarer" from Old English poetry. "Henry, listen to this passage on youth. It sounds like us. The Anglo-Saxons had our number all those years ago.

Oh, wildly my heart
Beats in my bosom and bids me to try
The tumble and surge of seas tumultuous
Breeze and brine and the breakers' roar.
Daily, hourly, drives me my spirit
Outward to sail, far countries to see."

Blake continued to read dramatically for a couple of minutes before Henry interrupted him with a friendly invitation.

"Blake, they really knew what we're about. It's been really great getting to know you over the last few days. Maybe you'll decide to join me on the continent later? But I've got to get down to my archeological dig down around *Le Musée de Préhistoire de France*."

"Henry, take care. Write. Let's stay in touch! Have a great time!" bid Blake, parting from his new friend with a strong heartfelt handshake. Both boy-men sensed the warmth and exuberance of a bond that would endure, of a unique understanding that brought them together to share the ideals and adventures so meaningful to those who have just ended their adolescence and who are entering their young manhood.

Having purchased a train ticket in London that included the crossing to the continent, Henry boarded an oldish large boat. Overriding his desire for some solitude and time to think for himself was his enthusiasm at the human variety that boarded the ship. It was his first time to be on a sea-faring craft. There were loads of student types in dark-green woolens or bright Moroccan or Mexican or Greek blankets serving as ponchos to ward off the chill of the foggy afternoon. There were Indian, Pakistani, and African students, some of them families with young children, and even incongruously, a few upper-class American women. From The Seven Sisters, they were unsuccessfully trying to mask their delicate skins under long, shabby plaid skirts under which they had an extra pair of worn jeans. The rough channel that day uncovered their attempt at imitating the proletarian chic of the English and French students–sending them to the edge of the deck to relieve their stomachs of excess contents.

Taking in this panorama, Henry sat outside on the deck across from an attractive English couple who exuded wholesomeness. They, too, were covered in old thick high-collared gray sweaters and were huddled together under the ever-present green blanket. They must have had experience making this crossing. Henry just wanted to ruminate about all the travel and people he had "been through" in the last few days. First, he was angry with himself for not telling Blake and the others about his best learning experience as an undergraduate in university that had put some of his ideals into practice.

I must have sounded like a big schmoozer: all talk and no action. If Blake overheard my conversation with Pierre, he must have thought I was a real hypocrite talking about the national commission on violence and not having done anything about it. But perhaps it was better I didn't say anything about it in front of that silly, southern-California trio. Things were pretty tense just as it was. Maybe I can explain things to Blake, if we meet later or if we write.

Henry was thinking of his stint in the South tutoring Sonny, helping him prepare for the first year of his community's integration of schools in Fayetteville, of his work in helping to organize the Negro community there, and of his tutoring Jewish juvenile offenders in Los Angeles. What was wrong with tutoring? You would have thought it was a crime given his family's reaction. His rich Uncle Steve from Atlanta was basically angry that

51

Henry wasn't getting paid for his work. Uncle Steve believed that since Henry was poor himself, he should work only where there was sufficient remuneration. His brother-in-law and cousins were pissed off at his "kicking up shit" too close to home; and his gentlemanly uncle from Mississippi was furious at his disturbing the status quo. Sonny's and his relationship had been terrific. Henry could play the role of a big brother, and Sonny had been introduced to the other side of town. Sonny had introduced Henry to the Negro town within a town, located in the valley in back of City Hall, hidden from the view of the affluent hills and the small-town shopping area on the top of the other side of the rounded enclosure. Sonny and Henry would walk to different libraries and read or work on math and talk about their families and the changes that were going on. When John, Henry's co-worker at the UCLA library, had mocked his "reformist" work as "petty bourgeois," it didn't bother Henry too much at the time. John was a true believer who never saw the problem with one-party states as a solution. He just kidded John back, "You want the South to be a one-party, super-conservative scene. Well, you can have it, along with my Aunts, Sue and Genevieve, and Uncle Max and the brutal police who enforce the system." He suspected John was bereft of any sexual outlet. Maybe that was the source of his pimples, because he ate well and exercised regularly.

Then there was that L.A. scene. He met real so-called delinquents. The only delinquent thing he could think about the place was the way the social worker had made them, the volunteers, so uptight about "being manipulated" by the toughs. Little Josh wasn't too different from the kids he had grown up with; well, maybe the social worker was right to some extent. Josh was always trying to get him and Rachel to buy him cigarettes. He and Rachel would always reply, "Isn't the air in L.A. bad enough?"

Poor, sad Rachel had the beautiful face of a second-generation, Turkish Sephardi Jewish girl. Her great weight was always so gracefully tucked under a dark home-made dress from which her rounded olive face and huge black eyes shone like those of a great opera star she wanted to become had it not been for her obediently complying to her parents' practical wishes. Josh wanted to hug Rachel, and rightfully so, for her voice beamed with the love of a Lena Horne and the passion of a Deborah. One day Josh had, indeed, tried to pounce upon Rachel whose operatic cry turned the home for first offenders into a laughing bedlam, at which point the authorities ran in and grabbed Josh. Rachel did not want the incident reported. Life for these kids was bad enough, she said. *Yes, it was true*, Rachel remembered, the social worker had warned them of "acting out."

Henry reflected to himself, *Well, if I did volunteer tutoring for the kids in the dorms, and they said they got a lot out of it, was it so bad to do it in the ghetto? I can understand where the Panthers' and the Black Muslims' anger is coming from, but I don't agree with their separatist program any more than I do with the white southern segregationists. Sure, it's great for all the groups to have the churches, clubs, cultural events, and associations of their own choice, but to turn our public institutions into hostile ethnic and racial groups destroys the public solidarity in the best of our national institutions. No, I don't like the blah, conformist, upper-middle class Anglo-Saxon white image projected as an ideal in much of the media, either, but we can change that with some pressure and hard work. However, I don't like the attitudes and inferior status of women among some Black Muslims and southern whites any more than I do among some orthodox Jews. Why are so many people apologetic of Eldridge Cleaver's chauvinistic attitude toward women in Soul on Ice?*

The channel waves began to toss the ship, and some mist sprayed over the side where the young couple was sitting. The rosy-cheeked young woman began to giggle and "her man" embraced her in a long, deep-throated kiss. Where had the stereotype of the undemonstrative, publicly correct English gone? Oh, days of liberation never looked so good. Then all of a sudden, the young woman withdrew her tongue from her male companion's mouth, shook her head throwing her long golden locks in a vigorous swirl, giggled again, and stared Henry right in the face: "You're a taciturn fellow, aren't you? A little on the shy side, perhaps? You're an American, aren't you?"

Before answering, Henry thought, *Damn, it's those ugly lime-green pants that were on sale before I left L.A. Why did I buy them?* He laughed half embarrassed, glancing at the deck.

"I'm having a good conversation with myself, I guess. Usually, I'd talk your ear off. Lots on my mind. It's all so new to me. I find this boatride terribly romantic. You must, too?"

They laughed again. "We're going to the continent for the first time."

"Where are you from?"

"From Durham."

"This is my first time, too. I'm headed for an archeological dig in the south of France."

"We're lifting to Yugoslavia."

"Have you ever hitched before?"

"Much experience in that field!" They laughed again.

53

Henry thought to himself, *In California you'd think anyone laughing this much had to be stoned or something, but they seem to be amused just by the humor in life.*

"What are you ruminating about so deeply, if you don't mind our asking? You looked so preoccupied with something."

"Oh, I was. So much to think about—lots of worries, troubles, and confusion, I guess. This trip is therapy for me."

Thomas, the young man, and Jane, the young woman, roared back with laughter, and Henry was carried away with it by a contagious bout of his own, quite infrequent guffaw. After a few minutes, the three managed to get themselves under control. The other passengers around them were annoyed at such noisy merriment. As he was catching his aching side and restraining himself, Henry wondered, *Wasn't that an inappropriate response of them to laugh at my woes? Oh, I guess not, maybe that was their way of shaking my body to make me feel better, to get me out of myself. I do feel better now.*

Jane was thinking, *He looks like the American version of a proper British public school boy. What's behind his shell?*

"I'm concerned about the right decision to make about the War in Vietnam, to serve or not, what to do and why. What's wrong and right in our country and the world at the moment. I graduated very young and began graduate school last March; then Johnson took away graduate deferments."

"Then you have real cause to be worried! Indeed, you do!" the couple responded at almost the same time.

"Yep." Henry's upper lip tightened as though he held back a tear that might have wanted to accentuate his mood.

"We'll be docking shortly."

"Will we be lifting the same way?"

"We're not sure. Let's get out our maps."

"If you're headed for Paris and northward, then you'll probably want to lift eastward to Ghent, and then head south to Paris through Lille. Since lifting's much better in northern Europe, we're going to head due eastward to Liege and on to Germany, then down through Austria to Yugoslavia."

"You're right. That looks like the best route."

"Come along with us through Oostende. They say you have to hurry debarking because it is urgent to try to get the sympathy of one of the drivers who has seen you aboard the ship."

"I'll follow you."

It was cold and the sky was overcast with gray billowing clouds that fluffed up one upon the other as the ship pulled in the late afternoon at Oostende. Dashing out of the boat, the three travelers loaded down with heavy backpacks romped out to shore before the first automobiles could debark. Walking backwards so that they would face the oncoming traffic, Thomas whispered to Henry, "Make sure you try to cast a pleading, warm, sympathetic, innocent stare directly into the eyes of the driver."

And Jane added, "That always gets them. It does most often."

Within about five cars, a British car driven by an elderly husband offered a ride to Jane and Thomas, who, before hastily stuffing their possessions into the car, wished Henry a "jolly good trip and much luck."

Worrying whether he was conveying too much of his own anxiety at hitching, Henry said to himself, *This is ridiculous. Do exactly what Jane and Thomas said.* After ten minutes more of practice, near the end of the line of cars coming off the ferry, a cheerful English family on their way to Switzerland offered him a ride to Ghent.

For this cordial Anglican priest and his wife, Henry was obviously a relief as a babysitter. As the jovial priest was helping him lock his pack in the trunk, Henry glimpsed at the two boys, about seven and nine years of age, who were beating each other mercilessly as their mother pleaded, "Here, here. This is no way to act in front of company." Surely as soon as Henry boarded— invited as he was to sit between the two lads—they straightened their backs as though their own nanny had suddenly been imported to settle the altercation at hand.

"Hi, my name is Henry."

"Oh, I'm Peter, and this is my younger brother, Edward."

"How do you do?"

"How do *you* do?"

"And I'm Evelyn. So very pleased to have you. Where are you headed?"

"I'm on my way to the south of France via Paris. As you can hear from my accent, I'm an American. Hi, guys, guess from what state I am."

To the delight of the pastor and his wife, Henry managed to keep up this guessing game, with all kinds of offshoots and variations, to Bruges. At that point the game gave way to Henry's starting up a song contest between the two boys. Their parents joined in to create a four-way song festival that lasted all the way to Ghent.

With such a joyous mood in the automobile, and with their relief at the reprieve from several hours of bratty bickering, Evelyn and her husband, John, insisted on driving Henry to the campground nearest to the motorway and paying the camp fee. "Please, it's late in the evening. We've been students ourselves, too. Let us do this."

Not wanting to upset his hard-earned night's sleep, Henry graciously accepted the offer and bid everyone goodnight and a happy journey. It was already about 8:00 P.M. He quickly rolled out his sack on a piece of plastic under a large tree. Freezing in the cold of the evening air, Henry tucked himself inside his thickly quilted, old green bag, and suddenly fell into a deep sleep, awakening only to the starting sound of an automobile emitting a strange diesel smell. His first thought was to get up early before the cars would be heading to their destinations. Henry quickly rolled up his bag and stuck it under the main part of the backpack on a little aluminum bar designed to hold it up. Within a few minutes, a Renault Four with its oval top tin-can-like sweep bounced to a sudden halt. A young bearded man around thirty years of age, who turned out to be a Belgian teacher, opened the door and announced that he was headed for Lille, France. By the time they arrived at the border of Belgium and France, he was surprised to have to ask the border patrol for a stamp in his passport. Just about two hours after getting this ride, he was left on the outskirts of Lille, an old military and textile town, which had changed hands from Flanders to France. Now only somewhat more than 150 miles from Paris, Henry waited endlessly. The overcast sky mellowed the giant elm on the slope where the gray stone church stood keeping the young man company. Imagining a landscape painting in a museum, Henry kept his thumb out from 10:00 A.M. to 2:00 P.M. and watched the irregular traffic thrust itself over the hill of his fantasy frame.

Suddenly an old Peugeot screeched to a halt. The driver and a companion—two Parisians in their mid-twenties—were on their way back to the metropolis. The young American stuffed his possessions and himself into the back seat. Tired and learning to be more cautious about the appropriateness of when and why to speak, Henry did not say anything and listened to the couple's conversation in French dotted with Parisian argot. They were going on and on about whether or not 60,000 Renault workers should return to work and how long the radio and TV employees would continue their strike. In about three hours, they left him to fend for himself at Gare du Nord, Paris' train station for northern destinations.

In the late afternoon in the great city of dreams, Henry wondered if he should just walk around all night and take in as much as possible before leaving the next morning for his dig in the south of France. In a torrent of thoughts, he pondered on taking a bed at a youth hostel or just hopping the first train for the south of France. He didn't want to activate his Eurailpass yet, so he could travel after the dig in the Périgord. He decided it was prudent to board the lowest-class train available to the dig right away that would leave for Bordeaux that evening and connect with a "milk run" omnibus train to the little village near the confluence of the Vézère and Dordogne Rivers where the Museum of Prehistory of France was located. It was about three hours before this train left, so he had to make it over to the *Gare d'Orléans* from the Train Station of the North. Hopping the metro over to near the *Île de la Cité* he gave himself a twenty minute tour of *Nôtre Dame* Cathedral and then walked by the Seine past the *Jardin des Plantes* over to the Orleans Station. Even his haste translated itself into more of a light expansion of freedom and zest. He felt that this must be his city, as though he had been born, grew up, and thrived in it, but he would have to wait to see it properly at the end of the summer, after his dig. This was just a friendly, tempting introductory appetizer. He was already pulled by the city's seductive lure. Springing up and down, even under the weight of the pack, his frame bounced to a temporary carefree lift.

He barely made the train on which he collapsed into a plain green-upholstered, straight-back seat facing a dashing young man who he would learn later was an Alexandrian of Arabic background, but who resembled a Greek statue. From his backpack, Henry withdrew a copy of the *New York Times* he had found lying on a bench in the *Gare du Nord*. A recent arrival must have dumped it there. Dr. Spock's, Rev. William Sloane Coffin, Jr.'s, Mitchell Goodman's, Marcus Raskin's, and Michael Ferber's ages spanned almost three generations, yet they all were finding courage to speak out against the war. As he turned the pages, he focused on the article on page six about the Saigon Information Minister, Ton That Thieu, who had been a Vietnamese delegate to the Geneva Conference on Far Eastern Affairs in 1954, and who was now Vice Dean at Van Hanh University in Saigon. At his address at the East West Center at the University of Hawaii, Mr. Thieu had said, "Our peasants will remember their cratered rice fields and defoliated forests, devastated by an alien air force that seems at war with the very land of Vietnam."

"Villagers will remember their hamlets uprooted from the earth, all to no purpose. And our city dwellers and our intellectuals will mark how, while saving Vietnam, a half million American soldiers are suffocating it with their fantastic wealth, their gadgetry, their promiscuous virility, and their destructive innocence."

Thieu went on to add to what Henry followed from everything he had been studying in his undergraduate curriculum, "If a greater share of American aid was provided to make it possible for Vietnamese to study sociology, in general, and the problems pertaining to their society, in particular; if American intellectuals were to take a greater interest in the problems of societies in transition and the sociology of Vietnam, then, perhaps, we would hear more sensible and helpful talk and see more effective action."

"Habib, those two women in the corridor are shouting at each other over your backpack," interrupted the young man sitting across from Henry.

"What?" responded Henry, so absorbed in the newspaper article, he had failed to hear the loud racket outside the compartment.

"The French woman does not think that you ought to be permitted to place—excuse her expression—your dirty pack on the rack, while the girl from Quebec grabbed it back from her saying she had no right to take another paying passenger's baggage."

With this information, Henry leapt up, thanked the fellow and thrust the sliding door open, bowed at the young woman from Quebec in her late teens and looked angrily upwards at the middle-aged French lady. He inquired, "*Qu'est-ce qui se passe?*"

"You have no right to put a dirty *sac-à-dos* on the rack for baggage," she screamed in French. Keeping his cool, he responded in the Gallic tongue to the younger woman, "First, thank you for keeping my possessions from being thrown off this car, ma'am." Then turning to the older lady, he replied, "I can assure you that my backpack is most sanitary!"

"What? How dare you say that? Backpacks are all filthy!"

Henry moved his hand downward in a sweeping fashion and bade his feminine defender welcome to the compartment, "*De rien,*" she smiled in her *joual patois*, "Can you believe the nerve of some people? Who the hell does that bitch think she is anyway? She is probably a reactionary who hates all young people because they wear their hair long. *Mon Dieu!*"

"Excuse me, *Madame,*" he formally addressed the older woman, "You are most welcome to join us as long as you don't throw our stuff out the window." On that point, the lady huffed forward to another compartment.

The conversation on the train continued in French mainly between the handsome, dignified Alexandrian, whose name was Adel, and the jovial, fresh-looking maiden from Quebec whose name was Francine. Her rosy rounded cheeks complemented her full breasts half-covered by a light cotton pullover. Henry was intrigued by the great differences in the *pied-noir* patois of the young Alexandrian and the Quebec accent, which in some way reminded him of southern American dialect in English. But watching the subtle advances made by the Egyptian, Francine politely and adroitly out maneuvered Adel. The action of the young *Québécoise* titillated the sense of humor of Adel and Henry who were rolling with laughter.

Sobering the air in these enclosed quarters, Adel asked Henry about the famous baby doctor's trial for his anti-war activities in America . "Yes, Dr. Spock feels that the American war is illegal and immoral and that the U.S. is destroying a country that never intended to harm it. I must say I agree with him wholeheartedly." As Henry was making his remark, the train was pulling into the Bordeaux station, and he would have to change to a local train to the village of Périgord. Thanking Adel and Francine for their help and good company, Henry heaved his pack onto his back and got ready to jump off the train to find out when and where the local train left. Luckily, he had about an hour and a half before the *omnibus* left for the village—just enough time to have a *café au lait* with a bagette. *Délicieux*!

As soon as he felt awake from the hot beverage, he walked briskly over to the platform to wait for the train. It consisted of two fading beige cars with green stripes. These were quite filled with passengers who looked like real peasants from the great works of French art. Somewhere in the back of his mind was the diffused light with pastels framing the hardworking farm-laborers and farm-servants in Millet's *The Gleaners*, *Angelus*, and *The Sheperders* which blended the realities of Naturalism with the sentiments of Romanticism. Sitting right in front of him were the poor, single toilers who were the subject of that art.

CHAPTER 13

As the train came to a stop in Périgord, Henry's mind was withdrawing from morning lethargy that slowly leaves large frames and heads. Gradually sleep seemed to recede from his brain. He would have loved to be invited to someone's home for a long shower or hot bath, although more important obligations had to come before comforts. When he inquired, the station attendant pointed the way to the museum. The small houses, stuck closely together in the town, made him recall the sleepy atmosphere and quiet of the South of much of his youth.

Finally, he reached the museum, a semi-decaying building that, nonetheless, stood like a monument mediating between nature and *la civilisation française*. Outside was the wife of the famous archeologist who, as a resistance fighter hiding in caves during the Second World War, had rediscovered how to shape Stone Age tools. She tried to help him find his dig. No, she was not aware that a professor had come from the University of California for an archeological expedition. No, her husband had not heard, either. But, perhaps, if she were to call Bordeaux, she might find out something more, if he would not mind paying for the long distance call. For Henry every few pennies counted this summer, and this call would probably be several dollars.

"O.K., please go ahead." The professor asked him for about five dollars to pay for the call, which yielded no more information than he had already.

Sorry, she said sincerely with a comforting motherly look, "Maybe, if you return to the Museum of Man in Paris someone would know something about the dig. I also must inform you, regretfully, that our famous caves that you probably want to see are closed for restoration," she said gently, accenting her tone with her strongly pronounced eyebrows.

"Thank you ever so much."

"Good luck!"

His morning head cleared. The warmth of the southern sun with the medieval ruins on the hill overhead tempted him to stay in this place that lingered undisturbed in history. There were no crowds, few denizens, but large warm droopy trees abounded. *No, I'll try some more in Paris, and if it doesn't work, I'll see the city and then hitch up to Scandinavia and try to get a job to make some money,* Henry mused to himself.

There was a local train returning to Bordeaux in the evening. The afternoon sun was splendid, warming him throughout, somewhat humid but drier than the suppressive heat of the American southern summer. Before early evening, the humidity had lessened, making the trip back to Bordeaux and Paris feel faster than the trip there. He slept most of the way.

Arriving in the early morning, Henry went to the *Musée de l'Homme*, the greatest ethnographic museum in France, where he spoke to about twenty professors. Again, no one had heard of the dig.

Henry began to feel as angry as dejected. *How stupid! Somebody should have informed the students and French colleagues about something!* he ruminated.

O.K., it's not the end of the world. Improvise! First, let me go back to the Youth Hostel to make sure I'll have a place to stay. Hopping the metro in the direction of the foot of Sacrecoeur, Henry got off and walked to Pigalle down the wide boulevard. A young North African tried to sell him a cube of opium to smoke. Trying to feign a blasé response, Henry politely refused while trying to fake his real revulsion at having been accosted by a real pusher. Several prostitutes widened their smiles and broadened the open-leggedness of their stance. Their overly made-up complexion and strength *du parfum bon marché*, though almost stereotypical, evoked a light upset stomach in him. Amused, but nervously repressing the thought of how diseased they appeared, the young man comforted himself with the thought that he would not go native. The street was both alluring and repulsive, exciting and anxiety-provoking. Within the crowd lay hidden a throbbing excitement but brooding violence, dramatic, yet life threatening. On reaching the hostel, he glanced around at the darkened walls. Paying his dollar, he left his equipment in the locked room and took a glance at the third bunk of a high-ceilinged room. *From what century could this building be?*

He figured he could afford four days in Paris before going north to look for work. He was exhilarated by the personal freedom to engorge himself on the beauty of the history, the people, the language, and the culture he had come to love during his studies.

Did Paris really come from the old word of the *Parisii* bargemen for boat? Just because the Parisian coat of arms depicted a sailboat tossed by the waves and its Latin motto meant that "It floats and does not sink" and just because its old name, *Lutetia,* came from the Greek word for whitened stuff, which Rabelais likened to the skin of the bargemen's wives, did not mean that these etymologies were true. So what if they were fantastic dreaming old wives' tales? The dryness of American social science dismissed them with disdain but, thereby, lost their color and dreaminess. But there must be some truth in what the battered book with browned edges and mildewing leaves pretended was the real history of the city.

Just imagine that at the center of Paris there had been a flat and wooded island where the *Parisii* had constructed their earthen huts. Just think that you could drink the Seine's waters and that the forests on both sides of the river were well stocked with game. Henry walked and read conjuring up the battle between Vercingetorix and Julius Caesar in 53 B.C. *Wow, there are still aqueducts and arenas left which the Romans built. On every street there was a name and a story that had been expressed in the dashing prose or poetry of Villon, Balzac, Hugo, Baudelaire, and Proust, and the sounds of Berlioz, Delacrois, and Daumier*. Henry's chest expanded as the air around inflated him with so much to take in and so little time.

This trip was turning out to be so different from the one in London. All by himself in a foreign country whose history, literature, and monuments had inspired him. He was alone communing with things and listening to people surreptitiously, while in London his time had passed appreciating the past and present with peers from whose lives he was learning as they interacted with the symbols of their past presents.

This morning at the youth hostel he had been annoyed at the crude seventeen- or eighteen- year-old provincial French woman's anti-Semitic remark, "There are so many dirty Jews here." The young woman had uttered this comment to her friend with a facial expression of disgust. Henry did not know whether to laugh or be frightened and revolted at the ignorance of this small towner's perception of North African Arabs as Jews. He was sure he must be the only Jew in this hostel. Yet it left him with the urge to be on his own and to look and absorb the best of the civilization of France, which had had such a long love-hate relationship with that of his own people. The Jews had been accepted as individuals but not as a nation in law, and, in reality, had been intermittently despised and discriminated against as a nation.

Over the next two days he promenaded down the Avenue des Champs-

Elysees to the Place de la Concorde, walked back to the Trocadero and Eiffel Tower through the Camps des Mars and over the backstreets to the *Hôtel des Invalides* and the *Palais du Luxembourg*, the *Sorbonne*, and the *Cluny Museum*, back over to the right bank to the *Halles Centrales*, *Place Vendome*, *the Opera*, and *La Bourse*, devoting his last day to the *Louvre*. While in this huge collection, Henry visualized that the art course which he had dreaded taking but had come to enjoy, had been etched in a spectacular monument beginning with a low section of Gothic to finely nuanced minute details engraved with monarchs and heavenly figures, painted, engraved, sculpted, carved, and raised in variegated architectural forms, framed in garden tombs. Suddenly, all these forms projected triumphal arches, domes, columns, places, stone, hangings, and tapestries to the Sun King. From there the emotions and drama of human lives were represented flying in their individual nobility in a quickened powerful crescendo. Everything was related to everything else: the language of this period was too exhausted for poetry but had transformed itself into the plastic arts of Gabriel's Trianon, Watteau, Boucher, Chardin, Houdon, Clodion, and Fragonard's voluptuous images tinged with emotion.

Henry's aesthetic ear heard music. Dum, dum, a lowered slow repetitious beat succumbed to tight classic cords of the Revolution and empire: centralization, archeology, and rationalism. Through this realistic drum, enthusiastic forms, nevertheless, conveyed epic ideas. All of a sudden a heightened staccato pranced from high to low, while the whole orchestra swept from one of its mighty wings to another: delicateness, sensitivity, colors, tones, landscapes of the country, and bodies in outline, upward in victory or reposed in death, the gamut of human form.

It was all too much, but still enraptured him! The chill of Roger Bloche's *Cold* changed into the warmth of Rodin's *Kiss*. If you chose to walk backwards through the rooms in that order, the serenity of Carot's *The Arras Road*, or his *Souvenir of Italy*, metamorphosed from Naturalism to Romanticism. Everywhere he went there were names that echoed melodies of beauty, like that of Puvis de Chavannes, in places of majesty like The Pantheon; in every street that he walked, the French had been able to turn stone into fanciful vaults and arches in thousands of different shapes, forms, and colors that made Henry feel in harmony with his surroundings.

By the fourth day, reality began to return. He dropped by the American Express to see if there was any news from home. After an unpleasant wait in the stuffy office where well-clad men and women asserted their right to push and shove the less ornately attired behind, Henry finally made it to the front desk where the clerk returned with a letter from his friend Fred. Shoving his way outside, he read the airletter in the heat of the afternoon sun.

June 20, 1968

Dear Henry,

Just a quick line to wish you a great dig and carefree jaunt around Europe. Things are pretty much the same here in Tinsel Town. The air is particularly thick with grime that must contain some new chemical that is especially irksome to my sight. Still this is home. I thought you'd be interested in the enclosed clipping from your group of rabbis from today's New York Times, I know it's none of my business as a non-observant Lutheran to influence your religious decision about the draft, but, I think it will really matter to you deep down inside. The old group at the library is much the same. Miss Winkle is slowly getting over her suicide attempt. We all take our turns visiting her over at Psychiatric Services. I hate to say it was pretty humorous when she requested a copy of A Thousand and One Way to Make Enemies. When I went to take it to her, another patient on their open ward came up to me and asked if it were for Miss Winkle. I said 'yes,' how did he know. He said that our good 'ol boss had been going into all of the bathrooms putting up notices 'Don't forget to flush the toilet,' 'Take your toothbrush back to your room,' and other such kindness. Well, her affirmative commands did get us to write her last published bibliography for her on time, didn't it? She had her nerve not even giving us a footnote, though. Did you hear that when Norma found Miss Winkle in her white marbled-tiled apartment with loads of exotic pet birds flying around, Miss Winkle was lying, wrists slashed, in the middle of her king-size bed with white satin sheets? They say that Norma got her the ambulance in the nick of time. For us Norma has become the great heroine, but Miss Winkle is trying to avoid her. She doesn't want her to come on any more visits. Life is hard to explain, isn't it?

Take Care!
Your Buddy, Fred

Henry now unfolded the clipping and started to read,

"Rabbis Ask End of All Bombing in North Vietnam: Group Asserts Administration Has Redistributed Targets Instead of De-escalating."

Great, thought Henry, *at least our Reform rabbis aren't keeping silent*. He read on: "It is our conviction that our military intervention in Vietnam has never been justified and that negotiations should and must lead to the withdrawal of all military forces from Vietnam so that the people of that land may be free to determine their own destiny."

Henry read further,

"On the other hand, the Union of Orthodox Jewish Congregations and the Jewish War Veterans have strongly supported the Administration's policy."

Well, I guess the old saying is true, "Two Jews, three synagogues," Henry chuckled to himself for one minute, and then reflected, *It's funny; I've never really known any Orthodox Jews very well and so much of our Reform theology is a critique of their beliefs or behavior.*

He stretched in the afternoon sun and decided to spend his last afternoon in the metropolis taking in a few of the great and small buildings lauded by his decrepit old guidebook, which, nevertheless, sounded as much like a text of contemporary American social science as that of art and architecture. Paris, like all cities, had changed. It had gone from antiquity through the Gothic to the Feudal to the Classical to the Monarchical to Neo-Classical to Naturalistic to Modern styles. Kings and princes and ordinary folk wearied of one style and opted for a different one, but in this constant change there was a sense of organic wholeness that was lacking in the American form. Still, even the classic regularity had been a relatively recent contribution by Baron Hausmann: the wide avenues and regular streets, and the decoration of ordinary houses. This would be transitory, too: there were forces building toward the skyscraper which derived in an important way from maximizing the value of urban land. But generalizations are overcome by the force of the actual structures. They leave messages for the listening visitor.

On his return, The Pantheon grabbed Henry. Here was the sign of France's great dead. Below were the vaults of J. J. Rousseau, Voltaire, Zola, Victor Hugo, and more. Henry wondered, *Will I be in some less well-marked grave soon, too, without any chance to contribute anything to my country or the rest of humanity except killing others whom I don't want to kill for a cause I don't believe in?* He thought of the fake wooden coffins, holding fake, molding corpses, which the art students had sculpted out of green plastic garbage bags filled with guacamole dip and surrounded by wreaths of potato chips. And of the wooden Crosses, Stars of David, and Islamic Crescents, which had been planted all over the UCLA campus this graduation. The Pantheon was solemn, holy ground, dark like the grave, which recalled a person's end. *That's why all the guides are spending so little time with the little old ladies from Atlanta here—it's too grim for them, and they probably don't know or care to know who St. Geneviève was in the first place. They probably think she's some typical 'Popish icon' who shouldn't be there in the first place.*

The Greek cross and the enormous central dome above and the Corinthian columns all around seemed to speak to his mind that there are some things for which it is worthwhile to die. It's secular here now. A voice from within whispered to Henry, *Your death should be worth enshrining, not for obedience to the dollar and multinational corporations but for following what your heart and mind lead you to cherish.* Time stopped. The darkness was cold. Reality fused with this space. His head, looking at the stones below his feet, focused on the late afternoon outside.

Walking past the Bibliothèque Ste.-Geneviève, he stopped briefly to admire the library that dated all the way back to 1624. It was time to walk back to the intersection of the Boulevards St. Germain and St. Michel, where he could get a good coffee and overhear the latest student rap. No sooner had Henry sat at a table than a scruffy young man plopped in the chair next to his, "Don't mind if I do," he chuckled in a southern-American drawl, anticipating some hostile anti-American *resentiment.*

"Actually, I was in the mood to be alone, but, if you need a place, take it," Henry stated matter-of-factly.

The fellow had stubble of a day or two and Henry could smell alcohol and tobacco on his breath from across the table. "Well, la-tee-da, who the fuck do you think you are, bastard?"

Henry ignored him. Suddenly this "type" pinched the buttocks of a passing mademoiselle, who was wearing a simple, blue cotton dress. She slapped him as fast as he had touched her.

"Well, little miss sassy ass," he roared.

"Sorry," he turned to Henry, "my name is Phil Grimes. I used to be from Georgia before I did my stint in the steel mills of Gary, Indiana, and stupidly shacked up with a *deutsche Mädchen* during my army stint. Fuck! Is that a bummer?! Man, it's killing me!"

"You're troubled about her?"

"Shit, man, she's my wife now. And they really hate us Americans in Germany except those cunts who really need a good fuck!" At which point this ungentlemanly redneck heaved his afternoon's fill of wine all over Henry's shoes. The table reeked of the vomit and Henry started to get up to leave.

"Hey, man, I'm sorry if I offended you. I didn't mean to. I'm just a mean son-of-a-bitch. Hey, man, I want to make it up to you." Phil plopped a twenty-dollar bill down on the table. "Look, there's more of this coming if you can get me out of this fuckin' whorehouse, man," offered Phil, as he heaved a second round of puke toward his acquaintance,

Perceiving a human being underneath Phil's veneer of pseudo-masculinity, Henry thought, *Maybe here is my way up north. I'll have to put up with a hell of a lot, but, who knows, maybe it will be worth it.*

Phil was thin and lanky with red spots on his neck and orange ones on his freckled face. For his rather slight frame and stature of five feet, ten inches, his hands and biceps were disproportionately large from hard manual work or training. Probably his chest would have been equally out of proportion were it not for his chain-smoking of unfiltered Camel cigarettes having collapsed it. When he breathed, one could hear a slight hee-haw rasp that squeezed his leathered lung cage out to his ribs as his diaphragm inadvertently kept the oversized machine playing like a neglected accordion. He must have been in his late twenties but looked much older, like a man who had set out to destroy his own body.

"Phil, I'm Henry," he replied, extending his hand while withholding his last name in case he turned out to be a racist. "I'm headed up north night now. Which direction are you going?"

"Get me out of here, and I'll take you anywhere."

"Does Scandinavia sound alright?"

"Fine with me."

"When can you leave?"

"Let's go over to the St. Severin where I'm staying and get my stuff, if those fuckin' whores didn't steal it."

Henry kept thinking, *I've got to keep my cool. I need to make it north where I can earn a few bucks. I'll never make it through the summer on ninety dollars outside the archeological dig.*

The St. Severin was a Latin Quarter hotel on its way down. They walked up a winding inner-court staircase, where the dingy, taupe interior led down deserted corridors. Suddenly a bang, wham, thump, crashed into the inner courtyard from what appeared to be the room to which they were headed. A battered piece of luggage remained intact.

"You bastard, why didn't you tell me you were married?" shouted the auburn twin sister. Thump, her twin hurled her left heel right into Phil's cock and the first twin plunged in with her blow. He bent over, covering his groin with both hands. Henry put up his arms trying to block the next salvo and pleaded in French, "Ladies, please, what did he do to you?"

"Don't ask us. Just go down and collect his shit from the courtyard like all his other lackeys," they shouted while dashing out of the hotel. Henry helped Phil rest on his shoulder.

"Do all women act toward you this way?"

"I guess I talked too sweet to her last night and she must have found my wife's picture in my things while she was snooping when I went out this morning. Her sister is one of them pruddy, lil' small town girls from Kansas. She was a German major in college, so I guess she deciphered my wife's letter for her sis. Shit. Let's get out of here, man."

Henry helped him to check his room. There was nothing left in this darkened space. Back down to the inner court to collect Mr. Grimes's remaining possessions, Henry neatly folded Phil's new Parisian wardrobe into his leather suitcase. It all seemed so incongruous with this fellow's way of life. "Do you have your car keys?"

"Here, man, I'll drive. I'm sober enough to."

"Phil, I want to go with you, but to be honest, I'd feel better if we went and had a double espresso before you drive out of town."

"Sounds good. I'll get a sandwich, too."

Sipping the coffee and gobbling down a thin slice of ham on a piece of French bread, Phil was not hiding his whim to leave immediately. Politely watching, Henry gazed at the serious student at the next table who was reading Jacques Derrida's *De la Grammatologie*. He yearned to strike up a conversation about the book and its author but kept his mouth shut, not wanting to step onto a territory which might intimidate Phil's many neuroses. *I'll put it on my reading list*, thought Henry, taking out a hand-sized notebook into which he jotted down the name of the author and title. He loved linguistics and grammar, which most people found dull. *Is that what that book is about? It'll just have to wait.* He glanced at Phil who just said, "Ready."

"Sure," Henry responded, swinging his backpack over his shoulders while Phil picked up the tab for both of them. Henry reciprocated by carrying Phil's loaded suitcase.

The Volkswagen bug whisked off with a startling thrust into the intemperate chaos of the Parisian boulevards. Out on the main highway,

Henry was sure that Phil would either get them both thrown into jail for reckless driving or kill them both in a multi-car collision, but somehow Phil had many lives. He smoked one Camel after the next—inhaling the smoke deeply, and exhaling the bluish-white smoke through both nostrils until his cigarette burned down almost to his lip. Unable to bear the thickness of the smoke without coughing, Henry lowered the VW's window, so he could breathe. Phil carried on a three-hour monologue all the way to the Belgian border just north of Lille.

"I was born in a small town in Alabama. My mamma and pappa were as good to me as anyone could be. Then pappa died when I was fourteen and mamma remarried a city slicker from Atlanta with lots of money. I had to prove to them that I could make it on my own, so when I finished high school I went up to Gary, Indiana, and worked in the steel mills. I was just as tough as the meanest and toughest fella there. I worked alongside of Croats and Serbs and you name it. They didn't bother me, and I could outdrink any of them.

"I got into the army before the Vietnam thing was big, and I was stationed in a small German town. There was a sweet lil' seventeen-year-old chick who kept following me on the weekends and those people from the town are so fuckin' narrow-minded that if a local girl goes out with us, they call her the American's slut or something even worst. So I said, 'What the fuck? If they're gonna treat her that way, I'm just gonna haul off and marry her'—screw that whole fuckin' anti-American, crappy lot. After what they did, they still think they're so fuckin' superior. What the hell, I married her. At first, it was real nice. We had a lot of good times together, but her parents and ol' school friends hounded the hell out of us. They said I was an uneducated, crude wife-beater. Well, she became a real nasty bitch and, hell, I lost control a time or two, and the whole fuckin' town was about to lynch me. I'm real scum, man. You chose to ride with the goddamn filth of the earth."

The sun had set, and they stopped briefly at the border. Phil was complaining that he had to slow down on both sides to avoid the cops. Phil's self-preoccupation showed no insight, causing his own and his rider's tension to rise. As it got dark, it was difficult for Henry to feign genuine attentiveness, particularly because Phil liked to talk endlessly while listening to the rock radio broadcasts by Euro-American stations.

"You've had some really rough times recently," Henry commented, trying to be non-directive, as he had learned in his psychology courses. It was difficult for Henry not to say what he believed, and he wondered if he weren't just trying to flatter this deeply troubled individual for his own end of a ride to where he wanted. Maybe there were just nasty, inconsiderate, mean people to whom their inconsiderateness and harm to others should be pointed out directly. But then he remembered Professor Zalman's warning: never attack a mental problem head-on. It will only lead to denial, repression, and defensiveness. But wasn't this being immoral and dishonest? If Phil was "sick," and this was the only way of getting someone who had beaten his wife and was living a self-destructive life to "listen" to his own behavior, then maybe it was O.K. to be non-directive. On the other hand, Phil had lied to one of the Kansas twins to sleep with her, had exploded at the constraints and prejudices of small-town German life in a way that had caused physical harm to his intimate, and insulted strangers on the street in a desperate attempt to draw someone to hear him.

Phil turned up Dionne Warwick's "Do You Know the Way to San Jose," just after passing the Dutch border. He also pressed his foot down on the accelerator. "Don't worry, man, I've driven this route a hundred times and have never run into a cop."

"Would you like to stop for a coffee or something?"

"Hey, that's not a bad idea, but I wanna keep goin' after that all the way to Travemunde." He pulled off the road at the next small village where there was a small restaurant still open.

After entering a brown exposed-timber-on-white-plaster building with a high slanted orange roof, Phil ordered two coffees. The middle-aged, chunky waitress brought out a black brew with cream and sugar cubes in separate blue porcelain containers. Before Phil could utter something harsh, Henry needed to acknowledge Mr. Grimes's mastery of local down-home delicacies.

"This coffee is delicious."

"You go ahead an' have a pastry too. It's on me. You're not bad company," Phil laughed.

"Thanks. I'll be finished in just a minute. Then we can hit the bathrooms and leave."

Back on the road, Henry inquired, "Phil, what are you going to do about your marriage?"

"That's the sixty-four thousand dollar question."

"You seem pretty unhappy. Have you ever thought of taking your wife back to America?"

"She says she wants to stay near her parents. She's never been outside her little part of Germany. She says she won't go."

"Can you really see yourself staying over here?"

"Not really."

"Have you ever thought, like, maybe this marriage just isn't working, and that it would be best for both of you to end it?"

"The thought has occurred to me, yeah, but I just feel so protective of her despite everything."

"But do you think that it can work?"

"No, not really."

Around four A.M. they reached Travemunde on the north shore of Germany. It was cold and foggy, so they just pulled over to the side of the road and rolled out their sleeping bags by the side of the car.

They woke up so late in the morning that they missed the first ferry to Denmark. Henry thought that Phil might want to save the cost of ferrying his car to Denmark, and it would be a good chance to travel with a more stable person. He asked, "Phil, it seems really unfair of me to ask you to pay for the ferry to Denmark when you hadn't even thought of going there in the first place."

"Fuck, man, you're the first person who's talked sense to me since my commander kicked me in the ass a few years back. It's O.K. Money is somethin' I'm not hurtin' for. Besides, I hear that they have good bars on these boats in Scandinavia, and I haven't checked 'em out yet."

It was thrilling to drive the small car on board the huge boat, and to rush up the heavy metal stairs to the decks to watch the other passengers. Phil made a beeline to the bar, so Henry agreed to keep an eye on him ever so often while he walked around the ship. As it was still quite cool outside, he sat near the entrance to the upper decks watching the well-dressed families and elderly people board. Hungry, he pulled out the big glass quart of milk and the loaf bread he had bought in Travemunde and began thinking how fast everything has been happening the last few days. Across the aisle from him stood a group of Danish women in their sixties smoking small cigars and laughing, yes, at him. They laughed and laughed before Henry caught on. Yes, there was a young man sitting on the floor drinking milk while they, old ladies, were standing there smoking cigars and drinking schnapps. Overlooking the scene, the young Danish crew hostess was perturbed at her countrywomen making a young guest feel uncomfortable. Stopping her reception of the VIPs, she walked over to Henry and inquired if he cared to join her after she was finished with her main duties when the boat pulled out of port.

"Sure!" he blurted out—relieved and flattered to be asked by such a beautiful and charming woman.

Ingrid had a sweet smile and sincere blue eyes that managed to penetrate the heart of her guests, while keeping a respectful distance. As the boat's receiving hostess, she spoke fluent Danish, of course, as well as German, English, and French, and made herself understood in Swedish and Norwegian. With all her sophistication, she maintained the down-home quality of a village girl from Gedser while being a cosmopolitan woman whose livelihood depended on making people of many different nationalities feel comfortable and happy away from home. After her duties were over, she walked up to Henry and joked in a President Kennedy-style American accent, "Do nice boys always drink milk and eat wholesome bread when they are away from home from their mommies?" Then she suddenly switched to a perfect May West impersonation, "Why don't you come up and see me sometime?" Except she added in her gentle Danish accent, "I'm serious, let's go to my cabin." Henry could hardly believe this was happening to him. It was right out of the movies. They walked down several corridors and made several turns, going down a flight of stairs. Ingrid opened the door to her small room indicating a small couch on which he could sit. "You look like a man of my taste. Did I say that right?" she laughed.

Henry felt jovial but awkward in his speech. "What is your taste?"

"Oh, I like men of ideas who have serious expressions while enjoying the basic things in life."

"Well, you certainly were nice trying to make me feel at home despite my being the brunt of those old ladies' joke."

"That's my job, but if you don't mind my saying so, you're cute."

"Well, you're plain beautiful!"

Henry kept wondering when was the appropriate time for words to end and their mutual admiration of each other's youthful form to be physically expressed.

Ingrid sat on her bed and threw off her sweater, lying back on a pile of pillows and looked her male companion in the eyes. "Let me guess, you're from California and you're Italian or Jewish."

"How did you ever guess?" Henry wondered as he felt the gentle rocking of the ship tilt towards the left.

"Well, you had California written on the name tag on your backpack, and you have a rather Mediterranean appearance. I like it. It's like all the statues I spend so much time studying in classics."

"You are the golden-haired enchantress that is supposed to accompany the statue on his various adventures."

"You may sit by me if you wish." Ingrid signaled with her hand.

Henry moved over to Ingrid's bed and moved up in a yoga-like position facing her, knees touching knees. They looked into the other's eyes. Ingrid giggled and joked, "Is this one of those California Zen trances I've been reading about?"

When it came to sexual intimacy, Henry liked absolute quiet, or rather he liked to talk with eyes and touch and usually to fantasize—but wasn't what was happening just like a dream, *ergo* no imagery beyond the immediate? He just smiled back at her and swam deeply into the blue lake of her eyes as though he were floating on the small almond rafts of his own sight. Their hands and fingers interlocked as though they were registering the depths into which they had dived into each other's presence. A warm feeling that radiated outward from their hands was like two currents immersing in the same body. Closing their eyes, they rolled back on the soft pillows, their youthful beauties of two regions complementing one another as they delicately rubbed noses, twittered eyelashes, and rolled cheek against cheek. Hands moved from hands to interlace in flaxen hair and incipient curl. Every crevice in the house of their mind was mesmerized by the drug of fingers and palms upon the shapes of thought.

Gently unsnapping the top of her dress as they lay on their sides forehead to forehead, Henry slowly lowered Ingrid's zipper, then suddenly pulled off his own sweater, turtle-neck shirt and undershirt in a unitary motion. Her small and firm breasts pressed against his cheeks as she unzipped his jeans and fondled his manhood. As she felt the contour of his back and carefully lowered his pants, his erection shot up greeting her ear and face as she lowered her mouth onto the site of his progeny. She licked as though she had bought a big lollipop at the country fair. Then, as she began to suck, she sighed with delight at the offer of her first Middle Eastern lamb. Raising her from under her arms, Henry moved his orifice to hers, their tongues slipping from top to bottom, further and further down, heartbeats supporting the intensity of the embrace. Ingrid shielded her first circumcised flesh and then warmed it with her folds, tucking it further and further into her innermost heat. Breath whooshed in and out, faster and faster, top, side, bottom, one commanding, then another. Toe pressed toe, foot, foot, thigh, thigh. Strengths trembled, bodies writhed and quaked, then reposed peacefully, cradled by the North Sea, mists and sea breezes cloaking their encounter into the dreamy afternoon of youth united. They slumbered a half-hour under Ingrid's fluffy down comforter and sparkling, slick, shiny white sheets. A muffled alarm sounded for her duty.

"Henry, I've got to get her back to my post. Here's a towel and soap if you want to wash up in my lavatory."

Waking up from a life-tale that must-have-happened—but-could-it-have-occurred?—Henry turned on the hot water, removed the condom, and washed his member. Did this feel good, too! After washing with the soft large washcloth in several full sinks of hot water, he felt as though he had had a full bath. His next thought was to check up on Phil, lest he roll off the ship in a drunken stupor or get into a fight with another passenger.

CHAPTER 14

Walking up two flights of stairs, Henry found Phil lying with his face in the fold of his arm, asleep in an alcoholic stupor. The bartender asked, "Is this your friend? Could you please take him over to one of the chairs or benches? You better pump him full of coffee. And you better do the driving in Denmark!"

Shoving Phil's rather light frame over his left shoulder, Henry carried him over to the adjacent area and propped him up on a bench next to the window and ordered a pot of coffee. Sitting next to Phil, he shook him sufficiently to arouse him enough to smell the aroma of the well-brewed coffee and to pour some into his mouth with one hand while holding his head up with the other. Slowly, Phil began to wake and hold his own cup. Meanwhile, noticing a copy of *The New York Times* on an adjacent table left by an elegantly clad Manhattan family of four, Henry tucked it unobtrusively under his arm and went back over to Phil.

"Hey, man, what happened?" inquired Phil in a low rasping voice.

"I guess you must have imbibed one too many and fell asleep."

"Get that haw-tee-daw vocabulary. Man, I got pissed as shit. An' where were you—servicing a local dame?" Phil joked while gulping down a second cup of coffee and smoking a cigarette.

"Well, something like that. If I told you the whole story, you wouldn't believe me, so let's leave it at that. Suffice to say it left me in a great mood. They just announced that we better get down to the car. Are you sure you can drive?"

"No problem, man, I'm in great shape."

The loud thump and jerk of the docking boat served as a signal to motorists and train engineers to warm up their machines to go to shore.

As they rolled through the little town, Henry monitored Phil's driving and was prepared to grab the steering wheel and step on the brakes at a moment's

75

notice if the need arose. They passed by meadows filled with flowers interspersed by cozy farms.

"We should make it up to Copenhagen in about two hours. Phil, if you drive me all the way to Stockholm, that's where I think I would have my best chances for getting some work."

"I'll trade that for some more of your shrink rap, man. What's in that New York paper I saw you pick up? It's hard to pull in an American station without a short-wave up here."

"Clifford said he detected some slight gains in the Paris talks with the North Vietnamese which point to secret sessions ahead. But at the same time there were fierce battles fought just outside Saigon."

The paper's from yesterday, the twenty-first. That family probably flew directly to Hamburg last night and drove to Travemunde to catch the ferry. So what else is new? wondered Phil.

"Well, there's a big election campaign going on in France."

"Pretty much the same ol' crap, huh?"

"Sounds like it. You feel like talking about you?"

"O.K."

"You're headed straight for the bar today?"

"Sure 'am. 'Felt great last night. I got a bad headache now."

"Is that the way you get your kicks? By the way, would you like me to drive?"

"No, man, I'm alright. Headaches are usual for me in the afternoons."

"All the time or just when you drink?"

"Just after I drink a lot."

"Was any one else in your family a heavy drinker?"

"No, just me."

"Did you drink before your marriage?"

"Yeah. I started serious drinking when I worked in the steel mills along with all the other guys. We would drink after work."

"When did you start drinking heavily?"

"Only when things started getting really awful between Angela and me. Basically, I used to be pretty much of a down-home Dixie boy—but a bit on the tough side."

"You're not anymore?"

"What are you trying to get me to say, that I'm a fuckin' alcoholic?"

"Are you saying it?"

"I'm not sure. I still feel I'm in control. I don't drink all the time. Then I'll go on a binge—like the whole of last week."

"Why are you clinging to Angela when everything's pointing out that the relationship is not working out for you? She won't go live in a place where you're treated like a decent human being, and her relatives and friends won't accept you, even when you were a respectable soldier. The situation has led to your being so frustrated, you've exploded and hurt her physically, and she stays there and seems to enjoy the sympathy she gets for being a devoted wife who's sticking through it, even though she made an initial poor choice."

"Divorce is something nobody ever did where I came from."

"But you've not been loyal to your wife, and you beat her."

"That's true. I don't mean to, but I guess there's jus' this mean streak in me, the Devil or somethin' ."

"But you can't get the self-esteem you need by living in a place where everybody just hates you for what you are, and your wife won't go any place else. Don't you think that all these unsolvable problems have caused what you've called 'this mean streak' in you?"

"Probably, but what can I do? There's no way out of it except for both of us to do our own thin' ."

"But if you stay together, as you are now, 'doing your own thing,' as you put it, don't you think that one or the other of you might end up doing something that you'll really regret?"

"Could be."

"You mentioned divorce. Why doesn't it occur to you that it's a possibility for you? You know, separation, legal or otherwise, might be a possibility in between divorce and being blocked, where you two are 'at' right now."

"God, I jus' never thought that a member of my family would get divorced."

"What's so weird about that?"

"I guess I jus' wasn't brought up that way."

"You mean you feel like you would be sinning a horrible, unforgivable sin?"

"I never thought of it that way, but maybe you're on to somethin'. I haul off and screw somebody that's not my wife without givin' it a second thought but deep down inside me feel that it ain't right to divorce. That's strange, man, real stupid."

"Could it be that you learned these things by picking up what somebody else thought was right for you without giving it a second thought yourself? And that even these people think these things are right without ever asking themselves why?"

"Hey, man, you're not as dumb as you look."

"Thanks for the compliment. If you were to want it, do you think Angela would consent to a separation?"

"Maybe yes, and maybe no. I doubt it, though. She's a Catholic, and I'm a Baptist—not that I ever go to church. She's pretty religious. She goes to church a lot with her folks. When we first got married, I'd go with them, but it felt so foreign, it didn't mean anythin' to me, ya' know what I mean?"

"Uh huh."

"Are you sayin' I ought to ask her for a separation, and if it don't work, then get a divorce."

"Didn't you come upon that yourself?"

"Hey, man, guess I did, come to think of it."

"I didn't suggest that's a solution to all your problems. But it seems to me that you're in a relationship that is only causing pain to both of you. Given that you both are sticking to your guns about basic issues that affect some very important things about the way you deal with each other, that is the least bad of your alternatives. What do you think?"

"I might give it a try, man. It sounds like you have some sense in you."

"To change the subject, I'd like to take in some of Copenhagen this evening, which basically means I'd like to walk all over and take in as much as I can before going on to Stockholm. Besides, you could use a good night's sleep before driving all the way up to Stockholm."

"I might walk around a bit with you, then I'd like to hit a strip joint or two. I've heard this place is famous for its sex clubs. I'd like to check out that scene, man."

"Fine with me. Let's head for the youth hostel when we get in unless you want to camp right outside the city and take the train in."

"Sounds fine with me. We'll get a place and then go out on the town."

Phil rolled his little Volkswagen into downtown Copenhagen and parked near the Botanical Garden. The young men quickly found the youth hostel listed in Henry's guidebook to Scandinavia and made a reservation for the evening. Once back in the car, he drove around the city's center past the King's Garden and Rosenborg Castle, the Rådhus, the Marmor and Christiansborg Churches, the Castle and Frederiksholm. Henry read that even though the city's history goes back to the eleventh century, Copenhagen does not look so old because both the Swedes and the British destroyed much of it, and it was rebuilt several times.

The two travelers agreed to split up and meet back at the hostel. Henry walked through Tivoli and was particularly struck by an old turn-of-the-century bandstand. As he stood there listening to a musical group, a middle-aged, suburban housewife from Chicago, accompanied by her daughter, around his own age, asked him for change. He replied, "I have about ten crowns in change, but I can't break a hundred crown note."

The daughter, Janet, chirped in, "How about lending me those ten crowns? Come over with us to the slot machines, and I'll win you some money."

"What if you lose?" Henry wondered aloud.

"Then you can walk back over with us to our hotel, and we'll get some change there."

"I win, you win. I lose, you stay the same."

"That sounds like a safe investment," remarked Henry, who had never gambled before in his entire life.

Janet's mom, Mrs. Kirk, put in the first five crowns. She lost all of them.

Mom, let me do this one, O.K.?" intoned Janet in her high nasal accent. She put in a crown, and inside a machine a funny metallic click grew louder. Coins fell from the slot. They kept tumbling out, so Mrs. Kirk blocked the rushing load with her generous bust. One coin fell into the slit in her more than adequate endowment tickling her, at which point she began to giggle gleefully. Janet kept jumping up and down squealing, "Didn't I tell you? Didn't I tell you?"

The gush stopped, and they all plopped down on their bottoms and began to count. Neglecting her suburban proprieties, Mrs. Kirk withdrew the crown from between her breasts and giggled, "Does that add up to three hundred altogether?"

Janet then placed the coins in three neat stacks of one hundred. "Is that agreeable to you two?"

"You bet," they responded.

"Well, divide by 6, that makes about $16.66 each," figured Janet methodically in the fashion of the experienced teller that she was at the main branch of the Continental Bank on LaSalle Street in downtown Chicago.

"Well, you got your change, and I made fifteen bucks plus. That's not bad. Thanks a lot, you two."

After concluding their business deal, Mrs. Kirk suggested that they all go for a snack. They promenaded over to the Ferry Inn and bought some dark beer and long red sausages while they listened to the heavy-set singers' folksongs. They studiously avoided any serious conversation, realizing that great differences of opinion about most questions of the day probably separated them as a bank employee and suburbanite versus an academic. Still, they managed to have a good time together, enjoying the pleasant atmosphere and their mutual fortune.

Henry walked Janet and Mrs. Kirk back to their hotel right off the square where the Rådhus, the town hall, was located, and then strolled back to the youth hostel just before it shut its doors for the evening. There was no trace of Phil.

As the lights turned off, the Americans started their horseplay while a group of Germans shouted, *"Wollen Sie gefälligst den Mund halten!"* (*Shut Up!*)When this tactic didn't work, a fight broke out between the noisy Americans and the Germans who wanted to sleep. Feigning sleep, Henry managed to avoid the foray until the hostel manager turned the lights on and informed everyone that fighting and noise were forbidden and that anyone caught doing either would be put out on the street instantaneously. It was already 1:30 A.M., and the people involved in the battle began to settle down.

When he cleaned up for breakfast, Henry was surprised to find Phil sitting on a bench in the dining room. He had thought that Phil had decided to drop him here and return home. Phil had dark circles under his eyes but looked unusually relaxed. The only thing he managed to say was, "Man, what an orgy! It was fuckin' unreal. When do we head north?"

Hating to be a nag but concerned about their safety, Henry asked, "Are you sure you're in shape to drive?"

"You said you wanted to go to Stockholm. Let's go."

Within a few minutes, they were back on the road and drove north in Denmark to Elsinore, stopping briefly by the Kronborg Castle, which Shakespeare had immortalized in *Hamlet*. Although Phil did not remember *Hamlet*, the mysterious towers by the sea were a good setting for his fanciful recall of his pleasurable evening in Copenhagen. Within a half hour via the large ferry, they were in Skåne, Sweden's flat southern provinces, the granary of the country.

Driving eastward across the country from Hälsingborg to Kristianstad and on up to Kalmar, Phil kept smiling as he continued to remember his adventure and occasionally pressed his hand with verve between his legs—covering up his secret with the map resting on his lap. The bookish Henry was busy devouring his guidebook which related how this region once belonged to Denmark, how the city of Kalmar used to control access to the northern coast, and how the people and dialect of this region still wrestled their independent ways from the capital. Intermittently, Henry would sight a landmark described in his book and comment on it to Phil. About the only thing Phil did was chuckle, "Sometimes your balls get the best of ya'. Ho! Ho!"

At midday they grabbed some small, open-faced sandwiches in a small restaurant in Kalmar. Just outside the town, there was a tall woman in granny glasses and a thick brown sweater standing by the road with her thumb slightly distracting Phil away from her tight jeans and trim legs. Without asking his traveling companion, Phil screeched the VW to a halt. The woman inquired in perfect American English, "Are you going to Stockholm?"

"Sure are, ma'am. Step right in!"

Glancing up from his guidebook, Henry introduced himself and Phil.

"My name's Annette. I'm from Philadelphia where I attend Temple University."

"Less impressed by her *curriculum vitae* than by her shapely features, Phil started imagining another thrilling evening. He turned toward the back seat and asked, "Annette, what is a young lady like you doin' hitchin' all by herself?"

"I'm in Sweden because I am interested in social democracy, in democratic socialism, and in their welfare state. Why do you find it peculiar for a single woman to be hitchhiking?"

"Honey, I don't have to tell ya' that. You're a college girl."

"Men respect women in this country more than at home. They have progressively given women more and more power, although they still have a long way to go, and violence is not a major part of their contemporary way of life. And, by the way, I don't like being called 'honey,' and I am no longer a girl; I'm a woman," Annette replied matter-of-factly, not picking up on the differences in education between Phil and herself.

"Sweetheart, I don't care where you are in God's world, it ain't safe for a young lady to be out on a lonely road by herself. Weren't the fellas in these parts Vikin's and didn't they sail down to jolly ol' England and rape and kill a lot of people?"

"That was centuries ago. They're a neutral country now."

"There ain't nothin' neutral about your looks, darlin'."

Halfway overhearing their conversation, Henry, though still absorbed in sightseeing and his guide, could sense the anxiety rising from the backseat.

"Annette, don't mind Phil. His bark is louder than his bite. He sort of grows on you."

Everyone laughed a sigh of relief, but Annette was not the appreciative sort of hitchhiker who would charm her hosts just to stay in the car. No, she wanted to communicate and proselytize particularly to her own people from her own country. She was positive that in most cases Americans were ignorant of the advantages of democratic socialism over their own liberal democracy.

"Isn't it obvious to you that there are no slums here and that *per capita* this is the wealthiest country on earth?"

"Can't rightly say, ma'am, 'cause we jus' got here this mornin'," Phil chuckled back.

"But haven't you already noticed how everyone looks much healthier on the average than in the States? You know it's not by chance that they're that way; they fought hard for socialized medicine and got it. They fought for job security and retraining and got it. They fought for longer paid vacations and got it. And policies like these influence everyone's health and well-being."

Phil found her self-righteousness cute. It made him recall one very attractive Jehovah's Witness who used to ring his doorbell with another fellow Christian in search of saving souls in Gary, Indiana.

"I think you're right, Annette, but wasn't this much easier to achieve than at home because it is a much more ethnically and racially homogeneous society?" Henry joined in.

"If Americans weren't so damned racist and so wrapped up in trying to acquire private goods of little real value, then maybe they could reap the benefits of the collective materials of real value like basically free public gymnasiums, swimming pools, sauna baths, medicine and education. Personally, I think all this ethnic revival is a way in which the power elite keeps the American people divided into mutually suspicious camps," Annette retorted, looking Henry angrily in the eyes trying to decipher to which of the reactionary white ethnic groups he belonged.

"Annette, where are you staying in Stockholm?" Phil asked—thinking he would offer to treat her to a nice hotel in hope of some action.

"I have a student apartment with three other women near Djurgården, a really lovely park."

"Do you know of anyone with whom we might be able to crash?" Henry popped in.

"Oh, sure, no problem. I have a few male friends in the twin apartment building. They are looking for some guys to sublet their flatmates' rooms to for the summer. It's a steal, too! Just $50 a month for a super modern, clean apartment next to a beautiful park!"

"Wow, I'll take it now."

"Well, let's wait and see what they have to say when we get there."

Phil's plans were suddenly foiled, but he immediately started to revamp them. He was thinking that he would take her out to dinner and then ask if she would show him the park.

"Annette, I really desperately need a job. I thought I was going on an archeological dig in France and my whiz of a prof forgot to leave word with anyone exactly where his dig is taking place, so I've got about ninety dollars to last me two more months. Do you think there's any way I can earn some bread in Stockholm?"

"It might be hard because you're supposed to have working and residence permits and enter the country with a job offer. But, in fact, there are ways around it, and because all the Swedes desert Stockholm in the summer, they need people to carry on services, so they make it easy for foreign students to work them. In fact, I know of a home for the elderly that is in great need of personnel this month because several people more than planned took a vacation."

Around eight in the evening Phil pulled up to the *studenthem* where Annette was living for the summer. To his amazement, Annette invited both him and Henry up for a shower and dinner and immediately got on the telephone to her friends, Lennart, Öve, and Klaes, to invite them to join the potluck in order to check out Henry to see if they would rent him a place. Phil could hardly believe his eyes when they passed four bedrooms into a commonly-shared kitchen where Annette's three gorgeous apartment-mates were sitting drinking coffee. It was as though he walked to meet the Northern Lights, which suddenly incarnated themselves into anthropomorphic forms. Annette threw her countrymen some extra-large bath towels and bars of soap and walked into the kitchen to make pancakes.

The hot, steamy water never ran cool and both Phil and Henry came out totally refreshed. Annette asked Karin to start cooking the pancakes, and Karin and Birgitta offered to set the table while Annette ran in for her shower.

Phil was so awed by the physical comeliness of his human entourage, he could not say anything. Besides, it was so romantic the way they had laid out an impromptu meal with candles as nice as a top restaurant back in Georgia.

For all of her feminist rhetoric, Annette turned out to be a whopper of a hostess. First, she formally introduced all her own newly-made friends to Phil and Henry.

As a way of reminding Phil that his recent luck in sexual escapades was no solution to his problem and notifying Annette not to get hurt, Henry asked

Phil, "Well, have you made any decision driving me all the way up here?"

Without getting angry at the thought of being tattled on, Phil understood the several levels of meaning in Henry's ambiguous question and appreciated his leaving him the responsibility of bringing up the fact that he was married. "I'm going to ask for a legal separation, and if she doesn't grant it to me, then I'll file for divorce. My mind is made up."

The seriousness of Henry's question with its *double entendre* was immediately seized upon by Annette's friends as a sign of concern for her. After a few brief sentences in Swedish to Öve and Lennart, Karin and Klaes looked back at Henry and said, "*Välkommen*, Welcome to our flat, if you want to sublet a room for $50 this month."

"That'd be great. Could I pay half now and half at the end of the month? I'm traveling on very limited funds."

"Sure, by the way, don't say anything to anybody in the building about subletting. It's against the rules formally, although a lot of people do it."

"Gee, these pancakes are good, Annette!"

"Try them with some lingonberries, those little red ones."

Henry, who never drank coffee in the States, was drawn by the flavor of the strong Swedish brew. "Could I have a second cup?"

"Watch out or you'll end up a coffee-holic here. I'm not kidding."

As the table broke up into several two-way conversations in both languages, Karin addressed Henry in a low tone of voice, "Annette tells me you need a job pretty badly. Don't worry, I think I can get you something at the home for retired people where I work part time. They really need some people this month, and there are no Swedes in town who would want to do this kind of work for only a month. It's really not bad. You clean up the old people's rooms and visit with them. I think you would earn about 1000 crowns—that's about two hundred U.S. dollars—a month, if my boss can pay you out of petty cash, so you won't have to bother getting work and residence permits, which take forever. Do you mind getting up at seven to go with me to work in the morning? It's just a few subway stops from our house."

"Sounds fine with me. That's just about all I need to get through the summer, if I'm frugal."

"Oh, you'll have a great time here. There are lots of wonderful things you can do free or for a small fee," Annette remarked.

"It's just what I need now. It'll give me time to think about what I'm going to do about military service, about whether or not I'm going to answer Uncle Sam's call."

CHAPTER 15

Everything worked perfectly. The efficient administrator who was Karin's boss sized Henry up in about five minutes in her office. Great, he looked sturdy and would be a substitute for the janitor who lifted heavy things for her when needed. He was very friendly, and she would bet money that he had a way with old people, and he had already learned a few well-pronounced phrases of Swedish, which would do fine for small talk. There was enough money in petty cash to pay him, and she would throw in two free meals on the job from the prepared meals for their sick residents, several of which were never touched in the first place.

After all the confusion and disorganization of missing his archeological dig in France, this fortune glistened like an oasis of security. Besides this luck, there was something hauntingly familiar about the layout of Stockholm and the people he was meeting—as though he had lived here in a previous life.

This state-run *pensionärshem*, or pensioners' home, resembled the best of upper-middle class facilities for the elderly run by churches or ethnic associations in the United States.

The first day he was taken around and introduced to all the residents, each of whom had wonderful life-tales and personalities he would learn about over the coming month. He watched the Finnish young women attendants gently comb the silken white hair of a 94-year-old woman. He was impressed by another ninety-two-year-old's having read most of the classics of Western literature in her retirement, even though she had had only an eighth grade education. Kjerstin, his boss, asked him to rearrange some furniture in the common room and to walk with a few of the weaker people to the local food cooperative a few blocks away, to make their purchases, and to help carry their groceries if need be. He ate lunch with Karin, his benefactor, in the beautiful flower garden overlooking the water.

"It's more than I could have hoped for. Thank you. *Tack. Tusen Tack! Tack ska du ha!*"

Karin smiled a warm, radiant smile acknowledging that his heart-felt gratitude made her feel she had helped a worthy person.

The workdays went well. Of course, like any job, there were people to watch out for and those who needed to be handled with kid gloves. He felt a little uneasy about having to help contain Herr Lundqvist, an old lumberjack who had to take an early retirement because "he wasn't all there in the head." The middle-aged Swedish women attendants had been most distressed that Herr Lundqvist had refused to change his long underwear, shave, or bathe in over a month. It was high time for the boss to take things in hand. Kjerstin, a benevolent bureaucrat, had had to weigh the delicate differences of Herr Lundqvist's individual rights—however objectionable to others—against the democratically expressed, strong opinions of her staff. Yet, hygiene and respect for the line of institutional authority demanded that Herr Lundqvist be bathed and his long underwear be changed, and Henry would be the principal instrument by which this decision would be enacted. Then there was also *Fröken* Sundberg, who had attempted to live out several of her fantasies about her former male attendants. Therefore, Henry was told that he should never enter her room alone, and should always be accompanied by at least one female attendant—no matter how serious Miss Sundberg claimed her condition to be.

After work, Karin and Henry dashed home on the attractive, clean subway and began to prepare an evening meal for a few of their little group. The simplicity of the spread was highlighted by its attractive layout—blocks of the pale yellow *Jarlsberg* and caramel-colored goat's milk cheeses placed by Scandinavian cheese-knives, next to which lay a wooden knife for cutting through soft butter. Henry prepared an American tossed-salad, and Karin boiled small potatoes and put out some rye-crisp hardtack and a shrimp pate in a squeeze tube. Underneath all this bill-of-fare sparkled a polished pine table. Bringing some very thinly sliced meat from a downtown store, Öve and Klaes joined them.

Öve was a tall country boy from a big family. He had made the national soccer team but had given up sports to study at the university. He had come from Dalarna, a kind of folklore haven of the countryside. Karin, his girlfriend, was the only child of a couple of Stockholm schoolteachers but had the freshness, propriety, and innocence of a country girl. They had met their first year together in university and were for all practical purposes "married." They had slept together several years, although proudly but discretely had made it a point that they do not believe in marriage and give each other "freedom" to an open relationship. In private, Annette later would joke to Henry about Öve and Karin's relationship. She said everyone knew that they had been faithful to one another because the roommates had seen them sleep exclusively together for over two years, yet from this good-looking couple's talk, you would think that they had experimented with a good portion of the rest of the youth of Stockholm. In their absolute wholesomeness and trustworthiness, they exuded an atheistic commitment to their own purity and quest for social justice that inspired Annette, who, while almost worshiping them, was still driven by a libido that hindered her behavior from emulating theirs. Annette admired the limit setting, the exact-edges, and the uptight underlying rigidity that nevertheless provided the motherly and fatherly security one sensed near this couple.

Öve and Karin were so different from Birgitta, who was first of all "dark"—olive-skinned and black haired. Her temperament was Latin—she was emotionally effusive, wild, and full of *joie de vivre*. Her eyes were big jade jewels deeply set into shaded ovals decked by long lashes. Birgitta was always surrounded by different admiring men. Henry kept admiring how each of these apartment companions in her own way had managed to turn her small place into a delicate corner of imaginative color and shape, as attractive, yet more original and less ornate, than the finest student dwelling he had seen back home. Yet, Birgitta's "roomies" found her room to be disorderly and disheveled. They were also outraged by her pet guinea pig, which deposited its fecal pellets along the corridor walls. Karin was exceedingly irked when Birgitta's mother, Fru Söderberg—who suffered from a long history of mental distress—had made repeated advances at Öve and Lennert wherever her daughter let her stay in her room. Having her mother over for a nice meal and conversation and then dumping the attractive and interesting but emotionally laden fifty-year-old on her roommates relieved Birgitta's guilt towards her mother's "condition."

As it would turn out over the summer, Fru Söderberg liked Henry because he was Jewish. A Swedish national, raised in southern Europe, Mrs. Söderberg, still a young woman, had returned to Sweden on the eve of the Second World War. A Swedish Jew was the only one who would employ her with her funny accent in Swedish spoken with a humorous Italian staccato. She came to know this man and Jewish culture and was, in fact, more knowledgeable and familiar with Henry's background than were her daughter and the other young people in the flat. Henry's mother had been labeled as mentally ill for a large part of his life as well, and perhaps, for this reason, he felt sympathetic to Fru Söderberg's episodes of unpredictable crying or exuberance. For Henry the days from late June to late July turned like pages a favorite storybook that a child beseeches its parents to read over and over. Often Klaes would take him swimming at one of the huge public pools after they both got back from work. Sometimes Lennart, Öve, Birgitta, Annette, and Karin would tag along too, and they would sauna afterwards— all this for a crown. Then they would split up into smaller groups for the evening—sometimes taking long walks in Djurgården or going up Kaknästornet, the modern tower, beneath which the modestly-lighted city flickered in the pitch of the night. Often they would lie in the grass and gaze at the clear stars and the constellations or take a coffee and sweets at an elegant round wooden hut to the accompaniment of Spanish guitarists.

To everyone's surprise, Phil, who ended up staying one week, hit it off with Annette. Karin, who found Phil to be a crude, racist pig, was shocked, but Öve understood the situation to arise out of what the French were calling *ouvrièrisme*, an excessive, uncritical admiration and deference to working-class mores. Despite her strong anti-Israeli sentiments and general discomfort around Jews, Annette ended up taking Henry out to Gamla Stan, the Old City, right after Phil left. She took him to the discotheque to which Phil had initially taken her against her own preference but at which they ended up dancing every evening. She was trying to explore this excessive passion.

"Henry, you'll probably get a laugh out of this, but I think Carl Linnaeus may have been right in his book *Lachesis Naturalis: Philosophia Humana*. He wrote that when *genitura* presses, mania is induced. When young women 'in this state meet a man whom they like, they get chlorosis, grow green in the face, indeed often leap into the lake and drown themselves.' He said that a '*halitus incalescentis concupiscentiae* begins to rise within her, coming from the *genitura*.'"

"Annette, for all of your outward rationalism, you're basically a passionate person. Phil turned you on because he's strong and earthy, and despite the puritanical image you project, there's a lot of repressed lust smoldering inside you."

"I'll have to admit Phil satisfied me. But isn't this whole thing selfish? We'll probably never see each other again, and we enjoyed each other like we had one of those scrumptious green-icing creme cakes that I love in the local shops but can't afford very often. And all of this for free!"

"It's what Freud called 'polymorphous sexual perversity' and Engels described as 'the communism of pre-literate sexuality.'"

"But didn't Lenin liken free love to drinking out of a rusty tin can?"

"So what if Lenin said it? He helped form the one-party dictatorship that was the basis of Stalinism. He put down the uprising of the sailors at Kronstadt, didn't he? Why do you worship his repression?"

"Let's not get into a political rap, O.K.?"

The serious conversation of the night terminated with that comment, but they had a wonderful walk in the warm evening air all the way back to their redbrick dorms, which faced each other. They felt a warm brotherly-sisterly type of protective closeness of being so similar but so far apart in this fairyland that they both grew to love more with each passing day. As Henry left her at the door, he just smiled and inquired, "Hey, I'd like to take a look at the Linnaeus book you mentioned."

"O.K., you'll love it. It's really a precursor of the holistic health trip. See ya'."

Every evening Klaes and Henry would do something different. Of all the people in the apartment, they had the least in common, yet grew to like each other the most. They were both about the same stature. Klaes had the appearance of a slight Viking raider. He had long red hair and orangish freckles all over his body. He was quiet unless pulled into a conversation by Henry who had to weigh finely when he was talking too much in Klaes' presence. Klaes conveyed knowledge without words. They would go to a new part of the city like Skansen, the replica of the historical architecture of Sweden, and without saying anything, Klaes gave a whole lesson to Henry. They talked a lot about the War in Vietnam and about life and love just through feelings and experience. Klaes was strikingly handsome but too shy to meet women other than at "meat-market" like bars where it was understood that the purpose of the encounter was sexual. But Henry introduced him into the fun of society—into joking and laughing and doing things with all sorts of people, an evening outing with Yugoslavs, or French, or Germans, or Finns. Klaes's two great loves of the summer were met through Henry's work or social circle. At a party thrown by a German co-worker of Henry's, he met the equally bashful and equally beautiful redheaded Finn, Elisabet.

Annette was to share with Henry a short passage from Linnaeus humorously describing the character of the Swedish people. Of the *Suecus* he wrote "…he eats like an Englishman, drinks like a German, dresses like a Frenchman, builds like an Italian, smokes like a Duchman, takes snuff like a

Spaniard, tipples *akvavit* like a Russian." That passage gave Henry some insight into Klaes. Klaes was Henry's first close friend who smoked, took snuff, and drank more than infrequently, who dressed spiffily, and who had rather simple culinary tastes. But Henry felt that Klaes was more intelligent than he permitted himself to become. Klaes sensed intellectualism to be unnatural and false, but was, nevertheless, attracted to it. On the other hand, he could not see himself working his way up on a construction site, where his father was a foreman, as his older brothers had done. Klaes didn't want to stand out. Only toward the end of his stay in Stockholm did Klaes show Henry his moving poetry. Klaes despised almost religiously so many of the conveniences of American life which he thought to be superfluous or the outer signs of a corrupt society that was miserly toward its poor, its working class, its sick, and its elderly. Checks were one of his pet peeves, and he chastised Henry a whole day for the thought of opening a checking account. Klaes and Henry became inseparable, though. They both loved table tennis, nature, and politics.

And such a tumultuous month for politics it was! The Gaullists had won a smashing victory, yuck. But Trudeau won in Canada with a decisive margin for his program of a just society. Hippies shouted obscenities on a TV show and the New Left planned a convention protest in the U.S. A virulent anti-Semitic campaign broke out in Poland. Sweden granted asylum to ten more U.S. deserters. The Saigon Premier ousted fifty to one hundred district chiefs. Young American men began to burn their draft cards. The Soviets agreed to parleys on the limitation of missile systems and a ban on the spread of atomic arms. The future of the non-violent movement for civil rights in the U.S. was placed in doubt after Dr. King's assassination. And the problems of transportation and national sovereignty were snarling aid to the millions of starving people in Biafra.

One early evening, the group of apartment mates and friends took a stroll down Strandvägen by the water of the Saltsea to go to a five-crown concert. As they walked in two's, Klaes confided to Henry, "I hope you decide not to go to Vietnam. It's not right. The American army is doing the dirty work for the profit of a handful of multinational corporations. I served in the Swedish army a year after gymnasium because we all have to or work in a conscientious objector position like tending the King's sheep. It was shit, but at least we didn't go around plundering other countries pretending that we're helping them out."

"Klaes, do you think there's a chance for democratic socialism to happen in Vietnam?"

"There's certainly a better chance if a lot of guys like you keep saying 'Hell, no, we won't go.'"

Annette, overhearing their talk, couldn't resist butting in, "Well, men, I finally read something in my beloved Linnaeus I disagree with the implication of, but I must admit he expressed himself eloquently. I memorized it."

She quoted, "I saw mankind consume all animals, all plants, and all earth. The beasts of prey lived on herbivora. The birds of prey lived on small birds, which ate seeds and worms. The plants lived on the soil. Hence I went first to the soil, where it all began. The humus under a microscope was only *desumta animalia et plantae*."

She switched references, "I must say that Carl believed in the struggle of all against all. I tell you, I don't think all human history has been like this. There have been golden ages when people cared about creating beautiful things, learning the truth, and helping others. If we give in to the big bullshitters like the militarists of every country, then the just, beautiful world we're seeking has no chance. Henry, do you want to get your ass shot off to help a few right-wing dictators and their armies? Why be the lackey of Standard Oil and others?"

As they passed Strömmen, Henry looked at the calming waters of the harbor over to the Palace. "If only the whole world would spend its evenings taking in nature, walking with friends, and listening to music."

Klaes peered into Henry's eyes. "Heh, man, my parents and grandparents fought for these things the same way our generation is fighting to get your country to negotiate with the Vietnamese of all political parties."

Henry was stunned to hear such a forceful conversation from Klaes who usually expressed himself in curt phrases and non-verbal messages by taking Henry to places and sites in Stockholm that were clearly superior to the average urban American's environment. This would leave Henry with the obvious conclusion that Klaes's city was much nicer. You could get around without polluting the air with noise and filth because bicyclists, environmentalists, and planners had fought against the congestion and blight promoted by big oil, car manufacturers, and advertising.

Listening with friends to the folksy Pier Gynt in the back row of the Concert House brought home the security and familiarity of the Scandinavian romance with nature.

As they left the concert, Henry picked up the conversation from where they had left off, "Klaes, on one hand, I'm tending in the direction of your advice. I'm especially angered that Johnson is ruling out the solution of a coalition government in Saigon. The evidence suggests the U.S. doesn't really care if there's a democratic government or not. Everything I've read leads me to believe that Eisenhower did not go along with the Geneva Conference's call for free elections after the fall of the French colony in Vietnam because everyone knew Ho Chi Minh would win the election. And everything I've read leads me to believe that Ho Chi Minh was more of a nationalist than a communist. He wanted American aid to modernize Vietnam, and I think he would have compromised with some form of capitalism in small and medium-size business and a more moderate, gradual, and only partial collectivization of agriculture, particularly in the south. But the domino theorists drove Ho Chi Minh further and further into confrontation with the U.S. You know, I think they really are fighting the social democrats more than the communists because they fear that if they lose to them, they'll lose their great profits and power, even at home."

Not saying anything, Klaes smiled and threw his arm over Henry's shoulders. Tightening up at the first expressive physical touch he had remembered ever receiving from another adult male, Henry quickly withdrew and then immediately felt terribly awkward that he had not been able to accept or reciprocate what must have been an unprecedented feeling of brotherly solidarity by Klaes. Klaes sensed that he had passed a tabooed cultural line, which would only be repressed as a gauche move on both of their parts. The episode closed as he stuffed a wad of snuff under his upper lip.

Changing the subject Henry asked, "How about going together to Narvik? I want to see Norway before I leave. I'll activate my Eurailpass and we can spend a couple of days hiking around above the Arctic Circle."

"Let me see if I can talk my older brother Johann into driving us up in his old Volvo. He needs a vacation and is too shy to take off any time. And that way you won't have to take a week off your train pass. Would you like to come spend the weekend at my family's home on the south side?

"Sounds great!"

CHAPTER 16

The weekend soon arrived, and it was the first time Henry remembered being with a big family since he had left the South. He was a little anxious as was Klaes, but Klaes had told his family so much about Henry and Henry so much about his family that they felt that they knew each other already before meeting.

Theirs was a two-story, gray, concrete house, one of several on lots along a winding street. Husband and brother-in-law had built the house by hand in the years after the Second World War. Large gray stones jutted from the ground among the birch, pine, and apple trees. Klaes's "Mamma" greeted them with a warm "*Välkommen*" at the front door. Of medium stature, a blond woman in her late forties, full of energy and activity, she showed the wear of the hard work of raising three grown boys and two girls while maintaining a large home. Fru Ericsson had only had an eighth-grade formal education but had read as widely on art as most college majors in the United States. To top off the perfectly arranged home, furnished in modern Scandinavian, she was quite an accomplished painter who sold her own artwork in the neighborhood shopping mall to which she rode on her bicycle. She had her studio on the ground floor between Klaes's room and the "*bastu*," or sauna.

Klaes's "Pappa" was a tall, six foot two man who was getting a slight paunch from Fru Ericsson's tasty, but carbohydrate-full round of potatoes, pancakes, whole grain cereals, rye-crisp, butter, cheese, and almost yogurt-like buttermilk. Klaes' father always had a big smile and hardly ever spoke. He conveyed an air of warm authority and skill in his building trade in which he had risen to a foreman's level over the years.

Klaes's oldest brother, Tommy, had followed in his father's footsteps on the job and was what everyone had hoped all the boys would become—stable, unassuming, hardworking, a good family man and provider. Johann,

93

the second born, was less talkative than his older brother but was equally practical—following in his dad's and oldest brother's paths. He was studying to become a building engineer in his spare time. He had a good sense of humor and liked to laugh and take snuff. The two older brothers looked quite alike: blond, blue-eyed, freckle-faced, of medium stature.

Klaes and his sister Asa were most alike. They were filled with *wanderlust*, a taste for adventure, the arts, literature, and a hope of doing something different with their lives. Yet both were pulled by a family magnet that deflected to the practical, yanking them to stay within bounds and not wander too far into the dangers of the wider world. They were both more high-strung and unsure of themselves than their siblings, although Klaes more so than Asa. Both were heavy smokers. Lillian, the youngest child, a pre-teen, was spoiled and indulged, getting her way with everyone.

This was the biggest family into which Henry had ever been allowed entrance, and he felt immediately drawn to its sense of deep security, *trygghet*, that Klaes confided to him was what deep down inside he wanted the most.

Inviting Johann and Henry to follow him out to the backyard, Klaes began to throw darts at a target behind the house. As their match progressed, he proposed the trip north.

"Well, we were up in Norrbotten just before *farfar* died," Johann reminded Klaes in Swedish.

"That's true, but we've never really been above the Arctic Circle. And you love to go hiking."

"It's possible, but I can take off only seven days at the most. That'll mean two days driving up there and two days back which will leave only three days for hiking."

"That's enough time to get a feel of the place to let us know if we want to go back. And you always said that you would like to go up there."

"Well, O.K., if it's only a week's trip at the most. I'll ask dad if I can get a week off. He's not going to be thrilled, but then again, he might be secretly proud we're going up to see the part of the country where he grew up and grandfather died. Hey, we're going to get to see the Midnight Sun."

Understanding more and more Swedish every day, Henry understood from the gist of the conversation that Johann had agreed. They would leave on July 22nd and get back by the 29th at the latest.

CHAPTER 17

The route north was spectacular. They drove up the coast through Sundsvall—all the way past Umeå to Luleå where they stayed with Klaes's and Johann's cousins who, dressed in their best clothes, had prepared a giant *smörgåsbord* in honor of their Stockholm cousins and their American friend. Then they cut inland across Sweden to Mo-i-Rana in Norway. Along the way they stopped and admired the elegant combinations of ground flora framed in the striped white and black of birch. The shades of green and muffled delicate white and pink petals cloaked the bog: Wood Cranesbill, Fungus Boletus, Grass of Parnassus, Arctic Bramble, Dwarf Cornel, Labrador Tea.

"Annette would be going crazy," chuckled Henry as he thumbed through her Linnaean travel book, which identified the botanical magnificence of the countryside.

Seeing glaciers and fjords, driving and then putting the old Volvo onto the ferry, they were awed by their surroundings and spoke little. Occasionally Johann would turn on the radio. The big story was the Soviets' pressuring the Czechoslovaks to stop their liberalization program. Henry sensed that nothing should be discussed, and infrequently Klaes would mumble, "*Det är jatte skönt och tyst.* It's really so beautiful and quiet." It dawned on Henry that this must be their way of praying. Neither Johann nor Klaes went to church, and Henry gathered they were non-believers from Klaes's rare allusions to the subject. Yet, within the vast expanses of forests, lakes, fjords, and vistas of utter radiance and contrasting colors, in the long twilight of crispy air, there were thunderous roars and crystal tingling that vibrated in and out of Klaes's and Johann's spirits just like a vibrant Gregorian chant to praise the creation of God Almighty. The highness of their souls, their lapse into a mystical meditation flowed back and forth from their simple holiness. This voyage was a pilgrimage just like the call of the Muslim to Mecca, the

Catholic to Rome, and the Jew to Jerusalem. Klaes and Johann were ascending to their purification before their Lord and to the roots of their forefathers. In their quietness they surpassed what Henry suspected to be a falseness in the stillness of the Western devotees to Zen Buddhism. Their communion with nature expressed everything they were, had been born to be, and become. Henry noticed how both brothers had practically abstained from tobacco since they had left their relatives in Umeå. Something wonderfully weird was transforming them. There was a unification with the place and a breakdown in the barrier of time. Henry sat back as the anthropological observer he had been trained to be, not going native along with their ritual, but deeply appreciating their letting him witness the otherworldly change in themselves. He was carried along listening to their still voices within, which were translated into the swish of the passing wind or the murmuring or roar of the waters under them. Their human exteriors melded into the solidity of the rocks, the uprightness of the trees, and the force of mightily flowing rivers and streams.

Finally arriving in Narvik, Johann parked the car in the lower town. After their long drive, they went to the first café they came across, and Johann ordered coffee and sweet rolls for all of them. To Henry's astonishment he overheard two Texas accents and the deep mellow tones of an educated New Yorker. He turned around and saw two very young, Scandinavian-looking women accompanied by a pleasant-looking Negro woman in her late-thirties or early forties. All three were laughing vigorously. After the long mysterious communion with nature and his brother friends, Henry had experienced over the last two days, the lighter side of people from his own country was a welcome sound. Turning around, he inquired, "What's so funny?"

"Oh, just an in joke. Where are you from?"

"We've just spent the last two days driving up from Stockholm. I'm Henry from a bit of everywhere USA and these are my Swedish friends, Johann and Klaes, who're brothers."

"Hi. I'm Jenny. This is my sister, Rosie, and our favorite teacher of all times, Bea or Miss Thompson."

Johann, who was even more reserved than Klaes, couldn't believe that he was easily meeting two attractive Scandinavian-looking women—who turned out to be American—and the first Negro he had ever personally met in his whole life. By now familiar with his buddy's ease with striking up relationships with most anyone, Klaes just played along with more engaging interest and asked, "Where are you staying in Narvik?"

"Up at the youth hostel. It's absolutely homey, and the surrounding area is spectacular. Their place is way over half empty, and the manager is super-nice and will point out everything to you," described the two Texans.

"Hey, you guys want to stay up there?" the cheerful schoolteacher asked. "Sure."

"Would you like us to show you how to get there?"

"We have a car."

"Oh, don't take it. Park it down here and hike up the hill with us. It feels great."

All six of them wandered out in the cracking chill of the late afternoon air and began to climb. "It feels like walking on a giant sponge up here."

"You're just high off the air," Bea chuckled. Dressed in a tweed skirt and green sweater, Bea's face exuded the warmth of wisdom, motherliness, and propriety of a successful public school teacher. Her deep voice commanded respect while simultaneously exuding affection.

Rosie and Jennie were sororal twins who had been in Bea's class when their family had been stationed in West Germany for three years. Their grandparents on both sides of the family had settled in Texas in the late nineteenth century and this was their first chance to see the land of their ancestors. Who would be better to go with than their teacher-friend? They had written to Bea from Texas and had quickly received a reply that she would love to see how her "little girls had grown up."

As they turned their backs to the hill and gazed at the North Sea, the expanse was breathtaking. They were but mere specks in the huge vault of sky. Reversing their stance, continuing up the hill, they climbed upward way beyond the large house sitting by itself in this enormous stretch. This path must be a ladder to an infinitely enlarging Heaven.

The hostel manager checked in the young men and their backpacks, and the sixsome then set out again, this time prancing and jumping on the soft-lichen covered ground and then racing down into the town.

"You won't believe the teenyboppers in this place. It reminds me of Biloxi, Mississippi, where our family went on vacation last year," Rosie chirped.

"It sure does," interrupted Jenny. "The guys just sit around drinking and then churn all over the town on their motorcycles."

"They're probably just bored. It's the 'nothing else to do around here' mentality. They must be spoiled living in one of the prettiest places on earth and taking it for granted," commented Bea as the guys just listened.

As they entered the modern part of town down by the water front, Bea observed, "Did you know that the Norwegian troops that were aided by British, French, and Polish detachments recaptured Narvik from the Nazis in 1940? The Allies' victory was the Nazis' first military defeat of the Second World War."

Johann whispered something in Swedish to Klaes who translated. "Yes, my brother reminded me that the reason Narvik was militarily significant was because there are important iron-ore mines a little across the border in Kiruna in Sweden."

Henry was breathing deeply, tasting the freshness of the air and tilting his head backwards to take in the rows of snow-topped peaks above the town and the stupendous, but muted, multicolored panorama of the sky in this land of the Midnight Sun. While everyone was enjoying the company and the view, all of a sudden a drunken sailor, whose clothes reeked of fish and breath of alcohol, began shouting slurs and epithets at Bea. Had a Klansman snuck up here from the intolerant southern climes to disturb their peace and fellowship? They all pretended not to hear, and then the sailor began an even fouler, louder, and more offensive salvo. Stunned between embarrassment over their ancestral homeland's discovered manifestation of bigotry and their frustrated anger over not being able to do anything about it, the younger women puckered their lips.

Without saying anything, Klaes walked over to the old, strong, weathered man and punched him with one slug as hard as he could and then came with another just as fast. But the tall sailor mustered enough strength to block both blows and to launch two of his own. Klaes ducked, and then the sailor began to vomit. Johann signaled to the other five to get out of here before the local teenybopper brigade spurted on their mopeds—two blocks away—to lynch the tourists. They ran up the side street to a nice, small hotel.

Disgusted at his own inaction, Henry wrestled off his inhibition and put one arm around Klaes' right shoulder and the other on Johann's left and jumped. They sat down at a cozy, elegant table, and Bea took Klaes's right hand into both of her own and clasped it. Then she laughed it off, "Well, it exists everywhere, I guess. No hiding from it. It's worse in some places and times, under certain laws and customs, than others. There are ugly, mean people everywhere, and there are good people everywhere. Thanks for standing up for my honor!"

The next morning the two groups of adventurers parted but carried with them the mostly pleasant memories of their stay in Narvik. The women set out to explore the northeasterly part of Norway while the men wanted to hike in Sweden's Jämtland the next day on their way south.

CHAPTER 18

Again, the brothers entered their quasi-religious trance with nature, although Johann occasionally would turn on the radio mainly to crack jokes about the sound of Norwegian. Klaes got involved in one news broadcast and translated it for Henry, "Well, here's another good example of the brand of democracy your country's fighting for in Vietnam. The Norwegian Radio reported that there was a South Vietnamese lawyer named Truong Dinh Dzu who ran as a peace candidate in the elections. He came in second while General Thieu won by 34%, but it is alleged that Thieu got 2/3 of his votes fraudulently and—had he run a legal campaign—he would have had only 10% of the vote. Now he's expected to send Dzu to prison because Dzu favors withdrawal of American forces from South Vietnam as Hanoi troops withdraw to the North. Then they would reconvene the Geneva Conference of 1954 to work out a new settlement. The South Vietnamese Government would be made up of a coalition. The radio announcer also quoted several reliable sources that claimed that there is enormous corruption and that debate is basically absent in their assembly—not to mention there's basically no legislation to improve the lot of the peasantry."

Henry remarked, "I guess it's a question of whether or not you believe a given group, like the big landowners in many parts of the poor countries, has the God-given right to what it acquired by inheritance, custom, or force. Well, I don't think that their rights are inalienable any more than I think the various classes in the developed countries should be exempt from paying a graduated level of taxation. And I don't want to give my life to protect their fat-cat interests. If the South Vietnamese can't get their act together and make some necessary changes, the Communists will win, and it'll be just as bad as under their corrupt rulers, except they won't have the mass of black market graft that filters into their economy from the American military machine. But if all the competing factions can be pressured into negotiating, I think there's hope for a parliament with a reformist policy in favor of better land distribution and social policy."

As they pulled into the province of Jämtland in Sweden, they drove to the valley at the foot of Mount Are and busily readied their campsite before going on a late-afternoon, quiet hike in the freshness of cool air. An administrator of the campsite strongly suggested that they take a guide with them lest they get lost, but Johann calmed this fellow's anxieties by insisting that he was an expert in orienteering and that there was no possibility of their wandering astray.

Without uttering a word, Johann stepped into the position of a gentle peacemaker, and swinging his arms in different directions, led the group forward for a brisk tramp in the woods before dinner and early bedtime.

Over the course of the next day, the friends climbed up and down Are and spoke little except for Johann's joking putdowns of Henry's and Klaes's lack of dexterity in ascending and descending the peak. Johann's one-upmanship was an irritant to an otherwise marvelous climb.

Back at the base, Johann started to become anxious about making it back to his job in Stockholm on time. But all in all, everyone was having a splendid time, and their rediscovery of the outdoors was deeply appreciated by all three young men. Klaes read over the newspapers from the last few days while they sipped coffee and had rounded cream puffs at a local café. Glancing through the headlines, Klaes was glad to report that the news was actually relatively cheerful: the Czechs were optimistic after the end of their talks with the Russians.

On the long drive back to Stockholm, the young men stopped to visit Eyvind and Karl, Klaes's friends in Darlarna with whom they were invited to make a trek around Sweden's traditional tourist area. Technicians at the Domnarvet Steel Plant, Eyvind and Karl were six feet tall, blue-eyed, blond soccer players who took pride instructing their guests in their region's rich history. It was thanks to the Falun copper mine that Gustavus Adolphus could afford to carry on his imperialistic adventures that contributed to the victory of Protestantism in the Thirty Years' Wars. The red paint seen all over Sweden on houses and barns was taken from ingredients that remained after this mine had been exhausted. And many of the *Dalkarl* found their way to the United States during the mass emigration of the nineteenth century. Eyvind and Karl bubbled with slapstick humor, yet carried themselves with smooth and upright steps like the firs of their province. In appreciation of the great time they had on their last visit to Stockholm, they bestowed upon each of their visitors a beautiful, palm-sized carved, bright red horse with a blue, green, and yellow saddle.

Worried about how they would have to pay them back, Klaes and Johann were a little uncomfortable at their friends' generosity and kept pleading that Eyvind and Karl should not do this. When they insisted, the Stockholmers finally accepted with at least ten thousand thanks, if Henry had properly reckoned the number of *tusen tack* with which they reciprocated. Henry said *tack* just two times.

All the way back to Stockholm, Henry nostalgically looked out the car window and rejoiced in how close he felt to this country and its people and how much he admired the social system they had struggled to build over the course of this century. For the first time in his life, he had learned to appreciate the value of quietness, of non-speech, even though he was so awkward without words. He felt close to the friends he had made this month, and he sensed he could depend on them. Yet, he was growing to understand that their great mutual affection was based on their enormous differences. His enthusiasm and verbal plays complimented their restraint and measure. His appreciation of nature was that of a monotheist in awe of created beauty; theirs that of unknowing-and-uncaring-to-know celebrants of the immediate that was, *punkt och slut*, "period and end," as they said, "period dot" in our vernacular. How much more their lust for life in the here and now and in the materially pleasurable, resembled that of contemporary California than did the sober, reality-prone grayness and heaviness of Toronto. Should he go to Toronto, or "face the music" of the American army, or come back to his friends here?

Well, there was still a little more than a month to decide and a lot more to think about. As the evergreens and birches, hills and dales rolled by, he drew a sketch in his mind of his proposed August. He would activate his Eurailpass on the thirtieth, head south through Germany to Switzerland, spend a week in Italy, a week in Spain and Portugal, turn back over the Alps to Vienna and then up back through Germany to Berlin, over back to Paris, then Brussels and Oostende, and hit the ferry back for England. He would sleep free as much as possible on the train to save money, and he would leave two days in London to make the final decision about Vietnam.

Parting was a sad affair. Henry owed his job and two hundred dollars savings to Karin's suggestions. He was in debt to Annette for finding him a wonderful place to stay. He felt enormous gratitude to Johann for a wonderful trip up north. His roommates, Öve and Lennart, held a special place in his memory for their hospitality, tact, and company, and his mutual friendship with Klaes was something mysterious and tremendous, which neither wanted to let go.

As his friends walked to the modern central station in Stockholm, Henry felt as though he were leaving home, as though a part of him from an earlier existence had been uprooted from where it belonged. Behind these dreams, there was much to decide and realities to face. Klaes wrapped his arms around Henry's shoulders and squeezed a strong, warm, masculine hug. Overcoming his fear, Henry reciprocated with strong, slow pats to his soul brother. Nothing was spoken. Karin, Birgitta, Annette and he exchanged gentle kisses on the cheek. Öve and Lennart just shook hands warmly with Henry. The three young men looked at each other with mutual affection. The overnight train departed for Copenhagen.

CHAPTER 19

Henry was the first to take a seat in a compartment in the first-class coach to which his Eurailpass entitled him. He grabbed a seat by the window facing in the direction of the engine. Soon afterwards he was joined by a thin man in a somewhat baggy, out-of-date, gray suit. He was wearing a fedora. *This fellow could be Uncle Herman*, thought Henry, remembering the uncle with whom he had lived during his childhood until his uncle's death when Henry was a pre-teen. This middle-aged man had dark, deeply set eyes that made him appear ancient. He remarked to Henry in Swedish with a strong German accent, "I believe we belong to the same tribe."

"It appears so. Do you speak English?"

"I understand it better than I talk it."

"Where did you grow up?"

"In Mannheim."

"That's funny. Part of my mother's side of the family came from there," Henry responded, then quickly asked, "Did you come here because of Hitler's rise to power in your mother country?"

"That's right. We were saved by the Danes and Swedes, you know."

Henry stared out at the passing countryside as the clickity-clack of the train made him drowsy in the late afternoon.

"*Jag heter David Mendelsohn.*"

"Hi, I'm Henry Green." Then he inquired, "How has your life worked out in Sweden?"

"Quite well. My small family and I are happy. I have one child, a son, about your age, and a wife. We are not wealthy, but we lead a good life. We are all healthy."

"What do you do? I mean what is your line of work?" Henry asked, remembering that some Europeans he had met misunderstood the Americanism referring to their occupation.

"I am a teacher of German in the *gymnasium*."

"Do you have any relatives in America?"

"Sure, cousins. We write once a year. We lead such different lives. They make much money over there. They own several stores. But they are not very cultivated people. They don't read, go to theaters or concerts."

"Did you ever visit them?"

"No, not yet. But I'm hoping to send my boy one day soon for a visit. He went to the Holy Land last year for the first time."

"I bet you and your wife work hard and give everything to your son."

"Why not? But that's not why we never visited America. I guess I still hold a grudge."

"What do you mean? Why?"

"They never let me or my family in before the war. They never bombed the railway lines to the camps. They could have saved millions, including most of my family. They didn't."

"Why weren't the railway lines bombed?"

"They thought most of us were Communists, which is a lie. Many of their leaders were deeply prejudiced against us because of cultural and religious differences. During his visit to America even Freud found as much or more dislike of us there as in his native Vienna."

"I think Freud may have exaggerated about that. There are good sociological studies that indicate a real decline in hatred and discrimination against our people at home since the Second World War. We're at a highpoint in America because our values for free expression and our ability in commerce, science, and the professions are shared by the deepest values of American culture," Henry retorted, defending his mother country.

"Listen, young man, we felt the same way in Germany before the war. We aped what the majority did. Many of us didn't feel any different from the majority. We lost respect for our own traditions and faith. And let me tell you, when times became dark, even that butcher Stalin let in more of our people than America."

"But Stalin let in basically only the skilled whom he could use—from what I've read—and many of them starved at that."

"Whatever that *meshugena* did for whatever reasons, he let in many of us, and he liberated Auschwitz. And he did not single us out to starve. When people starved there, everyone did."

"But he instigated the Doctors' Trials. He wiped us out culturally. He set the grounds for forced assimilation."

"You misunderstand me. I'm not trying to defend that madman. I just want to point out that more of us survived thanks to him than thanks to America. And when the State of Israel was fighting for its freedom it was Czechoslovakia, not the U.S.A., which provided the necessary arms. I don't think I'll ever visit America out of respect to my dead brothers, sisters, and parents, may they rest in peace. I have found freedom, peace, and security in what one of your writers called 'our middle way.'"

"But Sweden took only a few of us, too. And I've learned this summer that that was done against the wishes of our own community members here who were looking out for their own skins and against the fears of the Swedish medical doctors who were afraid of the competition. Their businessmen profited from trading with the Nazis, and a few of their aristocrats were pro-Nazi."

"Look, young man, you cannot imagine what it was like in those times. Sweden is a small country with a small population. They were trying to survive and maintain what they could of civilized values when most of the rest of Europe had reverted to barbarism. No nation had its hands entirely clean, but some were much cleaner than others."

"Excuse me for asking this if it offends you, but I really want to know why from one who was part of that community, why you would have gone like sheep to your deaths. This spring the French students were chanting repeatedly, '*Nous sommes tous des juifs allemands,*' which was their way of saying they were being persecuted, but unlike the German Jews, they were not going to their deaths without a fight."

"Your question reveals the ignorance of those who pose it, yet there have been many answers to it. This is painful for me to answer, and you have your *chutzpah* to ask, but I will attempt a response. The Polish Jews fought back. The Partisans fought back. We could not believe that our neighbors and friends and the culture and people we loved and had contributed to so greatly could turn their backs on us. It all happened so quickly, and we were left abandoned."

"Why didn't the heads of the Jewish community get together with the heads of the workers and other groups to try to assassinate Hitler and the heads of the Nazi Party shortly after the Reichstag fire? After all, after Hitler had destroyed democracy, wasn't anything fair play?"

"We all knew there had been other waves of extreme anti-Semitism in German history, and they passed. So we thought this one would pass over eventually if we kept quiet, negotiated with, and obeyed the authorities.

Besides, we were very divided like any nation. There were liberals, conservatives, social democrats, communists, and even small numbers who voted for the Nazis, believing that the current difficulties had been brought on by the emigration of their brethren from 'the East.' And many believed that something far worse than *Kristallnacht* would have been brought about by active resistance at the time."

"But after that, why did they passively accept being transported to Eastern Europe?"

"Listen, the Final Solution took place in gradual stages. We were first robbed of our citizenship and livelihood. This weakened us psychologically. Most of the people were further weakened by the horrible transports east. Many died in passage. Those crowded into the Warsaw Ghetto were not 'maintained' as the Germans pretended, since a large percentage starved daily on a ration which could not sustain human beings. And those in the East who were murdered by the *Einsatzgruppen* had correctly remembered that things in the First World War had been better under the Germans than the Russians, so they were more prone to follow the Germans' orders in the Second War. The Final Solution had never happened before in history! No human group had been gassed and reduced to ashes by the policy made possible by industrial technology and organization. At every stage of the way the Germans disguised what they were doing up to and including the gas chambers. There was never any official German letter that clearly and directly described what was happening. Whenever they meant extermination, they spoke in euphemisms like resettlement, information center, showers, and the like. And in countries like Denmark and Bulgaria, where the gentiles stood up to the Germans' policy toward our people, the great majority of the Jews were saved," related Herr Mendelsohn, hands quivering. When Henry saw this sign, he knew he must stop talking about these things and respect this man's limits which had been set after so much suffering.

Henry himself felt taut like a rope pulled so hard it was about to break. Herr Mendelsohn thought to himself, *These American young people are so insensitive and poorly informed. Doesn't he know there was resistance in every concentration camp? Is he so unfamiliar with our tradition of Kiddush Hashem, of sanctification of the Holy Name, of being a martyr in defense of our faith?*

This conversation left both the young and the old man exhausted. So they both sat quietly looking at the soothing Swedish countryside and soon both fell asleep.

Next morning the train pulled into the Hamburg railway station. The efficient industrial-strength steel arches above the green or olive brown coaches matched the methodical pace of the people in the space. Throwing his backpack over his shoulder, Henry shook hands with Mr. Mendelsohn and smiled a formal *"Hej så länge."*

After the heaviness of the conversation of the night before, Henry remembered his wealthy aunts and uncles boasting to one another that they had no desire to visit *Deutschland* after what had happened. Then the thought dashed out of his mind. He was here and would stay only a day on his way to Italy. He wondered how the Germans had gotten the reputation of being so anal about cleanliness. In comparison to the Swedes, although everything was in order, the public places were all a bit grimy, not like the spotless ones seen up north. The youth hostel was large, airy, and spacious, and even surrounded by nature, yet there was something extraordinarily cold and lonely there in contrast to the north. Here nature was present but more distant and less pulsating. Industry and the variety of lower human urges were let go here in a way they never would be permitted to be up north except in bed in the grasp of a lovers' tryst. In this way while the harbor was not as choked with industrial grime as in the large cities of the American Midwest, they lacked the relative gleam of the Nordic lands. Everything had a price, even human flesh on the Reperbann. And everything was packaged, but without the contained French flare. It was muffled and somewhat grim. There was something in the cut of the clothes and their tints that reflected average regularity without spirit. As Henry walked or rode the elevated train, he sensed a combination of tenseness in human beings and things which was intermittently interrupted by someone's shout or roaring ignition and exhaust of an automobile. The scale was smaller than that of Americans but larger than that of Scandinavians.

Intently taking in the various street scenes, Henry didn't think why he was walking so fast from one neighborhood to the next in Germany's second largest city and seaport. There was something powerful but murky in the waters of the Elbe as it flowed out to the North Sea. As he rode in the tourist boat around the harbor and gazed at the ships of many sizes and shapes loading and unloading machinery, chemicals, and processed foods, he conjured up the Elbe as a dirtied, thickened Jell-O which was stirred up over and over. Even the fishing boats had lost the verve and romanticism of those he had seen in Scandinavia.

The guide on the boat explained that this town had become the basis of the

Hanseatic League. There was also a familiar success story noted in the guidebook. The English cloth merchants who had been kicked out of Antwerp, Dutch Protestants, and Portuguese Jews had contributed greatly to Hamburg's economic prosperity. The town had Germany's first stock exchange, many technical and medical institutes, a university, and an active cultural life.

There was a passive, pleasant curiosity that let Henry absorb these details as though they were something one should know yet not be enthused about. So why was he spending time just viewing? Yes, it was a giant lesson: one must not forget that. It was part of his general plan—be cultivated, sense the geography of space and geology that had formed the site of so many events about which he had read. Open yourself up: not every minute must be an exact account producing work, prestige, or money. To live also means to relax, to breathe, to experience. God's accounting book does not record each second like the behavioral slice he had meticulously dissected in his undergraduate course on group dynamics. There must be time to view the world, to expand horizons. Luckily, although it did not occur to Henry at the moment, contemporary American and European society had given youth an extended period to do just this, in hopes that this enrichment plan would lead to new things and ideas from which everyone could benefit. Suddenly, Henry's mind began to stir. Did the conversation he had had yesterday with Herr Mendelsohn leave him in a bitter, depressed, defensive mood to view this city, which had, after all, been the birthplace of Felix Mendelsohn and Brahms? Maybe Herr Mendelsohn was right that one could no longer relax in the city of the master of the lullaby.

The crowd bustled off the harbor craft onto land. Henry walked over a few blocks to a restaurant for a bratwurst and beer, when all of a sudden, a smiling, energetic guy about his own age plopped down on the wooden bench across from him, looked him into the eye, and said in English, "Come, come. Life isn't so miserable! This is a great place to live. You Americans are so serious these days. We're the ones who're supposed to be the heavies. I'm Hans."

"Hey, I'm Henry. Thanks for cheering me up. I got into a heavy conversation last night that has been bugging me all day, but I won't admit it to myself."

"Would you like to see a bit of our lovely city? I'm heading out to the University to pick up something and then I have the rest of the afternoon off. You're welcome to ride around town with me, and I'll point a few things out to you."

Henry felt lucky. His friends told him that he had a sympathetic sort of face that drew people. Often he could sit in a public place and people would walk up to him and start a conversation.

Hans must have been a very active child. Even as a young adult he couldn't keep still for a moment. As they hopped into his old Renault-4, which was a swept-back rusting tin can, they bounced up and down as Hans drove at an incredibly high speed. Then he turned on a dime and made his passenger feel that they would surely turn over in this old wreck. They didn't. Henry gripped the bottom of his seat with both hands. Hans turned on the radio and thumped his fingers on it and his front window. *Is this guy a speed freak?* wondered Henry to himself.

The afternoon was passing as briskly as the ride. Although Hans liked the radical tone of student politics at the moment, he also liked many things he regarded American—speed, confidence in technology, and an attitude of practicality toward having to serve in the army. Yet, he hated the war in Vietnam and was a big advocate of *Ost-Politik*, an opening up between the Federal Republic of Germany and the Eastern block countries.

Hans was most preoccupied with his relationship with his girlfriend, Angela, and his best friend, Friedrich. As he and Henry drove to a late afternoon tea at Angela's apartment, Hans let his acquaintance in on this part of his private life. It was strange: Angela was the opposite of everything that Hans was. She was studying to become an international translator, but unlike many young people Henry had met in Sweden, she didn't exude any thrill in engaging a native in conversation. She continued on in German. Actually Henry enjoyed hearing them speak their language and trying to figure out how much of it he understood. But there was something terribly cold and rigid about Angela. She, or at least her parents, must have been loaded. This small apartment reminded Henry of the properly-furnished lodging of his wealthy, aging southern cousin. There were small, darkened paintings of country life hanging all over the walls. As they sipped coffee and slowly and properly consumed the ginger cakes and cream tort, Hans told her about the complicated engineering problem on which he was working. Angela's face was turned toward Hans in a trance of feigned attention with side-glances of harshness. There was something terribly conceited and insensitive in Hans's going on and on about an incomprehensible, boring mathematical problem, but there was also something amusingly-cute and child-like about him. Angela's friend, Anne, was frigidly polite to Hans, and Henry sensed that she was revolted by this sick relationship but understood the geometry behind it.

Henry was catching on, too. Angela was seeking a monetarily-secure MRS. degree and an early marriage into at least an upper-middle class family. Besides, Hans was handsome and in good shape. So he was silly, unbelievably fidgety, and occasionally a bore. She would keep him in line: well-dressed, an attractive home, and all that. She could keep on working after a couple of *kinder* and have her flings on the side. Neither she nor Hans had any religious convictions against it. Indeed, their only belief was in the rational application of mankind's mind to the material world. They also believed that an individual should enjoy the fruits of his or her labor. A worker's benefits were often deserved but should be divided up better than in America in order to provide for social order and justice.

Anne did not say much, except an occasional jab from the viewpoint of economics and business. She couldn't decide about doing something either theoretical or practical with her life. Henry found this whole scene intriguing. Here he was, wrapped up in memories from his youth and young manhood in the South. Here, in another time and another country, was a class of people reacting to a slightly-modified scenario of what he had often seen as a youth. Woman gets her man. But there was something so anachronistic about their behavior and something of a totally hypocritic sham. While not professing a faith in *not* getting traditionally married, as had his friends in Sweden, this couple would hint in words that that's what they admired, while their actual actions moved on an opposite course. As soon as they finished their sweets, Hans jumped up, grabbed Angela, squeezed her tightly and gave her an engrossing kiss on the lips. On the side, Anne emitted a face of disgust at Hans's impropriety, and Angela's stiff body and mouth emitted a giggle of victorious conquest.

As quickly as they had entered this graying-brown flat, they left in the *R-Four* to pick up Friedrich at the machinist shop. Hans had been friends with Friedrich since childhood, and like Angela, he was a totally different person compared to Hans. Hans's father was *nouveau riche* and had made it as a contractor in the expansion of home-building during the reconstruction of Germany following World War II. Friedrich's family had remained working class, and he still lived at home, not having pursued university studies. Friedrich was intelligent, liked travel and reading and had spent some time working in England. He was a clean-cut but plain-faced young man of medium stature and dark brown hair. Even though he was a skilled worker, Friedrich exuded a tiredness-with-the-world feel about him. He could become excited about some things but inherently he saw his own and the situation's limitations in everything. Hans suggested that they go out for a few beers. When they arrived at the beer garden, the wood-paneled bar was already filled with the afternoon working crowd on their way home.

Hans asked Friedrich in German, "So what do you think of my little Angela?" His eyes anxiously suggested the answer he wanted to hear.

"So she is already *your* little Angela?"

"Did I say that?"

"*Ja, ja,*" replied Friedrich, while Henry unintentionally let out a "Uh, huh."

"Are you already that serious about her?" Friedrich wondered. "I've seen you go through a few of these in our times together."

"No, with her it's different. There's something solid about her that I like."

To himself Henry reflected, *Yeah, like a rock. But I better keep out of this. I shouldn't upset his romance. He's really been nice giving me a tour around town and a glimpse into his life here.*

"You two are very different," observed Fredrich.

"Yes, but so are we. I guess I like people who can calm me down and keep me in order," Hans replied.

"She has classic good looks, Hans," remarked Henry.

"That she does."

"Hans, I've got to get home early tonight. *Mutti* is having a special dinner for *Pappi's* birthday. I'd like to invite you two over, but you know how they are."

"Yes, well, maybe I'll drop Henry back over at the Youth Hostel and then the train station. He's going on the night train to Zurich and then south on to Italy. Then I'll stop by your place and bring your father over a bottle of schnapps. He'd like that, wouldn't he? You know, I envy you and could kick you in the seat of your pants at the same time over your behavior toward your parents. You're the only one your age in Hamburg who still calls his folks *Mutti* and *Pappi.* I know you love and respect them, but you should have more a life of your own, too."

The three fellows hopped into the *R Four* and Hans dropped Friedrich off at home and then started to drive Henry back to the hostel. "I just don't understand my friend Friedrich. Like tonight, he loves his folks but hates their narrow-mindedness. He would have liked to have you over, but he knows his folks, especially his dad, don't like foreigners. To be honest, I think his father still loves his memories of his having been in the SA. Friedrich is not like that at all, as you saw. But he has never really challenged them on their past. I guess they bestowed a lot of love and attention on him and he feels very protective towards them because of it. I would have liked for you to see life in a working-class family here. Sorry."

"Oh, that's O.K. I'd planned to leave this evening, anyway. And, about his parents, who's rational when it comes to parents in the first place?"

"You understand!"

Henry ran out, fetched his backpack, and checked out of the hostel. Then Hans drove him to the station to get his train.

CHAPTER 20

The train ride south through Germany was quiet and provided Henry with some time for thought. Trains—special conveyors of people, so comfortable and energy-efficient—permit passengers to stand up or sit down, stretch, read, eat, and walk. And the old compartment trains offer a small space in which just a few strangers might chat, converse or just wonder in silence about the personalities of the people with whom they are temporarily enclosed. On this part of the journey, Henry found himself in a compartment all to himself. So wrapped up in sightseeing, meeting new people, and reminiscing about his month in Sweden, he had little time to follow current events about which he was usually a wealth of facts and figures. He glanced at the newspapers and magazines, which had been left in this compartment. The rainy mists of northern Germany began to hush the travelers under the graying green of the early evening countryside. The place names conjured up hundreds of events, heroes and villains of his school years: Hanover, Kassel, Frankfurt, Darmstadt, Mannheim, Heidelberg, Stuttgart, Wurttemberg. For each of these names there were places and people he knew in Middle America. After all, Americans of German background outnumbered even the white Anglo-Saxon Protestants.

His mind skipped from the map to the window and back to the newspapers. Yes, the world was changing in so many contradictory directions. The political sociology he had learned—packed full, though it was, of nineteenth-century conservatism—contained some truths. France had just voted the Gaullists a big majority in the National Assembly. Yes, there were backlashes in history. Things just didn't progress from less to more equality, from lesser to greater tolerance. Hegel had put his finger on something: yes, history started with a thesis against which was generated an antithesis, which would produce a new synthesis. Isn't that what was happening with the movement for civil rights in the U.S.? King's Gandhian peaceful resistance was a thesis that was giving way to its antithesis, Black Power. This took place in the realm of ideas, but Marx was right in criticizing Hegel that the idea was lived through real people and materials. Would the movement of the hippies lead to its antithesis? Would hippies shouting obscenities on TV shock the moral consensus so much that it would lead to a reaction? This is what some of the professors on campus had said, but, so what, didn't the staid morality that pretended it didn't curse but did, deserve to have its hypocrisy attacked? On the other hand, if such free speech set back civil rights and social justice in the world, shouldn't it be modulated, as the psychologists liked to say? Henry tended to think so, but how do you control social movements? They have a force of their own. Henry had grown up most of his youth in the old South. Southerners did not like their complacency rocked, and when it did get upset, nasty things like the Ku Klux Klan became active. While he admired the free-swinging lives of the hippies, their drug culture frightened him deep down inside. But he was most afraid that their unconventional antics would scare off the mean majority into nasty-spirited policies against equality and minorities.

At this point, I am pretty sure I'm going to join the chorus shouting, 'Hell, no, I won't go.' I basically think that America should negotiate a coalition government in Saigon and give the democratic forces the military muscle to insist on a republican or parliamentary democracy. President Johnson and his advisors are clearly opposed to such a solution. In fact, they publicly ruled it out. Basically, if Thieu stays in power or the Communists win, there will be huge numbers in jail and killed. I think that both are about equally bad. But I'm not going to give my life to support what amounts to a Third World fascism. Although you can't transplant an exact mode of society from one part of the world to the next, if you were to exile me and give me the choice of going to Argentina or Yugoslavia under Tito, I'd pick Yugoslavia any day of the week.

By now the night had surrounded the moving cars and Henry walked through the train, stopping in between cars where a conductor had opened the upper section of the door. He smelled the fresh-tasting air of the countryside. After deeply inhaling the cool, fresh air, he walked back to his compartment and stretched out on the seat. He fell asleep. Sometime in the middle of the night a stocky young woman entered his compartment, and he sat up, trying to strike up a conversation. She spoke no English and found Henry's attempt at broken German very funny. They giggled, then laughed, then roared.

Perhaps this Bavarian country lass found it beyond belief to find herself alone in a compartment with a silly, young foreign man who could only botch her language. She was so paralyzed by laughter that she couldn't muster the strength to leave. After about an hour, they managed to settle down on opposite seats for a long snooze in the pristine air of the Alps.

Henry woke up in the morning in the majesty of the northern Italian Alps. The German woman must have stepped off the train while he was still sleeping. As the train went through the passport inspection by the Italian officers, the compartment began to fill up quickly. Indeed, after the stop in Milan people were crunched into every available space. The windows were rolled down; and men were smoking in the corridors. As the train moved south, the seriousness of the time in Germany was being replaced by a bustle, movement, talkativeness, and presence of the old and the young, as people squeezed tightly in the openness of society.

Just as the train had changed character and become dense, so did the next two weeks in Henry's life take on a packed mixture of a college curriculum squeezed tightly into an uplifted new shape of centuries of ideas, forms, tongues, and constantly-shifting new configurations.

Henry was surprised at his excitement upon entering Rome. Having had to take four years of Latin to graduate from high school, he was seeped in the grammar, history, and religion of this city, all of which had been foisted on him and several of his close family members against their will or by the fate of changing circumstances. The closeness with which Catholicism and Italians and Italian-Americans were interwoven into his own family relationships and life history left him with a joy of familiarity fraught with millennia-old competition and conflict between Catholicism and Judaism: similarity and difference, majority and minority, not infrequently persecutor and persecuted. What had attracted Aunt Cathleen to embrace The Holy Mother Church so fervently after having been raised a mainline Protestant and after her divorce from her Jewish husband, one of Henry's uncles? Why had Aunt Kathleen's children, raised in proper Catholic schools abandoned their faith for a nebulous, agnostic materialism? Had his own sister—who had disliked the rigor of discipline in her Catholic high school—converted to The Church Universal only for the convenience of marrying her observant Catholic-born husband? No, the protection, order, and clarity of its hierarchy provided structure where the openness and lack of order in her Reform Jewish upbringing had left her with a feeling of emotional instability in her glaringly unsupported childhood. Of all these people, his Uncle Bernard's most enduring wife exhibited the most clean-cut case. Her successful immigrant Italian family's Catholicism left her with only comic and distasteful associations: the upturned rhinestone glasses of her stepmother or the delicious scandals of lesbian nuns and alcoholic or homosexual priests. For her the glory of Italy's art and beauty, the hearty pastas and buttery sauces of its cuisine, and the effusiveness of its passions fit in well with the upper-class California culture of her husband, a Jewish doctor. As these thoughts passed through Henry's mind, the back of his head was struck by something that felt like a finely-boned hand. Again it hit, and the word, *imbecile*, was hurled at him thrice by a tastefully-dressed, middle-aged woman who had his wallet in her other hand. "You must be a stupid American or Canadian," she continued in English. "God knows, I'm married to one. Put this damned wallet in your front pocket or you won't have it very long in this city. Where are you going?"

"I'm headed over to the youth hostel."

"Listen, help me carry some things and I might be able to solve your housing problem. You'll get to see some of the city, besides. I am Faustina Smith. My husband is originally from Toronto."

"Hi. I'm Henry Green, most recently from Los Angeles."

As they walked from the train station toward the Piazza della Republica, Henry took Faustina's shopping bags as she pointed out Guerrieri's Naiad Fountain to him. Faustina loved to walk but did not like to bear the burdens of her many purchases. They walked a long way through some small back streets to a splendid semi-enclosed market where small-scale merchants stocked their various food specialties. She bought more things, from tortellini to fish, and they trudged on this hot day all the way past the Marmertine Prison. They must have been walking an hour, but Henry hadn't even noticed, taken in as he was by this woman's staccato comments and jokes about this architect or that monument. All at once they were at her doorstep on the Via dei Foraggi. On the outside the building was a crumbling, dirty, yellow-painted structure. But on the inside, Faustina's three-bedroom, high-ceilinged flat greeted him into a world of painting, plants, and heavy wooden furniture.

"Do you like it?"

"It reminds me of one of those interiors that houses the soft colors of an impressionist painting."

The telephone rang and she conversed about twenty minutes in Italian, then she picked up Henry's and her conversation at the exact point at which they had left off.

"*Grazie. Grazie.* Would you like to stay here a while and help me out? I'm one of those real Italian mommas who misses her little boy. I have a son about your age who's in charge of my gardening when he's here. He's in Canada now visiting his relatives there. You two even look alike. I just spoke with my husband who approves of the idea which must mean that he's already bored by the quiet summer we'd planned to spend alone."

"Well, I have only a few days because I've already activated my Eurailpass, but if you're willing to swap a little of my work for room and board and give me enough time to see the city, well, fine."

"We'll do better than that! We'll show you around. And the only thing you have to do is take down the trash, water our plants, and pull the weeds. That's all little Rodolfo does when he's at home, anyway."

Faustina was funny. She had lived all over the world and thought of herself as a modern woman. In many ways she was an untraditional Italian. She was the highest ranking native Italian at the Canadian Embassy in Rome, and her husband was a cultural attaché for the Canadian Embassy. Faustina was elegant and excitable, adding just enough flair to the proper sobriety of the Canadian Embassy to keep the English and the French Canadian staff laughing at each other and at her. She was like a comic release valve which let off the necessary steam in her work world in which all true feelings and thoughts had to be constrained according to an ethic of propriety. Faustina was approaching her mid-forties with the dread of a *bella* who had no desire to give up her beauty, elegance, and muted non-conformity to the dictates of the human condition.

"Henry, *prego,* you can put your backpack into Rodolfo's room where you'll be staying."

"Here are the houseplants I'd appreciate your watering, and come downstairs with me and I'll show you the garbage container and the outside garden in the courtyard. There was a large pot of lavender, hyssop, lilies of the valley, primrose, and anemone located just below their flat. The other neighbors left their part of the courtyard in its typical Roman appearance of studied disrepair, so as to discourage thieves from taking the residence as a site of opulence. After they finished their rounds, Faustina, who had the next few days off, inquired, "What would you like to see the most?"

"Everything, but let's start with the Forum."

"First eat and then we'll set out. Which forum do you mean?"

"The main one."

"You're lucky it's just a few minutes from here. We call it '*Il Foro Imperiale.*'"

The adopted mother-son team set out in the early afternoon entering the Forum near the Arch of Septimus Severus. Faustina knew every inch, every name from the Temple of Saturn to the Arch of Titus. In this elongated garden of trees and remains—some intact, others in ruins—both Faustina and Henry entered into that dream state in which the border between their present and yesteryear was dissolved. They were stepping into history. They sat down below the monument to the Roman conquest of Jerusalem. Henry felt stirred and uneasy, projecting himself into the frescos. By the time Faustina had demonstrated her expertise—she must have guided thousands of visitors in this "her back yard"—it was time for them to return home to meet Thomas Smith for dinner.

Thomas was a tall, straight-forward man, who had to make it a point to exercise just enough so as not to overburden his wife's youthful image. He, too, enjoyed being a father and was secretly happy to have the flat alive, once again, with youthful vigor. His wife's Latin flair suited both his marginality to his own extremely austere upbringing and his natural propensity to follow along with the flow of people and events. Having been a soldier in wartime and then a diplomat, he exuded confidence and had a disarming personality.

"How about taking Henry to a restaurant *per il pranzo*?"

"O.K., *Babbo*," laughed Faustina, leaving Henry in the dark about this joke between them.

Thomas Smith strolled in an upright, almost military fashion—his left arm interlocked with Faustina's right—across the *Piazza Venezia* in front of the *Vittoriano*. "Why we've lived so near that monstrosity all these years, I'll never know," chuckled Faustina.

"Yes, it does have almost a pre-fascistic quality to it, *carissima*," replied Thomas.

Henry couldn't believe he was hearing these kinds of remarks from people who had spent the largest part of their adult lives in government circles. Even more audacious than the daredevil drivers of Fiats and other mini-sized cars, Mr. Smith dashed in and out of traffic on foot—somehow managing to avoid being hit and quickly arriving at a respectable neighborhood restaurant about three small streets off the piazza.

Breaking the protocol appropriate for her sex, Faustina pounded the spoon against the side of her glass of water. Thomas ordered for everyone. For antipasto, *carciofini sott'olio e olive*, small artichokes in oil and olives. Then, for Faustina, *una minestra in brodo*, a noodle soup, and a vegetable soup for himself and Henry followed by *scampi fritti*, fried shrimp, for

Faustina, broiled tuna steak for Henry, *un fritto misto* for himself, and a spaghetti with clams for everyone to try. Finally, a bottle of white wine to cap it all off. Not wanting to offend his hosts, Henry waited to speak until spoken to. When he saw Faustina take a bread stick, he took one himself.

"You're about draft age, aren't you?" inquired Thomas.

"Yes, sir," slipped out of Henry's mouth even without thinking.

"Oh, I gave up those military titles long ago. Just call me Tom."

Faustina looked deep into Henry's eyes and, with the latest North American vocabulary her son had brought back to Rome the summer before, she confided, "You can be cool with us." This password put Henry more at ease.

"Well, what do you think of this Vietnam thing?"

"Sir, what do you think? My major problem this summer is deciding what to do about it."

"Well, many, probably the great majority of us in Europe and the Commonwealth, don't like it. I am old enough to remember your President Dwight D. Eisenhower's saying, in I believe early 1954, that he was bitterly opposed to involving U.S. forces in Indochina. Even John Foster Dulles said, 'No.' Well, you're in it now, and I think that if you're in it, then you bloody well should use enough force to win. But I'm opposed to your being there in the first place because the old empires, those of France and Britain, have passed on in history, and the United States should not assume the role of supporting every reactionary dictator in the developing countries. People have a right to self-determination."

"Sir, I don't understand if you are for or against the War."

"In plain English, I'm against it, but your leaders have gotten themselves in a mess, and yours being a democracy, the majority of the people in your country still support that quagmire. All I'm saying is, if you've convinced yourselves that you're saving the world from Communism, then you ought to use sufficient military might to win. However, I would say that your vacillation at doing so indicates that you're not convinced that this is the basic reason for which you've been fighting in Vietnam. Many of us suspect that America is up to old empire building without believing in empire in the soul of her values."

This kind of answer baffled Henry: there was good and bad in the American involvement, according to Thomas Smith, but the bad outweighed the good, if he had understood him correctly.

"You know," continued Thomas, "General Eugene Henri Navarre, commander of the French forces in Indochina, lost at Dien Bien Phu within four months. The French casualties were around 158,000 of whom about 58,000 were dead or missing. And America had paid for about 80% of the French war. Today you can see religious Buddhists and Catholic social activists organizing effective opposition to the Saigon dictators. When the Buddhists burn themselves up before a television camera or a newspaper reporter, the message all over the world is that you don't have to be a Communist to oppose oppression."

Faustina interrupted her husband, "Henry, look, we Europeans have sinned grievously in the complicated histories of our different countries. Now we're throwing back at the United States much of the self-righteousness it threw at us over the years after the last great war. We still respect your country for its great accomplishments and its freedom for the individual to expand. However, the limits to the American liberal notion of freedom are striking: you have millions of unemployed and poor people who live in deplorable conditions. You don't have to be a statistical wizard to realize this! Just open up your own eyes. And we can also see many more people working, enjoying health benefits, and a more beautiful environment where the state has adopted these goals, as it has in western Europe, particularly in the northern countries. So what is America protecting the world for? I'll tell you what—so that your largest companies can drain the underdeveloped countries of cheap raw materials and labor! Henry, don't be taken in by those bastards!" At this point Faustina, obviously quite excited, took several quick gulps of white wine.

Thomas interrupted, "Darling, calm yourself down. I am sure Henry is weighing the various reasons his country is involved in Vietnam."

A tear rolled down her face, "But I don't want to hear that he got killed helping a tyrant stay in power. Imagine our Rodolfo in this situation!"

"But Rodolfo doesn't have to make this decision!"

Winding some spaghetti onto his fork with the help of a spoon, Thomas continued, "Henry, did you hear the news today? Nixon was nominated yesterday on the first ballot to head the GOP ticket, and he has picked Agnew as his running mate. He has pledged to end the war through some plan he claims to have, and they'll run on a law and order platform. The Democrats are deeply divided on many issues. So what is on your mind?"

"Well, I feel uncertain. I am deeply opposed to the war. I've been accepted by The University of Toronto to continue my graduate studies, but it is a big step. I've loved my undergraduate and beginning grad studies at UCLA, and it's unfair that I'm being penalized for finishing my B.A. early, in a little over two-and-a-half years. Every day I become more and more convinced that if the U.S. would genuinely support a coalition government in South Vietnam—sort of like your accepting Communists who win seats in a democratic election in your governments in Italy and France—that this would be a just resolution. But the conservative Democrats won't hear of it, and it looks as though they have the upper hand, so that leaves me with the choice of leaving the country or staying and being drafted and then arrested for refusing to serve in the war. And to be honest with you, I don't think I could emotionally survive serving a prison sentence. You know, political prisoners might be put in with murderers in America. The judges tend to sentence to the better prisons only people found guilty of white-collar crimes—you know, people who steal money from a business or who are found guilty of some crime involving finance. I am still fighting my induction, but if I'm not successful, then I think I'll go to Canada, although I still feel mightily queasy and nervous about putting myself into this situation."

Quickly changing moods from one of grief to levity, Faustina lunged forth, "*Carpe diem*, that's what the ancient Romans said, 'Seize the day!' Eat, drink, and be merry, and all of that. What would you like to see tomorrow?"

"Well, if I get up early and finish my household duties, do you think that we could walk over to Vatican City and spend the day there?"

"*Pater Noster*," intoned Faustina in a mock Gregorian chant, then crossed herself.

Amused, Thomas and Henry didn't laugh for fear of appearing inappropriately irreverent to a faith of which they were not members, although upturned lips could be discerned on both faces.

"If we have time, I'd also like to take in the Colosseum, the Pantheon, and the St. Angelo Castle."

"That's probably too much. But we're only about a fifteen minutes walk from the Colosseum, and we could go from there to the Vatican. I doubt we can make it to the Castle, but let's see how much time you'll spend in the Holy See."

Mr. Smith paid the waiter and he guided them on a slightly different route home by the Theater of Marcellus and the Jewish Ghetto. Upon arriving home, Henry shook Thomas's hand with gusto and thanked him for a superb evening. He was about to do the same to the Signora, but Faustina put her perfectly made-up, slightly rosy cheek forward, as if to say, "Don't deny a

121

Mother her parting son's due." Henry implanted a warm filial *beso* at the designated spot and retired to Rodolfo's room.

On the morning of August 10, Thomas Smith knocked at the door of his son's room at 7:00 A.M. so he could get Henry off to an early start. "Come on with me over to an espresso bar, and we'll grab a coffee and a roll. That'll put you back here about 8:00, and then you can get Faustina up. She'll let you into the inner-court where you can do the weeding. At Thomas's quick clip they entered within minutes the brown interior with a big glass mirror. Mr. Smith's routine was to skim the headlines of all the major papers which the owner of the café kept stacked on a corner table for his customers. As Henry sipped the strong dark brown liquid from a miniature cup, Thomas Smith gave him a downcast look, "Henry, the world seems to be suffering from hardening of its arteries. While Tito and the Czech leaders meet today in Prague with an outpouring of popular emotion, Moscow warns against any liberalization and insists upon the Communist Party's central role in governing. In your home, Senator McGovern is preparing to run as the peace candidate against Hubert Humphrey. When the Russians and the Americans sink their boots further into the mud, someone else is going to get trampled upon—you can count on it."

"Gee, it's getting late. I'd better get back to get Faustina up."

"Here, I'll get the bill."

"Thanks, that coffee really gives you a bang. It was delicious."

Finding his way back almost as fast as he had been led to the coffee bar, Henry had to ring the bell several times before awaking Faustina, who hurried down in her billowing caftan to let him in and into the back courtyard. "I'll wake up by the time you're finished," she said sleepily.

Having had a part-time job doing some gardening one summer when a teenager, Henry knew a weed from a flower. He methodically extracted the unwanted herbaceous growth from the small plot and plucked a few dying petals from the flowers. Within an hour he had finished, and Faustina was ready for an outdoor excursion.

Wearing a white summery cotton dress, Faustina pranced down the wide boulevard toward the great Flavian Amphitheater. Soon she and Henry were climbing up the Colosseum's four stories and dashing among its tiers of marble seats. "Could this place really seat 45,000?" Henry asked, amazed that some of his ancestors might have been among the Jewish slaves who built this arena.

"That's what they say. If it overflowed, they probably threw the excess mob to the beasts," Faustina remarked in something between a joke and a serious statement about the brutality of its history. After running all the way to the base, Faustina ran across a great plaza to a bus stop where they caught a vehicle packed to the brim with other ordinary Romans and befuddled tourists.

They soon reached St. Peter's Square. Henry and Faustina walked to the middle and turned around in circles several times, and then, without saying anything, Faustina led him into the enormity of the enclosed golds, reds, blues, and greens in marble and gold adorning the interior of the basilica. Standing on the Wheel of Porphyry, the great red Egyptian disc on which emperors knelt when receiving investiture from the Pope, Faustina confided to Henry, "It is not all these centuries of monuments in stone and precious metal that inspire my faith. Let me show you what does." She took him over to Michelangelo's *Pietà*. "Whenever I come here, I see in this mother's forlorn, downcast eyes a sadness ruled by gentleness and devotion, a resignation that she must lose this perfectly sculpted young man so that all humanity might be saved."

"Faustina, do you believe in the words of The Roman Church, 'In God the Father Almighty and in Christ Jesus, his only begotton Son, our Lord, who was born of the Holy Ghost and the Virgin Mary, who was crucified under Pontius Pilate and was buried, on the third day rose from the dead, ascended into heaven, is seated at the right hand of the Father, whence he will come to judge the living and the dead, and in the Holy Ghost, the Holy Church, the forgiveness of sins, the resurrection of the flesh?'"

"Oh, that form of the creed is its Greek form written in the fourth century by Bishop Marcellus of Ancyra. You know, Henry, we Romans tend to be anti-clerical. My husband raised as an Anglican and Rodolfo has been taken to a variety of Christian and other churches and places of worship, depending on where we were or the practice of the country at the time. We have spent too much time in North America to be militant atheists or agnostics, and we have spent too much time here to be extremely observant. We are a tolerant, ecumenical family. By the way, you brought up the creed in reference to my love of the *Pietà*. You know there are many different creeds depending on the time and place, and they became incorporated into the Sunday Roman mass in the eleventh century because an emperor requested it of the Pope."

"But every muscle, curve of flesh, and fold of clothing which Michelangelo was able to fashion out of this white stone is your personal creed, that of the caring mother."

"I never thought of it that way, but maybe you're on to something."

"What is *your* mother like? Is your relationship like that of Rodolfo and me?"

"Not at all. My dad died when I was a baby, and my mother's mother a year after him. Mother had already had a few breakdowns. After all this death, widowhood, and financial hardship, she cracked up again and was hospitalized most of the time until I was a teenager. My sister and I were placed with one of my father's brothers and his second wife, and when my aunt and my sister didn't get along, they sent her to a Catholic school in the same town in which my mother was in the state hospital. I would see Mother several times a year from the time I was a little boy. Mother—I only occasionally called her 'Mamma'—was always emotionally effusive. She would hug and kiss me when we were alone when I was little, but when she would fall into her depressions, she would then say that we didn't love her."

"Do you know if her doctors ever diagnosed her by any psychiatric terms?"

"Yes, she was labeled a manic-depressive, but one of the main reasons I got interested in the social sciences is because my readings in university convinced me that most of my family's and my mother's problems were social in origin. In the South, when we were growing up, it was very difficult for a widowed woman to get a job, particularly if she was from a minority group like ours which was expected to take care of its own, but, in fact, often didn't."

"You are a member of a minority group?"

"Well, not the way the term is being construed now in legal battles at home, but in the sociological sense of a group which has a history of being discriminated against, yes. Both of my parents and many of our relatives are Jewish, although I have aunts and cousins who are Catholic and Protestant. I myself as a teenager was sent to a very Protestant high school with my survivor's benefits from Social Security and minor contributions from several relatives."

"But do you have a good relationship with your mother?"

"Yes and no. I love my mother; I feel sorry for her condition. I feel responsible. But to be honest, it is extremely hard to cope with Mother when she gets depressed. During my teenage years, when I would spend the summers at her apartment with her, she would swing from taking me around town to show me off to all her friends and relatives. Then she would cry bitterly saying that neither I nor the other members of her family cared for or loved her. This verbal abuse is really difficult for an adolescent to handle, believe me! But Mother has gotten amazingly better this year since President Johnson's full employment programs have opened up jobs for her and others like her. She holds down a job she enjoys—selling hats in a large department store. She hasn't had any huge ups and downs since she has gotten this modicum of self-respect. When lithium maintenance came out before this job program and she was put on it, she would go around like a zombie and said that she felt controlled and manipulated. You could see her dried-up lips which she and everyone around her attributed to this external mind and body constraint. When she was on this stuff, you got the general feeling of listlessness without mood changes."

"Henry, it sounds to me that you're insinuating that in America the powers-that-be in private industry, like the large drug consortiums and government, would rather spend huge sums of money for medications, which, in turn, make zombies of people. You think that if people were trained to work with the mentally ill and change their real life situations that their chances for improvement would increase."

"You've hit it on the nail, Faustina!"

Faustina threw a kiss at the *Pietà*, and they moved on to the Sistine Chapel.

"Henry, I always sense movement in this chapel."

"Yeah, life here seems like it's in perpetual motion filled with so many scenes important in the spiritual struggle of mankind in the West and Near East," Henry observed.

"The fading greens, blues, beige, browns and gold attract you to their action but put you in a special time-space where you're here and long ago at the same time," Faustina added.

"All of these paintings are splendid but none really speaks directly to the central moral issue of our time, the War in Vietnam, unless it's that picture of God surrounded by angels giving the touch of life to the naked Adam. Maybe Michelangelo was trying to say that we are put in this beautiful spot to choose on our own between right and wrong, and, in trying to do just that, we can make grievous mistakes or be right."

Enclosed by all these paintings bringing the Supernatural so near the earth, Faustina became edgy. Henry sensed that she wanted to leave. After the Sistine, Faustina walked him at a very brisk pace through the huge Vatican Museum. As they took in the floor of this enormous collection, Faustina was obviously taking this part of the tour to be more of her exercise time than a detailed visit. By the time they made it over to the St. Angelo Castle, it was closing, so Faustina took Henry by hand and pulled him on a laughing run toward the bus stop from which they made their way to the Piazza Novona.

"I want to treat you to *gelato*, our thick, creamy Italian ice cream, Henry. We'll come back here later."

Catching a glimpse of the dreamy fountains with marble statues and monuments set in the long track of asphalt-like pavement surrounded by buildings, Henry followed Faustina into an elegant *gellateria* with large spotted eighteenth-century mirrors behind small, rounded tables encircled by upholstered chairs with cushions of green and purple. She ordered two huge portions of *gelato*, for herself a hazelnut and spumoni combination and a lemon and *canneloni* for Henry.

"It's wonderful. It's the best ice cream I've ever had."

"I thought you'd like it. I've taken Rodolfo here since he was a little boy."

"Henry, what does your mother think you should do about the war?"

"You know, we've never discussed it directly. She was indirectly glad when I threatened her rich sister and her husband. I told them that I'd take them to court if they didn't give me my Social Security benefits, which they had been taking illegally for years. They told everyone that they were giving this money to my mother out of their own pockets. But she feels nervous about much of the rebelliousness among today's students—particularly the drug subculture. I find that funny because she knows I don't take drugs, but she worries over the possibility that I might because it's constantly in the press. She now claims that she and her sisters' families were for the Civil Rights Movement. But I distinctly remember getting into several bad arguments with her, my aunts, uncles, and cousins, who with two exceptions, were opposed to the Freedom Riders and civil rights workers, whom I supported as early as elementary school."

"You know, parents worry that their children may be harmed by things that are over and beyond them or because they may too readily follow the crowd."

"You're right, but it's hard to live with suspicions about you when you know you're not like that."

"It sounds, Henry, like you're being forced to break away from a rather narrow background by the very nature of your intellectual curiosity, your own personal history, and the fast-changing world we are living in. It is painful for all who are involved. But as long as your family shows love and respect toward you, try to reciprocate. Unfortunately, it is often hard to distinguish between what is meant as love and harm. I know that from my own family members who disapprove of my having married a Protestant and a foreigner and who don't like my modern ideas about women at all!" Faustina counseled Henry, as she gracefully dipped the metal spoon into the light brown dessert.

"You have one of the happiest family lives I have ever seen. You've really found a good balance between being a mother, a wife, a worker, and your own person. Do you mind if I ask you a personal question? You seem literally to worship motherhood, yet you have opted to have only one child."

Faustina looked askance as a tear disturbed some of the light make-up on her face, "Henry, *Dio Mio*, how I wanted another child; how both Thomas and I had planned and worked to have other children. We've been to the best doctors in the world. After such a perfect son as Rodolfo, who would have thought there could be complications? To be honest with you, something terrible happened to our bodies when we were stationed while the Canadian government was constructing its so-called peaceful nuclear reactor in India. You know, now people are just beginning to discuss the bad effects man-made technology can have on nature, including us. In those days everyone thought that nuclear plants didn't harm the environment. Now I have personally spoken to some of the top scientists and physicians in the world, and they are discovering more dreadful effects of nuclear radiation on nature, including human beings, every day. The governments have hushed it up for economic and military reasons. But I can tell you that the safety standards and building practices at the plant in India were shoddy. I was there every day for two years. According to the medical examinations I've had, I have been exposed to a much higher than normal level of radiation. Cancers could flare up in my body at any moment. Thank God they haven't so far, and thank the Lord I never took little Rodolfo even near that plant. I left him with a lovely Indian woman in a nearby village while I was at work. I have come to accept our infertility, and every day we are glad to have another healthy day of life."

"Oh, Faustina, I am sorry. That explains why you've never adopted another child."

"Yes, Henry, at least we have gotten Rodolfo through his young manhood, and should we die early, he will be well provided for by our insurance. We're fortunate that both Tom's and my family members adore him. Perhaps, you'll find it peculiar, but we don't dwell on the matter. Thomas and I are lucky enough to be good-natured people."

"I plead ignorance. I haven't read any serious literature on nuclear power since my high school physics course, and, frankly, it was very technical or depicted nuclear power as the wave of the future—clean, endless, cheap energy, that sort of thing."

"Lies! *Caro*, wait, just wait a few years; stories like ours will break. Something horrible is happening without people really questioning it."

"You know, it's strange, but when I was in Sweden, I got into an argument with some young Swedish soldiers my age who were claiming that nuclear power and arms were bad. I'd never really thought about the issue and didn't even question my academic knowledge then because they sounded uneducated, and I was picking up on some anti-American vibes from them, which made me reject their arguments out-of-hand. I'm going to look into this question when I get some time. Right now I'm so preoccupied with this Vietnam thing. I'm doing well to deal with that huge problem alone."

"Henry, just about five minutes back from here where we were at the Piazza Navona, I can show you Borromini's Church of Saint Agnese and Bernini's Fountains of the Four Rivers and the Moor. Would you like to see them as well?"

"Sounds fine," gulped Henry as he was beginning to grasp Faustina's style of pushing her intimates to their emotional and intellectual apogees, catching them and pulling them back to equilibrium by changing the depth and focus of the conversation which she somehow masterfully orchestrated. They walked out onto the flat plain that had been the Campus Martius of classical times and which still retained the shape and some of the remains of Domitian's circus of the first century.

"Henry, besides the tourists there are plenty of ordinary Romans here."

Sitting on the edge of the fountain, they enjoyed watching the passers-by and cleared their heads of heavy thoughts, then leisurely walked back to the Smiths' home. When they arrived, Thomas, who had been reading the evening paper, immediately jumped up to greet them and to suggest a light evening dinner and a stroll. Faustina, who was accustomed to cooking at home, decided that it was only appropriate to pamper herself and their guest during her vacation. *Why not splurge tonight?* thought Faustina. *Andiamo a Mamma Caesarina!*

Hopping a bus over to the Statione Termini in the Piazza dei Cinquecento, they passed the sedately lit Servian Wall, which dated back to the fourth century. They watched the muted light that revealed bustling activity all around. Finally, when they reached the restaurant, Faustina, who had been looking forward to an evening of culinary splendor, was taken aback when the hostess mistook her for a foreigner and sought to sit them in the primarily

American section of the establishment. "It must have been you two Anglos," Faustina whispered, jabbing Thomas and Henry in the ribs. Finally, they were seated in the section for the local people and Thomas Smith immediately ordered a large bottle of red wine to begin their meal, which he immediately poured for all of them.

"Henry, I've been doing a lot of reading about Vietnam, which you may have noticed if you had a chance to browse in my library."

"No, I didn't even know you had more than a passing interest in the subject."

"Come on, this issue is the main question of our time. Let me try you on some basics. How many changes of government took place in South Vietnam between November 1, 1963, when President Ngo Dinh Diem's army overthrew him and Air Vice Marshall Ngugen Cao Ky seized control in June of 1965?"

"Gee, I guess I was too busy trying to get through high school to have counted."

"Well, the answer is nine. What did the agreement between the French and the Viet Minh conclude on July 21, 1954?"

"Didn't they agree to split up Vietnam into northern and southern military areas?"

"At the 17th Parallel of Latitude, to be exact. And you left out the main points of providing for a cease fire and permitting refugees to pass from one zone to another. I should know this because an international commission of Canadian, Polish, and Indian members was created to supervise the agreement. What were the problems that arose from the Geneva Accord?"

"Diem let the landed elite wreck land reforms and accepted American money to build up a spy network and armed forces. Then he refused to participate in an all-Vietnamese election and that led to a guerilla movement by the Communists who, according to all accounts, would have won these elections."

"Yes, you have learned something about the conflict."

"I recently took two courses, one on Asian geography and another on Asian ethnography."

"Did you know that in North Vietnam in 1956 there were some local revolts against collectivization of agriculture?"

"Yes, but generally the north went forward economically from 1955 through 1965. There were around 900,000 refugees to the south. Diem favored Catholics and alienated Buddhists there."

Faustina, intrigued by all these facts and figures, felt obligated to underscore her point. "Look here, I've read some of Tom's books, too, and even the conservative ones describe Diem's regime as totalitarian, a term your leaders generally apply only to Communist governments. Diem made loyalty to him and his family the major obligation for all, and his brother Ngo Dinh Nhu organized a party to spy on everyone, including army officers."

Thomas Smith interrupted his wife, "Henry, I can draw several generalities from my reading of Vietnamese history. First, since the 11th century there has been a very strong central power at the head of a unified administration that enabled the Vietnamese State to stretch a thousand miles from the Golf of Tonkin to the South China Sea. From Confucius they got the idea that this absolute power was based on a mandate from Heaven. Vietnam was cut into two only two times in its history, and these governments fought one another for years and years."

"Tom, that's just it. The States are so ethnocentric to believe we are going to impose a division of all nations undergoing civil wars into non-communist and communist halves, along the lines of the European model of Germany at the end of World War II," commented Henry.

Faustina interjected, "I was impressed by the strength of women in Vietnam's history. Did you realize that two of the Vietnamese rebellions against China in the first century were led by a noblewoman and her sister who had themselves proclaimed queens of an independent Vietnamese kingdom that lasted for three years? And in the third century the next resistance to total Sinicization was, again, led by a woman?"

"No, I did not know that. You know, the right-wingers at home believe that the Vietnamese are and will be basically puppets of Red China."

"Who said you should expect ideologues to be rational, Henry?" Tom observed, munching on a long breadstick.

Henry savored all these facts and generalizations more than the antipasti in front of them. A round scoop of *spuma fredda di salmone*, a cold salmon mousse, lay on a small leaf of lettuce in front of them. Occasionally, the black olive on its top would stare at them like an eye inquiring why it was left to the company of the yellow lemon slice and red tomato. Despite its exquisite appearance and delicate taste, the salmon dish was consumed slowly without comment—indicating the seriousness of their conversation to all of its participants.

Thomas Smith picked up the lull as his wife and guest took a quick bite of the pinkish ball.

"You know, the farther you go back in Vietnamese history, what stands out is its high degree of mixing of many different cultural and social characteristics. Yet, despite all this diversity, they already fused an ethnic identity about two millennia ago."

Faustina, who had a knack for blending the pressing questions of the day with her reading of history, jumped in the brainstorm, the aim of which was to save the life and values of this young man who so closely resembled their son. "What seems to me most relevant for Henry's decision is the fact that the French—falsely thinking that they were benefitting France—drained Vietnam. There were no civil liberties for the native Vietnamese who were excluded from industry and trade. You see, the resistance to French rule naturally saw capitalism to be foreign and undemocratic."

"Henry, I can cite you a long list of facts and figures to back up Faustina's contentions. If you're interested, I can show you their sources when we get home. What I don't understand, though, is why your government didn't use its good relationship with Ho Chi Minh to woo him away from a Leninist type of Marxism. Until recently I had no idea that when the 'Vietnam Revolution League,' established under nationalist Chinese pressure, proved incompetent to gather information on the Japanese in Vietnam and to rescue downed pilots, the Allies relied on the Viet Minh. Directed by Vo Nguyen Giap, the Viet Minh organized a network of political agents and guerillas who were useful to the Allies.

"In 1943, Ho Chi Minh was released from prison where he had been put under orders from Chiang Kai-shek. He was made the chief of the Dong Minh Hoi, and the United States of America's Office of Strategic Services gave him money and some weapons for anti-Japanese activities inside Vietnam. Of course, he used his office to help the Viet Minh, and by the second half of 1945, they were able to win Hanoi without any major opposition. The Emperor abdicated in favor of Ho Chi Minh's government in Hanoi. And in the south, a Provisional Executive Committee of South Vietnam in Saigon was dominated by the Viet Minh and placed itself under the authority of Hanoi in late August. Very early in September, Ho Chi Minh proclaimed the independence of Vietnam and all the Vietnamese understood that the Communists were in the top position. But the Potsdam Conference of the victorious Allies let the French reoccupy Indochina. Even Chiang Kai-shek didn't want the French back in Indochina and didn't interfere with the new government. Several days later, the British armed the French soldiers who had been interned by the Japanese and later in September the French began their re-conquest, driving communists and anti-communists into armed resistance."

Without her husband or young friend even noticing it, Faustina had ordered a meal which soon began to arrive. *I Primi*: green gnocchi, gratineed with butter and cheese. "Excuse me, you two, aren't these *gnocchi verdi al burro e formaggio* absolutely splendid?"

Thomas and Henry, tasting their first mouthfuls of the spinach and ricotta gnocchi, rolled their tongues from side to side, smiled at her and at the stout, loving picture of Mamma Caesarina hanging on the wall.

"Wouldn't it be nice if mankind could eat its disagreements away in some kind of culinary contest?" Faustina laughed. Her utterly serious company suddenly shifted moods to an unanticipated guffaw. What an absurdly delightful thought!

Just as quickly as the conversation had turned to humor, it switched back to the heavy historical reality. Faustina again led the turn in the conversation, "We lived through the period of the first Indochina War, Henry, as young adults in diplomatic circles from 1946 through 1954.

"*Dio Mio*, Henry, people had thoughts that were so Manichaean at the time! The world was a battleground between lightness and darkness. And we, coming as we do from what at the time were considered such different backgrounds, and from countries which were not superpowers, became so cynical that we retreated into irony about the dour truthsayers on both sides."

"We did come up with quite a few good jokes about them all the same!" Thomas chuckled before Faustina summed up for Henry what it had been like when they were young adults.

"But the France that we both loved seemed like a silly tyrant over Southeast Asia. And those of us with progressive ideas compared the likes of the French colonialists and militarists, like Admiral Georges-Thierry d'Argenlieu, the high commissioner for Indochina, with our despised and recently deposed despot, Mussolini, for whom I and my family had had the utmost contempt from the beginning. Nor could we help notice the ties between quite a few of the French militarists and colonialists with their collaborators of Vichy. You are no doubt aware that despite the fascist regime in Italy, the French were much more culpable in collaborating with the Nazis in their persecutions of *La Comunità Israelitica* than were the Italians."

Henry nodded, "Yes, there are more investigations and literature backing up this claim all the time. That's one of the major things that really disturb me about American foreign policy of that period that has formed the groundwork of the current American policy. Many high-ranking American governmental officials assisted powerful Nazis in getting out of Europe and hid them elsewhere, including the United States, to use them in its cold war against Communism. And I believe some of them also shared quite a bit of the Nazis' racism. Of course, the Soviet Union followed the same policy in its satellites and republics, except that it didn't let as many of the big Nazis off scot-free. It adapted a policy of forced assimilation, cultural destruction, and physical extermination of the leadership of my community there."

Going beyond Henry's guardedness on the subject, Faustina emphasized, "Of course, you must consider the survival of your own group in the first place—that's a basic fact of life for any nation or ethnic group. But the main point here is that liberals, such as you and I, must respect the rights of a nation to self-determination, in this case one as populous as that of Vietnam. And the French simply didn't want to do that. They wanted to retain their colonial rule while the Vietnamese wanted their independence and unity.

"This was true of the anti-Communists as well as the Communists. Why, I can remember when the French reunited Cochinchina with the rest of Vietnam in the late forties under the former emperor Bao Dai that even the Roman Catholic leader Ngo Dinh Diem denounced them," Faustina said in one dramatic breath.

"The fact is that Ho Chi Minh was the father of the Vietnamese War of Independence," Tom said, knocking his knuckles on the table. "The Geneva Accord of 1954 reached the agreement that the Viet Minh would withdraw north of the 17th Parallel. The French and State of Vietnam troops were to go to the south of it, while refugees were to be permitted to move from one zone to another within a certain period of time. Nevertheless, all indicators suggested that the Viet Minh would win the all-Vietnamese elections. These were to take place in July 1956. Of course, Diem refused to participate in those elections."

Looking into Faustina's face, Henry noted the scrunched up eyes and pinched lips accentuating every fact and figure that popped forth from Thomas's incredible memory for names, events, and places. She was intently admiring her husband's cool recollection. As they continued this discussion, veal rolls in tomato sauce were set on their table along with gratineed Jerusalem artichokes for Faustina, beef braised in red wine sauce with fried finocchio for Henry, and sautéed calf's liver in onions with rice and peas for Thomas.

"*I Secondi?*" Tom asked. "I thought this was going to be a light dinner."

Despite the absolute sumptuousness of the meal and the artistry of its serving, the three ingested and digested one another's thoughts, information, and insights on Vietnam more than the culinary splendor of Italy.

Thomas wanted to infuse the history they had drilled into Henry with some personal observations, "We were in Vietnam for a week or so on our way to Hong Kong in 1966. It was during the time when Nguyen Cao Ky broke the resistance of the Buddhists around Hue and Da Nang."

Then a bleak memory erupted from Faustina's mind, "It was in the late spring, *Caro*. It was awful. There was no freedom at all. If you disagreed with Ky, you were labeled a Communist sympathizer and thrown into jail."

Thomas continued, "These were the conditions that led to the formation of the National Liberation Front. They represented several groups but were directed by Communists. They wanted South Vietnam to become neutral, all foreign troops to leave the country, and to gradually be reunited with the south."

"You know, some of the student information about the Viet Cong is wrong in that weapons and military advisers have been coming down from the North and have really increased during the last two years," Thomas cautioned. He continued, "In a deep sort of way, that's beside the point because no knowledgeable person has ever seriously doubted that the vast majority of the people want one nation."

Picking at the splendid meal before him, Henry looked puzzled and worried, "That's the whole issue. When President Johnson ordered the bombing of North Vietnam in February 1965, he thought he could stop the soldiers and arms from the north. For him it was a practical question, 'North Vietnam is Communist; South Vietnam is our friend. We're strong; we can stop beliefs in one nationhood by the appropriate amount of force.' I've read that there are around half a million of our troops now in Vietnam. The National Liberation Front and North Vietnamese seem to really believe in what they are fighting for while the South Vietnamese soldiers don't appear equally determined. Given all the graft, corruption, and lack of freedom in their country, our propaganda must seem like a pack of lies to them, even if they like the cash and some like the pop culture we are bringing with us."

"Although I don't like Communism, I think that the vast majority of the Vietnamese people would like to see their country united. If their leadership is made up of Communists, they are Communists who seem to really want to turn to the U.S. and other western countries. For that reason, I believe their policies can be directed in a more democratic way, in the manner we helped to promote in Yugoslavia. If this damn war continues, many more Vietnamese, Americans, and others will die, and there will be much less chance of conciliatory policies to develop," Thomas remarked.

"Gentlemen, please don't let these mean times destroy Mamma Caesaria's creativity," Faustina smiled, trying to get both the younger and the older man to finish the main course.

"This is scrumptious," Henry remarked.

Forcing a smile, Faustina thought to herself, *Eat, enjoy, for in a few months you may die.*

"It's really first rate, dear, as always, except tonight let's forego *le dolce.* I really can't afford the calories."

Slowly finishing their meal, they gazed at the highly respectable roomful of evening gourmets' devouring varied repasts. Faustina, who usually loved to guess the occupations, personalities, and pastimes of each of Mamma Caesarina's clientele, remained silent letting the lines of the just terminated conversation turn again and again in her head.

By 23:00 hours they were back home tucked peacefully away in their comfortable beds, while bullets were crackling and bombs exploding in the swamps and mountains of Vietnam. Incompatible philosophies expressed in economic realities drove the testing of one another's military and ideological might on the terrain of the southern hemisphere.

CHAPTER 21

This was the last morning in Rome of tending flowers in exchange for room, board, and companionship. Henry combed the soil with the metal teeth of the five-pronged hand hoe as though it was the long, silken, white hair of the 96-year-old, gentle bakerwoman at the retirement home in Stockholm. Let the roots breathe. Let these *genitalia florarum* scandalize the conformity of the ochre apartment-dwellers to celebrate dear Faustina's enthusiasm for the beautiful and Thomas's elegant propriety. Every leaf stood perfectly alive. He trimmed the yellowing ones and removed the cigarette butts that marked the remains of the charred matter feigning civilization. Faustina peered down on his handiwork and smiled a sweet, soft caress of gratitude, then said, "Let's go up to the *Campidoglio*. It's just around the corner."

Thus the morning began with their marveling at the three palaces designed by Michelangelo. At each corner images registered like slides in his mind's eye. There was the statue of Minerva between the effigies of the historic rivers of the Nile and Tiber. Entering The Capitoline Museum Faustina lectured him on the changes in sculpture between the 9th century B.C. and the 4th century A.D. By the time they left the Museum, Henry was more interested in watching a civil marriage ceremony across the square at the Town Hall of Rome. As they left the simple ceremony, the commanding figure of Marcus Aurelius' hand stretched out toward them. Faustina stopped in front of the statue of the Roman Emperor of the second century A.D. She remarked, "You know, I'm named after his wife who bore him eleven children. My parents scarcely knew anything about his life, but they liked the name, otherwise I'm sure they would have chosen something else. Have you ever read his *Meditations*?"

"Just some excerpts. How could he have stressed tranquility and equanimity and still persecute Christians?"

Continuing her unassuming insights, Faustina replied, "Historians say that he believed that because Christians opposed Emperor-worship they were dangerous to the state religion's established order."

"That makes me think his Stoic stress on wisdom, justice, fortitude, and moderation as a means of living in harmony with nature is b.s. If you're going to persecute people for what they believe in, that's not wise, just, courageous, or moderate. And what bothers me so much about this question is that a few professors whom I really respect for their erudition put Marcus Aurelius on such a pedestal. One of them is a friend who has a hashish problem he doesn't think is a problem because Aurelius says that to be of equal mind is foremost. To be 'laid back' might make you mellow company, but it doesn't make you more just. It often gives you an excuse for not sticking your head out for a particular individual or cause," Henry observed.

"You're quite right, but overall Marcus Aurelius received the top marks among the emperors of his period from most historians. Remember, he was living in very corrupt, cruel times," added Faustina, who put M. Aurelius in a proper historical context.

Walking down from the *Campidoglio*, they quietly strolled along, passing the *Circus Maximus* over to the *Viale delle Terme di Caracalla*. When they gazed up at the beige-brown, enormously thick walls rising up to the blue sky, Faustina picked up their conversation where they left off. "*Caro*, behind all this beauty and luxury of Emperor Marcus Aurelius Antoninus Caracalla was cruelty and gore. Can you imagine that here in the inner hall they could choose hot or cold water perfumed and colored; and over here to the side they had steam and massage rooms where they were worked over with perfumes and ointments. They had libraries over there, stadiums, gymnasia, schools, and conference rooms. Yet, Caracalla, who was one of the two sons of Septimus Severus, ordered the murder of his own brother, Geta, and around 20,000 of his followers early in the third century. That wasn't his only crime, but I don't want to go on."

As they entered the darkened rooms and peered down at the triangular, brown, green, and taupe tiles with fanciful infant-like riders on lion-like horses, Henry inquired of Faustina, "Do you see a lot of similarities between our times and then?"

"Some, Henry, some greater than others, depending on what you are talking about, but I hate superficial comparisons of the decline of Rome and its Eastern Imperial kind of excesses with those of our own day. These are usually given by ill-informed, right-wing politicians or churchmen to scare the masses into a harder acceptance of a rigid type of discipline they must impose on them to keep their oppressive organization of society going for their own benefit."

"So, you are not afraid of all the talk of libertine sexuality, say, when it affects Rudolfo?"

"Goodness, no! He is his own person. From his Italian side he has acquired a zest for life, for the senses, for the beautiful, and from his English Canadian side, he has learned the importance of being practical, measured, and reasonable. I'm not bragging about him. It's just the way he is."

"So, you're not afraid about his experimenting with his body?"

"As long as it's with other healthy bodies. No. No." Faustina laughed. "This a not a preoccupation, even to Thomas, who tends to give him occasional cautious warnings about these matters. The drug controversy is something else. While we don't worry about it in Rodolfo's case, when we read about what's going on in the U.S., we're a bit baffled by it. We tend to think of drug addiction as a sign of degeneracy, as a sign that someone has lost his self-control to something outside of himself. There are stories about it in every family, and I think most people tend to associate drug experimentation with the highly addictive drugs and the lowest of the low on the social ladder. Of course, every rich family has tales of a son or an uncle who has a private habit, and there is gossip about their connection to the Mafia. But these are just stories. What we hear coming out of the United States is something new to us—those 'mind-expanding drugs for entering new worlds of consciousness,' substances taken in the religious rites of different small-sized sub-cultures—these things aren't being taken as weird, but more, perhaps, as some new fad sweeping a crazy country."

"I brought a new book to read this summer. It just came out of our anthropology department. Its author, Carlos Castenada, gave it the title, *The Teachings of Don Juan*. I think its good points instruct us to appreciate the religious ways of a Native American culture. But I don't like its methodology, which it calls structuralist, and I don't like the pseudo-aping of the book by the underground drug culture. They've taken a substance being used in a religious rite, peyote, and removed it from its religious setting. When they do this, they just make it another marketable product. By taking it out of its spiritual context and removing it from its home base, a lot of its psychological support is lost. Besides this, whenever I have met 'the heads' at any political meeting, they're the ones who tend to just hang on for the good vibes of community spirit that come from being a part of a social group, but when you ask them to help out or what they think about something, you get a 'Heh, man, that's heavy' response, and after that you usually don't see them again, or you see them at the 'party' of the demonstration, if they even bother showing up. I might be wrong about this as a group phenomenon, but most of 'the heads' I've met come from upper-middle or upper class families and are primarily in the movement as just another 'trip.' Don't get me wrong. There are notable exceptions, and maybe, they do add a relaxing quality and fun to social protest, but I don't think what they're into is nearly as creative as all the publicity to the contrary, and I've seen a lot of personal destructiveness in quite a few of their trips. I'm not for stamping out their experimentation. If that's what they want to do and don't hurt others, fine. However, often they do hurt others when they become dependent on their drugs, and society must step in then. But the most effective way for society to control this subculture is not through heavy-handed arrests and false information. A positive educational campaign could demystify the attractiveness of the scene by showing its ugly realities. Intelligent people could stop mocking otherworldly and ecstatic experience, and they could promote warmer spiritual leaders and institutions. Maybe I'm just too uptight, but I find the heads' message empty. From my personal experience, I think of people into drugs as being untrustworthy and unconcerned about social issues."

"But, Henry, what about the reputed orgies to which you were comparing what went on in these baths?"

"Maybe I should experience some before I can comment on them!"

They both laughed, then he continued, "Maybe I'm blind, but I think it's really exaggerated. I'm not so sure our generation is so much different from yours, except we're getting married later and we talk about our sexual lives somewhat more openly. I actually saw one 'love in' in Griffith Park in Los Angeles. I just sat down on the grass and watched and felt really joyous about it. I can't say that it turned me on sexually, but it did surround me with what's being called an 'Aquarian Spirit.' Anthropologists doubt whether there ever was anything like primitive sexual communism, and I didn't see it there, but I did see so many tabooed differences with which I had grown up melt into an erotic embrace. That was wonderful. For the first time I witnessed real people of European and Middle Eastern backgrounds making love with Blacks and Asians in all sorts of combinations under trees and in the grass. There was something splendid about it. Was it just lust? Was it still the old game of dominator and dominated? Maybe in some cases. It certainly wasn't institutionalized in the wider society outside that park. And this summer in

Scandinavia, I learned to feel more at ease with my body and sexual self than ever before in my life. I've had three serious girlfriends in university, and I don't think any of us was using the other. We all enjoyed learning about ourselves and our bodies to some extent, but when things started getting serious, we both started seeing the chains around us in which our own individual choices had shackled our possible long-terms relationships.

In all three of my relationships, the problem has centered around my being much more a left-leaning liberal or social democrat and not worrying about being economically well-off in comparison to the woman with whom I was going out. All of my girlfriends have come from a background which was at least economically secure enough that they didn't worry about having money for a nice place to live, food, clothes, education, entertainment, and travel. I never had most of those things, except education, on a regular basis. So it didn't bother me to do without them. And I don't want to slave after these things the rest of my life for someone else; so it's led to a series of about one-year relationships. I guess I never really tried to describe this part of my life before. It's just happened that way, and we've all grown from our experience. This summer in Scandinavia was the first time I've had a 'one-night stand,' and I didn't initiate it. I liked the greater equality of men and women in Scandinavia, but even there nationality creates big differences. I sensed that the Swedish women were too strong for me, although I really enjoyed becoming companions with them, while the Danish women seemed softer and easier for me to relate to as a lover. I guess my experience in the other Nordic countries is too limited to generalize."

"Henry, what you're confiding to me is pretty much the same message I'm getting from Rodolfo. Here in Rome things are not as open as in the northern countries. They are done more discreetly. Oooh. We've got to be getting back."

"Faustina, thanks for another beautiful day. And thanks for being such a good confidante."

The older and younger friends hopped a crowded bus in the heat of the afternoon sun. Faustina looked at her watch and decided that Henry should try to squeeze in at least a quick run around the Palatine Hill, while she would rest and clean up for the evening. Still intent on taking in as much of the city as he could before leaving, the young American eagerly followed her directions and dashed about the area which had been the site of the homes of the wealthiest of ancient Rome's citizens and, later, of Diocletian's Palace. He enjoyed taking breaks watching the extraordinarily varied group of tourists. Serious French classicists debated the correctness of the description offered by their Roman *professore*. A lovely, upper-middle class German mother and her strikingly handsome teen-age son appeared as somber lovers in a revived classical tragedy. A loud busload of enthusiastic union households from a Boston parish included some Italian-American wives taking pride in showing their Murphy-named husbands the beauty of their own roots. After a sweaty run around the paths and byways sheltering decaying monuments and trees, Henry stopped at the great terrace looking over to the southeast toward the Appian Way. This must be Septimus Severus's Belvedere—beautiful to see, yes it was.

Looking down over to the left, he remembered the Circus Maximus where he had visited. He regarded the subtle color of the now wild flowers that had once been cultivated for the Emperor's gardens. Henry's rushed impressions stacked simplicity upon the complexity that once was the centralized organization of a mighty city. Its empire, that had dominated the world, left splashes of brilliance that it had extracted from and united the distant regions it had conquered and then assimilated into its fold. It fell, but pink oleanders and tall cypresses would grow on the lands. Only nature, God's handiwork, is eternal. It was hot, but the temperature did not disturb the ruins' mysterious lesson.

Back at Faustina's and Tom's, the house was in frenetic activity. At the last moment Tom had to meet with a few moneyed philanthropists who were visiting the academy. Faustina had to accompany him. "Why don't you spend the evening in The Ghetto? You'll recall it's only about a fifteen-minute walk from here. You can take a shortcut at the foot of the Theater of Marcellus."

"If it's O.K. with you, I'm going to nap and shower first."

"A marvelous idea," responded Faustina, who then puckered her lips, "I hate these last minute, polite little meetings that Tom has to drag me to infrequently. *C'est la vie*! I know you're planning to leave tomorrow. We'll all get up early and talk. We should be back here by 11 this evening at the latest. *Arrivaderci*!"

When they left, Henry stretched out, shoes off, clothed on Rudolfo's bed. Closing his eyes, he was surprised to almost converse with air which had been kept remarkably cool by the thick walls. Silence. Later, the tepid shower was perfect—not too warm, not too cold. Still tired, he picked up August J. C. Hare's *Walks in Rome* which Tom had recommended as the best guide that had ever been written in English about Rome. Opening Tom's old black-bounded book with a red stripe, he turned to the pages of The Ghetto and imagined from the Smith's brief tour where such-and-such an event had occurred.

What a complicated history of ups and downs and downs and ups! Just think, there had been Jewish settlers here even before Pompey the Great brought Jewish slaves after taking Jerusalem. By the next century the Jews of Rome lived very well except for two short crises. Agrippa's daughter Berenice or Veronica was even Titus's mistress. Julius and August Caesar were tolerant to the Jews, but Tiberius and Caligula were harsh to them because they refused to recognize the Emperor's divinity. Things got bad, though, when their dissenting kin, the early Christians, got into conflicts with the Jews. These events called for magistrates. Then Titus destroyed Jerusalem and brought thousands of Jewish slaves who were used to build the Coliseum. At the same time Vespasian permitted the Hebrews to practice their religion but made them pay a tax into the Temple Treasury to Jupiter Capitolinus. Domitian banished Jews to the Coelian where they had to make a living by soothsaying, love-charms, magic potions, and mysterious cures.

Under the early Popes the Jews enjoyed considerable liberty, particularly because they were thought to be good physicians. Up until the early fifteenth century the physician to the Vatican was usually a Jew. Innocent III forced them to be segregated and wear a badge, but their first real enemy was Pope Eugenius IV, who reigned between 1431 and 1439. He forbade Christians to trade, eat, or dwell with them and prohibited them from walking in the streets, from building new synagogues, or occupying any public posts. On top of these indignities in 1468 Paul II made the Jews run as horses during Carnival to the hoots of the populace. On Rosh Hashana, September 9, 1553, all Talmudic literature was confiscated and publicly burned.

With this history in mind, Henry first walked over to the Place of Weeping where on July 25, 1556, the Roman Jews were first forced into The Ghetto. The Dominican Pope Paul IV, who reigned between 1555 and 1559, required them to live only within the present Ghetto. If they had to go outside, men were required to wear yellow hats and women yellow veils. Sixtus V treated the Jews better, for they were then regarded as "the family from whom Christ came." He allowed them to practice many trades, deal with Christians, and build houses, libraries, and synagogues. But from 1592 to 1605, under Clement VIII; Clement XI (1700 to 1721); and Innocent XIII (1721 to 1724) the only trades which they could practice were in old clothes, rags, and iron; and Benedict XIV (1740 to 1758) added drapery to these. Under Gregory XIII, who ruled from 1572 to 1585, the Jews had to listen to a sermon every week and on every Sabbath, as police-agents were sent into The Ghetto to drive men, women, and children into the church with scourges and to lash them if they appeared to be inattentive. Only in 1848 did Pius IX, encouraged by Michelangelo Caetani, Duke of Sermoneta, stop this requirement. He also removed the limits of The Ghetto and the oppressive laws against the Jews until, pushed by the Jesuits, he reimposed some burdens.

As Henry walked in the warm night air down the narrow streets, he remembered the platitudes of his youth, of how his Rabbi had always favorably compared the elaborate rituals of Judaism and Catholicism, and he remembered being shown Pope John XXIII's honest but hopeful words on the history of the relationship between the faiths. He had read that despite its fascist government, the Jews of Italy had fared better than those of France during the Second World War. Sitting down on the edge of a small piazza that was the site of an excellent restaurant attracting throngs of people, he just watched the elegantly-attired Romans enter the soothing yellow light. The denizens of the neighborhood were mainly indoors and the storefronts were closed. He would return tomorrow on the way to the train station to get a glimpse of their faces, the stores, and the houses in which they had dwelled but not owned so long. Reflecting on the history A. J. C. Hare had recorded, Henry concluded, *Even in some of the best places in the civilized world, the life of a minority is precarious. The 'logic' of history is often irrational. When things would have been expected to be bleak for the Jews of Rome during the Middle Ages, they were generally good, and when things would have been expected to be better during the Renaissance and Enlightenment, they were worse.*

By the soft, small street lamps, Henry found his way back to the edge of The Ghetto. There was a sharp descent by the Theater of Marcellus where the darkness was only intermittently interrupted with light cast onto the wall. Who lurked in this dark sunken ruin? His heart began to beat faster. Dashing across the long, sunken space, he felt relief upon finding the street. Had there been someone behind that column? He walked at a quick pace, almost a run, to Faustina's and Tom's apartment. It was already 11 P.M. and the Smiths were still not home. Rearranging his backpack, he was all set for setting out from Rome late the next morning.

Despite his jovial and affable play for the dollars of the holiday classicists of The Millionaires' Club, Thomas arose before either Faustina or Henry. He had a good feeling that he had bedazzled the few remaining elderly members of The Club or those who still resided on The Boulevard who realized that the classics were still a pre-requisite for civilized citizens or subjects of Her Majesty Elisabeth II—however they preferred to think of themselves.

Dr. McBride, who was now in her 82nd year, could still recite long passages of the Ciceronian orations, and as one of Toronto's first women physicians, she had had one of the city's most successful practices in obstetrics. Dear Dr. McBride, who had never married and had no surviving relatives, sat down with him at the end of the evening, took out a copy of her will, called over one the country's top lawyers, and then and there bequeathed to the Academy a sizeable percentage of her estate. Although there had been no other concrete manifestations of such immediate magnanimity that evening, Mr. Smith sensed that several other of the party-going-would-be-intellectuals were sufficiently impressed so that more money would be forthcoming. Whew, now there was no pressing need to kowtow in the near future to the various levels of Canada Council, not knowing where you stood with this or that bureaucrat, whose petty likes and dislikes, covert or manifest, he always detested deciphering—never sure if he had pleased or offended them. With the pleasure of a well-orchestrated move, he turned the lever of their home espresso bar, and flicking the steam into milk, he smiled with satisfaction over his triumph of last night. He dripped three small cups of coffee and neatly placed the crusty rolls, butter and his favorite Scottish marmalade on the heavy, wooden table, then tapped on Faustina's and Henry's doors. *Bongiorno*!

In a cozy, velvety rose robe, Faustina wondered out to the dining area and embraced her husband, as though he had just returned home as a conquering hero. "Well done, *Caro,* well done!"

In his clean jeans and plaid shirt, their young guest bounced in his heavy brown boots over to the table with the air of an adventurer setting out to new parts. "How did your reception go last night?"

"Splendid! It was one of those rare evenings when everything went well."

"How about you? What did you end up doing?"

"After cleaning up and relaxing, I read the guidebook Thomas lent me and then walked over to The Ghetto by the Theater of Marcellus. I'd like to walk back through there on the way to the train station this morning."

"Are you sure you don't want to stay on for a few more days?"

"It's really tempting. You've been wonderful to me. Thanks ever so much. I hope to be able to return to Rome one day, but I'd also like to take in as much of the rest of Europe I can squeeze in while my Eurailpass is still good. But I'll take a rain check on your invitation."

"Sure, anytime, we want you to meet our Rodolfo, too."

Dressed in a light-beige, cotton suit, Thomas stuck out his arm and shook Henry's hand with the strength of genuine fatherly affection, then withdrew it and added, "Henry, good luck with your big decision, whatever it is. Just be sure that it is really what you believe in."

"*Grazie*, Tom, you've really helped clear my head on a lot of points about that decision. I'll write you what it turns out to be."

"*Caro*, I'm going to walk to the station to see him off. I'll call you for lunch."

Faustina hurried her usual prolonged morning ritual and scurried out of her bedroom. In a few minutes Henry heaved his blue aluminum frame backpack over his shoulders as they walked from the Via dei Foraggi back over to The Ghetto.

They both watched the faces and form of bodies that held the stories of millennia in their eyes and posture. The stacks of linen almost touching the high ceilings reminded Henry of the Browns' disheveled, but excellent quality, small-town dry goods store of his youth. Faustina led Henry out of this quarter down new sidestreets and struck up the morning conversation.

"Henry, keep up your spirits. There's so much more to life than politics. You know that here in Italy the Socialists, who were collaborating with the Christian Democrats, lost badly, and the Communists won almost 30% of the popular vote in our general elections this year. People were just irked at the Socialists giving in too much to conservative Christian Democrats and letting them put off the law for tax reform too long. Although things have changed since Carlo Levi wrote *Christ Stopped at Eboli*, southern Italy is still economically backward, and they need development now—not tomorrow. And everybody knows we need to reorganize our government. But even though Giovanni Leone heads a one-party Christian Democratic cabinet, we still enjoy our lives, our food, and our fun."

"Do I seem down, Faustina? I really don't feel down, except I'm going to miss all the warmth and good times you and Thomas have shown me. Maybe we can stop for a quick espresso and that'll perk me up!"

"Great idea! And I want you to try some panetone before you leave." In a few steps they sat down at a neighborhood café, sank their teeth into the buttery yellow sweet bread washed down by the thick, dark, bittersweet liquid, then proceeded onward toward the Quirinale and the train station.

"I'm headed for Florence this afternoon and will be there tomorrow morning. Gee, it's been great! Let's just say, until we meet again," Henry intoned quietly in Faustina ear and kissed her cheek amid the muffled roar of the packed station.

As Faustina wrapped her arms around him, *"Arrivaderci, Caro,"* sighed forth from her lips and then suddenly she turned and briskly walked out of the Termini's great entranceway.

Glancing upwards, he noticed it was already 9:55 and the train for Florence was leaving at 10:05, but he had no idea from which platform it was leaving. His heart began to pound as he turned around trying to figure out the giant timetable. Giving up, he ran over to the first officials and besought which was the right platform for the train to Florence. He ran outside behind the terminal to the endless green line of coaches and when two people confirmed that this was the train, he managed to grab hold of the metal grip and hop on just as it began to pull out of the gigantic terminal.

CHAPTER 22

The train ride from Rome to Florence took about three hours. Henry had lost all consciousness of time and immersed himself in the countless images of natural and human beauty heated by the intensity of the summer. He had become an ardent reader of maps and took great pleasure in finding his place in the exact spot of a vista, painting, sculpture, or monument. In this city of art and home of the Italian language, hues of red roofs against blue skies were interspersed by the Tower of the Old Palace, the cupola, and the Cathedral of Saint Mary of the Flower. The sun and the humidity only intensified the verve with which the names and scenes hastily carved themselves into visual-auditory memory. Listen to the sounds: Pi-e-tà, cam-pa-ni-le, Ben-ve-nu-to Cel-li-ni. Each syllable intoned a note, a bounce over the Piazzale degli Uffizi. Clear sky, greens of the land, flesh of human bodies, and angels faded into an undying history. The plastic slides of his art course suddenly became real paintings by people of a particular time and place. Yes, Botticelli had really painted the *Birth of Venus*.

Suddenly the memory of his sixth-grade geography play presented in front of the full auditorium exploded into his memory. What an embarrassing thought! Susie and he were the Italian peasants speaking in a ridiculously feigned, Italian-accented, southern American English. How stories they had learned had the facts sugarcoated beyond recognition! Despite Cosimo's and Lorenzo the Magnificent's bringing mercantile, artistic, and scientific prosperity, their Medici family members were driven out of town and Savonarola was burned at the stake right here on the Piazza della Signoria. He'd never remember all of these objects! None the less, Henry rushed through the Etruscan collection at the Archaeological Museum, then as quickly as he had entered, stood some distance away and watched the reflection of the museum in the crystal azure of the water, somewhat muted by the evaporation on this sweltering day.

Drifting over to the Pitti Gallery, he peered at walls of paintings more as a moving slide show in which he would intermittently select what he found most captivating. Outside he moved on at a slower pace to the Boboli Gardens and spent the rest of the afternoon watching Florence from the slopes of its hill. Could this really be the city that nourished Dante, Boccaccio, and Petrarch? He ran sweating more vigorously all the way back to the doors of the Baptistery—remembering what he had read about the Renaissance, and then fixing the name, Donatello, in his mind, like a song, he repeated it to a melody, Dona-tello, sculptor of the re-awakening, Dona, Dona, Dona, tel, lo.

This was not loneliness. It was ascension to beauty. It was communion. Absorbing the beauty of now and yesterday, his ninth grade English teacher's favorite poem came to him, "Beauty have pity for the strong have power." Yes, Mansfield, you are unfortunately right. But here are spots where beauty can hide for a brief glance by every person who wants to seek it.

It was a hot, lazy afternoon, which exuded a natural lethargy, the only antidote to which was youthful enthusiasm. But the steamy air and the elevated centigrade would have overcome even Marco Polo. In a slightly dusty store window, a bottle of mineral water focused ever more clearly into Henry's field of vision, so even the splendid vistas would be temporarily traded to quench his thirst in a shady spot under a tree by the River Arno. The grating sensation on his skin felt raw through his sudden sluggishness. By late afternoon, the sweltering humidity cooled to a stickiness like water drops from a broken shower.

Henry strolled up and down the small streets from the Ponte Vecchio all the way past the National Library, the University, and back over to the Palace of the Congresses. After dark, he tried to pretend he wasn't afraid but his pace quickened, and he stuck to larger thoroughfares. Even though this city was a treasure, Henry was pushed by a force to move on. Maybe it was simply being overcome by the reluctance to touch only the surface of a place so filled by the exquisite, or was the weather just too unbearable?

Was it the thought that he might miss out on something while he had this magic carpet for only one month? Why not learn more about Italy and less about other places? No, the urges say go, even if it is a flight from Florence, the City of the Lily. Breaking the crusty, thick *pane duro*, he sat intermittently opening and closing his eyes while listening to the crunch of his teeth as he bit into the heavy peasant bread. The last train left at 20:40 hours and would put him in Venice after midnight. After he carefully put the rest of the fresh loaf into a bag which he stuck into his backpack, he slowly walked out onto the platform and watched a small group preparing to board the Venice train.

He thought about one of the fictive aunts of his childhood, Tanta Margherita, a short, stout Italian-American woman who lived with her daughter, Maria, a masseuse at one of the large, local hotels, and their beloved terrier, who was the sister of the dog, Jill, of his own childhood. Jill and her sister, Gillian, one fat and the other thin, hopped and jumped and licked each other every time they got together, which was about once a month. Tanta Margherita was old and sweet, for as long as Henry had known her, and, in some way, had had a long-standing connection with his family. Was her dead husband Henry's grandfather's good friend? These stories became increasingly confused as over time new details and inaccuracies were constantly added. There was always a new, tasty snack whenever his aunt, uncle, Jill, and he would visit, and then, it all stopped. Why? He never understood. Had his real aunt been overcome with her foreboding sense of sin and evil and suddenly cut off the relationship as she was prone to do? Why should these memories suddenly creep into his mind? Could it be the dim light with suspended dust and smoke hanging in the heavy, warm evening air that reminded Henry of the stagnant, weighty atmosphere of Tanta Margherita's den where the combustion of her constantly-lit Lucky Strikes slowly yellowed the white lace curtains?

When the train pulled into the Florence station, he rushed into a surprisingly empty compartment, stretched out on the long, cushioned seat, and fell into a deep sleep. The conductor stirred him awake to check his ticket and once again in Venice, where he got off at half past midnight.

Chugging along the Mediterranean coast the next evening, the young man reflected on how his jaunt to Venice had left him exhausted and with a low-grade headache. How could his brief time in such a romantic place have been spoiled? First of all, it was his own fault. Why did he accept the invitation from that utter bore from downstate Indiana to crash on the floor of his cheap hotel room? Yuch! The thought of petting the fur of what felt like a cat, which turned out to be a rat crawling over his sleeping bag, still sent a shiver of disgust down his spine. But what had been as bad as the rat was wasting the only day of his life in Venice accompanying this grumpy 20-year-old boy around this city of 118 islands. Why did he always feel obligated to entertain someone who had done a minor favor for him—and in this case being thanked by a miserable rat at six in the morning—for a few hours extra sleep? Why couldn't he learn to drop unpleasant people once and for all? Why suddenly feel responsible for someone whom he did not know from Adam, with whom he had basically nothing in common? Why couldn't he have dropped Denis after an espresso or a glass of wine—oh, yes, Denis didn't like Italian wines. Denis had seen nothing special about the Grand Canal! Didn't Denis think that Saint Mark's was too ornate? And Denis thought it was "too damn hot to enjoy anything. It was just like a sauna bath." Henry had wanted to explore the first ghetto in the world, but the only thing Denis wanted to do was to sit in a shaded café and unfavorably compare Venice to Gary, Indiana. To Denis' credit was his portable chess game, which he liked to play while sipping his lemonade. Oh that twang! Squeak! "Mamma wouldn't approve of that. Dad doesn't think very much of what students are doing these days." His attempt at wisdom had been, "So why did they call it a republic if they had a *Doge*?" Neither tall nor short, neither clean or dirty, Dennis had sported polyester pants and an off-white shirt which was brown around the collar and somewhat rancid with perspiration from his reluctant tour of this town which grandma had insisted that he see. It was as though Denis had remained impervious to the time in which he was living. Not one issue of importance outside of his brothers, sisters, aunts, uncles, cousins, and grandparents had parted from his puckered lips all day. Flabbergasted, Henry had somehow been pulled into his warped shelter for twenty-four hours, had been his cheap guide, and was supposed to be grateful for getting to know a real supplier of the world's breadbasket.

Had there been something about Denis that was attractive? Maybe his blind stability, his total security in his own world of medium-sized, mid-western agri-business, and his almost total disregard for other places' history, art, and music gave him a special quality of enrootedness in the unsure world of fads and fleeting fancies in which they were living. And, perhaps, Henry had eased Denis' way in this place which was so foreign to him, but which meant a great deal to Denis' grandparents of Italian, Polish, Irish, and Scandinavian strains. These hardy folk had populated the small farms northwest of the Alleghenies for the last six generations. The young men parted courteously as Denis mourned the absence of American beer. To him wine was for winos.

CHAPTER 23

Henry had wished a polite adieu to Denis, and, distraught by the fatigue and mental stress of his strange, sudden inability to assert himself, boarded the train for Spain. Getting off the train in Milan for a few hours, he walked quickly around its famed Gothic cathedral and gazed at the inhabitants of Italy's biggest and most industrialized city. Pushing his way through the densely-packed streets, he was soon back on the train, headed for Spain via France's *Côte d'Azur*.

As the hot summer air cooled, the train sped toward Marseilles past the luxury spots of the nineteenth century European royalty, contemporary film stars, and jetsetters. At the border of Italy and France, the French patrol had quickly checked passports, and Henry had fallen back asleep after walking between the cars and smelling the balmy air of the Mediterranean night.

In the morning Marseilles greeted Henry with the fast pace of an old city where the facades of the buildings and boulevards rushed by him like the quickly-turned photos of the album of France in the 1930s that he had glanced at before leaving the States. These things were used, aging, in parts gracefully, in other parts comfortably, like the stub of the unshaven men in the train station. Even where there was a burned automobile parked on a side street, the oldness reflected a lively port city atmosphere where people of North African and many other nationalities walked alongside faces from the various French departments in not-the-latest, but quietly-intriguing clothes and motions. Even the view of the modernistic Le Corbusier housing complex, seen from the cathedral overlooking the city, did not shake his impression of Marseilles' being a treasure of a viable past, an underrated provincial city, perhaps not unlike Louisiana's New Orleans, where he had been a camp counselor during the summers of his teenage years.

In a neighborhood café near the train station, a very tall, slender, blond, blue-eyed man about his age sat his blue and yellow backpack down by the table neighboring Henry's. They had both ordered milk coffee and baguettes and were slouching in their rusty chairs while studying the variety of their human entourage. Given the tighter cut of his clothes and the khaki safari-like jacket, Henry had no doubt that this fellow had recently been to one of Stockholm's army surplus stores.

"*Vous êtes suédois, n'est ce pas?*"

"*Oui,*" replied the tall fellow, "*Comment est-ce que vous m'avez reconnu?*"

"I spent a month in Stockholm this summer," Henry continued in English. "Where are you staying?"

"On the train. I am just spending the morning here in Marseilles. Since I can't afford the price of their *bouillabaise*, I'm headed for Spain."

"Actually, I'm going that same way. When does your train leave?"

"There's one in about an hour and a half."

"Want some company?"

"Sure."

They walked up the majestic, white staircase and crossed over to the station to check the timetables, while exchanging their names of Lennart and Henry. There was a train with both first- and second-class accommodations leaving at the time Henry had thought. "I'm lucky I got a month's Eurailpass for a graduation present and can travel either first or second class on all the trains except the Transeuropean Express, the TEE."

"I have just enough for a second class ticket."

"It makes no difference to me. I've been hitchhiking all the time before I activated this pass. Let's double-check with the conductor if my pass is valid on this train and if we can travel together in the second-class coach."

After verifying their travel information with the ticket vendor, Lennart and Henry were reassured that they could leave together on the coming train. To their surprise, a two-car, self-propelled train pulled up to the platform at the designated time of departure. Expecting an ordinary long passenger train, they inquired again if this was indeed the train with the first and second class accommodations for Spain. Two officials quickly sent them scurrying aboard the railroad cars which were not air-conditioned against the sweltering summer temperatures. The car was already filled with many American passengers who were complaining bitterly about the unbearable heat while making makeshift fans and stripping down to a minimum of summer clothing. Unlike all of the other trains he had ridden in Europe, this one was built in a semi-American fashion without compartments with many rows of double seats per car, some of which faced each other. Lennart and Henry found two remaining places, next to a large, dark-haired man who appeared to be in his late forties. Unlike other uncomfortable passengers who were squirming out of anything but the lightest cotton fabric clothes, this man sat stoically in a gray double-breasted suit and a white shirt. When they asked in English if they could take the seats facing each other, he replied in a multilingual phrase, "*Bienvenue, meine herren*, please sit down, *por favor*."

The lads thought that this must be a joke coming from this most unassuming man. They inquired, "Are you from all those places?"

"Боже мой   (*Boze mój*), *tutta la terra* is *min hem, panowie*."

The young men smiled at each other, both wondering whether this iconoclast was altogether there. "Lennart, we have to change trains in Avignon around 15:10 and have 38 minutes there before the train leaves for Barcelona.

As they were getting their schedule coordinated, the polyglot with his hair parted down the middle pulled out an old tin of *pâté de foie gras* teeming with maggots. He began to spread this concoction over a stale bagette stuffed in his right coat pocket.

"*Camarades,* Вы хотите   (Vy   Khotite) *essen un poco* of this delicious *smörgås*?"

With protruding jugular veins and the corner of their eyes turned down, the rugged young campers gushed forth a simultaneous, "*Nej tack*; no, thank you."

Henry was thinking, *The natural food freaks are saying you are what you eat. Maybe this guy doesn't think very much of himself if he is eating maggots and liver paste out of a tin can. On the other hand, I guess it's no worse than bird nest soup.*

Lennart's stomach tightened and his throat and lower abdomen convulsed in an upward motion. He excused himself and scampered down the aisle to the toilet. The bizarre world denizen quietly consumed his unusual bill of fare with gusto. In a few minutes the young Swede returned looking pale and somewhat bent over unlike his usual straight posture. When they arrived in Avignon, Lennart remarked, "That was the most disgusting thing I've ever seen."

"It didn't look very good to me, either," Henry laughed, then asked, "Do you think that guy's mixed up language was for real?"

"Real crazy."

"I sort of got the feeling he was trying to make a statement like we should all try to understand one another. He has invented his own version of *Esperanto*. Weird guy! I got the idea he was a Yugoslav who'd gotten stuck in a camp for displaced persons and who never would adjust to any country except as a guest worker."

"I'm not sure. Wouldn't you say he was schizophrenic?"

"I don't like psychiatric labels. I don't think they mean very much. The guy seemed to get along O.K. on his own, even if his eating habits weren't exactly conventional."

Again checking on their connection, they were told by a conductor that their train was another two-car variety. And again when they boarded, their *wagon* was filled with many irritable American travelers overcome by the blistering afternoon heat and poor ventilation. This car was particularly packed, and there were more people standing or resting on their knees in their seats than on the last train. There was a rotund, middle-aged official who intently studied each ticket as he slowly made his way through the car. He glanced at Henry's Eurailpass and then asked for Lennart's ticket.

"I am sorry but this train has only first-class accommodations and you will have to pay the difference, for you have only a second-class ticket," the conductor said in French.

"Hey, we both were told that we could take this train and that it had first and second-class accommodations."

"I am sorry, but that train was changed. And this train has places only for first-class passengers. May I see your passport?"

Lennart handed the conductor his black, hardback Swedish passport. Then the conductor opened it and took out his pen, as if to begin to write something in it.

"What are you doing?" Lennart inquired.

"Just marking down that you owe the Government of the French Republic a few francs," the official replied in French.

"You can't do that. I have already paid my fare, and we were specifically told we could travel together on this train."

Henry turned to Lennart and added, "If I were you, I'd get my passport back. I don't trust that creep."

Once again Lennart requested that his passport be returned and the conductor replied, "The difference will be 100 *francs français*."

"*Monsieur*, if you don't give me my passport, I will be obliged to take it back myself," Lennart said in French.

At that moment the conductor stuck Lennart's passport into his inner-pocket and proceeded to the next car. Lennart ran after him and tried to reach into the official's pocket to recover his passport. The conductor hit him.

Henry began explaining the situation to the passengers, for the most part, upper-class Americans, who, exasperated by the lack of air conditioning and their condescending treatment by the rude conductor, cheered Lennart on to victory. After retrieving his passport, Lennart left the fat conductor lying in the corridor and holding his side still smarting from Lennart's last blow. When he finally got up, the official, whose haughtiness had been somewhat deflated, retreated into the second car.

As soon as the train arrived in Montpelier, the conductor's revenge became apparent. Armed police boarded the train and escorted Lennart off their *chemin de fer* to a special jail for foreigners. From the beginning of Lennart's arrest, Henry and the other American passengers pleaded the justice of his case. Very proper, though somewhat strong-armed, the police insisted that they would have to wait to talk to the police prefect for foreigners who would not be back for several hours. They invited Henry to wait to plead Lennart's case before him or to contact the Swedish Consul General in another town. Lennart didn't want to disturb his consulate for such a simple matter about which anyone with the slightest bit of reason could see that he was right, so he requested that Henry deal with the proper official.

Sixteen hours later, Henry rehearsed in French the details of the case in front of the police prefect for foreigners.

"Even if your friend had been right, he should not have resorted to taking back his passport with force."

"I don't think he wanted to, but the conductor gave him no alternative."

"You should have waited, gotten off the train in Montpelier and filed a formal complaint with me and with the French National Railways."

"And how much time would that have taken us?" Henry inquired respectfully, and quickly decided not to confront the prefect any more beyond this point.

The prefect demanded that Lennart pay $10 more and then he released Henry's new traveling companion. Feeling guilty that he had egged Lennart on, Henry split the fine with him.

"You Americans have to have an explanation for everything, don't you?" Lennart smiled.

"*Fy, Fann,*" was Lennart's only immediate comment, which he accented with a heavy hit on the wooden bench.

"Did I help ruin your trip?"

"It's not your fault. I think that they are terrified of young people here at the moment. But that bastard who took my passport just wanted to show everyone that he was in charge. If I had offered him a bribe, there would have been no problem!"

CHAPTER 24

It was almost two in the morning when they left on the train departing Avignon for Barcelona. Lennart read down the timetable and thought, *If we're supposed to get into Barcelona-Sants at 9:39 tomorrow morning, we're going to miss the Costa Brava.*

"How about getting up early and hopping off at one of the little coastal towns north of Barcelona? After the last day, I just want to lie down in the hot sun, swim, and admire the señoritas."

"Sounds like a healthy prescription for recovery to me. Aren't you still pretty upset about the way the pigs treated you?"

"Yes, they were pretty corrupt *grissvin.* Or do you say it 'fat swine,' the whole bunch of them."

"You know, even if it was only a ten buck fine, that was ten bucks they didn't deserve and we needed, but what are you going to do? If we had made a big deal over it, no telling how long you'd be sitting in the clink and how much trouble your consulate would have gone through to get you out of jail."

"Face it, we did the practical thing. We cut our losses. The way the prefect was playing the game with us, it was impossible to win."

"Yeah, they well merited to be called pigs. It was like they had a whole racket going to steal tourists' money."

"Let's forget the whole bloody incident. Otherwise, they're going to spoil our vacation."

The whole significance of the event did not strike the young men. Neither believed that every event and action of human existence should or could be interpreted for some deep-level meaning in general. In fact, while Lennart found interpretations occasionally entertaining, he never liked to engage in them himself unless someone's behavior got out of hand. Then he was usually able to come up with a good joke or indirect comment to let the other person know he was concerned about something. On the other hand, Henry loved to play around with interpretations—the way a good chess player seriously tries out various strategies. However, Henry became so engaged in the intricate moves that he would often forget he was simply trying to grasp something. Lennart had been enjoying this vacation up until his stint in jail. The international youth camp in Holland had been a load of fun. The songs of freedom and brotherhood had added just enough prolonged inspiration to solidify the light work and occasional tryst he had savored. Even though he was tall and gaunt, his regular pleasures of life—mainly tobacco, beer, sex, and marijuana—had seasoned his body to some imperfect blemishes of early aging—mainly the darkening of his deeply-set, turquoise blue eyes and yellowing index and middle fingers. He very infrequently would note these and wonder why his eternal moderation in these goodies still affected him more adversely than others, given that he had taken care to pass as much time as he could at sea or in the pristine mountains or woods. Oh well, he was enjoying his life, even if it did bring with it an occasional unpleasantness such as these greedy and dishonest small-town officials.

CHAPTER 25

White foam and light-brown sandy beaches stirred the gleam of the blue Mediterranean. Henry and Lennart put their backpacks under a thicket of bushes near the ruin of a castle and walked back a few miles to the long beach of soft, hot sand. They took turns swimming, one guarding the other's clothes and valuables, and then walked through the narrow, crooked streets of this tourist town. The stinging heat of the sand and the cooling wetness of the sea contrasted with the flies, urine, and feces covering the unkempt public w.c.s. Lennart preferred the creature comforts of home in Scandinavia. This sentiment was reinforced dramatically the next morning. At first light the next day, two soldiers' rifle barrels rustled Henry up from a deep sleep.

"You are illegally encamped on the estate of Senor Miguel de Castile."

Replying in quite good Mexican Spanish, Henry objected, "But I didn't see anything posted. There were no signs or fences."

At this protest the taller soldier hit Henry's scapula with a rifle butt, so as to warn him not to object, just to get off this land immediately.

"*Sí, señor*," replied Henry and quickly rolled up his sleeping bag, not even attaching it to his backpack.

The lads strolled back down to the train station. Lennart held up his head. "Henry, I've had it with cops in this part of the world. I'm going to go back home."

"Well, I wish you would stay and see the rest of the Iberian Peninsula with me, but I hear where you're coming from. Let's compromise. Spend today in Barcelona with me—it's still early—and tonight we can try one of those paying camp grounds a little outside the city."

"O.K. But if anything else goes wrong, it's back to *Norden*."

"That's a fair deal."

The two vacationers strolled down the beach and up toward the road continuing in silence as they soaked up the warmth of the early morning sun. In about an hour's time, they found a stretch of beach with only a few swimmers and sunbathers. Propping up their backpacks on their sides, they took turns baking and prancing into the force of the surf. Lennart closed his eyes and took a deep breath—wondering if he would ever come up as the strength of the tow pulled him backwards. At the end of his wind, the current shoved him forward with a mighty thrust until the pebbles and sand glued his long frame in a place for the next ebb and flow. *It feels great!* was the only thought that entered Lennart's head. Neither the tumble of the previous day nor the rough awakening this morning surfaced in his mind as he dived in and out to the roar of the sea. He swam the length of the beach and back.

On the beach, the American friend lay tanning with the rays of the sun passing from warm to hot so that the sand, as it passed between his toes, cleansed with its pebbles of fire. *O.K.*, he thought, *it's not a contradiction. Just because Barcelona was pro-republican and anarchist back during the Civil War, doesn't mean that the policemen are workers' syndicates today. Franco won, and he and his fascists still hold power today. Those pigs this morning were just some latter-day versions of his old-time creeps.*

So far this was the only European country in which Lennart had been where the place and geography appealed to him more than the people and the culture. He was feeling ever more strongly this way. The bullfight didn't appeal either to Lennart's macho mystique or Henry's historical curiosity, especially when it meant parting with their limited funds. So far the beauty of the land far surpassed the comeliness of people or buildings. Lennart had joked that the trinkets in the stores were like refurbished blessed virgins, and even Lennart's healthy sex drive had taken a distinct second place to the sand and sea. Between catnaps and roasting in the sun by mid afternoon, the young men began to arrange their possessions and decided to try one of the "European camping grounds," where they had heard you could rent a space for your backpack at youth hostel-like prices. Loading their packing onto their backs, they hiked up to *el camino.*

The road was packed with tourists, and the adventurers were not really sure if hitchhiking was allowed. With an eye out for the ever-present militia, they put out their thumbs, and, by chance, within a few minutes, landed a ride with a British family, the Jamiesons—mom, dad, and son—to go all the way to the camping grounds just about a forty-minute drive from where they picked up Henry and Lennart..

The camping ground was marked with a simple sign and reminded Henry of the run down private camping sites in the South of his youth where the trees and the entrance ways always were powdered with an excessive amount of dirt. They walked into the equally dust-covered cabin where each paid a dollar for the privilege of dumping their backpacks in the sand near the beach and using the piped-in water.

"You know, Lennart, today my mind kept flashing back into what happened to us over the last two days. I lay there with my eyelids closed and saw the bluish-black of my veins enclosed by a muted-red background. The heat warmed every inch of me. I would be thinking of nothing, then suddenly something some of my professors said or something that I had read about social control would flash into my mind. 'Society always exerts control over its members and visitors by a variety of written and unwritten rules.' Children and strangers often learn these rules by breaking them and being punished for their infractions. Nixon and Agnew—like all the conservatives before them—are trying to frighten the public, which is afraid that social change means that law and order will collapse. Nonsense! The civil rights workers and we antiwar types are making the nation live up to its higher laws. All nations, like modern France and America, which were built on doctrines of natural laws, are supposed to subscribe to the idea and reality of a higher law."

Not totally following Henry's philosophical harangue, Lennart suggested that they walk out by the seaside. Just as fast as the day had warmed up and the heat waves had throbbed in pulsating layers above the sea, the night temperature had cooled and the air was getting even a little nippy. Lennart took out one of the unfiltered Spanish cigarettes he had delighted in purchasing for about the equivalent of an American quarter. Curving his hands over his match, he lit and drew lightly the smoke into his lungs, forming a temporary little cloud in his mouth, then gently blew it forward. "You get what you pay for! This shit tastes like raunchy, dry straw."

"Why don't you just throw them away?"

"Then I wouldn't have any more. Better these than nothing."

Lennart wasn't the inveterate smoker that Klaes was. When Klaes had smoked, it was the sensual ritual of a confirmed addict from whom the bluish white was emitted over several breaths in long gushes from the deepest part of his lungs. Never deeply inhaling but never wanting to kick his habit, Lennart smoked for an occasional diversion. He thought non-smokers were potentially boring and puritanical, although he had friends like Henry who fell into his category of O.K. abstainers.

They quietly lay back on the sand dune and watched the darkening sky of the early night put on its own star show to the lulling tunes of the sea.

"Are you rested up enough to go into Barcelona tomorrow morning?"

"Why not? *Ja.* I do feel much better now. You want to get an early start?"

"Sure, I'd like to take in as much of the city as we can."

They strolled back to their sleeping bags, which were in the spot next to the British family who had given them a lift. The Jamiesons had now assembled a large tent immediately next to their car, just about six feet away from "the boys'" campsite.

After cleaning up, the young men turned in for an early doze and quickly fell into a deep sleep. The coolness of the night air and the softness of the sand under their tarpaulin formed a comfortable bottom that gripped and shaped the contours of their bodies. In the distance, the muted tones of a portable phonograph record player or radio blended the classical notes with the starry sky and the ebb and flow of the waves.

Suddenly there was a screech and a flood of white light and the strong smell of diesel fuel. Someone was screaming at him in German, and Lennart was screaming back also in *Deutsch.* Henry felt a great weight on the lower part of his body, and his legs began to ache as though an overweight football player had tackled him. Mrs. Jamieson was screaming in English, "Back up off him at once! Get on with it!"

Henry's femur began to be pressed harder and more firmly into the sand. He was terrified, but he couldn't say anything as he realized a large car was parked on the lower part of his body, which had been pressed deeply into the sand. "Thank God for the sand!"

As Lennart yelled something back in German to the driver—who had been momentarily shouting at Henry and waving a ticket in Henry's suddenly-awakened face—the stout man retreated into the Volkswagen and rolled it off Henry's legs, now covered by sand.

Mrs. Jamieson was holding Henry and inquiring softly, "How are you, dear?"

Looking sharply at the obdurate man who had left his car parked on their neighbor, Mr. Jamieson could not believe that a driver would insist on his right to a campsite while he was crushing a presumptive trespasser under the weight of a motor vehicle. The site number on the receipt of both Lennart and Henry and of Herr Rattner was indeed the same. The attendant had mistakenly given them both the same place.

Andrew Jamieson, the teen-age son, was at Henry's side while Mrs.

Jamieson felt Henry's legs. "Do you think that they are broken?" he inquired gently.

Mrs. Jamieson reflected, "Dear, I can't feel any fracture. Henry, are you still in pain?"

Recovering from a light state of shock, Henry sat up supported by Andrew and touched his own lower legs which felt there but numbed. He was short of breath. "Let me see if I can walk on them. Andrew, could you give me a little support with your arm? Thanks." Henry took a few paces and smiled. "They feel like they're asleep and coming awake, tingling, prickly." He ran a bit in place to overcome the sensation.

Herr Rattner walked up and shook his hand in a strong grip and replied in broken English, "Sorry, sorry, that idiot gave us the same place."

Mrs. Jamieson stared sternly at Herr Rattner and pointedly suggested, "Don't you think you should drive him into Barcelona to see a doctor? It really is the least you could do."

Henry looked tenderly at Mrs. Jamieson and reported, "I think I am O.K. Really Mrs. J., you are so kind!"

"Are you sure, Henry?"

"Yep, I think the sand under us was so lightly packed that the car literally pushed my legs deep down like a wafer. I was very lucky. My legs are beginning to feel normal now. However, let's wait to see tomorrow morning. Tell this guy in German that let's all get some sleep and see if I'm O.K. in the morning. If I'm not, then he can drive us into Barcelona to see a doctor. Tell him to make his camp in front of ours, and we'll settle the whole thing with the attendant tomorrow morning."

Stirred from his deep sleep, Lennart confided to Henry, "You must be totally out of it to be able to sleep after that. Henry, you know I said I was going to stay on in Spain only if nothing else bad happened to us. Well, this is the end. I'll go in with you to see Barcelona tomorrow, but after that, it's back to *Sverige*."

"I can understand where you're coming from, Lelle—do you mind if I call you that? We've already been through quite a lot together."

"No, it's fine with me."

CHAPTER 26

In the morning Henry and Herr Rattner went into the camp director's office, and Henry let him know that his error had almost cost him two broken legs. The director apologized but noted that these mishaps do occur on occasion. "No real guilt! No real remorse! Just an accident with nobody responsible," mumbled Henry to himself. Henry and Herr Rattner went to bid the Jamiesons farewell, mainly to let them know that Herr Rattner would drive "the boys" into Barcelona this morning.

On their way into Barcelona, Lennart opened up to Henry for the first time.

"I come from a pretty bourgeois family in Stockholm. We have a nice home. My father is a manager for a large company, and we even have an old summer cottage outside of Stockholm, but I do have an uncle, my father's brother, *farbror* we say in Swedish, who was a volunteer on the side of the anarchists during the Spanish Civil War. He's always getting into bad fights with Dad and calling him names. They're only nice to each other when we all go over to visit my father's mother at the home for retired people."

"Oh, I know about those places. I worked in one in Stockholm. You hear of the weirdest family fights there. Do you like that uncle?"

"We always sort of respected him in a begrudging way. He's had a very hard life, although my dad thinks he brought most of it on himself. My uncle has always thought that being working class was something holy—not that he's religious! He's anything but that. But he worked hard his whole life with his hands, and he lives in a run-down old apartment around Slussen—you know, where all the alcoholics hang out—not that he himself has a drinking problem. He's taken pride in his volunteer work at our labor union movement over the years, and I guess Dad doesn't think he's all that bad deep down inside. He just thinks he's a fanatic who has paid an unnecessarily high price for his beliefs."

Lennart summarized in German what he had said to Henry in English and got back a "Uh huh" kind of neutral sound, which Henry interpreted as, "Yeah, you know we sent Franco's troops his deciding arms." Thinking Rattner just didn't want to be bothered with these jerks for whom he had to waste a morning of his vacation driving into Barcelona, Lennart took his reaction differently. Then Lennart wondered to himself, *I bet he's doing this lest his hasty reaction to the accident be paid back in damage to himself or property by people he regards as representatives of this new disorderly generation.* Finally reaching Barcelona, Herr Rattner deposited the young guys at the train station. With curt *Dankes* the young men hoisted their packs from the back seat of Rattner's VW, and, after checking their backpacks, headed toward the Ramblas, the main street of the old town. Examining Henry's gait, Lennart inquired, "Are you sure you're up to walking around after what happened to you last night?"

"Sure. Their only problem is that the air is as filthy as LA's. I'm pretty interested in Gaudi's architecture. I'd like to see *La Sagrada Familia* first."

Scratching his head, Lennart figured he'd just follow along with Henry's whims and take in as much as he could.

"You're right about this air. It's putrid. There are too many motor vehicles. It's too damn loud and congested."

When they got to the church—Henry was amused they called it *templo* in Spanish—he kept thinking, "How camp," and accidentally thought it out loud.

"What does 'camp' mean?" asked Lennart.

"Oh, it's one of those 'in' words in the States now. It was coined by Susan Sontag to mean a vision of the world in terms of style. It's supposed to stress the extravagant, the unnatural artifice. It can vary between high and low and be unintentional or on purpose. Come to think of it, Lennart, you and I and most of my friends in Sweden are the antithesis of camp."

"Why do you think that?" inquired Lennart, wondering whether Henry was being critical of him or his country by implying that they were not really 'with it' or up-to-date.

"I'm beginning to wonder if when people become concerned about equality and really are doing serious things to promote it, and when they are in harmony with nature, then they, at the same time, belittle the arts and fashion because they see them as showy and, today, literally plastic."

"Maybe you're right. Like this church—I can do without it. It doesn't speak to me at all."

"Yeah, I know what you mean."

"I think it's interesting, wavy, soft, and really out of it for its time, but I don't want to spend all day here, either."

From the Holy Family, Henry and Lennart kept up a brisk pace all day. They watched people sitting around the Plaza Cataluna, and walked down the Ramblas. Then they took in the twelfth century houses of the Monks of Mercedanos.

"You know, people look to me like they are under pressure and suspicious of me," remarked Lennart.

"Yeah, but at least you can see them talking to each other. You know, if you have to live squashed so closely to one another in poor conditions, you have some real things to worry about."

They spent awhile at La Pedrera in the Paseo de Gracia and then climbed the hill above the city on the road to Montjuich. Lennart began to look like he had had enough sightseeing, when Henry pushed him on, "There's just one more thing I definitely want to see today. It's the *Rosa de Manos Unidos*, and it's not far from here. It's in the park on Montjuich."

"O.K., but what is it?"

"It's a sculpture of Barcelonians dancing their *sardana*. It's their version of a circle dance. And this statue is supposed to have inspired everyone from Thomas Mann to Albert Einstein and Albert Schweitzer."

When the friends reached the Rose of the United Hands, they put their packs on the ground and just stared up at the work from different angles. In his typical terse style, Lennart commented, "It is really magical. I like it. I wish we had seen a real sardana today. Well, maybe another time."

Solidly joined together forever, the people concretely molded before him reminded Henry of the *hora* he had danced many a night at UCLA's house for international students. "Those were the days; you could just be together and get outside yourself. You could really share with other people from all over the world. All the complicated reasons to be guarded toward someone from this or that country just vanished," Henry sighed to Lennart. He concluded, "These circle dances let you have fun without being isolated."

CHAPTER 27

Lennart's train for Frankfurt-am-Main left at 7:00 P.M., and Henry headed toward Madrid at 10:30 the same evening. The two different young men liked each other and had an adventuresome trip, which swung from quiet, lazy days on the beach to shocks of unjust and unexpected encounters with the agents of the state.

On his own, Henry was catching up with the news from the wider world. In the Mekong Delta heavy fighting had erupted. Pope Paul appealed to give priority to humanitarian aid during the Nigerian/Biafran Civil War. Swedish Count Carl-Gustav Von Rosen flew in ten tons of food and medicine to Biafra by a secret route. In Yugoslavia, the dissident Milovan Djilas was in complete agreement with President Tito's support of Czechoslovakia's liberalization program. In Canada, Prime Minister Pierre Elliot Trudeau called for a bill establishing equality between French and English languages in the federal courts and public services of his country. Students in Mexico demonstrated against the government. The International Federation of Airline Pilots had made it known publicly that all flights between Western Europe and Algeria would be stopped until the 14 hostages aboard the Israeli airliner hijacked on July 23 would be released. Senator George McGovern made public his opposition to a platform endorsing the Johnson Administration's Vietnam policies. And the Portuguese Dictator Antonio de Oliveira Salazar collapsed in his home of what was thought to be a heart attack.

Illness, death, threats, combat, opposition, and aid reverberated around the world with energy shooting in every direction, while the great thinkers disagreed about whether or not all of the fuss had any meaning to it.

There was a distinct Midwestern American twang audible a few seats from Henry's. Glancing over the seats in front of him, Henry noticed sandy

167

hair and sturdy necks protruding a head above all the surrounding dark human tones. He walked up the aisle and asked, "Are you guys going to Madrid, too?"

"Just stopping there on our way to see El Escorial and The Alcazar and the Cathedral of Segovia. We just left the Pyrenees after traveling through Portugal. Take our advice: stay out of there now. A bastard soldier beat us up because we wouldn't pay off some petty official who for no reason had confiscated our passports."

"Yeah, that SOB was impossible. We finally had to fork over ten dollars each. The country's really nice, but, man, is it a nasty police state!"

"I just heard that Salazar had had a heart attack. Maybe that's why they're so uptight now because they expect a revolution or something while their dictator is physically down."

"The people were nice enough. It was friendlier than what we've encountered here in Spain, but watch out."

"I know what you mean. Something similar happened to my Swedish buddy when we were in southern France, and I almost got my legs broken here in Spain because some dimwit assigned us and another guy with a car the same spot."

"Well, that's travel, I guess. You get to pay a price if you want to see the world."

"I can do without the hassles and try to avoid them if I can. Well, have a good time playing knights in shining armor. *Adios amigos.*"

"Hey, man, have a good time, too!"

Returning to the thin, fraying seat, Henry thought to himself, *Darn, there goes my trip to Portugal. I can't risk losing my passport while all alone there. I think I'll just take in Madrid and then head back north. This heat is pretty intense, anyway.*

CHAPTER 28

It was too hot to spend the entire day walking in Madrid so Henry ended up spending a good part of the day at the Del Prado. Most of his time there he stayed viewing the Goya drawings. Outside, the city was surprisingly in a rush; there was construction and dust everywhere. This city had grown from about 400,000 in 1880 to nearly three million. After lunch he walked to a bookstore and thumbed through books on Madrid and Spanish art and architecture. His mind fixated on the description of this capital by the *fin de siècle* Spanish novelist Pio Baroja y Nessi in his *Perverted Sensuality* where he had written, "Madrid did not appeal to me. It took me a long time to get used to its atmosphere—its physical rather than its moral atmosphere. I did not like the harsh light, the glittering sun, and the dusty air. The summer in particular seemed to me very trying."

Henry did not like the city's moral atmosphere either, but, perhaps, he was a biased judge. While he was browsing, he had been particularly irked at a masked defense of the Inquisition. In a widely used reference book an English professor of Spanish history tried to excuse the expulsion of the Jews from Spain. He claimed that in a decree of March 31, 1491, after the fall of Granada around 165,000 Jews were given the "alternatives" of Christian baptism or exile. Reginald Trevor Davies had seen the national enthusiasm following Ferdinand's and Isabella's victory as fanaticism, although he subtly suggested that it was due to indignation at Jewish financial operations. Of course, Mr. Davies offered neither empirical or secondary evidence for the Jews' alleged improper economic activity nor did he elaborate on what he had regarded as such. The height of his insensitivity, though, was noting how relatively restrained the Spanish had been with the Jews. In his words, those expelled were called "emigrants" and, it was said, "…they were allowed to take with them their goods except gold or silver." Henry laughed, thinking to himself, *What did this guy have in mind, that in the fifteenth century you could ship your household possessions in a moving van or on a national highway? What about a house or business?* This former university lecturer at Oxford and former tutor at the St. Catherine's Society of Oxford continued to stress the leniency of these policies. In his estimation, "The use of the credit system made [these policies] less cruel than it would otherwise have been." Henry was boiling over with anger. He thought to himself, *Can you imagine in an important work like this that not one shred of evidence is offered to back up the writer's assertion about the credit system or how much of the Spanish Jewish wealth was in gold or silver? Mr. Davies doesn't know the worth of the wealth they had in gold and silver. He has no clue as to how much they could buy with it to take out. So he doesn't know how much they couldn't take out of the country. He doesn't know what percentage or how much of their wealth they lost. Mr. Davies wrote* The Golden Century of Spain *and* Four Centuries of Witchbelief, *but he neglects explaining was how much credit Spanish Jews would have received for their precious metals and other possessions that they could not take with them. They had to sell out under pressure in a rush to get the hell out of Spain!*

The whole level of this apologetic writing made Henry think of the pre-Civil Rights Movement southern version of slavery. He recalled educated people declaring, "Oh, it was really more humanitarian than the northern wage system," and "Oh, it would have died out if the Old South had just been left alone." *What b.s.,* he thought to himself!

Outraged that such history was being marketed as the mainstream version, yet intrigued at the selective meandering of its biased reasoning, Henry flipped back a few pages to the account of the Inquisition. Here the story began rather objectively, "The Spanish Monarchy was so strong that the Pope's power was practically eliminated." It was stressed that the Spanish people were deeply religious and that no foreigner could hold office in the Spanish Church. Yet, after a few lines, R. T. Davies begins to insinuate bad things done by the Spanish Jews. He stated that as a matter of fact during "the anarchy" of Henry IV's reign between 1454 and 1475 "the Jews gained great power and influence." Again, this reputed professor claimed, "They might compel—sometimes by means of their usury—their debtors to renounce the Christian religion." Here Henry saw an old medieval anti-Semitic belief without one bit of documented evidence. Yet its author, called a learned man, had repeated it. Davies went right on recording "Marranos (Baptized Jews) often preserved their old religious faith," as though that should be a crime under natural law!

Henry wondered if such an account reflected the lingering anti-Semitism of an English professor or the dominant version of Spanish history. He noted that this writer was as nasty to the Arabs and Moriscos as he was toward the Spanish Jews. As far as he could tell from a brief skimming of the surrounding works in Spanish, this version of history reflected the standard. According to this work, the Inquisition was frequently popular among Spaniards of "pure Old Christian descent," but that it met strong opposition in Aragon. Where more judicious scholars might record that rumor or hearsay attributed the murder of the inquisitor of Saragossa, Pedro de Arbues , who lived from 1441 to 1485, to the Marranos, Reginald Trevor Davies' racist description attributes it to "rich baptized Jews." Yet, Davies did not stop there! He claimed that the Inquisition was "no more unjust or inhumane than most other courts of the Europe of its day. The traditional exaggerations about it were derived from propaganda against Spain at the time of its greatness and from the works of Juan Antonio Llorente, who lived between 1756 and 1823, nineteenth-century liberals, and a number of historical novelists and dramatists."

Henry's chest pounded and his heart throbbed, "So Conservatives expect people to believe such misinformed interpretation as fact?" He was trying to remember the exact article and author he had read in one of his sociology courses. That author had actually compiled historical statistics showing the enormous numbers who had died in the hands of the Inquisition which had expanded its murder, fear, ignorance, and intolerance in proportion to the size of its growing bureaucracy.

Lelle was right. All the guides describe this city as conservative in mood and temperament. Why should I spend any more of my time here, if all I can expect is the distortion of the past and encounters with the ever-present Guardia Civil? Get me out of Madrid. I'm leaving Spain tonight.

Henry left the bookstore near the Museum and walked down the *Gran Via*. "Grundig," "Schweppes," and other international companies advertised themselves in large neon lights. It was no wonder that most of the names of the big corporations were foreign. Many of the conservatives of England and America supported the fascist takeover. They had too much to lose if the local people assumed control in a republican or anarchist state. The big concessions, low taxes, and depressed workers' wages would have ended their holiday.

It was becoming late afternoon, and Henry was on edge, sweaty, and getting anxious to leave. *Well, maybe one day I'll come back to Spain and get to see Portugal. The countries have some very pretty places to see. This trip has been a real eye-opener, and I guess I got a taste of what I should have expected—a real taste of what reaction is all about! Here I stepped into a vestige of fascism, and I got roughed up, scarred, and it frightened my buddy away. Enough is enough. I'm not a masochist. Get me out of here!*

The crisscross of electrical wires above the trains in the Estacion de Chamartin made the back of the Royal Palace and The Cathedral of Our Lady of Almudena appear to be captured in a prison set on the reddish-brown, triangular roofs of the train station. Only the dusty gray of the sky broke through. Perhaps God was reaching down at the people of Madrid to cover them for a bluer day when they would break from the bonds of these steel enclosures, which they themselves had built. The train for Geneva was to leave at 10:10 in the evening, allowing Henry just enough time to visit the Garden of the Island and the Jardin del Principe, the San Antonio Market, and the Town Hall.

CHAPTER 29

As the train pulled out of Madrid, Henry fell asleep. The images, which had settled in his mind, began to resurface in his dreams. At once the image of Goya's *Caprichos* frightened Henry and made him laugh as he found his soul fleeing. Intermittently watching the scene from the outside, he felt as though he were the victim of the Inquisitor's horrible enema. The human and animal faces mocked and accused the pleading man, who looked like his father's sister. The jackass teeth of the Inquisitor, brandishing the enormous enema plunger-torture-tool, was a caricature of the aging woman to whom he had spoken at his local draft board last spring. In his mind he flew ambivalently from being the personage of the Jew to being an external audience unable to escape the tension-filled scene. Afterward he collapsed into a warm receiving interlude of being a camper on a dark night when El Greco's Holy Ghost descended in the form of a radiant dove to a crowd of many different men. They waited on the stairs ascending toward heaven. The heads of these elongated faces were lighted by magical lamps with only the high flames of a menorah illuminating the nocturnal earth under the peace of the dove. The woman in the center must be Joan Baez in a prayer of hope for the salvation of these men. In the long darkness these stills ran over and over again in his mind's eye until he plunged into a restful pictureless repose.

Henry awoke to the crisp air of a Swiss morning—mountains in the background, freshness, warm rays of sun cooled by the heights, an occasional wisp of diesel fuel recalling the intrusion of civilization with its regular companies, banks, hotels, and embassies lined orderly in this, Calvin's city. Henry did not talk, just walked all morning through the town and by the shores of *Lac Léman,* and by afternoon boarded a boat and listened to the gruff sounds of *Schwyzertütsch*-speaking visitors from other cantons, scattered among the speakers of French and English. The intensity of the sun on the water attracted people, warmed and brightened on this clear day of blue skies. Its peace penetrated the skin and its restfulness offered a delightful respite from a world at war with itself.

After the tranquility of watching the industrious city, which was set between the lake and the mountains, Henry managed to squeeze in a brisk walk around the center of Geneva before grabbing a train for Zurich in the late afternoon. By leaving at five, he would get into Zurich at eight in the evening. In the long hours of summer light, he took in the beauty of the countryside standing in between coaches and opening the top of the Dutch-door-like side opening of the train, after the conductor had passed. What a glorious evening! He felt coolness and smelled the scent of evergreens as pastoral scenes of grazing animals on the hillsides whisked by him before the late sunset. Between the healthy whiffs of mountain air, Henry realized that such healthy moments were too expensive without a good tent for camping. Once in Zurich, awaiting the night train to Vienna, he dashed out of the station for a quick view of the square. With high, local prices like these, there was no choice for him but to continue on to Vienna and sleep on the night train, seeing the Austrian Alps only by the bright moon of the night. He didn't mind, though, for there was something special about finding quiet serenity while on a public train. He wandered off to a spot between cars, and opened the side windows to view the passing nature.

Sometime past midnight the cool sweetness of the mountains turned chilly, and Henry stepped into the compartment where he had placed his backpack. He yawned and quickly was lulled to sleep by the gentle regularity of the wheels clicking on the rails. The depth of sleep was more of a pleasurable total calm than a deadened lifelessness, and so, when the first lights were cast on the green meadows, the spruce, maple, and occasional green alder, the young man's yawn and stretch centered on the yellow glow of the early morning. It was 5:00 A.M. Seated across from him was a middle-aged man dressed in a brown tweed coat and tie. This gentleman's dignified mouth was upturned in a slight smile even with his eyes closed. Centering on the soft golden light on the green pastures and the high evergreens, Henry marveled at how trimmed and upright were these woods compared to the magnificent wild California forest in which he had been camping just before leaving home. Almost sensing that he was in 1928, then in 1938, Henry fluttered through a series of pleasant, then frightening thoughts.

There was something intensely familiar about this place, this central Europe about which he had read so much and yet had heard so many remorseful tales and horror stories. His last girlfriend had been a Jewish girl whose family was from Vienna and whose mother still had a sister there. Rhonda was so American and, indeed, such an Angelino. Her family had assimilated into the lower-middle class in Fairfax, affectionately called L.A.'s borsch belt, and Henry suspected that they had been much the same in Vienna. Not all the *Israelitische gemeinde* had been intellectuals or prosperous businesspeople. Rhonda's face and body reflected the most beautiful Middle Eastern features that were to become an Israeli stereotype. How could they not have been admired a generation ago? Henry imagined that the gentleman in front of him—who had such an air of poise and refinement and whose body was loose but upright even in sleep—must have embodied the grace of the last days of the Austro-Hungarian Empire. Could hard times turn a man like this into someone who would have pursued David's father or turned him over to the Gestapo? His friend, David's father, Ben, was a jovial man who had had to escape from Austria and via a long circuitous route had made his way to Palestine. Ben told half-bitterly, half-jokingly of how his Jewish father, had, in self-hatred, felt that the Jews had brought it on themselves; Ben's father who, unable to adapt to America, returned after the war to live in Austria. With an air of humorous disbelief, Ben would recount how one of his aunts had converted to Christianity and had settled in France, surviving there until a ripe old age.

Henry thrust his mind back to 1938, imagining that he was escaping at the last minute, but the stateliness of the tall trees and the utterly verdant pastures kept returning him to the luxuriant present. Freud had written that war made life interesting again. Henry thought that applied only to those who found life boring. Things were changing so fast and there were so many things happening; how could people not get excited about something in the present? Well, it was true that there were dull people who did get bored and would rather kill or risk getting killed rather than going to the same old job day in and day out. But even in olden times when people had no control over nature and were more believing in miracles and the intervention of God, didn't they find life thrilling enough—filled as it was with gossip and secrets and complicated human relationships to keep them stimulated? Yet, ever since the Neolithic Revolution, one group or another had found war an attractive way to effectively advance power and prestige, not to mention getting away from personal bonds. *Am I weird or something to be thrilled by science, language, literature, music, art and philosophy?* Henry asked himself. *The more I learn, the more I want to find out. I certainly wish I had a fraction of the time*

175

to do the things I want to do. I guess if you get off on raping unknown women and destroying and being brutal, war lets you do that. In my opinion, you have to be a pretty repressed person to want to explode like a steam kettle just because some big daddy you don't even know tells you you're a hero for doing those kinds of things.

As they neared Vienna, the older man across from him awoke and turned out to be as amiable as he appeared in his smiled-filled dreams. Wearing dark-tinted glasses, a young, rather stout man peeked into their compartment and inquired about the time. They invited him to join them. Jean-Guy was a nineteen-year-old Montrealer who was supposed to meet his sister, Sylvie, in Vienna. When it was discovered that neither Henry nor Jean-Guy had a place to stay in Vienna, their senior compartment mate, Herr Hauser, recommended a modestly priced accommodation with more privacy than the youth hostel. The two fellows were enthusiastic about Herr Hauser's suggestion and were delighted to be in the company of someone who had the manners of a baron yet who seemed so open and relaxed with foreigners of a younger generation. For someone who must have been a young adult during the 1930s, this man contradicted all the stereotypes. Maybe he had been a socialist or maybe he had spent the war in The United Kingdom. He spoke English with a strong British, upper-class dialect tinged with a slight Viennese German accent. Despite his formality, there was a levity about him that made them feel they were accompanying a storybook character. He led the visitors to their subway line, and Jean-Guy and Henry reached their destination—an old brownish, four-story stucco-covered building—in no time. Jean-Guy pressed the black button, which sounded the landlady, who, after examining them with a straight-faced seriousness, opened the door. As soon as she heard Herr Hauser's name mentioned, her entire demeanor changed. She became bouncy and jovial as she led them up the darkened, dank stairwell and down the corridor into a simply-arranged room with two separate wooden beds. The walls were very thick. Jean-Guy negotiated a flat rate of $2.50 U.S. each per night.

Jean-Guy was good company. He was well read and informed on a gamut of subjects from philosophy to music and art. Heavy-set, his body type was not the sought-after, male ideal of 1968 California. Jean-Guy was, in his own words, *pondéré*. This was his ideal. Henry understood this to mean well measured, sort of like his high school alma mater, *Integer Vitae*, the whole life.

Their day in Vienna was scheduled according to Jean-Guy's sense of appropriateness. They returned to the center of the city from The Barracks and began with two different coffees in Kursalon of the Stadtpark. Savoring the whipped cream, Jean-Guy slowly sipped his *Einspanner.* Henry was satisfied with a strong *Espresso.* A devotee of music, Jean-Guy wanted to see the statues of Johann Strauss the Younger, Franz Schubert, Hans Makart, and the Danube Nymph.

Sometimes speaking in perfect Canadian English and occasionally switching into French, Jean-Guy was full of tidbits about the lives of the great composers and musicians, "You know, this city tended to be mean to its musical greats when they lived and then immortalized them after they died." He would end his terse observations with an ironic chuckle.

From the City Park, Jean-Guy and Henry strolled down Zeditzgasse over to Stephensplatz past St. Stephen's Cathedral, the best example of Gothic architecture in Austria. For them, the old buildings became a pleasant, scenic backdrop to their conversation.

"Jean-Guy, you know, this city makes me think about the letters which Einstein and Freud exchanged in 1932 about why there is war."

"That's funny. It makes me think about music. But you probably have much to worry about *la guerre en Indochine, hein*?

"Yep, it's all so complicated. Take Freud. He was incredibly enthused about the Franco-Prussian War and the Napoleanic Wars. He greatly admired the Carthaginian Hannibal, whom he saw as a Semitic general defeating Rome and Napoleon's General Massena, who was reputedly Jewish. During the First World War he took a position that was initially favorable to the Austro-Hungarian Empire and the Germans. But, by the time of his correspondence with Albert Einstein, he called himself a pacifist, yet, he stated that 'there is no question of getting rid entirely of human aggressive impulses, which can be diverted so as not to express themselves in war.'"

"Henry, I had a very strict Catholic upbringing. I studied St. Thomas Aquinas. In *The City of God* he made a distinction between just and unjust wars. Your country's war in Vietnam is not a just war. Instead of bombing the country, it could easily woo Hanoi and the South Vietnamese opposition through a generous program of economic development. The fact is that your leaders don't have the moral force to do that."

Their conversation meandered tangentially through the nave and crossing. Jean-Guy became almost ecstatic as they neared the sixteenth century *Pummerin,* the Boomer, the largest bell in Austria, which he had wanted to see ever since he had become a music buff. More enthused about getting a general view of the city, Henry's breath shortened when they climbed to the southern tower, the Steffl.

"Jean-Guy, isn't this view stupendous? I bet you're hearing music all over!"

"I guess I'm not typical of our generation, but *ma mère* is such a good pianist and dancer that this city leaves me with *frissons* down the back."

"I don't mean to disturb your view, but back to what we were talking about. When our class read that Einstein-Freud correspondence on war last semester, I got pretty pissed off at Freud's snobbery about Einstein's insights into the minds of men. Freud was supposed to have said that Einstein knew about as much about psychology as Freud did about physics. To be honest with you, I think Einstein got closer to the heart of the matter. He observed that there is a governmental class in every nation that craves power and is hostile to any limitation of national sovereignty. Einstein thought that their interests go hand and foot with the small but determined group of individuals who regard warfare and the manufacture and sale of arms as an occasion to advance their personal interests and authority. I was really amazed how closely Einstein's thoughts were like President Eisenhower's warning to the American people when he left office. Our teacher wasn't sure if there had been any intellectual feedback one way or the other, though."

"*C'est bien étrange* that we're discussing this as we look over *Vienne*, but I guess it's appropriate. *Je veux dire* that this was the very spot where the Turks and Islam were beaten back from Europe and Christendom just four centuries ago. And the Hapsburgs had to thank the very Catholic king of Poland for their success. *À part de ça*, what did Freud have to say about the psychological reasons for war?"

"Well, Einstein threw the question at him. Einstein wanted to know how such a small clique could bend the will of the majority, which stands to lose and suffer so much by a state of war. Einstein suspected that the emotions of the masses could be swayed to sacrifice their lives because man has with him a lust for hatred and destruction. Freud answered him by a long evolutionary sketch, at which point he concluded that a community is held together by the compelling force of violence and the emotional ties between its members."

"But didn't he say all these had their sources someplace else?"

"Uh huh. Freud hypothesized that there were only two human instincts. Eros seeks to preserve and unite, while the aggressive or destructive instinct seeks to destroy and kill. Freud thought that both instincts operate together. He felt that when the aggressive instinct was turned on it would relieve the organism that was responding to it."

"But didn't Freud have an answer, a way to control it before it got out of hand?"

"No, Freud thought that there was no way to get rid of entirely the human destructive impulses. At best he thought you could let them be expressed in some other way than war. The way he thought you could do this is by encouraging the growth of emotional ties between people. Freud spelled out two types of emotional ties: the first was love without a sexual aim and the second is identification, that is, sharing important interests. He felt that a strengthening of the intellect which begins to govern instinctual life and an internalization of the aggressive impulses with its advantages and perils are the characteristics of civilization that are doing this."

"But, Henry, did Freud think that there were just and unjust wars?"

"Yes, he even thought that as long as some countries prepare for ruthless destruction, others had to be armed for war."

"You know, it's so beautiful I could stay up here all day, but let's try to take in the palace and the *Schönbrunn* before evening. What are your plans for tomorrow? *Tu sais, ma soeur* arrives tomorrow around noon."

"Let's see how the day goes. I can't afford to stay another night outside a youth hostel, so maybe Sylvie can take my place. But I'd like to see as much of Vienna as possible. You're good company."

Jean-Guy laughed, but Henry began to realize seriously how much he enjoyed J-G's cultivated, genuine interest in the things he appreciated—good art, music, philosophy, and history. Unlike Annette, J-G didn't jump at people and give them the feeling that they better watch out if they said the wrong thing. Totally unlike Denis of Indiana, who had spoiled his trip to Venice, Jean-Guy was interested in cultures different from his own. Unlike Klaes, to Jean-Guy words were a chief medium of sharing with other people what you enjoyed. But, unlike Klaes, Jean-Guy kept his feelings towards others so hidden that they really couldn't tell if they were liked or were just an acquaintance with whom it was worth exchanging a few minutes of this life.

For all of Jean-Guy's seriousness, it was obvious that this trip to Vienna brought out his romantic side. As he and Henry walked through the promenade of ordered green trees that had been clipped like a hedge, Jean-Guy pretended to waltz with an imaginary princess in his curved arms all the way from the fountain statue of mother and her child to *Schönbrunn* Castle. From his movements, Henry could almost hear the sounds of Strauss, Lanner, and Ziehrer floating in the air.

As they walked around the palace, Jean-Guy shared his ultramontane sentiments. "The Empress Maria Theresa must have been quite a person. She had sixteen children and seemed to get along with nearly everybody. She was a reactionary and a progressive at the same time. The farmers loved her. She demanded efficiency from her bureaucrats and made her upper classes act prim and proper. But she persecuted new ideas. I bet I know where Freud got his notion about creating bonds of identification to avoid war. Just look at the Hapsburgs. Instead of fighting other countries, they would marry into them. How do you like the Maria Theresa yellow color? Can you believe that Mozart and Hayden gave concerts here?" Jean-Guy whose ordinary matter-of-factness reached a level of true enthusiasm had associations and ideas spring forth at every corner they turned.

By the late afternoon, they returned into the Ring in just enough time to search out the seventeenth century Baroque palaces of the inner city and to take a glimpse at the National Library and the Spanish Riding School. During their long walk, they said little but Jean-Guy hummed and whistled one classical melody after another. Jean-Guy's cheshire cat smile and his large eyes marked his mood of utter delight. After an early evening walk down the Danube Canal, Jean-Guy wanted to settle in a tavern to try the rural wines.

After they had been seated a few minutes, the chubby French Canadian young man struck his palm on his forehead. "It just hit me why we got such a bargain of a place to stay. The building where we're staying is in one of those old structures the Viennese call "rent barracks," which were put up at the beginning of the century to house the workers coming from the eastern parts of the empire. They were built so heavily they were never torn down. I bet that the landlady is a poor friend of the guy we met on the train!"

"You must be right. But it's not a slum. It's clean, and she does have a lot of nice needlework hanging on the walls. Her homemade quilts are really comfortable. Do you think that you and Sylvie will stay on there?"

"*Pourquoi pas?* It depends on her, but I'd like to stay here for at least a week and get to listen to a few concerts and see the museums. Where will you go?"

"I want to see Amsterdam most of all. I even have the address of one of the aunts of the wife of my favorite teacher from high school. I was really close to her and her mom too. They came from Holland. But I feel that I should see Berlin first. There are a lot of things I'm interested in there, particularly from the 1920s, the period of the Weimar Republic."

"So you're going to leave tomorrow?"

"Yeah, there's a train leaving about half past five tomorrow evening that'll put me in Berlin at a little after eight the next morning. That way I can meet Sylvie. Gee, I'm envious you get along so well with your sister. That's pretty rare today, isn't it?"

"Now, don't go reading your Freud into it, but I think it's because we're only a year apart, and we have so many of the same interests. I guess our parents paid a lot of attention to us, but we don't think we're spoiled. Who does? No, really, they spent much time with us doing wholesome things. Our mother taught us how to play the piano and how to ice-skate and our dad, how to ski. You know, we're not like the English. We know how to have a good time—but our parents made us study, although they weren't severe with us and let us go out with our friends. Neither one of us was ever very wild. Now would Freud say that I'm driven by some incestuous drive for Sylvie?"

"Where would you ever get that idea?"

"One thing for sure, the one bad thing our parents did give us was a hell of a weight problem. Both Sylvie and I were called "balloons" in school. So I guess we've sort of mutually protected each other on that score. We both tell a pretty good joke. You know, everybody loves a fat man, and oh how a fat man can love?"

"I can sympathize. I've been through the same thing," moaned Henry, who continued, "Do you like the music that little orchestra's playing? It's called Schrammel—music from the name of some brothers who came up with it in the last century."

"Yeah. It's rather lighthearted and folksy. I like the combination of the guitars, clarinets, and violins. There's a big German beer hall in Montreal where that's pretty popular."

By midnight the young men made it back to their lodging and were up and out on the streets of Vienna again by 9:00 A.M. They spent the morning at the Imperial Palace and Apartments. Jean-Guy was fascinated by the crown of the Holy Roman Empire and its thousand-year rule. Henry was more taken with the Albertina. Both were overwhelmed by the Austrian National Library where, besides the books, they were awed by the Prunksaal Hall. With their minds stuffed with jewels, books, and paintings, the traveling companions set out to meet Jean-Guy's sister at the West Station.

Sylvie stood out in a crowd, even from the other side of the large structure. Her complexion gleamed, and she had a creamy tone of skin. Like her brother's, her eyes were huge, and Henry's evasive, American look askance had to refocus outwards in order to avoid revealing his innermost desires.

Sylvie was pleasantly plump and wore her rounded extra pounds—large breasts and belly under a loose, neatly ironed, thick tartan cotton dress—considerably longer than the style that had been popular in Los Angeles. She also had long, dark brown hair in a beautifully-laced chignon. Sylvie seemed much more comfortable with her size because she didn't stuff herself into the shapes popular with her age-mates. She would not permit herself be like everyone else. She said to herself that she literally had too much to hide, and growing up, she had developed an artful way to make herself at home anywhere. She preferred long, dark, flowery dresses and loose blouses.

Jean-Guy and his sister wrapped each other in a four-armed embrace and kissed on both cheeks. Then they just blurted out a loud guffaw. After initial introductions, it was decided that Sylvie would stay at their pension, and they would spend the afternoon at the Belvedere before walking Henry back to the train station in the late afternoon. They checked Sylvie's luggage and set out for the palace that housed the galleries of the Medieval, Baroque, and nineteenth and twentieth century Austrian art.

Sylvie was full of stories of her family and tidbits about the lives of the great Viennese composers. Both she and her brother were enamored with Franz Schubert. As soon as she had checked her baggage, she joked, *"C'est pas parcequ'il resemble à mon frère, mais, c'est vrais, n'est-ce pas?"* Then she withdrew a clipping of a painting from one of her music books on the lives of the composers.

Henry chuckled, "Yeah, he really looks like Jean-Guy, except his hair is a little woolier, and he doesn't wear granny glasses. Jean-Guy's rather rounded face and intense gaze could be those of Schubert."

On that note, Sylvie asked, "Do you mind if we go see his museum right away?"

The three walked over to the Nussdorferstrasse 54. Sylvie hopped as soon as they reached Schubert's old house, now a museum. "Can you believe that in 1815 he wrote four operas and *Singspiels*, two symphonies, two masses, 145 songs, a string quartet, and a lot of piano music," gasped Sylvie as she read through the literature around the museum.

Jean-Guy twisted around excitedly at his sister, "Wouldn't it be wonderful to be able to do in a lifetime what he did in 1815?"

Henry found the details of the life of composers informative, but their lives did not excite him as it obviously did this old-fashioned brother-sister duo. He walked over to the attendant to inquire whether or not there were any public concerts about town.

"Hey, you two, how about listening to an afternoon Brahms' concert in Volksgarten. It's supposed to be free."

"Pourquoi pas, on peut voir la ville après qu'il est parti," whispered Sylvie to Jean-Guy. "O.K."

After a brief promenade, the trio made it to the open-air concert where neatly-lined rows of wooden-backed chairs were still available. They sat down close to the orchestra. What luck! The opening piece was Franz Schubert's Symphony No. 7 in E Major.

Sylvie gasped, "No, I can't believe it!" By the second movement her rounded arms and thighs overflowing her own position were lightly rubbing up first against Henry then back to Jean-Guy as she began literally swaying in both directions between the stringed and wind instruments.

During the second number, Jean-Guy sat first in the middle, then on the edge of his chair, as his hands beat out the pounds of drums followed by his mimicking first the violins with the movement of his hands and arms, then the winds with his mouth. Having read the brochure on this performance of Johannes Brahms' Symphony No. 4 in E minor, Opus 98, Henry closed his eyes and tried to envisage what a Brahms' visit in the Austrian Styrian village must have been like. Instead, he pictured lovely ladies in white satin dresses frenetically dancing with a platoon of stately men in imperial garb.

"How romantic!" exclaimed Sylvie to Jean-Guy.

Attending to his sibling's enthusiasm, he replied, "How real!"

"Can something be romantic and real at the same time," wondered Henry, his eyes still closed. "In any case, I think Brahms' friends misjudged this piece. I don't think that its beauty escapes the amateur. If anything, most people here seem to be enjoying it."

The last piece from Hayden appeared to leave the audience in a lively mood, energized, and ready to go home and prepare an elegant meal or to undertake several hours of uninterrupted exercise. It had certainly left Jean-Guy, Sylvie, and Henry with a sense of deep appreciation for the sounds, which had moved audiences the world over to admire the genius of this city. The passions of this once mighty empire of many tongues had managed to express itself best to many nations and through time in the universal code of music.

"What a wonderful note on which to leave this city," commented Henry. Sylvie and Jean-Guy chuckled and stepped out of the crowd to bid him farewell at the West Station.

CHAPTER 30

It was twenty-five minutes after five on this glorious evening, and the train was due in Berlin's East Station at 8:13 the next morning. Henry had no doubt that they would be on time, so he began to reconsider if he really wanted to arrive in Berlin right away. Should he go to Mannheim first and explore one of the putative origins of his mother's father's family? He just realized that there must be some interesting connection between the story that his mother's family came from Mannheim and the story that his grandmother was Alfred Dreyfus' first cousin. According to one of the stories, his maternal grandmother had emigrated from the Alsace-Lorraine and his maternal grandfather from Heidelberg, Germany. Contradictions were inherent in genealogies, anyway. Wouldn't this be a great opportunity to investigate this story once and for all? One thing was for sure. There were enough embittered stories from his father's side of the family—affirmed vigorously by some and equally silenced by others—that they as Russian Jews had been ostracized by their co-religionists of French and German background in the southern United States. His father's sister had unpleasant memories of how her family, even those who married "across the lines," had been treated in an arrogant and haughty manner.

It was strange, Henry thought, how his father's "Russian" side—actually from a small Ukrainian village in the Tsarist Pale of Settlement—was so different from his mother's Franco-Alsace-Lorrainian-and-German side. His father's family was wild—they had lived their lives to the extremes. The four brothers had entered into different occupations: a furniture salesman, a wealthy businessman, a department store milliner-later-unemployed, a famous doctor, and the wife of an alcoholic traveling salesman. In contrast, his mother's two sisters were lights of bourgeois respectability. Accidentally sight-impaired at birth, her brother had settled down from an impetuous

184

youth and young manhood to life as a hardworking accountant, a late marriage, and adopted children. Then he became a widower and re-married a woman with children who provided them with grandchildren. The French and German side had stuck closer to its Jewish religious roots through several generations, while the Russian side was mixed between intermarriages and assimilation to non-observant middle- or upper-middle class America. A good portion of the men on the Franco-German side had graduated from Ivy League schools, while the Russians had made it through local high school or their state universities and had immediately gone to work. The Russian side was more emotional, effusive, and given to excess, but were more themselves and down-to-earth, whether it be in hearty eating or trying to reach the great American dream. Had not Mother constantly repeated the tale of how Father's brother, the businessman, had lured them to a small town in Oklahoma with promises of commercial success only to take all of Father's $3,000 depression era savings—mostly earned on WPA—surreptitiously to New York, leaving them stranded in the dusty plains? And Henry still cringed when he remembered the angry but muffled denial by another of his father's brothers when he had inquired into the veracity of this story. But Henry himself felt more a victim of the well-meaning manipulations of one of his maternal aunts' husbands who really believed he was helping his sister-in-law by taking her family's social security money and then giving it back to her for appropriate uses. Henry had to admit to himself that he liked the security, which his wealthy cousins enjoyed. At the same time, his own lack of security had left him more at ease with the unconventional, the bohemian, and the radical. Particularly he was drawn to the intellectual. He was one of the few on either side of his family who had sought solace in books and ideas. Yet, he was never contented with them when they ignored the injustices of the world. So, as the train rolled northward, he kept wondering whether to check the roots of his mother's family or the roots of German socialism. They certainly had not been intertwined in his family who were all—with the exception of Henry—unabashed believers in American capitalism and the American dream. He wondered about his father, though, who had been the poorest of his brothers. His dad had, after all, labored on WPA after his grandfather's small store had failed during the Great Depression. After that, he found a job in Rochester after the Second World War only through the intervention of a brother-in-law. Hadn't he had questions about the system? Henry's mother's class-consciousness was limited to her jealousy at her sisters' marrying well. Indeed, Aunt Olivia was to confide that her wealthy sister found it uncomfortable to be around Henry's mother, so great was her unstated resentment. Yet, Henry's mother, like her sisters, saw it as a family, not a societal problem. She expected them, not Uncle Sam, to help her out, and when their help was quite modest, she responded with barely repressed dislike.

Well, maybe he should stop and probe or maybe he should skip it and spend more time investigating the remaining traces of Weimar in Berlin. Well, maybe later, maybe, just maybe, on the last lap of his jaunt. would he explore his mother's heritage? That was the last thought that he remembered before falling asleep.

When Henry woke up, it was a morning filled with blue light and fluffy clouds. As the train pulled into the Zoo Station, he felt rested despite the long journey. As he walked from the train into the dingy Bahnhof, Henry was amazed to be leisurely strolling out into a city where less than a generation ago he would have been hunted down like a hated rat. Perhaps, this realization left him somewhat cautious, but not overly so, for he knew that this city had remained anti-Nazi in its majority more so than any other place in Germany. He was too much filled with interest in placing where so many things that he had admired had been located and then comparing any differences between capitalist and communist cities located next to each other. At the information stand he inquired where the youth hostel or other reasonable accommodation was located.

Across the way was a tall, very blond, blue-eyed woman about his age and height. She cast a warm smile his way. Henry returned her convivial greeting while observing the long list of private accommodations that were about the same price as the *Jungendherberge*. There was a cylindrical column outside where many activities and events had been posted. It was much neater and cleaner but lacked the charm and grace of its Parisian cousins. When he looked up from the announcements, who should be standing on the other side of the column, but the same woman with whom he had exchanged glances at the information counter. Their "Where are you going to stay?" popped at each other at the same time and made both of them giggle. After an initial exchanging of names, Henry asked, "Would you like to come take a look at the first address on both of our lists?"

Kristina's big breasts stood out in a tightly packed brassiere, not loose, like many of the young women her age that Henry had noticed on the train and in the street. These maidens appeared to wear nothing underneath. Kristina was also well dressed in a heavy, blue cotton skirt and blouse. She offered to drive them in her car to the Kreuzberg. To their surprise, the area around Chamissoplatz reminded them of the tenement parts of Paris, but the area was thick with birch and willow trees and small shops all around. Before they went up, Kristina offered, "If I like the place, would you mind sharing it?"

"No, if it's all right with you."

"No problem," she giggled.

After the third ring of the heavy black bell, a hefty, middle-aged woman escorted them up four flights of stairs into a plain but immaculately clean room with a big window and two fluffy beds. It would be about two dollars each per night, according to Kristina's translation. They paid the woman who quickly left them as they dropped their possessions on the floor.

"I'm not a real German," Kristina explained in near perfect English when the landlady had left. "I'm Polish, even though I'm a German citizen, and believe me, when I was young and new here, they never let me forget."

"Even after the war?" Henry asked.

"The more modern, the more subtle."

"But you wear such a big crucifix and you look so Nordic."

"Forget Nordic. I tried being like them. I'm just not. I lose my temper. I scream. I bubble when I'm happy. I look at you romantically when I find you sexy. I'm no atheist or rationalist, either. When I pray, I shake inside through the love and compassion I feel when I see the Black Madonna. I don't think coldly and rationally about things. I get excited and enthused about them and then do them."

Henry did find this woman beautiful, almost literally too much for him, and her feelings were so intense they stirred the air around them. Initially, he felt more revved up as though he wanted to skip all around the city holding hands with her and laughing instead of languishing in bed. She was very big. This scared him a bit and calmed his initial arousal. She radiated so much energy that he almost couldn't sit still. Her skin was absolutely lovely. It was a faint cameo, and her eyes were a delicate blue, like the sky on a summery day when mushy clouds float lazily dissolving into the surrounding azure. Her presence made him sigh. "Kristina, what do you do?"

"I'm a stewardess for Lufthansa. This is between you and me. I'm in Berlin doing something illegal. Don't worry. Anyone who can get away with it does it. I live in Cologne, but because Berliners don't have to pay taxes on their cars as we do in West Germany, I'm going to register mine over here."

"Don't you worry about getting caught?"

"No, I love taking risks. I'll just establish an address here and that's that.

Let's see; you're a student and an American Jew—right?"

"How did you guess that?" wondered Henry, his heart beating that this was the second time this summer his features and mannerisms had given him away in a possibly dangerous place.

"Listen, you're cute. You have curly hair with a bit of very pre-mature graying. You look terribly serious and innocent. And you speak American—all of these facts mean you're not Italian, Spanish, a Yugoslav or Arabic which are the other possibilities. Plus I serve people from all over the world—so I get pretty good at guessing these sorts of things. You know, my people have made love with, hated, and given your people a place to make a living since at least the fifteenth century."

"You know, you're the first Polish person I've ever met. I know only one Polish American. I was only a baby or a kid when we passed through Chicago and Buffalo where there are a lot of Polish Americans. In fact, I think I have known only four Polish Jews. The kosher butcher in the town where I grew up and the owner of the kosher-style restaurant were *poylishe Yidin,* as Sarah's grandmother used to say. Sarah was the little girl I used to play with when I was a small child. And so was Mrs. Lefkowicz who used to bring over her baked goods to my uncle when he was dying of cancer."

"Look, the Nazis thought of both of us as *untermenschen.* Your people was to be wholly exterminated, like our leadership, and the rest of us were to be their slaves, because, we were ethnically Slavs. With stupidity like that—that a whole nation swallowed—to think that they have the nerve to think of us today as dumb Polacks."

"Kristina, I find your story fascinating, but how would you like to tell it to me while we see Berlin?"

"I have to take care of this license problem, which might take a long time. Why don't you go over to East Berlin first. That's where most of the historic parts of the city are. It'll take you all day and then we can meet back here this evening. By the way, how many days are you planning to stay?"

"It depends. Maybe three or so."

Kristina left Henry off at Checkpoint Charlie, then headed over to take care of establishing her Berlin address and registering her automobile. It was only 11 A.M. by the time Henry cleared the border patrol through the pedestrian crossing. The wait was not too long, and it had been made pleasant by a good conversation with Diana, a serious student of German from the University of Indiana at Bloomington. She was a very plain, thin woman of medium stature who wore no make-up. She must have had a bad case of acne as a teenager.

"I'm going to the Pergamon. It's reputedly one of the best museums in the world. How about you?"

"I'm more interested in getting a more general impression of the city, meeting and talking to people, if possible. I'm curious about what life is like under Communism."

"Those big border guards should tell you something. Don't their uniforms look like those of the old *Wehrmacht*," she whispered in Henry's ear.

"Yes, they do."

But Henry thought to himself, *So far, they don't seem to be as heavy as the Guardia Civil in Spain, but who knows?*

After exchanging the necessary amount of their American money into East German marks, they made it through the inspection and were across the border in about fifteen minutes. Diana and Henry walked together down *Unter den Linden*, and parted company on the Corner of Friedrich Strasse. This promenade took him past the State Opera House, the French Cathedral, the Neue Wache, the Dom, the Church of Mary, until he finally reached the Alexanderplatz.

Here Henry stood in the heart of what had been the center of the fast-paced Berlin of the turn of the century, the very name of which Alfred Doblin's novel had immortalized. He sat down on a cold gray slab of concrete and gazed at the large square. As soon as had he become comfortable, two sturdy, but somewhat disheveled and haggard-looking young men approached him.

"Heh, man, you're an American, aren't you?" the first fellow inquired in a rather declamatory fashion in a heavy German accent.

"Yes."

"Could you help us out? If you buy us two cartons of cigarettes at the hotel at the customs' duty-free shop, we'll pay you back just after you buy them. We can't shop in there."

Without thinking about the legality of his action, without contemplating that these characters might be out to take him, but thinking it might be a good way to get to know some East Germans, Henry replied, "Sure."

At this point, the taller, sallow-faced man, somewhat jitteringly introduced himself and his friend.

"Thanks, man, I'm Hans, and this is my friend, Jürgen."

On the way to the hotel it occurred to Henry that buying cigarettes for someone did not portend to be the best way to make friends with them. Oh, it was rather utilitarian, and there certainly was nothing wrong in helping someone, but were these two fellows just using him? He purchased the tobacco and rejoined them on the square where they promptly paid and thanked him and bid him farewell before he had a chance to put his wallet back into his pocket. At the end of the day he would find out that he had lost several dollars because he couldn't cash back in his East German marks accumulated from this transaction.

After being left abruptly, Henry was disappointed that he had not been able to converse with these young men whose profession it must be to take tourists the way he had been. So he began to clear away from the main plaza and wandered down a side street past rows of black houses where a chimney sweep could still be seen clearing the flues. And there in the burned out remains were the old walls of what he suspected was one of Berlin's great synagogues. Was it *Kristallnacht* or the bombing of Berlin or both that left this silent ruin whispering like the chimneys of Nelly Sachs' poem?

O the chimneys
On the ingeniously devised habitations of death
When Israel's body drifted as smoke
Through the air—
Was welcomed by a star, a chimney sweep,
A star that turned black
Or was it a ray of sun?

Was it Leo Baeck who had written that the great dialogue between Germans and Jews was dead and would never be revived? Could as wise a man as he—who had suffered nobly the ordeal at Teresinstadt—have failed to discern the vestiges of that dialogue during his old age while teaching in Cincinnati and traveling about for Progressive Judaism? Or was Henry exaggerating what he perceived to be partial strains of German Jewishness in his mother's southern, American Jewish family? Or rather had these spiritual roots been almost simply become indistinguishable from the mainstream of America? One thing was becoming clear to Henry. Both sides of his family had devalued philosophy, literature, art, music, languages, and mathematics. Learning was secondary to a career goal, second to advancing materially and socially. In this way they had a very American, utilitarian, practical outlook. In this respect they were quite unlike the upper-middle-class of the pre-World War II Berlin Jewry. Still, they had their stories of who was smarter and more cultivated. There was even a funny tale his father's sister had related. When the learned Reform Rabbi Stephen S.Wise had visited their small temple, it was her "Russian" father, Henry's paternal grandfather, who had had to explain what the rabbi had spoken of to the rest of the congregation.

On the other hand, Henry saw so many things that were remains from the smaller Jewish communities in the German towns and small cities. First of all, the southern Jews of German and French Alsatian background talked about their roots incessantly. And, of course, Herr Mendelsohn had looked like one of Henry's relatives. Indeed, Nelly Sachs had an uncanny resemblance to his aunt. One of his aunt's mother-in-law had even written a genealogy tracing her lineage. The similarity was also written in their names. It was also evident in the southern German Jewish relative personal coolness and body tenseness, the correctness and conservatism of their dress; their dislike of questioning authority and their conformity to the ways of a successful consumer culture. When they did defer to a respected, learned person, it was more to his rank than what he had to say. A maternal aunt had married into a "German" family who had proudly produced a long line of temple presidents. There was even an accent on order and decorum in their public prayer.

These characteristics set them off far from the American Jews of Eastern European background Henry had known. So as Henry contemplated upon all the great American scholars, scientists, writers, and politicians of German Jewish heritage, he had to admit that was not his pedigree. Nor did he regret its not being so. In a way he was beginning to understand the ramifications of coming from an immediate underclass, yes *lumpen,* Jewish family of mixed Western and Eastern European background. It was anxiety-provoking for Henry—and he tried his best to flush it out of his conscious thought—that Karl Marx, whose writings he found so profound, had written a mean-spirited commentary both on the Jewish religion and culture and on the political unreliability of the *lumpenproletariat,* both characteristics of Henry's. Oh, well, hadn't Marx's father had him baptized as a young lad, and that probably pushed him to want to be just like everybody else in some ways. Yet, this fact which he had read about Germany's craziness was correct: this nation did not seem to understand or care for pluralism. Differences were not tolerated for long periods. They had to be rooted out—particularly when they were Jewish. First was theological attribution of deicide. It was passed down and practiced in the terrible massacres of the Middle Ages. At the beginning of his career as a reformer, Martin Luther's first accepted the Jews. Afterwards, he preached violence against them. Down through the Enlightenment, Germans partially tolerated, then reacted against the Jews until they exterminated them in the Holocaust. All this history bore witness to the intense and tense interaction between the Jewish and the German peoples. Just two years ago,

Gershom Scholem had said in Brussels that there had never been a true dialogue; that there had been Jewish listening, adopting, and understanding, but never vice versa; but that didn't preclude trying to do it.

Freud had said this ethnic prejudice was based on little differences like those between the English and the Scots or the Irish. Groups seized on such little differences to define their own identity. This explanation seemed superficial to Henry. From what Kristina had confided to him this morning, although they were working on it, deep down, they had not yet learned the lesson very well—not even toward other gentiles.

Yet, as he turned right on Leipziger Strasse back toward the "*Mitte*," the downtown, Henry kept noticing the diversity in people's looks that defied the bleak contrasts described in all the American guidebooks. There certainly were many small private shops—bicycle repair stores, photographers, beauty salons—which testified to the survival of small entrepreneurs under the aegis of a Bolshevik hammer and sickle.

How peculiar, as he walked in this society, which professes atheism, that he was overcome with religious thoughts. Was not his faith so close to the enlightened Christians that they were barely distinguishable? They called his denomination of Judaism "reformed," and it was curious to him that he never thought how close were its links to Protestantism until he had struggled through an article in Russian in the Great Soviet Encyclopedia on Judaism: yes, Reformation, Dutch Reformed Church, Reformed Judaism did, indeed, share more than verbal etymology. It was striking that Liberal or Progressive Judaism, the British and international nomers, were never mentioned in his southern American upbringing. That was too close to those trouble-making, boisterous New York Jews, according to the unarticulated sentiments of his southern kin. But did not Moses Mendelsohn and his Enlightenment interchange with Immanuel Kant offer hope for reason, for human progress, for a prophetic enactment of justice here in this world? Nearly all of his friends, Christians and Jews, firmly believed in this optimistic outlook for mankind. This was the French and American Revolutions' gift to humanity. So too, had these upheavals given the Jews all the rights of other citizens as individuals, although still not as a collectivity. Were there flaws in this ideology? There still was poverty, war, and genocide, but it never occurred to Henry to throw out the whole philosophy because of these inconsistencies. What was needed was more enthusiasm and effort to solve these problems. Then the Messianic Age would come!

It was turning into a graying, bleak, damp day, so Henry decided to see if he could find Diana in the *Pergamon*. In a few minutes he had entered the huge neo-Classical structure among throngs of identically clad children. First he shuffled his way to the *Pergamum Alter* which had been one of the Seven Wonders of the World. Despite the splendor of this relic and large collections of Egyptian, early Christian, and Byzantine art, he paid as much attention to the adults and children as to these ancient treasures. Inquiring about the children's groups, he learned from a proud emphatic woman that these were free, state-sponsored programs that provided instruction and childcare during the summer vacation. The kids were more orderly than a similar group of Americans but quite a few were horsing around and having to be corrected by their teachers. Henry also found the imagery of the heavy Prussian monolith—played over and over again in the American journalistic stories about East Berlin—to be contradicted by the life he was seeing around him. There were many smiling faces, couples holding hands, children and teenagers climbing or jumping where they should not. His impression contradicted the dour, drab equation of East German communism as a lifeless prison, which was the standard billing in the American press. Yes, he believed the reports that many former Nazis had been "reformed" as communist officialdom in the German Democratic Republic, but he had read similar reports about the Federal Republic of Germany. Great Britain was the only ally to have protested at legitimating people who had made the unforgivable moral choice of joining the Nazis.

Henry could not find Diana, so tiring of the Greek antiquities, Henry left the Museum Island and curved down the Karl-Marx Alle where the workers had revolted against their Communist overlords in 1953. Hardheartedly, Henry had the cynical thought that they had arisen against their Bolshevik tyrants but not very many against their National Socialist ones. It bothered Henry that America, which had helped organize the flight of more than a few Nazi war criminals, had preached so moralistically about the holiness of its cause.

Henry wanted to get to see the interior of these apartment blocks, which were so routinely condemned in the West. Unfortunately, he had met no one who would invite him in. Yet, standing on the outside, Henry thought that they were no smaller, and seemed much more solidly built, than the one and a half room decaying apartment his mother and he had shared. These cramped quarters reminded him of the short periods they had spent together in the American South of his youth.

From here it was not far to the Soviet military cemetery at Treptow. Yes, even though his teachers had dwelled on the history of the Second World War in high school and university, the great sacrifice in life of the people of the Soviet Union had never been mentioned, not once in class. He could not even remember reading about it in his well-known, comprehensive history texts. Yes, the Russians soldiers had fought their way into Berlin overcoming the fascists. There was an eerie quality of being haunted around here. Built from the marble of Hitler's Reich's Chancellery, this structure must have given the soldiers' memories a sense of triumph, although Henry wondered what the people of the capital of the G.D.R. really felt in the depths of their hearts when they saw this memorial. After all, it had been they or their fathers and mothers who had been defeated in their struggle for an evil cause.

From the faces of the visitors it was hard to read any sign of involvement in this thing which, after all, belonged to a doomed past. It was getting late in the afternoon. The morning rain had stopped, though the dreary clouds still loomed overhead. Evidently this was an unusual day for Berlin which tended to be hot at this time of year. Henry wanted to take in the last of the monumental architecture so he returned to the eastern end of the main boulevard which he jokingly dubbed "Lime Tree." By the time he reached the Museum for German History, it was closed. As the best example of Baroque architecture in the city, this old city arsenal was worth beholding from the outside. The German State Opera and St. Hedwig's Cathedral transported him mentally to the eighteenth century. But he was jolted from this trance by a sense of urgency. He ought to return to West Berlin to avoid missing Kristina. So Henry quickly beheld the Brandenburg Gate before returning via the checkpoint where more orderly, bland officials quickly passed him through the routine check.

Henry was somewhat fatigued by the time he reached Kreuzberg at 18:30 hours. It was a pleasure to lie down for a short nap before Kristina returned. The day had been filled more with monuments than with people, despite his efforts at meeting some of the "locals," and he realized somewhat disappointedly that his tour of the old Russian Sector was superficial at best. Before he dozed off, Henry promised himself he would not try to generalize on the basis of such a limited experience.

CHAPTER 31

Kristina arrived about a quarter past 7:00 in the evening, and, even though she entered dramatically into the large chamber, she had to tickle Henry under his arms and sides to wake him up.

"What time did you get back?" she asked.

"Oh, just about a half hour ago," he yawned.

"Let me pour some tea into you, and then we can see some of the night life," Kristina gesticulated as though she were brewing it herself. Then she thrust her hand into his and gave him a hardy yank up from the bed.

Sensing the strength behind her soft grip, the young man wondered if she wanted to be animated friends or something more. Meanwhile, Kristina offered a report on her day as they quickly washed before leaving.

"I got my permanent Berlin address through some friends of close friends. By the time we finished catching up on the lives of our mutual friends, that took me until early afternoon. Then, after lunch, I headed to the bureaucracies. By the time I got all the official forms and submitted them to the right authorities after standing in line, they were just about to close. Then I forgot where I had parked and after rushing around trying to find my car, I wasn't able to make it here until just now. But I am looking forward to our evening together."

"Me too. Where shall we begin?"

"Let's start off at a café on the Ku-Damm."

"Don't forget that I'm a starving student."

On that comment, Kristina grabbed his collar and threw him towards the doorway in jest.

"Golly, you're strong."

"I had to learn to be around the two bulls I have for brothers," Kristina interjected as they went to find her Volkswagen parked a few blocks away.

195

In a few minutes they parked near the Ku-Damm and found a comfortable and reasonably priced beer hall. The many colors of the shops and light exhilarated the new friends who entered the building and ordered two mugs. Seated and eyeing the other patrons, Henry struck up the conversation with some small talk.

"Kristina, is it glamorous being an airline's stewardess?"

"Let's put it this way: you get to see many places and deal with many very different people. Some are nice. Others are O.K., and others are impossible," reflected the tall young woman as her thoughts skipped out of the old room. Then she continued, "You know, I love Berlin; it makes me feel free. Perhaps, it's the only tolerant place in Germany, yet I hardly know it at all."

Henry smiled; he liked this woman's spunkiness. "Where did you grow up?"

"Oh, in and around Munich, in Bavaria. My parents came from East Prussia just after the war. You know, Bavaria changed a lot after the war. Now there are now about as many Protestants as Catholics. My family was Polish and, of course, very Catholic. It's funny, you know, here in Berlin, the French Protestants, Poles, Jews, Bohemians, and others were much more integrated and accepted than elsewhere in Germany."

"Well, it's a question of degree, I guess. Big cities everywhere tend to be more open and permissive of great diversity among people. But, from what I've read, deep down even the liberal German Christian theologians never came to accept the sort of religious tolerance of Americans. I mean the attitude that there are some beautiful things about your beliefs and behavior that I can really appreciate and enjoy to see, even if they are different from mine."

"I have relatives in Chicago. It's a particularly dreadful city. My cousin there jokes, 'What's yours is mine and what's mine is mine.' That's no joke. People have no respect for public property there except for a few monumental buildings they keep up in the downtown area. But there's a bad side to Americans' tolerance too. People say, 'Hey, you do your thing, fine, and I'll do my thing, but if life works out that things aren't going well for you, then too bad! It's probably your fault. There's nothing or very little I can do to help you.' That's the big difference between what's happened here in Germany and the rest of northern Europe in comparison to your country since the end of the last world war. I can see that when I fly to America. The drawback to the way of life the Germans, Dutch, Scandinavians, and, to a lesser extent the English and Swiss, lead, is that the government protects you from life crises like poor health and unemployment. Still here in Germany, people, especially the bureaucrats, act as though they don't have to be nice and kind to others on a personal level. I guess that's why people respect me on the job. I add that little personal touch that many of the other stewardesses just are incapable of giving because deep down they're just thinking that this is just a job."

"Do you still encounter much anti-Polish feeling?"

"Not as an adult worker on the job. I'm so Germanized now people think of my differences as being individual. But in elementary school and as a young teenager, I learned who I was in no mistaken terms. We were living with many other poor refugees from East Prussia—what's now Poland—and they hadn't forgotten all the lessons of hatred they had been taught during the war. Maybe those were the times, but I don't think that's all the explanation. What do you feel here?"

"For me, it's weird. It looks like such a modern, lively city. It's like being on the *Champs Elysee* and Fifth Avenue. People seem to be having such a good time. But, you know, I've been here such a short time, I really can't say. The only thing I've noticed so far—and it could be purely a matter of chance—but usually there's something about me. I don't know what it is, but I meet people. Today in East Berlin, the only people I met were these two guys who wanted me to buy a few cartons of cigarettes for them. I lost some money in the exchange, and then they dumped me. But what's important, we sort of met one another first thing, and you're Germany too, you're of the new Germany whether or not you feel that way 100%."

Very briefly Kristina looked Henry deeply into the eyes. Then their hands met about the same time in the middle of the table. Interlocking they held their fingers and hands crisscrossed—tenderness radiating around them. Gently pulling her hands toward the bill, Kristina grabbed it, jumped up, and returned to the table, enthusiastically suggesting that they drive over to the Funktürm.

"How much do I owe for the tea?"

"Come on. You're still the student. I'm the stewardess."

"*Danke schön.*"

The radio tower had been built in the mid-twenties for the Third Broadcasting Exhibition. By the time they reached it, the last of the clouds that had darkened the atmosphere on both sides of the wall had lifted. The white lights of new and restored structures outlined the turquoise-to-blue of the early night sky. They could see for miles. An elderly professorial couple delighted in pointing out to the visitors the landmarks of their city: the

Victory Column, the Congress Hall, the Opera House, and many others were all concisely explained. It was a pleasant evening.

Henry gave into an urge to put his arm around Kristina, but, not wanting to appear aggressive, he interlocked his arm with hers. He could sense her approval by the special softness with which her hand touched his forearm, but her gaze was turning outwards from one section of the city below to the next. Henry noticed her long, manicured, polished nails like those of a model. He thought, *She's the only person I've gone out on a date with who polishes her nails*. It struck him that bodily adornment like this didn't necessarily damn a person as superficial and affected. *Kristina must look proper for her job*, he surmised.

"Let's go dancing," Kristina exclaimed more commanding than requesting.

"Fine with me, but I warn you that I'm really lousy."

"With rock and roll, you can't go wrong. Anybody can fake it."

"O.K. By the way, Kristina, when do you have to be back at work?"

"Not until next week. How would you like to come with me to Prague?"

"Oh, I'd love it.

"I've never been there, and I met some people visiting Germany this summer who've invited me over. I already have the visa. You want me to leave you over at the Czech Consulate tomorrow morning to see if you can get one in time, and then we can spend the rest of the day sightseeing in West Berlin."

"Do you think I can get a visa in a day? Things are pretty intense there now."

"Oh, with their liberalization program, it only took me a day to get mine. They want our marks and your dollars, and that's the way to get them fast."

Kristina started her car and headed for the *Nollendorfplatz* where she had heard from the passengers about some great dancing spots. "You know, young man, I'm old enough to be your big sister."

"All the better for controversy. I like shocking people."

"Henry, we're very much like them, the younger generation of Germans, I mean. But we're different too."

"What are you talking about?"

"Well, they've tried to reject their parents' values; just the way your generation is trying to do the same in America. I'm a few years older than you are, I guess. I'm twenty-eight and you're twenty-one—right—well, events have changed a great deal in those few years. My parents were working class.

So they pushed me into getting a practical job at which I could make good money. Well, I was pretty and cheerful, and I lucked out at landing this position at Lufthansa. I suppose if I had been a few years younger—your age—I would have stayed in school. Maybe, I'll even go back someday, who knows? I have a good time at what I do, but someday, maybe, I'll settle down. Who knows?"

"But you're lucky, like you get to make the acquaintance of so many different people. It must be exciting meeting people from all over, like that couple from Czechoslovakia."

"It is, but it also gets very tiring. For every nice person, there are twenty bores. Meeting Marianka and Jan was special. They're very rare. You'll love them. We wish the Czechs well in their efforts to put a human face on socialism—as they express it. I am really very interested in seeing what's going on there. It's so near and, yet, I've never been there."

"Oh, there's the club my passenger told me about," noted Kristina as she swung into the nearest parking spot. The couple entered holding hands. There were lights of reds, yellows, oranges, pinks, purples, whites and blues flashing all over the ceiling and walls scattered by a glass-mirrored globe reflecting the rainbow in all directions. The music roared and the floor throbbed with whirling, shaking, wiggling, and pulsating motions of individuals of every size and hair color. The young adults were generally clad in blue jeans.

"I must be the only *babka* here," screamed Kristina to Henry above the shrill sounds.

"Isn't the music great? It's not my usual pastime, but this is fun."

"What did you say?" shouted Kristina, barely audible above the high decibels.

"Wait until we get outside."

It was already 10 o'clock, and, besides a rest break for some beer an hour later, Kristina and Henry did not sit down until midnight. The sweat began to roll off both of them until Henry's plain black glasses' frames and unbreakable lenses fogged over from the heat of his perspiration. He took Kristina by the shoulder and spoke directly into her ear, "Heh, if we're going to see anything tomorrow, we better get some shut-eye."

"What's shut-eye?"

"Oh, sorry, it's cowboy slang for sleep. Don't you want to sightsee tomorrow?"

"Sure. Besides, the noise is beginning to get to this old lady. Maybe her bones will start creaking with arthritis tomorrow morning, and we won't be able to walk anywhere."

Awkward about being proper, always noticing her crucifix, Henry put his arms around Kristina's waist. Again he felt a melting warmth that indicated his gesture was not untoward; Kristina was a real woman, and he was still a boy becoming a man. Yet, he sensed, despite the worldliness of her occupation, that Kristina had, perhaps, a different sexual ethic from that of his generation who had been taught that sexuality was healthy and that happy, mentally, well-adjusted people should engage in their fair share of it, if they felt the need. Kristina was nobody's fool. She read a lot and was by no means yearning for a nunnery. Yet, Henry wasn't certain if her cross meant that nice girls wait for marriage, or that sexual union could be a good communion of a brother and sister in Christ. But he wasn't in Christ. Jesus was just another great prophet for him. Only God knew what Kristina thought about sexual morality or why, and he was afraid to ask her, so he waited and gazed at the flow of traffic and the flashing lights of the city at night.

Kristina smiled and every few miles turned her head affectionately his way as she was driving. Soon they were back in Kreuzberg where she parked a few blocks from their room. As they locked up the car, Henry took her hand and they walked in silence through the lighted street and up the old stairwell of their building. Finally in the room, Henry began to take off his clothes down to his underpants and slipped into bed. Kristina turned off the lights and stripped to her naked body, barely visible in the light of the moon passing through the large windowpanes.

Is this Kristina's way of saying without words that I may touch her? If we make love and she regrets it later, will I go down in her mind as just a seductive, oversexed Jew who lured an innocent Christian woman into his clutches? I better clean up this matter before I end up producing an anti-Semite for some ridiculous ancient prejudice, thought Henry just as Kristina rolled over on her side to face him.

"Kristina, I have to ask you something. Do you feel that it's morally O.K. to make love with someone before marriage? I mean I'm worried because you wear that crucifix, and I don't want there to be any misunderstanding because I'm Jewish."

"*Kotku*, of course, I think it's fine. It's good! Otherwise, I wouldn't be in bed with you. Listen Poles and Jews have been enjoying one another's bodies for around seven hundred years regardless of what their old priests and rabbis told them. To be honest with you, I think that Jesus, God, and the Blessed

Mother of God all think it's fine. I'm a modern woman. I am a believer, yes, but I believe that to be a good mother and wife, you have to be educated sexually, to feel comfortable with your sexual side, and practice makes perfect," she giggled again.

"Kristina, I'm sorry I brought all this up, but I guess that just being in this city makes me hypercautious of what I do as a Jew doesn't make Gentiles hold anything against the rest of my people. I'm like you, but my scriptural interpretation on this subject is taken from Margaret Mead, the American anthropologist. She was a religious Episcopalian, the America version of the Church of England, the Anglicans, you know."

At this point they stopped talking and just held one another. Kristina's tall body was soft around her hips and thighs, and her breasts were like huge, snow-capped mountains, firm at the base but flexible and soft like lichens near a geyser on an altitudinous lake near the summit. He licked and sucked her nipples as his hands nudged themselves between delicate folds, and, then, ascending her *mons,* rounding it with gentle pressure, his index and middle fingers pressed downwards towards the source of her pleasure. She was thrilled! Her ecstasy expressed its passion in rising sighs, as his member—its executive having forgotten its ethno-religious preoccupations of moments ago—grew, tucking itself firmly into the cover of her side. Quietly tearing the seal of his shield, he quickly pushed it down to the base, and mounted his female companion of desire. Henry liked the friction generated by rubbing against her walls—slightly warm and soothing—which gave way with a slight resistance. He rode her like a well-trained mare who pants ever rising to the heights of her steed. Their tongues engulfed themselves in one another—exploring the nooks of their mouths. With gusto and strength, Kristina hurled her cowboy onto his back while cushioning his fall under her great frame. From this position she began to fall and rise with the grace of equine leaps over regularly placed arches. Her gasps and scream was a climax to the first round of this equestrian feat, after which the then rider, now stead, reversed his supine passivity, to reassert his gallops to its surge of the movements, whence they reassumed their human equality in lateral repose.

CHAPTER 32

Having neglected to reset it for her vacation, Kristina's travel alarm sounded suddenly at 7:30 the next morning. The shrill noise awakened both of them from a sound sleep but bestirred their adrenaline. It was already very warm outside, and they were both glad to get up so refreshed for an early start.

Leafing through the telephone directory, Kristina jotted down the address of the Czech Consulate. "Henry, I'm going to drop you by the Czech place to see if you can get a visa first. I'll come up with you. If it's going to take long, I'll go someplace and meet you later."

"Sounds great!"

After their breakfast, they were the first pair to arrive at the Czechoslovakian Consulate. In about a half-hour after filling out the necessary forms and leaving his passport, it was promised that Henry should have a visa by tomorrow morning.

"I love zoos. Do you mind if we go to the Tiergarten first?"

"You surprise me. I didn't think you were the type."

"Gurr. No, seriously, I actually worked in a zoo in the South for several months when I thought I was going to be a primatologist. I love everything about the places except the rats and the reptiles. I guess I've never been able to get over some primitive taboos about them."

Kristina dressed casually, and Henry put on a fresh shirt and pair of pants to appear respectable enough to be with this sharp-looking older woman.

"Let's take the U-Bahn this morning," Henry requested.

"Are you sure you don't want to drive?"

"No, I'd really like to see their system of public transportation."

In no time, they had hopped on the underground, grabbed a coffee and a roll, and began inspecting one of the best zoos in the world. When they reached the lions' cages, Kristina inquired timidly of Henry, "Last night, you were really worried about leaving me with the wrong impressions, weren't you?"

Hesitantly, Henry replied, "Kristina, it's probably this place, Germany, that makes me so conscious of who I am. I usually just try to blend in with what I feel is right. I don't start out thinking, 'Well, first of all, I'm Jewish, and God forbid that anything I do may hurt my people,' but you know what the hell happened, and being here just soaks that into me."

"But we're not in Weimar. It's 1968, not 1928."

"Yes and no. You know, the Berlin Jews used to joke, 'What part of the Jewish religion do you practice?' They would answer that they read the *Berliner Tageblatt*—the liberal paper of Berlin, every morning. And, you know, most of my family's not even kept up with that much of its prophetic or scholarly values. Most of them have just held on to the small or large business ethic and the will to get ahead, and that's it. They believe in the American civil religion. That means that they'll say they believe in God. The Franco-Germans go to their temple once a week. The Russians go once a year. We're really watered down Unitarians."

"And you think that's wrong?"

"Yes and no. No, because some people think not standing out so much has meant that we're better accepted. Others disagree and say that our basic values are similar to the core American values and that would make us better accepted anyway. And, yes, it's wrong because it has made a subgroup of people like my family wishy-washy in matters of real ethical importance. My family today is like a lot of the German Jews who fought in World War I. They never asked why when Kaiser Willy told them to go. They thought that it would make the Gentile Germans think the Jewish Germans were full citizens; O.K. guys. Well, it didn't. I had to go to a fancy dinner given at one of my wealthy aunt's country clubs, and one of my aunts started getting so upset and saying what a horrible generation mine is—protesting the war in Vietnam and promoting civil rights. And you know, she couldn't give me one rational reason why she supported the war. She was for it because 'her country was for it, and that was that.' Her servants live in poor houses because that's what they can afford on the wages she pays, and she wonders why the Negroes are up in arms."

"But do you think that we debauch ourselves sexually like in Berlin in the 1920s? I don't. It's an entirely different scene. You know, after the runaway inflation of the early twenties, the middle class was ruined. People were selling their bodies to those who could afford to pay. Big bankers were buying pretty young women and handsome sailors right down on the main street where you were yesterday. Everyone was bragging about his or her sexual exploits as the best subject of conversation. But we're not like that today. We are more equal because we can afford to be. When we practice a greater equality toward the sexes today, we don't have to buy our sex; it comes between two people who are willing."

"I agree with you. Instead of exposing which companies reap the profits from the war, the TV and radio hosts complain about our free sex lives. Most people I know should have a fraction of the libertine sex the media claim we have. The Lenins of this world compare too-free sex to drinking out of rusty tin cans. They're afraid of it. They can't control it."

The new friends continued through the zoological garden for another hour before Kristina wanted to move on.

"But, Kristina, we only got to see maybe two hundred of their 13,500 animals!"

Kristina jumped up like a chimpanzee with her hands under her arms and began to prance around him.

"Oh, I get the point. Where would you like to go next?"

She came up to him and whispered in his ear, "Out to the *Wannsee* so I can compare your bottom to all the others parading around in the nude out there. But maybe first let's go up the Siegessaule. It's not far from here."

In a few minutes they had walked through the park over to the circular avenue called the Great Star. There, on the top, stood the monument that commemorated the German victory in the Franco-Prussian War. The monument had originally been placed in front of the Reichstag. As they climbed the 210 feet to the top, Kristina commented, "See, it's just what I told you. The German state was able to come together only through its foreign wars."

Concentrating on making it to the top, Henry didn't say anything until they reached the top. "Wow, the view from here is something else!"

Looking at her guide book, Kristina began to explain the various sights. "Down below us is the English Garden which the Berliners call the Garden of Eden, after Anthony Eden; over there to the east is the Schloss Bellevue where the President of West Germany resides." Pointing her hand toward the southeast, she continued, "That's where the Berlin Philharmonic is lodged; and to the right of us you are looking at the Museum of Applied Arts, the National Gallery and the State Library. Then over there to the west is the Technical University, the Conservatory of Music and the Academy of Fine

Arts. Those pretty colored apartments are the Hansa Viertel which has some excellent architecture in it."

As he peered out over the city, Henry told Kristina, "There is something attractive but not sensuously beautiful about this city. Berlin's *Tiergarten* doesn't grip me like the Djurgården in Stockholm which feels authentically part and parcel of nature. For being in a big city, the *Tiergarten* is still pretty, but the iron bars on the cages remind you that the police force is not far away."

"I sense the same thing, Henry. It's an exciting, fast-moving city. But there's something desperate about its trying to work and have fun. A while back in Dresden I went to an exhibition and saw some of Otto Dix's paintings from Berlin in the 1920s. You know, everything, everyone seemed so lonely and by themselves. You in America talk about 'being cool,' well, those people in their outlandish fluffy furs and tuxedos thought that they were the epitome of cool, and they appeared so uncaring to the veterans of the First World War. They passed many of the vets who maimed or went hungry every day. That must have added to their resentment which turned them to a madman like Hitler."

"Even their best writers missed the point. I read a long essay by Thomas Mann in my class in literature, and he defined Germanism as 'The mean, the middle, the mediator, the bourgeois spirit, the spirit of the middle class.' It would have been nice if Mann had been right. Underneath this surface, there is the passion of a Wagnerian *Wotan*. I guess that's why both of us feel somewhat ill at ease here for different reasons. But this place still intrigues me. Did you ever see Fritz Lang's *The Metropolis* or any of the other important films from Weimar?"

"Maybe, I can't recall."

"I went to a series on Weimar just before I left L.A. Well, of course, the movies were in black and white. One was silent. That always creates a heavier mood for us who see nearly everything in color. But the story was something else. The capitalist was a mean, bad man who controls the workers who literally live in a machine hell. There's a crazy scientist type who tries to mechanize everything so that the workers won't be needed anymore. His action leads to the capitalist's then flooding their part of the city. So he has to create a robot priestess who looks like the flawless, virginal religious woman who preaches moderation to the workers who love and listen to her. Then there's the son of the capitalist who discovers all the evil in the world and, while trying to mend it, falls in love with the good woman. Oh, yeah, the father-capitalist fires one of his most loyal employees who goes over to the son's side. But you get the idea, that although the workers' world is just about to drown, at the last moment love will win out, as the capitalist's son finally gets together with the saintly young woman, and father and son finally come to an understanding. I guess it ends with a bleak hopefulness."

Intrigued by Henry's description of the movie, Kristina then set it into its historical setting, "But the Nazis hated all this and were getting together all the others who hated all that was modern and international about Berlin in the '20s. There really were many different discontents. Some hated anything democratic. Others flaunted their nationalism and loved anything militaristic. Then there were common criminals and some that had lost all their values. None of them liked the jazz or the weird theater or the Bauhaus architecture."

Contemplating Kristina's view of his account of history, Henry tried to update it, "That's what's so different today. You don't see the mob's being manipulated out in the streets or stadiums. It's by TV today, plus we don't have that much time. I'm not sure if I could. Do you want to see the Cathedral of Ice, the 1936 stadium?"

"Henry, you seem a bit anxious about going there. There is so much else to see and do besides all those depressing things. How about having some *wurst* and something to drink on our way out to *Dalhem*? The museums there are supposed to be fabulous."

"You're the guide. You lead the way."

The rest of the afternoon went by so quickly that it left Kristina and Henry with that lightheadedness of a swirl gushing from and into everything that is magnificent. Traveling by the underground, they gobbled up their sausages and drank their juice by the time they arrived at the farmhouse-looking station with a thatched roof.

Within two hours they had been through galleries of the best of Durer, wonderful Holbeins, and *chef d'oeurvres* by Cranach, Van Eych, Botticelli and Raphael, Titians and a whole collection of genuine Rembrandts among many others. From there they rushed over to the ethnographic wing to take in the pre-Columbian Peruvian pottery and the South Sea Island masks, totems, canoes, and houses.

By five thirty in the evening, they were strolling on the nearby campus of the Free University.

"How are you holding up?"

"This old woman is full of energy."

"Me, too, I feel that we just got started."

"I know what you'd love. I'm going to take you to a student *kneipe*, and we'll just get a beer and watch what's going on."

Henry took her hand, "I'm having a marvelous time with you. Don't you feel exhilarated by all the things we saw? I'm really high."

"Me too."

They entered the rather modern pub of straight functional lines. The tobacco smoke was so thick it would take a Chinese butcher knife to cut through it. "I guess they haven't heard about lung cancer here."

Kristina laughed, "Californians are too health conscious. When I visit with my relatives in Chicago, the bars I've been to there are as smoky as the ones here."

"Remember that film festival I mentioned that I took in before leaving L.A.? There was another great Fritz Lang movie from Weimar I saw. It's *M.* The subject is just as bleak as in the *Metropolis*. This time it's about a murderer of little girls whom the police can't catch. So because the police raids are upsetting the underworld's business so much, they organize the beggars and others to find the psychopath whom they eventually catch. But the police coerce an underworld type whom they catch into tipping them off on where the criminals are holding the psychopath. They get in the nick of time to an old deserted brewery where they are trying the murderer in a kangaroo-style trial. Practically everybody in that movie smokes tobacco like fiends. They really never stop. The only difference I see here is that some of the student types are rolling their own cigarettes over there and nobody is smoking big cigars or pipes."

"You and your movies. What associations! Do you want to know what that fellow over there is so angry about?"

"Which one? They all look like they hate one another at that table!"

"Well, the guy who just pounded his hand on the table is shouting that Czechoslovakia is ruled by the same type of exploitative functionaries as the kind who rule in East Berlin. He thinks that is not the kind of society that Marx had wanted. Therefore, their group should write a letter to President Dubcek expressing their solidarity with his and the Czech people's attempts to liberalize Communism."

"Why is that tough-looking woman with the red bandana screaming, '*Nein,*' back at him."

"She just called him—excuse the expression—a dumb shit-head. She says he's playing the reactionaries' game and just because he grew up in East Berlin doesn't give him any special knowledge or insight into the workings

207

of their type of system. She says that while she thinks that the Czechs have the right to change their system that there are reactionary elements in their movement who would prefer to resurrect capitalism there."

"Why are all her friends sort of grunting?"

"They think she overstepped human politeness and comradely solidarity in insulting the intelligence of their brother intellectual-worker, and that calling him a 'shit-head' was a petty-bourgeois, low-type of insult that didn't merit her own inherent worthiness. Moreover, they think that the guy— Bertram is his name—is correct, and the reason that she is so indignant about it is really because her man-friend has been sleeping with Bertram as well as with her. Her name is Angela. They are evidently in the same commune."

"My goodness. They seem to be quite a lively group."

"I guess it's because of people like this that my parents discouraged me from going on directly to university. They needed the money, but, you know, we Poles are more conservative about many things in comparison to the Germans."

"Kristina, this pub is really interesting. Thanks for taking me here, but the smoke is starting to get to me. I know myself. If I stay here too much longer, I'll end up catching a cold, and I don't want to get sick if we end up making that long trip to Prague tomorrow."

"*Na zdrowie,* to your health!" Kristina chuckled hitting their mugs together for the last few gulps of beer. "Why don't we eat on the way home. I hear that there are some good, cheap Turkish places in the part of town where we're staying. And we can try to get to sleep early in case your visa comes through tomorrow."

"Good idea. Let's go."

By early evening the couple had arrived back in Kreuzberg. Not far from the underground station, Kristina started running towards some point that had struck her eye. Not exactly sure what was the cause of her sudden burst of energy and enthusiasm, Henry sprang after her until they stood in front of a simple structure with the word, *LOKANTA,* inscribed in plain letters on the window. Taking his hand, Kristina led him in. Just inside the entrance there were a dozen or so piping hot dishes set on a big steam table. She mumbled something to the middle-aged restaurateur with a day's growth of beard. Her pronunciation sounded like, keh-BAHP-chuh. The fellow put some of the kebabs of roasted meat on one of the large, plain white plates, which had mysterious, brownish circular marks alongside slightly grayish cracks. They appeared to be recovered rubble, scrubbed and polished with care so as to be revived for the present age. Kristina's next request rang "kuy-mah-LUH" in his ear. At this command the server put a large piece of pita with some ground meat on his plate. Then this connoisseur of Turkish cuisine ordered "dew-EWN," a kind of egg and lemon soup. Promptly two bowls were brought to the table that she had indicated with her protruding arms and index finger. A few single men were smoking a pungent tobacco, drinking small cups of coffee, and munching on pastry. As soon as Kristina and Henry seated themselves in front of this feast, the owner of the restaurant came to their table with a large metal platter. There were the *Meze* from which Kristina chose a flaky pastry for herself and a stuffed squash for her companion. With a final magical utterance, Kristina's omen for the evening brought forth two glasses of a whitish drink. This was a mixture of yogurt and spring water.

Before Henry had a chance to comment on this exotic Middle Eastern bill-of-fare, Kristina clinked her glass of *ayran* onto his, "Here's to a great trip with my *Amerikanische Freund.* This is my treat to wish Czechoslovakia success—not like that Angela back at FU."

Pleasantly stuffed and drowsy, Kristina and Henry exited the Turkish restaurant and walked back to her car, which she wanted to park closer to their accommodations.

"Wow, it's really been a full day!"

"And I am full!"

"They used to joke with me this summer in Stockholm when I tried to practice my little Swedish. I would say, *"Jag är full,"* thinking I meant I am satiated by the food, but *full* in Swedish means "drunk," so all my friends would roar at this mistake which I made all too often. I'd end up laughing at myself too!"

"Just slight differences in similar languages often cause such comedies. I bet I'll get into quite a few funny scenes in Prague tomorrow trying to speak Polish and be understood in Czech. For example, I've been dying to call you *kotku* since yesterday but have held off because I thought you'd think me silly calling you "kitten"—it's our Polish diminutive for sweetie or honey or darling."

"If only my visa comes through!"

"Yes, let's get to bed right away so we can be the first ones at the consulate tomorrow morning. If it comes through, we can pull out right away," Kristina replied as they were mounting the stairwell of the pension.

Once in the room they hurriedly performed the rite of laving their mouths and faces, jumped into the wide bed, and began to hold one another in a gentle, prolonged embrace. Then, lying on his right side, Henry tucked his head between her arm and breast and placed his left leg over her thighs and knees as Kristina lay sleeping on her back. In Henry's dreams this position both recaptured the protection of the mother goddess—purified in Kristina's Catholic Virginal Mother of God—while offering her peaceful cover. Then they turned, Kristina on her back, Henry on his frontside, as though they restated their rights to individuality. By dawn, face to face, they entwined ventrally—their isolation insufficient to bring rest.

And so they awoke the next morning at 7:00 A.M.

CHAPTER 33

After a strong coffee and a roll creamed with butter, they rushed over to inquire about the fate of Henry's application. At 8:30 the doors to the building were still closed, so they began to wait outside. Kristina took Henry's hand, "Don't worry, someone should be here by 9:00."

"I'm just thinking how much I'll miss you if you have to go all by yourself."

"You don't want me to go, then, if your visa doesn't come through?"

"No, you know I believe absolutely in everyone's freedom to do what he or she wants as long as that person doesn't hurt anyone else."

"But won't I hurt you if I go?"

"I'd wish I were with you, but I realize these are the only few days you have to visit Prague and be with Jan and Marianka. And, if you were to write me a long letter telling me about your stay, I'd imagine that I had come along too."

"I don't know if freedom means so much to me. I could have just as much fun seeing all the things we have missed so far in Berlin. We've just barely touched the surface of the city. And I like being with you very much."

"I feel the same about you, Kristina, but I don't want to interfere with this trip you've been looking so forward to."

"Come on, cheer up. We're acting as though they didn't grant you the visa, and we don't even know yet."

As Kristina spoke these words, a straight-faced guard opened the door to the Consulate and the other people who had joined them lined up to be served by the Czechoslovakian officials.

Kristina translated for Henry into German as he refreshed the consular officer on the details of his application. The official walked back to a filing cabinet and pulled out his record and walked back over to a desk. Skimming through this file, her expressionless face then broadened into a slight smile. "Mr. Green, I am pleased to present you with your visa to Czechoslovakia. Have a good stay."

Beaming with a grand smile, though not uttering a word, Kristina translated for Henry. Slowly picking up his documents, he looked over the visa and thanked the polite, slightly pudgy, middle-aged woman with the semi-combed hair.

The couple walked upright out of the building, and when back at Kristina's car, they jumped. "Yeah, we can make our trip," yelled Henry.

"Well, we did miss the Charlottenburg Palace, the Philharmonic, the Berlin Museum, and a stroll in the Grünewald Forest."

"Don't you think we can try taking in just a few of these things before we leave? We could take off later in the afternoon."

"I'd prefer setting out early for Prague, but, if you insist, I'd rather like to see the Charlottenburg Palace."

"And I'd like to take in the Bauhaus Museum."

Spontaneously shifting their plans for an early departure, the two friends—having become serious Berlin tourists—drove over to the second home of the Prussian rulers. Kristina dashed about the long halls with Henry tagging along until she stopped in the New Wing in a room with the Boucher tapestries into which the love affairs of Bacchus and Ariadne or Naxos and Venus seducing Vulcan at the Forge were woven into fading tones. From Frederick the Great's old apartments, Henry tugged Kristina to the Egyptian Museum in the east guardhouse where they stood in front of Nefertiti's almost thirty-four hundred year-old bust. Kristina reasserted her fast overview guiding them through the Museums of Pre- and Protohistory and Greek and Roman Antiquities, where they stopped only briefly to examine some of the ancient Egyptian jewelry. By late morning they found themselves strolling through the formal palace garden past a grove of cypress and into the English Garden. A guide claimed that these had been restored much as in the time of Friedrich-Wilhelm III. Kristina whispered to Henry, "Those pretentious old goats are likely to say whatever they feel like to appease all the tourists. I know. I get that way sometime myself on the airplane when I have to deal with particularly loathsome passengers."

"Kristina, I know you're in a hurry to get out of town, but let's just see one last thing, the Bauhaus Museum."

"I don't see what you like so much about that Bauhaus architecture."

"Who said I like it? I'm just interested in the twenties in Germany. You know, they were expelled from Weimar in 1925 and from Germany in 1933," commented Henry as he dashed across the street impervious to the red signal. Kristina stayed waiting for the light to change.

On the other side a hefty sixtyish-year-old man grabbed Henry's collar and huffed, "*Achtung, Jüde!*" as he pointed at the street sign Henry had neglected. Aroused, a chill going down his back, Henry thought, *Imagine, after all these years, and it's still around here.* Crossing the street on the go signal, Kristina remarked, "Hey, that old man got pretty upset with you for crossing on the wrong light."

"Yep, he sure did."

A few steps beyond this incident, they resumed their discussion of the Bauhaus. "That's the whole point. They were trying to end the division between art and the technical aspects of the industrial age. I don't like a lot of their minimalism like all those plane rectangular boxes of steel and glass that look alike all over the western world. But I don't think that Walter Gropius or Oskar Schlemmer or most of their other members would have liked this boring new conformity that resulted in trying to ape their style."

"Henry, it's already three, and I need a coffee before we set out."

CHAPTER 34

The line of automobiles leading out of Berlin and crossing into East Germany was long like an interminable queue of L.A. smog-makers in rush hour.

Suspecting but unsure of whether or not Kristina was a virulent anti-Communist, Henry thought it better not to get into a discussion of politics and life in the Eastern European block. He would simply to wait for the discussion to emerge in their weekend with Jan and Marianka. Kristina was just too much fun to push into a too-heavy discussion. She tended to avoid serious talk by abruptly changing topics with jokes or pushes or tickles. Yet, Henry tended to be too cerebral to avoid these verbal jousts. Given the right moment, he feared his shield would give way. In his rigorous high school's puritanical, authoritarian atmosphere, he had been trained to suppress words for the correct occasion. This education was antithetical to his character.

Kristina concentrated on the road ahead and turned on her radio, which was broadcasting a lively rendition of a Brandenburg Concerto. Outside Henry found the contrast between the large collective East German farms and those of the smaller privately-owned farms in Western Germany an intriguing etch into the human landscape of mankind's contrastive social systems. Peering as driver and tourist on the lovely verdant countryside, they sat quietly watching the view as the road rolled underneath them.

About two hours outside of Berlin, Kristina suddenly noticed that the sky was filling with airplanes and in the distance in front of them, she caught eye of what appeared to be a convoy of tanks on the sparsely-traveled road. The snappy melody of the Brandenburg Concertos gave way to a gruff-sounding news bulletin. Kristina's calm, quiet, domestic-driving serenity shifted into a mouth agape with fear and foreboding.

"Henry, something strange is going on."

"What? Kristina, this isn't anything to kid about. What did the news broadcast say? The only thing I understood was the names of many countries."

Before she had time to reply, an East German militia car pulled her over to the side of the road. A grim, very tall officer said something to Kristina and pointed for her to drive forward. She followed his car a few minutes up the road to a small highway patrol structure.

Kristina had enough composure to tell Henry, "*Kotku,* if anything happens to me, call my family in Munich. Here's their address and telephone number. Ask for my brother, Andrzej. He speaks English well. They'll take care of everything. Don't say anything more to the East German authorities other than the basics. We're going to Prague, that's it!" Then she pulled into the parking lot, got out, firmly closed her door and walked briskly to the checkstand. Straight behind, Henry followed her.

Oh, Matko boska! Holy Mary, Mother of God, thought Kristina to herself in Polish. *Please, don't let them send me back to that village in Silesia where I was born.*

"Your passports, please," the military-looking officials requested in polite, if somewhat austere, German. "Please, come with me," the chunky, middle-aged matron signaled to Kristina.

"*Verstehen Sie Deutsch?* inquired the fiftyish stout man in military attire of Henry.

"*Ein bischen, aber ich kann russisch sprechen.* Я говорю по-русски (I speak Russian.)"

The heavy, gray-blue eyes of the state policeman carefully fingered the pages of Henry's passport, which he took to a small room in the back. Another man in his fifties with a round face and civilian attire came out and addressed him with a big smile and handshake.

"Welcome to the German Democratic Republic, товарищ Green. How long are you intending to spend in Czechoslovakia?" the official asked in a friendly German-accented Russian.

How weird he addressed me as 'comrade,' thought Henry to himself and then responded, "Just this long weekend with my friend, Kristina."

"I am sorry for this inconvenience but due to temporary difficulties, we will have to reroute you to the Federal Republic of Germany. You may sit over there while you wait for your friend," the officer apologized courteously. He was obviously delighted to have an opportunity to practice his Russian. He then shook Henry's hand and escorted him over to a

215

comfortable, cushioned seat before he withdrew to his small office on the other side of the partition.

Wondering how long they would delay Kristina, Henry withdrew his copy of the *Report of the National Advisory Commission on Civil Disorders.* As he began to read, his mind drifted and his eyes followed the stout woman who trudged to Kristina's car and began to go through carefully all of her luggage, seats, trunk and glove compartment.

An hour and a half had already elapsed, and Henry could no longer concentrate on his reading. He knew they had absolutely nothing to hide unless Kristina was carrying some contraband or forbidden literature about which she had not informed him. *Why are they being so lenient with me while spending so much time with Kristina?* he wondered. *It's time to do something,* thought Henry, who walked over to the counter, and, again speaking in Russian, asked to speak to the official who had dealt with him.

"Excuse me, but Herr Schmidt will not be back for sometime," the first attendant replied in slow German. She exuded a politeness underwritten by fear.

"What are you doing with Kristina?" Henry asked in Russian.

The woman apologized for not speaking either Russian or English, but replied in a very slow German that Kristina was fine and would be out at the end of their examination. "Please sit back down," the frightened public servant bid him as she left the front desk unattended to speak to her comrade behind the partition.

Henry waited another half-hour, and this same scene was repeated in approximately the same words. Again he rapped his knuckles on the front desk and another heavy-set woman came out apologizing for the delay but explaining that it was just a routine check that would be over as soon as they had verified everything.

Henry's mind focused on the boards out of which this barracks structure had been constructed. *Were these ash or elm or birch?* Then he began to focus on the coarse lines of Walter Ulbricht's face. There was sternness in its cold, rough features that contrasted with the benevolently industrious seriousness of Friedrich Engels or the studied schlumpiness of Karl Marx's public portraits of utter sobriety. *What in the hell are they doing with Kristina? What in the hell can I do about it?* Henry thought, searching for a public telephone.

He arose, rolled his knuckles on the wooden counter, and the second of the stuffy women officers finally came out. This round Henry assumed an aspect of authority and stated most affirmatively in Russian, "Kristina has been interrogated for five hours. Neither she nor I have anything to hide and have done no wrong. We would like to leave immediately!"

By now the older woman turned somewhat pinkish and her hands were trembling. She replied in German she would be back shortly. Within minutes both of the attendants came out accompanying Kristina who was sweating and had bags under her eyes. The folds of her brow were tightened with tenseness and her hands were clenched. She peered at Henry and then marched forward to the car. Henry stepped quickly after her but refrained from saying anything until they entered her automobile. As she started up her engine, she refrained from speaking anything except quickly wrote, "Maybe bugs; don't talk until we are back in West Germany!" Then she clenched both of his hands tightly.

The next hours stretched themselves out endlessly. Finally past the border crossing, Kristina requested a private gasoline station mechanic to check whether listening devises had been placed in her car. She suspected something unusual. Back in West Germany, Kristina breathed deeply, got out of the car, crossed herself, and then shook with a big chill. "I was so frightened," she sighed.

"You're safe now. I must be an imbecile. Me, who takes such great pride in keeping up on world events, didn't bother reading a newspaper since we met. I bet that's why that commune's rap in that beer place near FU the other night was so intense." Standing, Henry held Kristina in his arms for the first time in public.

"I just want to get back home to Cologne. You know, they weren't mean to me. They were even formally polite. It was just the situation. They were so damn thorough and slow. They asked me everything, and I was honest in my answers about everything except the West Berlin registration of my automobile. I just said that I would go back to visit my parents in Munich after they let me go. But they were ever so afraid of you. What did you do?"

"I spoke to them in Russian. That's what. None of them knew any English to speak of. The only one who spoke a foreign language was that guy in civilian clothes, and I suspect he was part of their state security police. So here I am, a young fellow with an American passport, who speaks Russian well. I think that fellow thought I might be a KGB or CIA agent, and he wasn't going to take his chances—plus he was just pretty proud about his command of Russian and was glad to have a chance to demonstrate it."

"Yes, it's beginning to make sense now. They see that I am a Polish-speaking woman, born in the Eastern Block. I have a passport of the Federal

Republic of Germany, and I am in the company of a Russian-speaking American. That's probably why those old potatoes were so nervous with me. They were probably as frightened as I was. They must have thought that if we were KBG agents we must have been testing them. If we were CIA agents, they must have guessed that we were trying to gather as much information as we could from them. We were just too unusual to be ordinary citizens."

"Kristina, do you mind turning on the radio so we can find out what's going on?"

"Sure, in just a minute. If it's O.K. with you, I'm going to head straight for Cologne. I'm still pretty edgy and just feel like being home. We still have the rest of the weekend for us."

Placing his hand on her thigh, Henry watched this lovely goddess drive like a pilot flying at such a velocity that, as the terrain streaked by, only the main features struck his eye. As they sped westward on the *autobahn*, Kristina reviewed the constant flow of news on the air. "Henry, no wonder they sent us back. The Warsaw Pact countries sent about 175,000, mostly Russian, troops into Czechoslovakia at 11 P.M. last night. They are occupying the major cities of the country that they call their ally. Can you imagine neither the Czech President, nor the Chairman of their National Assembly, nor the First Secretary of their Communist Party claim they knew anything about this move? The National Assembly and the Central Committee of the Communist Party have been called to discuss the situation, but neither the Czech Army nor the People's Militia has been called to resist this obvious invasion. That's why I must have seen all those airplanes and tanks this afternoon. I knew something horrible was happening, but I couldn't piece it together. This really makes a lie out of their so-called democracy. The radio broadcast says the entire Czechoslovak nation is supporting its leaders except for a handful of Moscow puppets."

"I just can't figure out why they would do such a thing. What do they have to gain from it?" Henry inquired beseechingly.

"For one thing, they can put down any attempt at open discussion in the East Block for a long time. Second, that protects their greedy bureaucrats from any criticism or change. And third, it's a not-so-subtle way of putting all of its satellites down, of telling them Moscow is still the boss and they might as well stay used to that fact."

Henry felt saddened by this whole turn of events but kept thinking that it would ruin his relationship with Kristina if this discussion continued to any depth. "Yes, the Soviet leaders are crude klutzes now just as they were in

Hungry in 1956. But I still don't think the Soviet Union is one big hell. The fact of the matter is that the Red Army beat the Nazis—thank God—and that in winning they were in military control of what is today Eastern Europe. Had Britain, America, and their allies been prepared to pay with more of their own human lives, they would have been in control of those countries, and the war in Europe would have dragged on longer. Churchill, Roosevelt, and Stalin had agreed beforehand upon this plan at Yalta, anyway. And don't forget that Slovakia had a strong Fascist Party, which rather willingly cooperated with the Nazis. It was led by Father Tiso, a Catholic priest, who was a Nazi-sympathizer. It's too bad that the Russians won't permit any dissent now, but maybe they will gradually allow more in the future if they don't feel so threatened by constant wars. The Czechoslovaks were brave to try their experiment, and there has been negligible bloodshed according to the news we have so far. If America were serious about supporting democracy now, it is time for it to help the Czechs. Our generals, the president, and the congress are great at rhetoric, but that's it when it falls out of their sphere of influence!"

"But, Henry, people have to stand up for their freedom, or it will be grabbed away from them. You have to stand up to the Russians, or they'll take and take and take some more. *Kotku*, I am worn out and depressed over this whole thing. I'm worried about Marianka and Jan, too. Maybe I can get through to them when we get to Cologne."

"That's a good idea. Would you think of sponsoring them to live in West Germany?"

"That's a good idea. I'll offer, but I doubt they'd accept. They're so wrapped up in what's going on in Prague, I don't think they'd leave even if they could—unless they're under a real threat, and I don't think they are because they're young artists. They're not all that political except for their nasty jokes about corruption and their offbeat art. They're pretty marginal bohemian types. I don't know why we hit if off so well except they are such a happy, fun-loving couple."

At the wheel, Kristina had become straight-faced and attentive only to the road—everything else was irrelevant at the moment. She did not really listen to all the details and contradictory interpretations of the Czech events that were filling every bit of airspace. Henry was trying to figure out the German broadcast but was grasping only the gist of the various news items. He began to wonder how the invasion of Czechoslovakia was going to influence the American elections, and, from his perspective, he was sure that only bad would come of it. It would give ammunition to the militarists who were convinced we couldn't trust the Russians, and it would give salvos to the hawks who demanded escalation of the war in Vietnam and wars in other places in the world. All this was so depressing and anxiety provoking that he shut off the radio and gently stroked Kristina's right knee.

With a few stops for gasoline, they had reached Cologne by the wee hours of the morning. Kristina was exhausted both physically and mentally, and after Henry had carried her luggage and his backpack into her apartment, she hopped into her bed, stomach-down, head-covered by pillows, and was impervious to Henry's late entrance. She did not even notice that he had interlaced his fingers with her own. She dreamed of the decrepit suitcases and unending lines of people like her parents holding her and her brothers' hands on their way out of the "new" Poland. Then the nasty taunts and names of her childhood neighbors came back. It was a very ugly world, said a black demon, and, suddenly, she fell into a maelstrom of infinite dark smoke. Within this vortex was total repose.

The light of the afternoon sun sparkled off the perfectly polished floor onto Kristina's handmade quilt. It was already three in the afternoon, and Henry lay propped up on Kristina's pillows of roses, irises, and daffodils. He glanced around her sparsely furnished room. The only decorations were a few large wall hangings that distinguished themselves from the weavings of Navaho Indians by having less intricate patterns of fewer shades and earthier tones. In her sleep Kristina's long blond hair softly swirled around her back and covered her breasts and sides. Only in her sleep did she let it all hang down. In her sleep her eyelids were tightly shut, and her mouth was pressed tightly onto her teeth. In the corner of her bedroom she had placed a plain wooden chest of drawers and on the other side of the bed was a small writing table. He walked over to the window and looked out onto the beige exterior of the apartment building from which he could see the Rhine River. Kristina had heard him stir and sprang over to the window to embrace him.

"Let's have a nice quiet day to recuperate. I'll show you the city where I've lived now for five years. I like it very much, and it's becoming a real home to me," she said as she poured the coffee into the filter and began to boil water. Have you ever tried this Swiss Müesli? It's filled with barley, oats, malt, and you name it."

"No, it sounds yummy. Breakfast is my favorite meal of the day."

"I'd hardly call this breakfast at 15:30 in the afternoon."

"Well, I guess World War III hasn't broken out yet. You want to find out what's happening?"

"I don't think I can listen to it right now. Let's just have some peace and quiet for a while. I want to take you for a long walk down our 'little Nice' along the banks of the river and then maybe around some of the old city; perhaps even out to where I work."

In her living room the telephone rang, and Kristina called out, "Just pour yourself a cup of coffee."

Henry could hear a dejected tone of surprise, followed by pleading anger, then resignation in the long conversation that was rolling on in the next room. He wondered if it had anything to do with the events in Czechoslovakia. But his mind quickly turned to more practical urges, like the irresistible desire to cut the loaf of dark bread which Kristina had put on the table next to a heaping round porcelain butter dish inviting to be spread with a short wooden knife. His will power gave in and he decided to munch a slice along with the strong dark brew in front of him.

About fifteen minutes later Kristina returned from the entrance corridor. Her face was long and dejected, but she took Henry's hand. "*Kotku*, I have to fill in for my girlfriend on the flight to London tomorrow."

"Oh, Kristina, why? Can't you get out of it?"

"I tried. She's tried all the other stewardesses. They're all scheduled to fly elsewhere, and she has to go into the hospital tonight. It's an emergency. They'll operate on her tomorrow or the next day."

They shared poses of longing, then Kristina sat down and circled her hands around her coffee cup and put her feet on top of Henry's under the table. She poured some milk on her cereal and offered him some as well. So domestic in her white robe and uncombed hair, she sipped her coffee and nibbled the grains.

Quickly finishing her wake-up meal, Kristina went back to the telephone and attempted to call Prague. After a few minutes she shouted, "Henry, all telephone lines are 'temporarily not in working order,' according to this operator. I'll try reaching Marianka and Jan later when we come back."

After breakfast they walked along the lover's lane down by the Rhine. Along its banks were blooming trees and flowers that gave the earthen path a Mediterranean ambiance. Like the few other couples in their view, they walked in silence, her hand on his shoulder, his on her hip. There was a clean breeze that left the air with a fresh sweetness from the smell of luxuriant vegetation.

"This city goes all the way back to Celtic and Roman times. It gets its name, Cologne, or Köln in German, from the Latin *Colonia Claudia Ara Agrippinensis*. Later it became part of the Kingdom of the Franks, and

Charlemagne made it an archbishopric. During the Middle Ages, it was one of Germany's most important towns and was tied with Lübeck for first place in the Hanseatic League. Today it's really the capital of this part of Germany."

"Can we ride the streetcar over there?"

"Sure, how about taking it over to the Dom, the Cathedral. It's the most famous landmark in the city and took over six centuries to complete. We can climb the tower there, and you can see out over the whole city. Do you mind accompanying me to the mass this evening? I need it. Maybe, it's the best way to help the Czechs—we can pray for their safety and protection."

On nearing the monument, they sat down on a bench across from the cathedral and admired its blackened majestic spires, which exuded the strength of stone that had withstood the tests of centuries of warfare. Kristina stood up and gently pulled Henry across the square into the immense space, a guilded crypt filled with the treasures of centuries of the spirit, of this center of trade and commerce.

CHAPTER 35

As Kristina prayed, Henry gazed upward at the immense vault of this French Gothic cathedral that had taken from the mid-thirteenth to the late nineteenth century to complete. It was as though this scattering of people would ascend to God by the lights hanging midway between the floor and the ceiling. Casting his eyes up and down the nave, he counted fifty-six pillars. The Christ and Mary over the high alter appeared to be almost laughing at a funny joke—or was he just seeing poorly at a distance? Meanwhile Kristina knelt in prayer. Her innocence sparkled and cooled her effervescent energy.

At the conclusion of the mass Kristina led him closer to Stephan Lochner's lovely *Dombild* depicting the kings of the orient bringing gifts to the infant Jesus seated on Mary's soft blue lap. Although painted, the faces resembled a medieval photograph of the ancient world. The angels looked like living cherubim flying in a sky of the deepest gold, and the dove of the cover hovered like an exotic white bird above pure lilies. Henry was unexpectedly touched by the animate quality of the delicateness and gentleness of these people until his good feeling was immediately changed into one of queasiness as they passed in front of a symbol of hatred. In a wooden relief on a fourteenth-century chair rest, an artist had carved Jews—depicted by the stereotypical pointed hats—sucking and embracing a swine, a sign of the despised Jew.

On leaving this great religious monument, they meandered around the fifteenth century restored buildings of the Old Market and through the closely packed oriels of the Luthereck and the Gothic houses of the Bendergasse. Kristina could sense the mixed emotions in Henry's tenseness, so she tried to soothe his hurt. "Henry, I know that old chair must have offended you. But don't forget during the massacres of the Jews during the Crusades that the bishops of Cologne and Speyer stopped the riots at their beginning and punished the rioters with death and dismemberment."

"It's strange how all these old things get to me," Henry replied. Then Kristina changed the topic of conversation, "Let's go back to my car, and I'll take you by some of the conference centers and out to the airport where I work."

Kristina was getting back to her usual busy self. Henry already sensed her drive that constantly pushed her into motion. She twisted here and bent there, while seeming to sweep inexhaustibly in all directions. Now her energy propelled her into imaginative shortcuts on public transportation that led them back to her flat within a quarter of an hour. Neither of the young lovers contemplated the outcome of their interpenetrating past the precipice of tomorrow. They were rapidly devouring the joy of being together in the here and now.

With rapidity and daring, Kristina swung her VW around the corners of the rebuilt and new city. Her driving left Henry with a kaleidoscopic memory of Cologne from the guilded relics of the three kings in the Dom to the purity of forests and spans. The eight bridges over the river dirtied the waters of the Rhine even more in Henry's eyes.

"Kristina, of all the people I've ever met, you must be the most on the go!"

"Sometimes it even leaves me whirling!"

In a few minutes they stopped at a small restaurant among stores in a modern suburb. Kristina ordered, and the waiter brought out two dark mugs of beer and a couple of long Frankfurters with two small buns and a strong, slightly biting mustard on the side.

"Well, they sure beat our hotdogs, but I rate them under Copenhagen's hot *pølser.*"

Snappily downing her beer, Kristina smiled and ordered another. Knowing his intolerance of drugs of any kind in any but the smallest amounts, Henry slowly swished the mellow liquid around his mouth as a chaser to the greasy meat.

After their fast food, Kristina—cheered up by two beers—pressed her foot more heavily on her gas pedal. The car dashed down the tree-lined side streets and back onto the main roads. This route delivered them at the large airport all too much in a jiffy for Henry's taste.

"So here's my bread and butter—isn't that how you refer to it? Let's get out here. I have to be out of here by 9:00 A.M. tomorrow morning."

"I'm surprised it's so much like our airports back home."

"America isn't the only place to have the last word in modernity, now is it?" Kristina commented as an enormous Lufthansa taxied down the runway near them. "There's one last place I'll show you tonight because we're going to have to get up by 6:30 at the latest tomorrow morning, if I'm going to get you down to the train station and get myself to work on time."

She skidded around a circle and drove a new way through some large contemporary housing projects back down to the central city where she parked. Kristina jumped out of the car, ran to Henry's side, yanked him out of the seat by both hands and then started skipping down a few dark side streets until they reached an outdoor mall—a long somewhat curving street for pedestrians only.

"Hey, this is neat. I like the round large pots of flowers and plants and the sleek, plain lampposts, but most of all, no cars between all these stores on both sides."

"It's pretty deserted now, but you should see it during the day when it is packed with people shopping and sightseeing from all over Europe and many other continents too," Kristina observed with an undaunted air of civic pride. The couple strolled down the promenade and back to her VW. Her spirited maneuvering of gears, pedal, and clutch caused her bug to leap forward. Within a few minutes, they were climbing the small stairs leading to her fourth-floor flat.

Kristina hung her jacket in a closet before placing her off-white slip and dress onto the wooden chair by her desk. Henry followed suit, and they stepped into the hot shower. Its waters gushed in a firm stream from the silvery rounded head with a circumference the size of a grapefruit. Kristina flung her head backwards and took the cake of soap with which she rounded Henry's feet in small circles. After lingering around his penis, she moved upwards under his arms both on his back and front up to his forehead which she outlined in rounded strokes. Then she placed the soap back in its dish. This was the first time Henry had ever showered with another person, and the sensuousness of her sudsing left him with a protruding erection that sought the mouth of her vagina. Controlling his urge, he too picked up the bar of cleanser and wound it both over her belly and buttocks until she giggled from the tickling of his glans next to her soapy major lips. After covering her limbs, he took her feet and sat in the bottom on the small tiles and massaged each of her feet from toe to heel before moving his nose into her large frontal opening. Her laughter rose uncontrollably and subsided only in mounting breaths as he inserted his tongue around this soft orifice. Unhurriedly, he worked his center of taste around her entranceway as though he were consuming a delicious scoop of bubble gum ice cream. Her breath shortening, Kristina shut off the shower and grabbed an enormous white fluffy towel, which she wrapped both around herself and her lover. Then she handed him another thick cotton towel, and they both thoroughly whisked off all the water from their bodies before the steam had begun to form drops of precipitation on her large bathroom mirror.

Henry wrapped his arm around her waist, and they stepped into her bedroom where they enlaced themselves face-to-face, tongue-to-tongue before Henry inserted himself into Kristina whom he then gently pulled down upon himself on the edge of the bed. Kristina worked her way up and down over him, until at the end of her prolonged gasp, Henry slowly pulled her fully onto the bed. In an interlude, they ran opened fingers alongside one another's still wet hair before Henry assumed the position of a British missionary at the height of the empire. His discharge was gradual but with such a mounting thrill that both Kristina's excitement and his pleasure melted into a sudden but joyous prelude to their last rest together cheek-to-cheek, fingers intertwined.

CHAPTER 36

For a farewell, Henry crossed the square back to the Dom whose dark spires jutted their edges into the blueness of the upper sky. He sat for a few minutes fascinated by its intricate carved stone and stained glass set against the backdrop of the plane flat surfaces and glass of its functional modern neighbors on the other sides of the *platz*. Once again he circled the church trying to recall how the flying buttresses supported the enormous walls.

Returning to the *Bahnhof*, Henry took one final glance at the cathedral through the panoramic glass front. High above in the middle, the round clock slightly interrupted the view with the handy reminder that it was half past seven in the morning. Becoming more proficient in reading the European boards of the arrival, departure, and track of trains, Henry figured out that he could leave for Amsterdam in twenty-five minutes.

As he observed the moderately-busy, circulating crowd, a dark-haired man in a crumpled gray suit coat and dark blue pants came up to him and inquired in Spanish, "Are you new in Cologne?"

"No," Henry replied. "Do you live here?"

"Yes," the fellow—around his same age—replied, "life is hard for us here, but we make better money than at home. I was sure you were Spanish."

"No, but you're not the first person this summer who thought I was from southern Europe. How long have you been here?"

"Six years."

"Have you made friends with any of the local people?"

"No, we say 'good day' at work, but my friends are all Spanish. That's the way it is."

"Well, it's been nice talking to you, but my train to Amsterdam is leaving in a few minutes. Good luck!"

"Good-bye," the young man repeated seeking other new arrivals at this point of entry—perhaps to share his apartment or just to make a friend.

Henry stepped up his gait to the proper track. The train was due to leave in seven minutes. By the time he had climbed aboard, most of the cars to Amsterdam were fairly filled with passengers from other places. He placed his pack in a compartment just as the train began to pull out of the station.

CHAPTER 37

As the train pulled out of Köln, sitting by the door in a full compartment and staring at the progressively faster passing urban landscape, Henry realized that he was changing. He was growing in ways that gave him pleasure and greater self-confidence. He was learning to understand his body and how to share it with women whom he found attractive and who found him appealing. The shortness of the two affairs through which he had drifted this, the summer of his sexual maturing, posed no problem either for him or the two young women. As relationships, they had been very different. The encounter with Ingrid in Denmark had been playful and fleeting; an enjoyable evening in which a socially graceful hostess had delivered him from the humiliation of mockery through the bliss of a surprise tryst on his first big boat. With Kristina, it had been different. Their ages and energy levels were different. Nonetheless, they shared similar activities. Part of their mutual interests consisted of their sharing the burden of their visitors' memory of their different group's pariah status in a place that once again avowed two closely opposing universalisms. Again fate thrust itself into their lives. Here chance had left them unequal proportions due to their socially diverging pasts carried by their present selves. Fortune had bestowed an extra load of fright upon Kristina. This fear was somewhat dissipated by the happiness of sharing her domestic life with a younger fellow whose forbidden attributes she had heretofore never been allowed to explore.

Neither Kristina nor Henry asked why they would never see each other again. Their values and selves had given each other joy because they both practiced and felt a real tolerance—a joy at indulging in and permitting to thrive what is so different from oneself. But there were limits on how often and on what occasions such leaps to the celebration of plurality could individually please or be materially sustained. For a special moment of growing up on the ceremonial occasion of one's graduation holiday or vacation, such frivolity was titillating. On a daily basis, however, such an extreme complement of values, beliefs, and characters would lead to an uncomfortable level of tension built on constant disagreements about fundamental issues. This must be why different categories of people and groups sorted themselves out in such intriguing spatial arrangements. In some cases distance did make better neighbors and, indeed, occasionally more intriguing lovers. For this meeting to occur both parties had to believe that this coming together was good. For both Kristina's and Henry's generation the body had become a politic on inter-group admiration. It had also occurred for their parents, but it was fraught with an excitement that accompanies violating truly profane sin.

As the train worked its way through the *Bundesrepublik* to Holland, Henry's mind turned itself away from the intensity of the romance and adventure that had filled his life the last few days and back to wondering about his decision about Vietnam. How, if in any way, would the new developments in the outer world demarcate the line between right and wrong? He would like to uncover a clear answer. The occupants of the compartment that he had hastily chosen had stern faces. The lanky, tall, blond-blue-eyed wearer of "granny" glasses was seriously enfolded in his heady copy of the *Frankfurter Allgemeine*. Next to him the shorter stockier woman, dressed in a tweed suit, had a frowning, disapproving air as she snuck a glance at the body of a semi-naked woman in her German *Ladies' Home Journal*-like magazine. *I wonder if that lady is Dutch?* thought Henry to himself. There were two middle-aged businessmen, clad in dark-blue suits, who were going through stacks of papers in their briefcases. Beside them was a scowling woman, probably an American in her early twenties, whose occasional furtive inspection of her unintended traveling companions belied a total dedication to the copy of Simone de Beauvoir's *The Second Sex* in her hands.

Overcoming his being intimidated by the unfriendly atmosphere, Henry addressed the young woman in English, "Have you heard or read any recent news from the United States?"

With the upturned sneer of an aspiring internationalist, this thin brunette in a simple blue-checkered, cotton dress appeared stunned and disgusted at being so readily identified as an American. In a tone of voice reflecting distance but courtesy, she responded, "Although I generally don't keep up on the United States of America, I have, in fact, been following events rather closely over the last few days. What would you like to know about precisely?"

"Like politics?"

"A few days ago I read that President Johnson refuses to de-escalate the war in Vietnam, and that of the major American candidates only Senator Eugene McCarthy has not been criticized by North Vietnam. You know the convention is on the 26th in Chicago?"

"Does that mean you're a McCarthy supporter?"

"Yes, but what I'm telling you is what the reporters are reporting—not my personal opinion. Whom are you supporting?"

"Well, I liked Robert Kennedy."

"And now?"

"Well, tell me more."

"The day before yesterday, when the Warsaw Pact invaded Czechoslovakia, your guys who were for Robert Kennedy, tried to get a compromise with our people. They want a halt in the bombing of North Vietnam, a cease-fire, and negotiations between the NLF and Saigon. But our side thinks it's necessary to criticize Johnson's policies, and your side thinks we should be mum on that issue. But, in general, the whole Democratic National Convention is really divided. Those of us against the war and for civil rights have been cheated out of seats through racist tactics in some regional seating, particularly in places like Georgia. It looks as though the TV debate between Humphrey and McCarthy is going to be called off."

"It sounds awful!"

"Life is not a bed of roses!"

"What's happening in Czechoslovakia?"

"For one thing, it has opened up a split among the Communists as big as the Moscow-Peking one. Romania and Yugoslavia quickly and firmly condemned the invasion, as did the Communist Parties of Italy and France. But East Germany, Poland, Hungary, and Bulgaria sent in smaller contingents of troops along with those of the Soviet Union."

"I suppose that's evidence that all's not black and white in their world. There seems to be many shades of gray on the red background."

From the slight turnings of their heads, the other passengers appeared to be trying to understand this conversation while feigning disinterest. Occasionally they would cast their eyes on the countryside out the window as the rolling wooden train neared Nijmegen.

"I'm Henry Green of Los Angeles."

"Oh, my name is Susan Pick of Boston, although I have spent the last year in France."

"How do you like living in France?"

"It certainly gives you a different perspective on life. I can't decide if I'll try to do graduate work in France or go back home. Living in Aix-en-Provence, where I do, is beautiful, but it's not Paris."

"What do you want to do in life?"

"Right now, I'm a little disoriented. Maybe that's why I find myself wanting to go back home and get involved in the McCarthy campaign. The French are very upset with America over its Vietnam involvement, and I must admit that it affects the way people act towards me here. Not infrequently, they'll assume you support our government's position without asking for your own view. Even though I love France and the French people, that makes me angry. But I'm even angrier and frustrated at America at this point, and I feel I must act on my beliefs now. Maybe that means I really ought to go back home and try to do something."

"It sounds like you're making a wise decision, Susan Pick."

Susan laughed at Henry's formality and replied, "So what are you going to do?"

"I have to make a decision very, very soon, before I leave Europe on September 9th."

"Which means?"

"I've got to decide what I'll do if I'm called up for the draft. I'm fighting my case at the moment. But I'm going to see Amsterdam, Bruxelles, and then go back to London first, all before September 9."

"Well, I'm going to Amsterdam for a day, maybe two. Do you want to do a walking tour with me?"

"That sounds great. I'm going to stay at the youth hostel."

"Well, I'd planned a pension or small hotel, but I have no reservations booked, so it might be fun to try the hostel for a day."

Henry thought to himself, *I bet this girl has money.* While Susan contemplated, *I better not tell him I've never stayed in a youth hostel before. He'll think I'm some kind of snob.*

Wow, was her tough grimace deceiving. She's turning out to be a nice person, Henry reflected.

CHAPTER 38

As the train pulled into Amsterdam's Central Station, Henry cast his eyes upward at the luggage rack above their seats and noticed the exceptionally large backpack above Susan's head. He wondered if it was hers and judged that it must be—given the more conventional garments worn by the other passengers in the compartment. *Will Susan think I am a stuffy, old-fashioned guy if I offer to help her get that giant backpack on? It must be twice the size, and I am sure, twice the weight of mine.*

Susan was anxiously waiting to disembark and set out to discover this town from where some of her ancestors had come to New Amsterdam. She had also read about the heavy countercultural scene in the contemporary city but felt unsure about coming so close into contact with it on a personal level. Gulping, she thought to herself, *Well, here goes!* The matter of the backpack had not entered her mind.

Henry inquired, "Susan, may I help boost your belongings in place or, perhaps, you'd like to wear my pack and let me try out yours."

Relieved to avoid promenading with such a weight on her, particularly when she had planned to take a cab to a pension, Susan responded, "Why don't you try mine, and I'll try yours? Where's the youth hostel anyway?"

"It's over on Kloveniersburgwal 97, 220b, according to my listing. It doesn't look too far away from here on the map."

The new traveling companions left the Central Spoorweg Station and trudged over the open place of the Stationsplein at as brisk a pace as their heavy loads permitted. Muted, the light reflecting off the canals was a darkened grayish-greenish brown, and mixed the reflections of the bricks of the houses. In contrast to the water, Susan's almost turquoise blue-and-white checkered dress added some brightness to the city's earthy tones.

"Susan, let's try to get some news at some point today. I also have to call

233

the aunt and uncle of the wife of my favorite teacher in high school. I hope they'll invite me over. I always love getting to know the local people."

"Sure, I can't wait to find out what's going on at the Democratic Convention in Chicago. Maybe if we stop by the American Consulate later on in the afternoon or, if we pass the University or City Library, we can get a paper."

In about a half-hour, they had reached the home-like structure with large glass windows that was the Amsterdam youth hostel. There was still a long morning line and, ignoring the proprieties of queuing, the youthful crowd packed in a hoard around the front desk.

"I hear that a lot of kids are sleeping in Vondel Park," intoned the gruff fellow in a New Jersey accent to his friend standing in front of Susan.

"You need a good tent and a sleeping bag for that, man!" the green-eyed, stringy red-haired fellow grunted back as Henry and Susan eavesdropped on conversations in at least twelve other languages. Bending her ears toward the French women her age, Susan was surprised to encounter the presence of both middle-class French students and some very haggard and hard-faced Parisian street people. When they reached the desk, they paid their fee and were assigned accommodations in different quarters for men and women. "Let's meet back here in about fifteen minutes," Susan suggested.

"Let's say, exactly by the door. There are so many people, it'll be impossible to find each other otherwise."

They proceeded upstairs and deposited their possessions on the bunk beds placed closely by one another in a very large high-ceiling room which had large windows letting in the light from the outside. There was space for all the people in the large crowd, which waited downstairs. In the bunk next to his, indeed that touched the very edge of his second top-leveled bed, was a muscle-bound American soldier who lay with his eyes barely opened, and his mouth in a dejected, downward turn. His lips were tightly sealed, and Henry was unable to distinguish if his expression was one of depression or repressed anger. *I wonder if it'll be safe to leave my stuff here. Well, there's nothing worth taking anyway.*

In the room for women, Susan found herself in a similar position. One brown-haired French woman of the medium-stature spoke in an almost incomprehensible Parisian argot. She was bedded in the bunk next to Susan's. Without ever bothering to introduce herself, she had, assuming Susan knew no French, called her a *niaiseuse* to her friend on the berth below. Keeping her sang-froid and dignity, Susan decided to take her backpack back to the main station's luggage-check lest her unwelcome verbal assailant decide to liberate her prosperous equipment. In its place, she left a large sheet of paper with her name and reservation number on the bed and then toted her pack downstairs thinking, *I don't care what that Henry thinks. I'm not going to invite that bitch to rip off my things, and that's that!*

When she joined the shove—holding her pack by its top bar and pushing forward—Susan was pleased to find Henry—a grin across his face—already at the entranceway. Without asking this time, he heaved Susan's pack onto his back. "What happened?"

"Oh, there is a girl I don't trust any more than a common thief who was assigned the bunk right next to mine. She called me a nasty name in French and gave me such a hateful look. Her friend got the bunk below hers."

"Too bad! Do you want to wait in line some more and try to get another place?"

"No. But do you mind dropping off my backpack at the Central Station before we take in the city?"

"No," said Henry, disguising his displeasure at having to waste some more time for the convenience of his new found, somewhat fearful, traveling chum. But he added, trying to soothe her, "The guy in the bunk joined to mine looks like he's on the verge of either killing himself or somebody else. I can't figure it out."

"For a supposed place of love and peace, some of the kids around here are frightening," observed Susan. Having read up on Amsterdam, Holland, she was beginning to feel some disappointment at its declining youth. She had always admired its religious tolerance, and its great traders, ships, and paintings since the time she had played the role of a little Dutch girl in her elementary school's pageant of countries at the end of her primary school.

"Susan, let's try out that little coffee shop over there."

"What a good idea."

They descended a few stairs into a plain-walled semi-basement with thick wooden tables and chairs. From the backroom floated a sickly sweet odor that blended and was overcome by a strong aroma of coffee. Scattered around the small room was a motley crew of pallid and pimply young men. Each youth was individuated from the next by bright but tattered raiment and long unkempt hair. Each was seated alone with the exception of a healthier couple rubbing knees under one of the tables.

"This couldn't be an opium den, could it?" Susan whispered somewhat apprehensively to Henry, and then she continued, "I read in a book that the

Amsterdam police allow the Chinese to use it but draw the line very strictly when it comes to the Dutch."

"They definitely look like druggies of some kind to me. Every kid here has washed-out, pale skin, and look at that guy over there. He has noticeable red marks near his veins! Do you want to stay here?"

"Well, we're here. We might as well stay unless somebody makes a threatening gesture," Susan pitched in a muffled voice, trying to regain her reputation as a courageous young woman after the upsetting incident at the youth hostel.

At this point, a thin, tall man in his twenties appeared at the counter. Henry walked over, unsure if one was supposed to order at the table or counter.

"Two coffees and rolls," he affirmed in well-articulated English.

The fellow slowly began to work on some other order, so Henry sat back down. In a few minutes their food was brought to their table.

"They don't seem to mind our presence, although that fellow at the door to the kitchen watched me in a very peculiar way as two of the customers walked back through that passageway separated by the hanging, long-brown wooden beads."

"Well, you are the only young lady here," Henry remarked.

"True, but it was a suspicious glance," Susan insisted.

"Do you think this could be a homosexual hang-out?"

"No, or if it is, these guys are into some kind of drugs before sex; that's for sure. They are definitely not what I'd call cute," Susan observed.

"Let's finish and get out of here. The coffee and rolls aren't bad, but the butter has some sort of rancid taste in it; I wouldn't use it if I were you."

"I was just thinking the same thing myself. Let's get out of here," urged Susan, gulping down the last sips of the dark, strong brew.

A few steps out of the coffeehouse Henry joked, "I am speeding already from their mysterious concoction."

"God, if my mother knew I had stepped into a place like that, she'd have died," laughed Susan—nevertheless relieved to have come out alive from the seedy, strange dive. They walked down Klovenierburgwal to the Nieuwe Markt and from there past the Gelderskade to Prins Hendrik Kade across the Open Haven and back to the Central Station where Susan checked her pack.

It was a lazy, warm day of muted blue skies filled with spongy clouds in a myriad of shapes. Studying Henry's reaction, Susan suggested, "I don't want to bore you spending the whole day at the Rijksmuseum, but it is what I want to see most about the whole city. It has the best collection of the art and crafts of the Netherlands."

236

"I'd like to visit it too. How about trying to get out by mid-afternoon, though, so we can see some of the other scenes?"

"It's a deal!"

As soon as they agreed on their route, they took a different way to the museum than the one they had walked in the morning from the youth hostel. Directly across from the station, they traced their way down Damrak to Rokin, through Leidse Street, then Place, crossing the Singel Gracht and turned left of Stadhouderskade over to the museum. They remained silent as they passed the four and five-story, brown brick houses with large, long rectangular windows and ornate gables. Susan followed the tops of the houses, first naming the sorts of gables she recognized—step, neck, bell, spout, and cornice. Then she would ask Henry to stop for a few minutes so she could sketch them. Occasionally she sighted an old signpost in stone with a little design depicting the trade of the person living there.

Meanwhile Henry was absorbed in dreamy, pleasant reminiscences of his favorite high school teacher and his Dutch wife, mother-in-law, and beautiful daughters. The Popovic family had been his succor in high school. He loved them dearly. Dr. Ljubomir Popovic, a tall, strong man who had aged and weathered the tides of the Second World War and Revolution in the Balkans, showed the lines of suffering yet endurance in the creases and crevices of his dignified face and the sharp lines of his nose and cheekbones. Immigration to three different countries on three different continents with all the tribulations that that had brought had softened his voice and his gait and left him with patience and gentleness. Perhaps this kind demeanor had made him appear too soft to the discipline-demanding southern WASPs who were the overwhelming majority of the school's students and teachers. For the very reasons these boys hassled him, Henry appreciated his sophistication and experience. Behind his back, his detractors called Dr. Popovic, Dr. Pop.

A lawyer by training and a polyglot by upbringing, geographical destiny, and the course of life, Mrs. Anna Popovic emanated warmth and charm. Occasionally, but not consciously, she would let her elegance slip through her daily life of mothering and teaching. Her wide smile and rounded face matched the curved contours of her hips and legs which she covered in thick suits of tweed and beige topped by off-white ruffled blouses into which her prominent bosom was tucked. The brown earth tones of her favorite dresses matched her brownish-blond hair. Henry liked to admire the quality of Mrs. Popovic's beauty as an integral part of a Quattro: first, the thinness and creaminess of the complexion and frequent laughter of her two daughters.

They blended into her own largeness of limb and comfortable fleshiness, and into her mother's divinely white hair and darker blue or black and white dresses of thick cotton or flannel. This attire draped over her somewhat heavier but even gentler mastery of movement. Grandmother and mother had blueness in their irises, which was mellowed by a slight grayness of tone. Only an occasional redlined broken vessel added a barely perceptible streak to the whites of the first generation. One of the young daughters had inherited the dark marble eye of her father's line while the other carried the lighter tones of her maternal side.

In the mildly Judaeophobic milieu of his high school, the Popovics had acknowledged Henry's Jewishness in an accepting and protective way. They knew, no doubt, of the moral disaster that had led to the Holocaust in their respective countries of origin. They had confidence in America generally, and in America's better record on minorities in comparison to their native Europe's. Nevertheless, their loving recognition of Henry's origins was based more on their liberal practice of different Christian traditions and of respect for the Jewish *kop,* which their higher educations had instilled in them. In an environment where Sunday church and morning chapel attendance was required, Anna, her mother, and daughters were not always seen. When they were, they were not always on time, and Ljubomir—if Henry had reckoned correctly—appeared regularly at chapel but less often at the early Sunday morning service of God. Though strong anti-Communists, they enjoyed carrying on argumentative jostling with Henry's Jewish-tinged liberalism. Proper manners and expressions had to be maintained for this discourse, and Henry remembered painfully having upset Mrs. Popovic when he suggested that Jesus had been a radical in his day. Understanding that he had broken the rules of propriety, Henry never repeated this observation in the Popovic family again, and it was quickly left unmentioned. Secretly, Ljubomir had confided to Henry in his senior year that when the Popovics were in Australia in the 1950s, he had been treated as a second-class citizen, despite his impeccable Oxford credentials. In contrast, Mrs. Popovic had been dealt with on a more equal footing with her northern European tact and looks. These experiences must have pushed them to teach in a southern institute for the blind when they left Henry's school.

When Anna's mother, Mrs. van het Reve served afternoon tea and her marmalade cookies or biscuits, it was always with the grace of the high *bourgeoisie* which sought to decorate their ordinariness of family life with a proper dose of royalty, served, of course, on Delft China.

Henry remembered the last tea served in the Popovic's home just after he graduated. The yellow light passed through the leaves of the old southern oak and shown through the large wood-framed windows in beams of off-golden yellow shaped by the leaves of the tree in the front yard. Tears welled in their eyes when they sensed that they were all growing older and passing onto a new inevitable stage of life which meant that they would never see one another again or only hear from one another through infrequent letters. Exchanging letters between beloved teachers and students may sometimes be accompanied by tales of success or of special happiness, which the hard events of life and history do not necessarily bring speedily, if at all.

Slowly Henry's mind shifted back from his lovely inner reminiscences to recalling that he must contact Mrs. Popovic's aunt, Mrs. van het Reve's sister, in order to set up an appointment for tomorrow. "Susan, may I try to place a long-distance call before we see the museum?"

"Fine with me." In a few minutes they came across a public telephone and with assistance from a Dutch passerby, Henry made his call.

"Hello, I am a student of Dr. Popovic's," said Henry, introducing himself. "Mrs. van het Reve wanted me to send you their greetings and news."

"Could you come for coffee tomorrow afternoon? My sister wrote that you were coming, Henry," replied Mrs. Zeh. "About one in the afternoon would be fine. You can get a direct train from Amsterdam."

"Oh, thanks so much. May I bring a friend with whom I am traveling?"

"Certainly," answered Mrs. Zeh in her deep, Dutch gutturally-accented English.

"See you tomorrow. We're looking forward to meeting you."

"See you tomorrow."

His breath rushed quickly through his nostrils, as his heart pounded and shoulders were thrust backwards. Had he made a good impression on the telephone? Only tomorrow would tell.

Henry's excitement at the prospect of meeting the relative of his favorite teacher was met with an exuberance of Susan's walking to the ringing mixture of drums, cymbals and pipes of the organ grinder about a half block from where he had placed his call. Not too far down the street they came upon the twin pyramidal darkened towers of the Rijksmuseum. The ground floor, where most of the Rembrandts were housed, was so packed with tourists they decided to go to the other parts of the museum, which were less mobbed. Their choice was rewarded with Ruysdael and Hobbema's landscapes and Van Ostade's peasant scenes. Susan's pacing of Henry at a fast-clip led them to Jan Steen's paintings of household life, which they found amusing. There were many fewer visitors in the rooms of Dutch history where the tale of the Dutch revolt from Spain so intrigued Henry that Susan had to yank him from the *Square of the 17th Century* over to the room of sea warfare and colonial history. Susan was particularly struck and upset by the artifacts of the Dutch presence in Ceylon, Japan, and China. With a flight scheduled to leave soon, she had no time to become totally immersed in any object before Henry pushed her onward to the exhibition dealing with the Second World War. Susan's unpolished nails, symmetrically cut in clean, rounded form, reflected off the newly shined display cases.

"Henry, we have only a half hour left if you still want to try to make it over to the consulate. Let's try to take in a few of the Rembrandts now."

"I'm following you," gasped Henry as they capered rapidly back to the first floor. By now the crowds had thinned and they found spaces in front of the *Night Watch,* or, more precisely, *The Company of the Captain Frans Banning Cocq and Lieutenant Willem van Ruytenburch.*

Susan thought to herself, *These men look so full of themselves; only that little girl looks like she's having fun*. But she remarked to Henry, "Well, I guess that in the Baroque it was really in to get in on a group portrait."

"That's true, but Rembrandt also added so much activity. This canvass was considered way beyond the standards of his age."

"Yeah, so much so, that for some time art historians thought that this painting had started his downfall. But that's a lot of baloney. The real reason was simply he didn't know how to handle money, no matter how successful he was."

In a few minutes they hastened on to Vermeer's *Maidservant Pouring Milk.* Susan stared intensely into the yellowish-green of the muted light and the thick, rounded brown bread in a sturdy basket. The exact stream of the pouring milk was focused precisely into the reddish-brown bowl. It was hard to see the eyes of the hefty, round-faced young woman, but Susan was sure her appearance and big arms meant sturdy control and exactness. Henry was grabbed by the painting as well, but not so intently that he forgot to note that it was time for them to take their leave of the Rijksmuseum for the day.

Leaving the *Maidservant Pouring Milk* was not easy for Susan. She could see herself being pulled into the quiet orderliness of the young, hardworking woman in that picture. Even though she would not let herself be yanked "back to the earth," as had some of her friends before she had left the States, she sensed that it would be easy to give herself up to the routines of being a mother and housekeeper. No disturbing thinking that had confused and upset her—particularly this last year in France—would, then, rupture her clear ability to pour milk and bake good, wholesome bread—not the chemically-filled, tasteless sort that had become popular in America after World War II. Hadn't the minister's wife of her childhood years encouraged the girls in her Sunday school class to believe that it was God's plan for women to bear children, maintain a happy home, and be loyal supports to their husband and family. Maybe that was a good calling. *Oh, how Simone de Beauvoir would be angry at me for having such doubts,* thought Susan. Then she giggled inwardly at herself, *No human being has to be privy to what I think deep down inside of me!*

Meanwhile, after trying in vain to find the American Consulate or Information Agency's address, Henry gave up when he located on the map the Municipal University Library. Not having noticed Susan's puckered lip, Henry suggested, "Susan, I bet this library would have all the newspapers we could possibly want, and it doesn't look too far from here. Look, we just walk down Spiegelgracht, swing a left on the Herengracht canal, go right on the Leidsestraat and than turn left, and it's a little ways down the street."

"You and your navigating!"

"Well, I don't usually have such first-rate maps like the ones you carry."

"I'm not sure whether to take that as a compliment to my good taste or a crack at my being so *bourgeoise!*"

"Come on, don't be so uptight. You're still angry about those women from France at the hostel this morning!"

"Not really, but let's get going anyway," Susan snapped back, leading the way out of the museum.

Walking at a leisurely stroll, they reached the library in about a half-hour and requested the latest copies of the *New York Times* and the *London Times* from the reference librarian who spoke excellent English in a bass tone. They sat next to each other at a large wooden table and began to leaf through the pages in concentrated silence.

Susan pulled out her ballpoint pen and a small brown notepad from her purse and began to jot down some notes on specific differences between her McCarthy views and the compromise attempted between the McCarthy and Humphrey people.

Henry's tension and anger rose from the moment he saw the events depicted in McCarthy's political ad, "What is this—a Convention or an armed camp?" Imagine five thousand National Guard troops being called up along with all of Chicago's twelve thousand-man police force on twelve-hour shifts. Just think of two thousand uniformed and plain-clothes policemen! He looked at the chain-linked fence and shared with the demonstrators the disgust and willingness to challenge these despotic attempts to contain dissent by Mayor Richard Daley. They reminded Henry more of Orville Faubus's calling out the Arkansas National Guard to block the federally mandated integration of Little Rock's schools. Yet he did not share Susan's hero, Gene McCarthy's enthusiasm, that the Democrats were going to beat Nixon.

Suddenly, his mind wondered and he glanced over to Susan who was furiously taking down notes on what she was reading. Her attention was so intense that the skin of her forehead and the muscles surrounding her eyes were taut.

"Pretty heavy stuff!" he commented.

"It's all so complicated. I'm trying to figure out the differences. I agree with a lot of the things the Democratic senators had to say about mutual withdrawal of American and North Vietnamese troops."

"Oh yeah, that was the day the seven Yippies and the pig they're running for president got arrested in Chicago," Henry chuckled.

"I don't know if their antics are so funny," retorted Susan. "They are mocking things many people inside and outside the Democratic Party hold to be sacred."

"To be honest with you, I guess you are saying what I really feel, but I am sort of bedazzled by their brilliance at the same time, and of having the nerve to criticize what deserves to be attacked in public."

"What good do you think that mocking the average American's values in public does, except to alienate the majority of the people, and drive them further to the right."

"O.K. you score your point! They are being holier-than-thou, spoiled, and really politically stupid, but don't you think that what they're trying to say is that the American electorate's consensus at the moment deserves a pig for president? That there's no way they're going to change it this election, so the best thing you can do is to make fun of it?"

"They may be right about the consensus, but they're playing political suicide. Many of the things they are attacking are good, like the religious pluralism of their pig, and they're wrong and intolerant to attack it. What they're doing sounds like nihilism. What Gene McCarthy is doing stands for the best of our traditions. He thinks that you should stand up for what you believe and defend it. O.K., the American public may be wrong on Vietnam at the moment, but they'll listen if we make our case clearly and strongly. And we'll wi..." Susan stopped before she added the "n" to win, and Henry interrupted.

"But, Susan, we've lost. We lost the nomination. Johnson sneakily inserted his hard-line plank into the party platform."

"But we'll win in the long run. The American people believe in helping the common man and woman. They don't want to trample the underdeveloped countries. They want them to share their material well-being. They want to give people a fair say in determining their future."

"I wish I held your confidence, but I do only partially. I think that the size of the military in the ol' USA is so big and powerful today that a lot of support for the war in Vietnam comes from just ordinary Americans liking to show people in other countries that we can flex our muscles. They better well do what we want them to do or else. This spring I almost got into a fist fight with the guy seated next to me on the 'plane when I was flying home to see my mother. He just didn't believe that students had any right to challenge the authority of their elected leaders. He really hated me, and he was the old redneck type whom you can be sure hated the whole list of minorities and civil rights types."

"But that's one man! Most Americans will listen to logic."

"Look, anti-communism runs so strong at home. Look, it's right here," pointed Henry with an outstretched index finger at the *New York Times* from the nineteenth of August. "Edmund S. Muskie of Maine says that the NLF should have no right to be included in the elections until a vague 'second stage of negotiations.' And look, he says we should not 'dictate the composition of the government,' as though the U.S. government didn't basically set up and keep the present South Vietnamese government in power."

"Well, don't you see what I mean, that's what McCarthy's supporter, Roger Hilsman, told Hubert Humphrey in a calm, well-reasoned way on the same day. By the way, Hilsman used to be assistant secretary of state for Far Eastern Affairs. It's right here in black and white. He said 'that the American intervention has failed' and 'has only succeeded in driving the Vietnamese peasantry into the arms of the Communists.' Then he addressed Humphrey's claim that the McCarthyites were trying to impose a coalition government on Saigon. By bringing to the vice-president's attention that the National Liberation Front in South Vietnam has such support, he demonstrated that the best we can hope for would be that non-Communist elements be permitted to participate in a coalition government."

"But it's only fair to insure that all factions be included in the government."

There was a pause, and Susan picked up at a different point from where they had left off; she was reading from her notes. "Did you notice that on the twenty-fourth Senator George McGovern said that by intervening in the internal affairs of small nations, the U.S. had encouraged Russians to do the same? He thinks there has been a willingness for the two large superpowers to carve up the world in a cynical game of power politics?"

"He's right on. I must have missed that page. And David Dellinger, chairman of the Mobilization Committee to End the War in Vietnam, likened Chicago to Prague. Read this, 'Everybody knows who was the guilty party when Soviet troops went into Czechoslovakia to prevent the Czechs from free expression of their views…And everybody will know who the guilty party here is if troops are used to prevent us from exercising our rights'…Chicago refused to issue them permits for a protest march. The police arrested eleven Yippies yesterday. Did you catch that report by John Finney on the twenty-third that the Democratic Doves agreed on a plank calling for a bombing cessation, de-escalation of the war, and mutual withdrawal of American and North Vietnamese troops?"

"Yep, but even they did not demand the formation of a coalition government. What they said was that the U.S. should encourage the South Vietnamese government to renegotiate a 'political reconciliation' with the NLF 'looking toward a government which is broadly representative of these and all elements in South Vietnamese society.'"

"I could even buy that," gulped Henry.

Susan thumbed glumly but hastily through her notepad, "And on the twenty-fifth Humphrey blocked a peace plank on Vietnam and said that he thinks that President Johnson's policies are basically sound. There's a reaction going on at home. James Reston summed it up well. He wrote, 'that ninety percent of the voters are not black, or young, or intellectual. They are white, middle-aged or older and middle class.'—Wait, let me find that other quote he cited from Richard Scammon of the Elections Research Center—oh, here it is: 'It's the combination that elected Governor Reagan in California…which may very well affect the national election. It is a combination of Watts and Berkeley. It's beatniks. It's hippies. It's draft-card burners. It's demonstrators. It's blacks. It's high taxation. It's easy sex and dope and kids running away from home. It's uncertainty, fear, madness, murder—all these appearing day after day on television and in the newspapers, adding up to a feeling that something is deeply wrong and must be changed.'"

"You know, even if Nixon and Wallace split the conservative vote and Humphrey wins, as far as Vietnam goes, there's not going to be a big difference."

"Henry, don't be so pessimistic. We can change the way people feel."

"I'm not so sure. The haves think that what they have they deserve and that the have-nots should get only a few crumbs. Worse, they think that their culture is the best in the world and that everybody wants what they have."

"But on the twenty-sixth things began to change."

"Yeah, like twenty people getting hit with nightsticks by the police?"

"The police claimed that a bottle was thrown from the crowd and smashed near one of the officers."

"It's possible, but none of my friends would have ever done anything like that. Look, they even grabbed Claude Lewis, a black reporter for the *Philadelphia Bulletin* and snatched his notebook. I admire the demonstrators courage; they called it a 'Festival of Life.'"

"But a lot of us McCarthyites were there the next day to protest out in front of the Hilton."

"Did you catch that story about Lyndon Baines' 'UnBirthday Party?'—where they called him a 'Freak.' Phil Ochs got out 3,000 people to sing 'I Ain't Marching Any More.' They chanted, 'No, no, we won't go.'"

"Well, maybe that was an appropriate response to Johnson's pushing through his hawkish Vietnam plank on the twenty-sixth. He even went further than what Humphrey wanted."

Susan raised her head and sighed, "Oh, Henry, what are you going to do?"

"I guess Messrs. Johnson and Humphrey pretty well sealed my fate. I disagree with the majority about the war in Vietnam, and about the causes of violence and poverty. That leaves me either jail or exile if I don't win my case. I just made up my mind. I am going to leave for Canada if I get drafted. I wouldn't survive jail nine chances out of ten."

"I know you must be worried, but at least you've now reached a definite decision. Let's go over to check out *Vondel Park* before it gets too dark."

All of these things are happening. What to do? What to do? were the thoughts that kept turning over in their minds as they wandered back down Leidsestraat and the canal. As they walked through the park, they saw quite a few young people wearing their hair in long and sun-dried fashion who were dressed in the many colors of India and Indonesia. Some, it was true, were smoking grass, although the odor was much less prominent than in some similar areas in America's big cities. Altogether this late afternoon-early-evening stroll was neither intense nor dramatic—unlike the press accounts of this place Susan had read. More young people were sitting quietly on the edge of the water, some soaking their feet, a few massaging their companions, and more smoking the conventional, if obnoxious, fumes of tobacco. There were old people and fat people, men and women, and some children with their parents, too. There were guitarists and organ grinders and the usual pop-park artisans selling their wares.

"It's beautiful, relaxing."

"Yeah, it's really different from what I had expected. It's pleasant and even down-homey."

"Maybe, it's the day and time of day we're here. We're really haven't seen anything very out of the ordinary."

"If it's very much like the tales about it at other times, fine! If they're just exaggerated, fine! We just needed a nice, quiet walk, and either we just lucked out or it's really more like this than its reputation."

As they began to walk back to the youth hostel, Susan saw a Chinese restaurant, which was hidden on an off-street. "Come on, it's on me. After all, tomorrow you're taking me to a tea at a real Dutch family's."

Not replying, Henry smiled and followed her to the small bedroom-sized enclosure with small dark wooden tables covered by dark red tablecloths decorated with small flowers. The wallpaper was dark and hid the pictures, which had become covered with a brownish hue from years of cooking in close quarters. The egg rolls and diced chicken dishes they ordered were simple but filling.

"You won't believe this, but all of a sudden I have an urge for a milk shake," Henry imparted to his hostess. Susan signaled the middle-aged Dutch woman who was the waitress.

"Do you know what a milkshake is?"

"Sure, I lived in New York during the last war. My husband can do you up something like it," she growled back over her wide waist. In a few minutes her Chinese husband passed a somewhat large beaker of something red in color. "Cheers," toasted Henry, raising his cup to Susan. "Here's to you, to America, to peace."

"Well spoken. Here's to our convincing the rest of America we're right,"

Susan retorted—supping the sweet, thick liquid that tasted more like a glass of milk loaded with sugar, vanilla bean, and syrup than the thick ice-creamy drink she was used to.

"I hope the drink isn't symbolic of our success," responded Henry, "Actually, it's not bad. It's too thin, but not too sweet. Thanks."

"Well, let's be off to the hostel and get an early start to the countryside and, of course, to your friendly bunking neighbors."

"How about the guy you're not sure about whether or not he is going to stab you."

"I'd almost forgotten."

Leisurely walking side-by-side with hands in their pockets, they watched the reflections of the lights on the canals.

"It's like I know this place and like this place. I'm really enjoying it like a tourist, not like it's home," Susan mused.

"Well, that's why you're here. Have a good time."

They walked back inside the youth hostel and bid each other good night.

"Let's try to meet each other downstairs about eight in the morning."

"O.K. I'll do my best to beat the pack's check-out. Sleep well."

"You too."

CHAPTER 39

As the local train pulled out from Amsterdam and wound its way south, the dense fog and heavy rain intensified the light within the train and softened its thinly-padded, upright, green and gray seats. Every bench was taken. Some passengers were standing talking to friends and family. The compacted interior thrust Henry and Susan's field of vision outward to the edge of the woods that were barely visible through the thick mist. Facing each other, Henry and Susan caught a glimpse of the varying scenes unfolding in the coach. The gentle jerk forwards and backwards provided a subtle tie to the reality of the moving vehicle. For Henry, the number of intermarried Dutch and Indonesians and Africans was a pleasant sign of permeability in the barrier of race to intimate communication. Focusing on the same thought, Susan wondered what percentage of the Dutch population was made up of these intermarried people, and how they and their children were viewed and treated by the surrounding society. The warm, stylish clothing, the proper attention to conversation with and the correction of children, and each other, testified to these particular couples' contented, middle-class existence. Were they just exceptions to the harder existence suggested in the book Susan had perused yesterday? Susan had the desire to pick up and stroke the little child with coffee cream skin seated next to Henry, but she didn't even have the courage to strike up a conversation with her very blonde mother. *When would those lines begin to erase themselves at home?* wondered Henry. *And were these couples the cheerful example of domestic bliss, which they appeared to be on the surface?* Susan then began to stare at the group of soldiers at the end of the coach. They were standing or sitting and laughing. She didn't seem able to take her eyes off the tallest of the group, a six-foot two-ish blond, blue-eyed farmer lad who reminded her of her cousin from upstate New York for whom she had nourished an unrequited crush from at least junior high school.

Even Henry could not miss the direction of her stare and began to get an insight into Susan's broad-shouldered tastes.

The chugging of the train southward through the gray, rainy day lulled Henry and Susan into a dream state only occasionally stirred by a gush of chilled wet air that shook the passengers, as one group stepped off and another boarded the train at each of the local villages. Some two hours outside of Amsterdam, the American traveling companions debarked at a small town station and walked down the long road past the neatly-spaced farms and houses until they came to a tidy two-story brick house set back from the main road by a large garden and trees. The rain had begun to clear and the low-lying mists began to ascend just about the time they got off.

The very student-looking duo, unaware of the obvious social identity of their clothing, rang the doorbell of the proper red—much blackened by age— brick home. Within the brief pause in which one wonders if it is appropriate to ring a third time, a dignified woman of medium stature in her late fifties or early sixties opened the door. Her cheeks had that delicate coating of just enough powder that somewhat dulls the shiny pink cheeks of a proper matron and permits just enough of her whitened down to tenderize any suggestion of undue stiffness conveyed by her warm, but occasionally coarse tweeds. Mrs. Zeh, like her niece, preferred two-piece suits of earthen-toned tweeds and ruffled off-white blouses.

"So very nice to meet you, Henry. We've heard what a diligent student you are."

"Mrs. Zeh, this is Susan Pick from New York. We met yesterday on the train coming from Germany."

"Oh, we are happy that you could come along with Henry, Susan," said Mrs. Zeh as she signaled with her hand that they should follow her upstairs to the family parlor. It was possible to see the roomy, but not enormous, rather high-ceilinged rooms which were packed with tastefully arranged paintings, tapestries, and metal knickknacks spaced at regular intervals along the off-white walls and wooden frames. Mr. Zeh, who was seated in a generously cushioned, wide armchair next to the table, got up from reading his paper to greet the young adults.

"Welcome," he repeated, as he regarded with circumspection their jeans and plaids. They all proceeded to sit down around a solid table upon which there were tea biscuits and tea. No one touched anything until Mrs. Zeh had carefully poured the Darjeeling into her delicate cups of blue-and-white china, which depicted scenes of merchant ships from the seventeenth century.

Although Mr. Zeh was dressed in a black suit with hyphenated golden lines imprinted from top to bottom, he wore no tie and kept his stiff, white collar open.

"Well, the Popovics are all very busy. Mrs. Popovic is teaching French and Spanish, and Dr. Popovic is in charge of Russian."

"Yes, we hear you won the Russian award the year you graduated, Henry."

"Oh, I worked hard, but it was Dr. Popovic's good teaching that did it. I really loved the language and literature. I love modern languages. I got the nicest present from Dr. Popovic for winning the award, a copy of Pasternak's *Dr. Zhivago*. I'm slowly making my way through it."

"Yes, it is a splendid novel. Have you read it, Susan?" inquired Mrs. Zeh.

"No, I've been studying in Aix-en-Province last year. It's such a lovely spot, but I've barely taken my eyes off French literature. I must say, I like their literature much more than their literary criticism, which is the 'in thing' at the moment. Or I guess I should say 'structuralism,' which has replaced existentialism as the general philosophy of the French. See, Henry, it's the bad influence of you anthropologists, like Claude Lévi-Strauss, or the people in literature, like Roland Barthes. It's penetrated into everything, even psychoanalysis, through the writings of Jacques Lacan. What disturbs me about the whole thing is that it is so pseudo-scientific. Their language is turgid and pedantic. When they come to deeper meanings, basing themselves on a linguistic model, they seem forged and false. I always come up with another interpretation of the same material."

"Hey, Susan, that's not fair. A lot of anthropologists, particularly the American cultural anthropologists, keep on writing their historically-informed deep descriptions of other cultures. Even I agree with much of what you're saying about structuralism."

"Well, that's good news. I beg your pardon."

"Susan and Henry, you are very immersed in your student world. We can see that!"

"Oh, excuse us, we just got carried away."

"Never mind. We like to see that people are still debating ideas. It keeps the mind functioning."

"Where did you learn such good English?"

"Oh, no, no," laughed Mr. Zeh, "Don't compliment us. We travel to England every so often for vacation."

"Mrs. Popovic confided in me just before I graduated high school that the van het Reve's had it very rough during the occupation. She said that they survived off tulip bulbs for several months. Did you go through that too?"

"Yes," said Mrs. Zeh, lowering her voice, so as to indicate that this question was too intimate to ask of someone you had just met. "It was extremely difficult for many people here. Thank God, we survived."

Not satisfied with this brief response, Henry realized, nevertheless, that it was not appropriate to pursue this topic.

"Do you have any children?"

"Yes, indeed, we have a grown son and two daughters. All of them are married and we have nine grandchildren so far."

"My goodness, it must take a lot of effort just to remember their names?" chirped in Susan, who was relieved that the subject of conversation had shifted from the Second World War, for she, too, had sensed the Zeh's discomfort at Henry's interrogation.

"Not at all! And we are lucky to always have someone dropping by!" replied Mrs. Zeh.

Susan noticed that Mrs. Zeh was much more talkative than her husband so she pursued the subject of her family, about which Mrs. Zeh showed such great enthusiasm. "What do your children do for a living?"

"Our son has pursued his father's trade at the international flower exchange. One of our daughters teaches on the secondary level and another is a full-time mother. What does your father do, Susan?"

"He's in business, too—always something new."

The afternoon passed by quickly in pleasant small talk about the hobbies and interests of the Zehs, Susan and Henry, the Popovic's, the van het Reve's, and their families. As it was nearing late afternoon, Henry felt sure they would be invited for dinner and to spend the night, but when, by four-thirty no invitation had been extended, he thought it prudent to excuse themselves—possibly hoping that this would provoke the expected invitation.

"Our train is leaving back to Amsterdam after five, so I think we should be off on our way. Thank you ever so much for the yummy tea and butter cookies and most of all for the great company."

"Think nothing of it. Tonight I'll write the Popovics that you dropped by," politely responded Mrs. Zeh as she rose to lead them back downstairs to the door.

Meanwhile, Susan felt sure that Mr. Zeh would offer to drive them back to the train station, but no such offer was made on the way to the entrance corridor. She resigned herself to asking Henry to help her carry her heavy backpack along the thirty-minute path back to the local train stop.

"*Dank U Wel*," Susan said smilingly.

"Take care," bid Henry as she shook the Zehs' hands.

Down the majestic garden path past the entrance gate, no word passed between the young travelers. As soon as they were out of hearing range, just a few minutes walk away from the Zehs' property out on the small rural road, Henry made an offer of consolation to Susan, "Here, let me take your backpack."

"I don't mind if you do. Can you figure out what happened?"

"Enlighten me, first, O.K.?"

"Didn't you think we were hitting it off so well, that they liked us?"

"That was my impression."

"Why didn't they invite us over to dinner and to then spend the night?"

"You tell me."

"I'm not sure, although Mr. Zeh didn't say nearly so much as his wife. Did you get the impression that he didn't trust students or something?"

"Maybe they thought we are some kind of licentious, unmarried couple who would defile the purity of their beds?"

"Ha, ha, who, us?"

"Well, he wasn't exactly all open arms—not cold, but somewhat reserved."

"Maybe it's just a cultural difference. Maybe the Dutch invite you over only if they know you well. After all, I'm a friend of her sister's and niece's, not hers. But still, it seems strange to me. Could it be a rural urban thing? Maybe out here in the country one should be more cautious of people if you don't know them, especially foreigners."

"But we're Americans. Our culture is so similar. We have such deep ties. Their family knows and loves you. You were their star student."

"Maybe I offended them when I asked about World War II. Or maybe I just looked too sloppy—I did try to put on my neatest clothes for them."

"Come on! We both look informal but clean. Maybe you're right about these different cultural rules. What would seem as something naturally polite for us to do, maybe means something else here. Maybe it takes a long time to cultivate relationships, even in Holland. Who knows?"

At the end of their baffled musings over whether or not they had been socially slighted, Henry and Susan reached the small brick and wooden station where their train was due in a few minutes.

"What do you want to do tomorrow in Amsterdam, or tonight for that matter, Henry? I could go on, but I think I'd like to spend another day in the city. It intrigues me."

"Would you mind going with me to the old Jewish Quarter?"

"Of course not!"

"Well, let's get to bed early then."

The evening was cool and damp, although the rain had ceased. They had reached the central station in Amsterdam by early evening, and luckily there were a few remaining places by the time they reached the youth hostel.

In the two hours before the doors to the hostel were shut, Susan and Henry walked aimlessly through the city streets—still reflecting its own images in a thousand directions. Their words were few. They just absorbed the quiet of the alleys and soft bustling of the lights of patrons of the nightlife or pedestrians whose pleasures were confined to the absorption of the scenes of others and to the form of aged buildings.

CHAPTER 40

In stark contrast to the dampness of yesterday, the new morning greeted the young travelers with a cool, quickly-warming breeze stirring blue skies filled with large, but distinct, pure white clouds. "Here we are in *Mokum*," laughed Susan. "Hey, it rhymes with *hokum*, doesn't it?"

"What are you talking about?"

"*Mokum* is what the Amsterdamers call their city in slang. It's a Dutch corruption of *Makom*."

"What's that?"

"You should know, after all, you're the Jewish one, right?"

"But I know only a few words in Yiddish."

"Dummy, it's not Yiddish, it's Hebrew for 'place,' like Amsterdam is 'the place,' get it?"

"I can barely read Hebrew. Basically I know just a few prayers in it."

"Oh, well, anyway, let's start off to the *Jodenbuurt*, you know that that's the Jewish neighborhood in Dutch."

"Yes. That I knew."

"Isn't it gorgeous out?"

"I can't believe it. Where do you want to start out?

"Why not be real touristy, like visiting Anne Frank's house first?"

"Well, it's pretty far on the other side of the central city, away from the Jewish Quarter, over on Prisengracht. Let's do the Quarter first. It's really near the hostel."

"Fine with me."

After a brief walk, they came upon Rembrandt's house. Sitting down in front of it, as though she had returned to the fond home of her youth, Susan took out her sketching pad and began to trace the small, barely-visible lines that separated each brick. These stood out in relation to the regular interspaces of stone, the elongated, dark windows with oblong, small shaded panes set at right angles to the brick. They were interrupted by the almost Roman stone portico and rounded decorations above the window. Though his attention span concentrated on her detailed drawing only a few minutes, Henry was intrigued at how she was able to capture the details that enriched what he generally ignored in everyday life. When he tired of following her preoccupation with capturing this place, Henry picked up her guidebook to read about Rembrandt. He lived here from 1639 through 1657 and had found many of the subjects for his Old Testament figures from the denizens of the Jewish Quarter. In this house, unlucky Rembrandt had undergone the tragedies of having three of his four children die in infancy and then his wife after the birth of his son, Titus.

"Just think, Rembrandt couldn't afford to pay the interest on his mortgage any longer and was forced to move and rent in the nearby working-class neighborhood of Jordaan," mused Henry to himself without seeing the parallel to his own life.

After Susan had finished her sketch, they briefly toured the house and walked over to where Baruch Spinoza was born. "Can you believe only a block away from Rembrandt's house is Spinoza's birthplace? One of the greatest philosophers lived so near one of the greatest artists. And their lives overlapped, too. Spinoza was born here at Waterlooplein 41 in 1632. I wonder if Rembrandt knew Spinoza?"

"I haven't read of any connection, but it's interesting to conjure up," responded Susan. "Have you ever read Spinoza?"

"I tried to in high school one summer, but it was just too heavy for me then. He put me to sleep, to tell you the truth. But I'd like to get back to him if I can find the time."

"Don't feel alone. I haven't read more than a few excerpts of his in one of those dreadful compilations of the great philosophers. Those little courses rarely give you more than a sheer taste of what they thought or were like. We were so hurried through the course, the instructor left us with no sense of their lives."

From Spinoza's house they drifted over to the Portuguese Synagogue from the same period. Henry walked very rapidly through the building not wanting to impose any of his own culture on Susan. This was actually the second time Susan had been inside a Jewish synagogue. In her senior year she had been invited to one of her college friend's weddings, which, in her opinion, had been a garish affair completely out of tune with the spirit of simplicity of the times. Yet, she knew that Debby had had this spectacle out of respect for her parents' and in-laws'-to-be wishes and was acutely aware of its tastelessness in the eyes of many of her friends. Still, Susan was disturbed by Henry's behavior here. After all, he had invited her to accompany him to see the Jewish Quarter, and, here he was, pushing her through one of its major attractions as though he were ashamed or unduly nervous about his heritage. It didn't make sense.

"How about going over to the flea market? It's just a few minutes from here," prompted Henry, anxious to get Susan away from this house of worship. Without waiting for a reply, he headed back to the front door so as not to give her time to respond. A few steps away, they were thrust from the quiet of the spiritual to the density of flesh as the crowd filtered through the old goods. From the tarnished steel rack, Henry took down a battered black leather jacket lined with a soft black material that could have been silk. Holding up the item, he inquired, "How much do you want for it?"

"Fifteen dollars."

"Hey, that's too much, I'll give you five U.S. dollars."

"No, twelve fifty."

"Sorry, that's all I can afford."

"No deal, I'm not a charity," replied the old man in an understandable, guttural English. Meanwhile, Susan was weeding through racks of Indonesian and Indian-like dresses or western aping of them, but couldn't settle on anything either. In exasperation, she grabbed Henry's arm and pulled him away from the old books he was now sorting through.

"You need another book like a hole in the head."

"You're right."

"Let's take a peak at the Jewish Museum now," Susan implored, as she was tiring from the smell of mildew ingrained into some of the books and old clothes.

Making up for being hurried through the Portuguese Synagogue, Susan spent a good deal of time admiring the exquisitely detailed drawings of the dedication of the place done by Bernard Picard in the early eighteenth century. The black-and-white small squares of the floor and high columns; the raised *tebah* or chest from which the Torah was read; every crease of the dresses of the women and seventeenth century wigs of the men; the talking, gesturing of the hands, stooping; it was all there. "Oh, how utterly masterful," commented Susan to herself, "and to think it was done by a French Christian. These were the heights that the tolerance of the Enlightenment produced."

Quickly passing through the myriad of sacred objects displayed in the cases, Henry was more intrigued by some of the books on the history of the Jews of Amsterdam and the Netherlands than by their art. Many of these little facts from his sparse Jewish education began to fit into the general pattern of Western Civilization to which he had been exposed much more thoroughly. At their expulsion from Spain in 1492, and then from Portugal in 1497, the Jews of the Iberian peninsula, the Sephardim, many of whom had become Marranos, those who practiced Christianity in public and Judaism in private, began to drift to the provinces of the Low Countries in large numbers. Many of the Marranos were prosperous merchants who greatly aided the economy of the United Provinces of the Netherlands. After they successfully revolted from Spain, the Netherlands granted them permission to practice their Judaism, first discreetly in private and then ever more publicly over the years. Later came the Ashkenazim, the Yiddish-speaking Jews of Central and Eastern Europe. Having immigrated in various waves, particularly in response to persecution, they were less prosperous and often poor. They arrived during the murderous pogroms when Ukrainian peasants under the leadership of Bogdan Chmielnicki revolted against the Polish rule, and much later, during the Russian pogroms of the 1880s. The Ashkenazim and Sephardim quarreled often and furiously, both against each other and among themselves. Perhaps because of their own persecution in Spain, the Sephardim enforced a strict adherence to their own laws and excommunicated their own freethinkers like d'Acosta and Spinoza. It was in the Netherlands that the Christians and Jews had reached the greatest understanding and respect for each other in all of Europe, with very few outbreaks of anti-Semitism. Amsterdam became "Freedom City" to heretics and freethinkers of all faiths from all over Europe.

Thrusting himself in the distant past, Henry chuckled lightly, picturing how he would have most likely become involved on the side that introduced the Enlightenment reforms of the period of the French Revolution that made the Jews citizens on an equal par with others. He projected himself backward into the struggles of the diamond workers to form their own union in more recent times. Henry noted with great interest how the histories stressed that even though the primarily Sephardi Jews had around twenty-five percent of the holdings of the Dutch East India Company that their shares were much smaller on the average than those of the Dutch Christians. He focused on the description that the Sephardim were considered to run their plantations in a rather humanitarian way. Knowing that there had been some very kind but also some very mean Jewish financiers during the period of British colonialism in South Africa, he wondered if these stories on Dutch Jewish colonialism were apologetic or accurate.

And he read event after event of how the Dutch and their royalty had stood on the side of the Jews against the Nazis, had hidden thousands, and had been the only European nation to call a general strike—a crime under the occupation. True, there had been Dutch Nazis, and some protectors had extorted money from the people they hid, but the Dutch record had been exemplary. Breathing deeply, Henry thought, *This is a place where I could live.* About this time, Susan walked back from her tour of the other part of the museum and suggested they better move on to the Anne Frank house.

Walking back to the other side of the inner city, Susan remarked, "All those objects were so interesting. I'll have to go to the Jewish Museum when I get back to New York. You know, I've never been there. I know so little about your religion. I've never really read much of the New Testament, much less the Old." She continued, "I guess our generation was taught to learn a little bit about people's beliefs all over the world, but not a lot about any one of them. But we did learn to respect other people's faiths—that much I'll say for the watered-down approach we were exposed to. I guess by playing our own differences down, it made everyone feel more at home in the public place."

"Susan, I think you're on to something, though, I have to tell you that in my high school we were required to attend chapel and Sunday morning service. I was given the choice between a semi-residential orphanage and a very WASPy prep school. My survivor's benefits from Social Security and some contributions from my affluent aunts and uncles paid for the prep school that I chose. So I had no formal instruction in Judaism from junior high on. Although we weren't obliged to read the Bible cover to cover in high school, we did hear important sections in our various required activities."

"Well, that's a lot more than I got at my public school and Sunday school. Not that anyone cared but the minister and a few old fogies, anyway," observed Susan about the time they stepped in front of *Prinsengracht* 253.

All of a sudden both of them felt a hushed stillness as they entered a shrine which began to move them more than anything else they had seen in Holland. They climbed the narrow staircase to her room and saw the little bust of Anne's head looking out the window of this house. It remained as it had been the day the Gestapo invaded the Franks' hiding place. Susan and Henry became aware that they had already survived longer in life than this teen-age girl of sixteen. Susan took a look at the clippings Anne had put on the wall and remembered how honest she found that girl's descriptions of her first sensations own womanhood—not unlike her own—when she was reading her diary in high school. For Henry, though, it was more of a warning of what the fascists in his own times would do if given the chance—unless blocked by an informed, alert citizenry.

As the golden light of the late, warm afternoon sun cast a diffused restfulness in front of the Franks' house, Susan insisted on taking a series of snapshots of Henry and he of her. Susan would come to associate this quality of loneliness with that of the precocious teenager who had lived here.

"Henry, you had your decision to make. This house has helped me make mine. It's off to the McCarthy campaign."

"So it really affected you, Anne Frank's house?"

"What do you take me for, some kind of cold stone? Of course, it did."

Henry felt privileged to make such an acquaintance as Susan, and to become platonic friends with her. He learned from her that even people who have vastly different beliefs and personal styles could think along generally similar lines, get along, and share memorable experiences with each other.

"I'm going to leave for Rotterdam on the train this evening and see if I can't book passage to Hull in England by a North Sea ferry tomorrow."

"Susan, I've enjoyed being with you and getting to know you. I'm going to miss your company. May I see you off?"

"Don't mind if you do carry my pack again," smiled Susan.

"What are you going to do when I leave?"

"I'm off to Brussels! Maybe you've pushed me into getting a train tonight, although I would like to stay longer."

Noticing the vendor of herring selling his wares on the street, Susan stepped over and purchased two long filets. She held one in her hand several inches above her mouth and began to chew to the other end like the old man who had just purchased one before her. Then she held the second herring above Henry's mouth and indicated to him to follow her example.

On their arrival at the central station, Susan wrote out her address and added, "If I can do anything for you, just write."

"Thanks. Good luck to you. I'd like to say, 'Old Buddy,' but we haven't known each other that long, have we?" responded Henry in a cheerful tone. Then he hugged her. Susan smiled and reciprocated. Henry carried her backpack out to the platform where the train for Rotterdam was about to depart.

"Goodbye, Susan!"

"Take care, Henry!" they said in a departing exchange in which tradition had managed to convey an authentic tenderness of the special quality of their brief encounter of three days.

It's two minutes to six, and the train is due in Rotterdam at a minute to seven. She'll have plenty of time to find accommodations. She's a spunky lady. She'll manage quite well on her own, thought Henry as he walked back to the spacious waiting hall. Then his conversation with himself resumed, *The last train is due for Brussels at eight twenty-eight. That'll put me in Bruxelles Midi at 11:30* P.M. *Well, the hostel will be closed, but maybe it's time to take in some night life. Talking about that, I haven't even seen any of Amsterdam's nightlife yet. Well, I've got two and a half-hours to kill. Here goes!*

Drifting out of the station and watching where the majority of male pedestrians of more leisurely pace and informal attire were heading, Henry soon found himself curving around a series of small side streets. There the black signs with large white lettering SEX SHOP made vividly clear the activity of the area. Particularly anxious single men with hands in the pockets of their simple cord pants and plain beige or gray jackets stood on the sidewalk looking at the varieties of pornographic literature and devises neatly arranged on a bawdy orange background. A few houses down the Zeedijk women of the night were seated near the windows of their literally rose-lighted rooms that were somewhat softened by light lace curtains. The sight was amazing and somewhat less brutal than the tougher faces of Hamburg's Reperbahn.

It was hard for Henry to realize that there were still segments of his generation who used the services of prostitutes. Surely, with sexual liberation, healthy people could find someone who would find them attractive in return. But these ordinary young people, especially men, passing nervously down this street, did not appear particularly ugly or ill. True, across the street were three sailor mates who were ogling at an outstandingly voluptuous young woman. Maybe they had become so horny at sea and had just docked or would be here a short time. Maybe they were forced to seek these outlets because their occupation had cramped their available leisure time. But there simply were not that many sailors cruising about tonight. The passers-by were young or middle-aged with an occasionally older man. Why did they have to purchase their sex? Had the sexual revolution not reached the nice Dutch of his age? Certainly, every sign to the contrary was all about him.

So who were these purchasers of flesh? Were they deprived husbands or timid or over-sexed men? The seeping tenseness of these streets was beyond Henry's world. They were the domains, perhaps, of the Southern American soldier who had been in favor of the war in Vietnam. The young man whom Henry had met on the airplane last spring appeared to be the type of person who could get into killing, yet for whom sex was most titillating when it was displayed as filth. Maybe there were still Calvinists who enjoyed entering this world of sin that was clearly demarcated from the world of purity of home and hearth.

Through these blocks of women vendors of their own flesh, Henry's gait was stiff and agitated. Although he knew about the markets of the meat of life, seeing one still left him with puritan feelings of dirtiness. He left these streets and continued toward the Lange Leidsewarstraat where he peered into a smoky bar with topless dancers. The rather drunken Amsterdamers in this scene were somewhat older than he, and he felt out of place, so he tightened his thighs and took a final stroll back towards the Leidseplein.

A California hippie at the hostel had raved about a "center of meditation." So when he saw a few spaced-out poncho-clad wearers of soiled jeans, he followed them into a den where East met West in spirit. Its yoga, tarot, astrology and a variety of other mystical trips seemed intriguing to him from a voyeuristic distance. Why did he feel so frightened by all these people he respected? One of the less colorfully dressed mid-western American lads with those telltale rosy cheeks and clear, bright skin descended an old staircase. What was down below? Henry eased himself downstairs and came upon a macrobiotic spread of the new standard health meal, green-grayish lentil soup loaded with bay leaves, black bread, cashews, almonds, walnuts, raisins, and apples, thick brown rice with soy sauce and seaweed, carrots, and lettuce. $1.50 bought a huge portion of this platter of nutrition: spicy and wholesome.

It was a half-hour's walk back to the train. This fascinating world tempted him to stay to engage these mystics in conversation, to stay up all night. But, instead, he felt pressed to get on. The train waited for him.

After retrieving his backpack at the baggage check at the central station, he met the train for Brussels. His soul was tormented by this curious sense of being ill-at-ease with all these worlds he found so captivating. Yet, the very anxiety they aroused in him perhaps expressed incompatible oppositions in these co-existing movements. Here in Amsterdam anything and everything seemed to go on as long as it did not hurt anyone else. This permissive tolerance permitted such great diversity which Henry, while admiring it, reluctantly admitted also frightened his provincial values and narrow ways which still managed to control his every step. One's life seemed to be ruled not so much by what one desired or believed as by what was instilled in one's inner being.

CHAPTER 41

As Henry approached the Art Nouveau building, he cast a departing smile at its brick, glass, and masonry, which reminded him of a gingerbread cookie castle. The warm air of the afternoon had cooled to a humid evening, so he reached into his backpack and pulled out his light beige polyester zip-jacket with the simple UCLA inscription in blue. In the impressive waiting room he gazed at the spacious rectangle. While he stood there contemplating the interior of this space, a middle-aged, tall man and woman, both stunningly-attired, approached him.

"Um huh," the fatherly gentleman uttered—clearing his throat quite loud, "Where are you off to, young man?"

"I'm headed for Brussels."

"Would you care to join me and my wife? We're on the same train."

Henry was pleasantly startled from his deep admiration of the building to be surprised by such a welcoming parental invitation from a fellow who resembled a not-too-old President Franklin Delano Roosevelt, one of his heroes.

"Yes, sir," he responded with his Southernism again slipping out in the deferent manner he so despised himself for not controlling, "My name is Henry Green."

"From Los Angeles, I see," noted the perfectly coifed, blond, blue-eyed motherly woman in her Manhattan dialect. She was neatly wrapped in a flowing greenish cape that blended nicely in with all the red bricks and color of the canal's water and flowers.

"You must be New Yorkers."

"From Manhattan to be exact, and we have a son and daughter just about your age, we suppose. Let's see, you're twenty-one."

"Right, ma'am—just last month."

"Henry, I'm Dr. Joshua Meyer and this is my wife, Dr. Helene Meyer. It's a pleasure to meet you. Now let's be getting on the train."

"May I help you with your things, sir?"

"No thank you. The porter has them. See you down there."

Henry glanced down the platform as they walked toward the Brussels car. He could not believe his eyes. This couple must be carrying ten large suitcases and a large trunk. It was the first time all summer in all of the Western European countries that he had seen Americans travel like this. Henry had mistakenly assumed this manner of travel to be a thing of the past. "Either this couple is enormously wealthy, or there is something weird going on," surmised Henry. *Why are they traveling by train?* he almost asked out loud.

"We missed our TEE connection, you know. We had planned to be here on time, but we just couldn't leave the incredible symphony at the Concertgebouw. It was simply marvelous—truly of the highest quality, and, to be honest, as good or better than the last concert we heard in Vienna this summer."

"The train won't be pulling out for another ten minutes, but we can get on if you'd like," Henry suggested politely.

"Yes, it is a good idea. I hate rushing."

The unlikely trio boarded the first class car designated for passengers to the capital of Belgium. In the lead, the Meyers took possession of their compartment with such an air of relaxed finesse that the conductor took Henry for a wayward son of some important American dignitaries who were sufficiently caring parents to have rescued their long-lost offspring from the depths of Amsterdam's vice. The real story was—it turned out—not too far off from this railroad employee's first impressions.

The train pulled away from the hushed yellow lights out into the pitch black of the countryside so that only the reflections of the Meyers and Henry could be seen in the windows.

For a while there was silence in the compartment after their initial chat and all of the three traveling companions were immersed in their last thoughts of life in this jovial city. In a few minutes Mrs. Meyer looked away from the fading lights back at her husband and remarked, "Perhaps, it's because New York has its roots here that we like this city."

"You may be right, darling."

"Henry, what did you think about Amsterdam?"

"I liked it very much though it wasn't my favorite spot in Europe. I wish

I had more time to see the Netherlands better, particularly Amsterdam, but I did enjoy what I had time for. You know, it leaves me rather happy. I'd been feeling down for a few days before coming to Holland and I met a very nice American girl there."

"So you fell in love?"

"No, I just met a young lady I had a very good time with, and yesterday, ever since we visited Anne Frank's home, I remembered her words on rereading them, and they made me so happy. They made my new friend even happier than me!"

"Yes, yes, what was that stunning passage? I know it like the back of my hand, but I can't recall it just now."

"'In spite of everything, I still believe that people are really good at heart. If I look up into the heavens, I think that it will all come right again, that this cruelty too will end, and that peace and tranquility will return again.'"

"That's right. Imagine such optimism in spite of such adversity."

"You know, seventy percent of Amsterdam's Jewish community was killed by the Nazis. Even though the Dutch held a general strike to protest the first deportations, they went on anyway. Even though seven thousand managed to survive, the others were murdered."

"We know this only too well. I'm an American Jew, and my wife is a German gentile by birth and upbringing."

Henry gulped thinking that he had made Mrs. Meyer uncomfortable. But she immediately set him at ease by resuming the conversation, "Henry, the Nazis drove the German Christian liberals and progressives out of the country, and of those who were brave enough to stay and fight, many died in the camps, too. My father made the choice to stay in Germany. He and my mother despised the Nazis. He felt he could minimize damage to our family's name and property. He felt he could help some of his Jewish friends by staying. When the devil comes to roost in a place, you must choose to stay there and fight or follow or leave. My father remained and resisted in a thousand little ways. He would have Jewish friends pose as servants and employees until we could have them smuggled to another country. In his business dealings abroad, Father always managed to sell this for the Weisses or that for the Rosens which, in turn, helped them get out of the country after things had become impossible. But I can still love and respect my father because he did not let them grab our minds. He and mother always pointed out the lies that we heard were false which is not easy for a child to understand when her nation defines falsehood as truth. They passed down to us the good values of brotherhood, freedom, love, equality, justice, and respect for all the peoples of the world."

"But you have a Manhattan accent."

"I was raised with the French, English, and German languages from my infancy, spoken by native-governesses. That does help, you know."

"I'm sure it couldn't hurt!" replied the young man. "What kind of doctors are you, if I may ask?"

"Both psychiatrists, although we are businesspeople as well," replied the husband.

Henry wondered if he had provoked their interest from some possibly abnormal behavior he might have inadvertently manifested. He didn't know what to make of Mrs. Dr. Meyer's "confession," and he would not inquire how she had come to meet and marry Mr. Dr. Meyer after the war. Instead, he thought to himself, *But the Dutch collapsed after only five days of resistance to the Nazis, and more than two hundred thousand Dutch citizens were killed, and thousands of their houses blown up. In the mid-thirties at their height in Holland, the Nazis got about eight percent of the votes. Yet, some Dutch officials put illegal German Jewish immigrants in internment camps and shipped many of them back to Germany. When their enemies were so much stronger, the Dutch resisted in the ways they could—fouling up production, and in killing Nazis 'in the underground.' But the Eastern European Jews' reaction is the only one people think of as passive.*

To fill the gap in silence, Henry inquired, "Where are your children?'

"Our daughter's studying music in New England this summer, but our son is in the City."

"You sound a bit worried."

"You picked that up from my voice, I suppose, perceptive fellow! We're worried about Frank; he's going through a drifting spell. What kind of student are you?"

"Well, I just graduated and have begun graduate school, but things are looking pretty bleak now."

"You mean the war in Vietnam?"

"Yes, that and the convention platforms."

"What are you going to do?"

"I'm fighting my draft case now. I should be given the normal four-year deferment, but because I graduated in a little over two and a half years, I don't know if they're going to give it to me. This summer I was supposed to go on an archaeological dig in France but when the professor didn't show up, I hitchhiked all over Europe. Most of the last month I've been using my graduation present, a month's Eurailpass. I've really been to every Western European country except Portugal. I was going to go there, too, but I met some guys from the Midwest who told me I risked getting my passport confiscated there so I decided to be cautious."

"I take it you've been doing the youth-hostel route. Well, we would like to invite you to see our way of life in Brussels. Could you be our guest there tomorrow and tonight?"

"Yes, sir! It sounds great." Henry almost gasped elated at the thought of not having to walk the streets of Brussels tonight because the youth hostel would be closed by the time they arrived.

Mrs. Meyer grinned, overjoyed to see an appreciative youth in this day and age when gratitude had become a passé sign of bourgeois domination.

The long patrician lines of Dr. Meyer's face did not appear moved one way or another by the words between his wife and Henry. Rather, he was listening and trying to interpret to himself the degree of intelligence and meaning of what was being said. Then his mind focused on the things around him. He began to take notice of the modern, rather Americanized-arrangement, of the newer parts of Brussels. At least here on the outskirts of town, it was the most American-looking city he knew in Europe.

After a few moments of silence, Henry came back with an answer for Mrs. Meyer. "Life is so complicated. I understand how you must love your father. When I was in Amsterdam, I learned that even many of the Jewish community leaders went along with the Nazi's round up of sixty thousand Jewish Amsterdamers because they really thought it would minimize harm to them. They really must have thought these people were just being shipped east." He thought to himself, *It's unbelievable how the leaders on those Jüdenräte deceived themselves. At least our generation of Jews has learned that we have to stand up and defend ourselves.*

About this point in their conversation, the train came to a rather jerking halt at Brussels' main station. Dr. Joshua Meyer waited for the crowd to clear and then stood up—silently signaling to his wife and Henry to follow his lead. At a bare snap of his fingers, a porter—the first Henry had noticed in Europe in all of his travels—shuffled up to the authoritative gentleman who gave him instructions about his and his wife's many bags. With his left arm stuck out at his side and tucked into his pants' pocket, his wife inserted her right arm through his angled limb. Flanking Mrs. Helene Meyer on her left, Henry served as her left-side guard. In a controlled position of self-assurance, the three entered the station.

Casting her large blue eyes toward Henry, Mrs. Meyer changed the subject of their conversation. "Henry, with all our business in France, we rarely come to *Bruxelles*. That's why I'm as excited about it as you. We have a reservation at the Brussels Hilton, and you can stay on the couch in our living room."

"Gee, thanks, Mrs. Meyer, that's great!" Henry replied enthusiastically.

Glancing to his left, Dr. Meyer smiled, as the porter flagged down a taxicab in front of the station. In minutes the fellow had loaded the car, instructed the driver to take them to 38 Boulevard de Waterloo, via a night view of the Grande Place. Unaccustomed to such service, Henry watched somewhat in awe at the rapidity and efficiency with which Joshua's large tip had activated the man's action, although he was bothered by the comfort with which he and the porter were showing deference to his hosts' unquestionable social superiority. Within minutes, they were at the square with its Baroque and Gothic Guildhalls and Town Hall, which shown like a golden box of jewels covered by the black satin of the night sky. For a few minutes they strutted around this compact place then got back into their cab. The cabby's speed was snappy but not furious, and he brought the car to gentle halts near the monuments floodlit in green or silver or gold. This was a city where light embellished the night in stately but jovial tones. Soon they had arrived at the modern weighty concrete and glass building, which exuded an American-European or Euro-American functionalism. The constituent strains of this architecture were difficult to identify properly. As before, the very notice of the Dr. Meyers' attire and movement called forth a ready train of helpers. Within five minutes, their luggage was removed and their reservations confirmed in a perfectly orchestrated sweep, and the suite with a large bedroom and antechamber was opened and arranged with few requests. At once, the Meyers were at home with all the convenience and comfort upon which the sleek modernity of the portable, electrified, clean and gentle order of contemporary America bestowed its class of effective entrepreneurs wherever they traveled around the world. *It must be for such citadels of ease that the powers-that-be are sending the boys to die in Vietnam,* noted Henry to himself. *It is comfy, but it's not worth dying for when you know only a few people have the chance to get any pleasure out of it.*

While Henry was reflecting to himself as he was washing up, Mrs. Meyer had the chambermaid convert the enormous sofa with pillows into a sheeted and blanketed fantasy nest for Henry.

"Sleep well."

"See you in the morning. We'll try to rise and shine at 8:00 sharp so we can get off to an early start."

"Good night," responded Henry as Dr. Meyer was shutting the door to their room. His arms pulled the long sheet cover of a light, fluffy blanket up to his neck. In the perfect temperature on the soft couch, he quickly fell asleep.

CHAPTER 42

At the sound of the muffled alarm, Henry, still sleepy, awoke on hearing the bustling activity in the next room. Last night had been his best sleep all summer. Before the Meyers had finished in the bathroom, he was dressed and ready to set out with his benefactors.

The day was cool and a bit overcast but was a welcome relief from the sweltering humid New York City summer from which the Meyers had left only three weeks ago.

"How does it feel to be in 'Little Paris,' Henry?"

"I certainly didn't expect to experience it first class, that's for sure. Did I ever sleep well last night!"

"Yes, it was rather cozy, don't you think, darling?" Dr. Meyer inquired of his wife.

"Maybe it was the coolness. In any case, it was a delightful rest. What do you suggest that we try to take in today?" Mrs. Meyer asked. After a brief wait at the sixth floor elevator, they descended to the ground floor and walked over to the long breakfast room. Its large windows stretched over the garden.

"On our itinerary, Jane already arranged for a driver to meet us and spin us around the major sites. After our tour, we're supposed to have lunch at the *Épaule de Mouton*. Is that agreeable to you, Henry?"

"That's terrific. I thought I'd have time just for the Grand Place, and I'd hoped to make the Breughel House."

Just as Henry was about to get in his plug for a visit to the Complex of the European Economic Community, a waitress who beamed a catching cheerfulness laid out a simple and elegantly arranged continental breakfast in front of them. The croissant was scrumptiously buttery and flaky, and the jam must just have been made from fresh fruit. There were large bowls of *café au lait*, and a bowl of fruit in the middle of the table. "Have you seen the EEC or Erasmus House before?" asked Henry.

"What a combination! No, we haven't. I'm not sure we'll be able to do it all today and still get in Helene's shopping."

Feigning sacrifice, Mrs. Dr. M offered a compromise, "I guess I could knock out some of it, but let's play it by ear. See if you can keep my interest off shopping."

"Let's be going now," said the host as he picked up the bill and handed a large piece of currency to the waitress. By this time the guide was signaling the doctors from the entrance to the restaurant. Without the slightest difficulty in recognizing his clients, the guide gestured to them that he was waiting for them at the exit.

"*Bonjour*, Dr. Joshua and Dr. Helene Meyer; they call me André."

"This is our guest, Henry. You have Americans from both coasts to show around."

"Ah, very well, your tour is beginning," the plump and jovial fiftyish man grinned as he whisked his trio into his large Peugeot. Within minutes, they were circling the center of the city which still had the shape of a heart. From there they drove down the Place de Broukere past Rodin's sculptures at The Stock Exchange and up to the vast International Rogier Center which would be considered an only moderately tall high rise in a big North American city. In front were parked streetcars, which Henry intended to hop on as soon as he was on his own again. Then the driver whizzed out to The Atomium. It reminded the Meyers of a gigantic model of the biochemical compounds that they used to study in medical school. Meanwhile, the driver recited the history of his city carved into its buildings. One could visit The Pottery Museum, the Episcopal Seminary, St. Gillis, St. Peter's Hospital for Leprosy, Brussels University, and the great tower of the Church of La Chapelle. They wanted to take in the Beginhof, the Academy of Arts, the Memling and Gruuthuse Museums, and the Churches of San Salvador, St. Anna, St. Walburga, St. Jacob, Ouze Lieve and Jerusalem, and finally the EEC and NATO headquarters. By noon, the Meyers were totally exhausted and bored, but Henry was delighted that he got a complete view of many things he would have missed walking around on foot and taking public transportation without a guide.

"André, we're famished. Couldn't you leave us off at the Lamb's Shoulder restaurant and pick us back up around three in the afternoon?"

"*À votre service, monsieur*," retorted the guide in a subtly subservient and dejected tone—picked up by Henry and Helene but overlooked by Joshua.

This guy ran us into the ground, thought Dr. Meyer to himself. Henry was privately bemoaning his probably having caused André to get into trouble with the Meyers because he had added his suggestions of the EEC headquarters in the suburbs to André's finely-tuned itinerary.

In minutes, André had Drs. Meyer and Mr. Green at the doors of a restaurant which was right in the neighborhood of the Grande Place. Even the ordinarily controlled couple exuded signs that their hunger would somewhat modify their selection of items from the menu. In the fashion of good French *bonnes tables*, the food was to be spiced with the joys of company. Tucking her long dress under her with gusto, Helene quickly accepted Henry's seating her, as her husband sat down facing her. Almost as soon as they were offered a menu, Mrs. Meyer, already well read on the best selection from the bill-of-fare, had drawn up a list of delectable foods, which could be served without a long delay.

First, they would indulge in the fish *Waterzooie*, a thick soup of a variety of the "fruits of the sea," sprinkled with fine herbs. For her husband *Tomates aux crevettes* should arrive quickly and satisfy his craving for the local mayonnaise and shrimp. Everybody should try the *boudin*, the blood sausage, which Helene hoped would arrive immediately before her man would be out of sorts from his tendency to have a hypoglycemic reaction to a lack of food. Henry should be overjoyed with a *biftek et frites*, which, while rather pedestrian, would probably not be on his plate if they were not there. For herself, she chose the herbed-streamed mussels floating in a sauce of garlic, parsley, black pepper, cayenne, and oregano. These delicacies she would share with the others in her typically generous *noblesse oblige* fashion. For her husband's main dish, she would risk ordering cod cooked in a mixture of lemon juice and beef extract. Instead of wine, she would shock the waiter and command a simple *Faro*. After all, beer was the national drink, and she knew her Joshua would prefer it to wine anyway. They would end their already late lunch with a *café au lait* of the variety *un filtre* and would wait for the evening to consume a cheese plate despite being pushed by the waiter to stuff in these extra calories.

Conversation was attenuated to the unspoken urgency of meeting the gentleman's need. Since theirs was the only occupied table out of the twelve in the establishment at this midpoint in the afternoon, others' demands did not overburden the waiter. He decided it would be worth his while to satisfy these simple American tastes. The hot creamy soup arrived in minutes with a wonderful, long, crusty *bagette* and butter. In the course of the next quarter hour, more bread and a filling blood pudding were placed before them as soon as the fish soup had been removed.

The humor of the doctors had already improved. Mrs. Meyer was delighted that her choice had perked up her husband and enlivened their guest. Henry deciphered the interpersonal messages to mean that they should wait for the master of ceremonies to be restored before they begin to chat. As the main platters came out one at a time, Joshua's opinion of André's morning tour had already scored higher than initially registered, so he broke the silence, "That André is thorough, isn't he?"

"Indeed!" laughed the hostess.

"I think it was my fault. I think I shouldn't have brought up the EEC."

"Nonsense, Henry, it was interesting. We wouldn't have driven there if it hadn't been for you."

"Are you sure you feel good about it?"

"Yes, surely. We did miss the main lunch hour, but look, we have this elegant little place all to ourselves. It's working out perfectly," observed Helene—savoring one of her mussels.

"This steak is very good, and I've never had such huge French fries with fluted edges ever in my life. This mayonnaise is wonderful, but I think the fries are good enough by themselves. Here try one."

Then the older and younger tourists began handing around little tastes of their various plates to one another. The waiter looked on in astonishment—hoping that his tip would justify the tasteless impropriety of these democratic table manners. And to make matters perhaps more strange than crude, the American nobleman raised his hand in great haste immediately after devouring his cod. This gesture made the waiter become curious if it were a sign of proper etiquette in North America to pounce into dessert and drink before engaging in conversation one's company.

"Madame wishes to choose some of your chocolates, and all of us would like a *café au lait*."

The phrase "at your service" was uttered as if some entertaining but gruesome scene were about to occur, which, in all hopeful attentiveness, would be duly rewarded. With the sudden desire to please tinged with a bit of imitative mocking *le garçon* brought forth a silver platter with a variety of artworks in chocolate. Helene stuck to the choices she had established as superb.

At this point, the filter coffee was brought out to drip in their presence. To test his sense of prediction, the waiter timed their consumption of these items and was reckoning on the amount of *pourboire* he could anticipate from this trio who appeared to be rushing through the entire meal. *Le garçon* was correct. They had completed all their repast by ten minutes to three, but he was amazed that he had underestimated their generosity by a full ten percent. They left a tip thirty percent of the total. Though delighted, he failed to understand such guests. Bemused, he bid them *adieu* with a wide smile and even escorted them to the door, opening it and bidding them *merci*.

André was waiting at the corner and was anxious that his clients not miss the Little Pissing Boy, one of Brussels' favorite monuments. But by now, he had picked up that it would be necessary to subordinate his own and Henry's itinerary to his paying patrons, so before pulling out he inquired, "Where would *Madame* and *Monsieur* like to go first?"

Pleased to have reasserted the proper line of authority, Dr. Meyer responded, "I believe my wife has her heart on visiting La Pléiade; that is the best shopping area, isn't it?"

"*Bien sûr, monsieur.* "

Before heading off to park, André left them off by a string of twenty-one shops scattered in an oval around the Royal Palace and Brussels' Park a few blocks away. Passing the variety of specialized shops, Helene commented, "Can you believe these names? They all tell you exactly what they do to a point!"

Dr. Meyer and Henry accompanied her past the shirt maker-supplier of the Royal Court, the King's Printer, and many more stores with precisely-indicated trades as the shopkeepers started the long process of displaying their models, samples of the latest dresses, nightgowns, suits, and raincoats. Trying to feign attention, Henry and André, who had now rejoined them from his car, found their heads bobbing up and down from their over-plentiful lunch. Joshua kept up a genuine attention watching his wife try on the different textures, colors, and designs of the fabrics. To him she was still the princess he had found in the relatively undamaged rural estate in Bavaria where her father had managed to hide his most precious possessions before the end of the Second World War. Her skin was a light creamy white; her hair still flaxen in which had grown a few strands of gray; and her eyes remained a deep, sparkling blue; her breasts prominent, but not motherly, after the birth of her two children. While Joshua studied with precision the line and cut of each garment, Henry studied Joshua's enthusiasm for this adornment. At this moment, André was picking up a few copies of the free brochure with a black-and-gold cover dotted with stars that described all the shops and locations. Glancing over at André's distraction, Henry found the cartoon advertising reflective of the lingering racist and colonialist attitudes probably still ingrained in the class of wealthy people who shopped in this area. In the sketches, poor Africans or Chinese were pictured lifting the heavy luxury items for Belgians dressed in colonial gear and the jokes all made reference to the natives' load.

No longer able to contain his excitement for his metropolis, and waiting until *Madame Meyer* signed the final forms to have a dress shipped back to New York, André made a suggestion.

"*Madame*, if you like shopping, let me take you to one of our *braderies*. You can see one of our typical street fairs and pick up some incredible buys at the same time."

"Are you sure I can find some porcelain worth sending some friends back home?"

"Most certainly, *Madame*. I'll fetch the car and meet you back shortly."

By the time Mrs. Meyer had concluded all the shipping details of her purchase, André had returned and drove them into a neighborhood, which, with its elaborate lights and outdoor music, made a lively contrast to the snobby atmosphere surrounding the royal merchants. All the activity of this village within a city neighborhood, awakened Henry, and he became taken with Helene's bargaining skills in acquiring for twenty dollars a set of what appeared to be very old Flemish porcelain. However, Joshua felt cramped in these two packed streets and thought it a bit unseemly for his wife to be haggling in a public market.

When Joshua's lips began to pucker and his eyebrows to squeeze inwardly, the unpredictably perceptive André turned to Mrs. Meyer and sought to punctuate her success with a terminal point, "*Madame*, you have acquired an excellent set of Flemish flatware for nothing."

"You really think so, André?"

"Yes, *Madame*, but now, since you've demonstrated your mastery of the market, I must show you one of the manifestations of the great legends of our city. Let us be off."

Following the lead of André's flattery, Joshua and Henry began to praise the simple decorations of tranquil Flemish landscapes baked in blue and white on Helene's bowls and plates while winding their way to the car.

At promptly a quarter past four, André rolled his *bagnole* back to the oldest burgher of Brussel's, the *Manneken-Pis*.

With his usual professorial delight, André lectured, "You see, it is said that a sick man's little boy wandered off from his home and got lost. Everyone in the city went to search for him, and at last his father found him stark naked, laughing and peeing all by himself. Other people in Brussels think that this kid stood urinating from an upper story window on foreign soldiers during an occupation, but, no matter what, everybody in Brussels loves him, and he has a whole collection of his outfits in the King's House on the Grand Place."

After André's rather measured talk, Henry chuckled while the two New York psychiatrists pondered over the significance of the constant flow of urine from the penis of a male child as a strong object of identification of an entire city.

"Of course, it does show disrespect."

"Pay attention to his devilish grin."

"But, *Monsieur* and *Madame*, the common people used to wash their clothes in the basin below his feet, and it has been stolen."

"Are you saying that you find our speculation too much out of context, André?"

"Not at all; I just want to bring to your attention the element of humor in it all. By the way, what time would you like me to drive you back to your airplane for Paris?"

"It's at seven o'clock tonight. Oh, Henry, we forgot to tell you we have reservations for this evening at the George V in Paris. Do you think it's too late for you to get a place at the hostel for tonight?" Turning toward Henry in a somewhat condescending manner, André inquired, "You are going to stay at the *auberge de jeunesse* this evening?"

"Could you show me where it is?"

Dr. Meyer turned to André and pulled out a ten-dollar bill. "After you drive us to the airport, leave him off at the youth hostel."

"Henry, I will be glad to leave you and your backpack at the entrance to the hostel, but first we will pick up the Meyers' bags at the Hilton, then drive out to the battlefield at Waterloo, and drop off your friends at the Melsbroeck airport."

On the way back to the hotel, Helene took Henry's hand, "Whatever decision you make about Vietnam, drop off and talk it over with us when you get back to New York." Then she took down her pen and wrote out her name and private telephone number on a small slip of paper that Henry put securely into his buttoned pocket.

"Be counting on my call. I've had a super time with you two."

"It's been like having our own children around, Henry. The pleasure is ours."

André's style wavered between acting like an arrogant, failed professor anxious to let the world know of his superior knowledge and a faithful servant somewhat uncomfortable at grasping the unvoiced commands of his social superiors. In any case, that chauffeur dashed up to the Meyers' room and carried down their ten bags on a rolling cart he requisitioned from the porters in the lobby.

"André, may I help you?"

"No thank you, young man, I'll be right back and we'll be off to the site of the great battle of more than 150 years ago."

True to his word, André proved to be more sprite than his rotund face and belly might indicate. Winding down the streets of the older part of the city, Joshua and Helene were struck with the dirtiness and drab exteriors in this part of town. The chilliness of the overcast late afternoon absorbed everything. Soon the ugliness gave way to the silvery green beech trunks and leafy branches of the *Forêt de Soignes*, one of the last remaining forests of ancient Gaul. The 11,000 acres were absolutely still as the four troopers sped to the battleground. When an occasional brook passed their field of vision, they were lulled into a restful calm.

The clock had the best of the travelers. It was nearing time for the Meyers to leave Belgium, and André wanted to make sure that his clients were at the modern terminal a good forty-five minutes before take-off. For Henry it had been an exciting experience to be "adopted" for a day-and-a-half by a wealthy, sophisticated New York couple. He sensed that for them it had been a fantasy of repairing their bruised relationship with their own son. Now it was time to part as individuals, returning to the vastly different paths onto which they're own lives and circumstances had embarked them.

As André carried their large load on another metal carrier, Helene stood upright leaning slightly forward. Henry stepped up and wanted to hug her but stopped and politely shook her hands. Their touch was warm and soft, as though her motherly attention and his filial receptivity had penetrated the lines of distinction that separated them. When Dr. Meyer grasped his hand, Henry felt the strength of a leader that conveyed the urgency for him to maintain his composure in making rational decisions about matters of utmost personal, national, and international import.

"Thanks," smiled the young man.

"Good luck," responded the Meyers as they walked to their gate.

On their way back to the car, André, beaming from what must have been the enormous *pourboire* the Drs. Meyer had put in his pocket, kept feeling the insides of his pants to the extent that passersby appeared to be attributing a self-directed sexual release to this exaggeratedly happy fellow. Not exactly sure how he should expect this flighty, older man to treat him, Henry strolled next to him in total silence. Back in his own vehicle, André relaxed and remarked in his near-perfect American English, "You certainly have nice friends, Henry."

"André, I can't figure it out. It's the one thing I do almost perfectly right in life. I meet nice people or they pick me up. I have met so many wonderful people this summer in all the countries of Europe where I've traveled. I've met a lot of nice Europeans and a lot of nice Americans. Of course, I've met a few of both I could do without, too, but it's been a fantastic summer overall."

"What are you going to do tomorrow?"

"I'll see some of the central city a bit more in depth—maybe the art museum. I'd like to see how some of the average people live around here, too. Any suggestions?"

"*Bien sûr*! Tomorrow you go to *Les Marolles*. It's what we call a *quartier populaire*. I think you say 'a working class neighborhood.' Just go to the Place Poelaert and look in front of the stone balustrade. You can't miss it."

Winding down a narrow, almost medieval street paved with cobblestones, André's Peugeot bounced up and down, swerved around the bending byways, and screeched to an abrupt halt. He deposited Henry's backpack on the small sidewalk and curtly bid him, *"Adieu,"* to which Henry responded a cool, *"Merci."* There was something in André's tone of farewell that implied, "Whew, that's the end of that freeloader who really fits in this shabby place."

The door of the hostel was made from a very tall, thick piece of wood dating back at least two centuries. On opening, it, the heavy entrance piece squeaked like the door of a haunted dwelling. The office was located a few feet inside the entryway off to the right. When asked if there were spaces available, the manager searched through a registry and answered, "You're lucky. We have very few guests today. Otherwise, you'd never get a space at this hour. We close in a few hours, you know," answered their keeper in his thirties who spoke very good English with a Flemish accent.

"Yes, here's my international youth hostel card, and here's the money I owe you."

Henry entered the large dormitory filled with old metal bunk beds with simple, thin worn mattresses. Flinging his pack on his bed, he decided that despite André's condescending judgment of his accommodations, he would trust the very serious-looking student, nature-, and traveler- types who were lingering around their beds and who were few in number, anyway.

He stepped out to the manager's office and asked how to get back to the monumental buildings of the city's center, which he realized were not very far away from this old accommodation for young people. The very proper manager handed him an old tourist map and traced a line from the hostel over to the Cathedral of Saint Michel and Saint Gudule. The cool evening was engulfed in a light, humid haze. Putting both hands in his pockets, Henry walked into the night for a leisurely stroll. Down the dimly-lighted side streets, he was soon in a wonderland of floodlighted monuments. From the cathedral of the city's patron saint of the thirteenth to fifteenth centuries, over to the laced stone of Our Lady of the Fine Sand, past the Royal Palace and the Museums of Modern and Fine Art, everything was enhanced in floodlights of many colors. The cheerful lights distracted him. He had learned about the conflicts between the Walloons and the Flemish in his class on ethnicity at college, but he had not had an opportunity to meet any real Belgians on an equal footing. André had been essentially the Meyers' hired hand.

Everything felt fleeting. Henry's summer was nearing its end, and he was about to embark on a frightening decision. Solitude was a comforting blanket on a mild late summer evening when he seized on the history of the buildings he passed to guarantee his anonymity. Their formal stately beauty overshadowed his personal stature. Noticing the hands of his watch, he headed back to the inn for youthful wayfarers. He had arranged everything properly on this quiet evening stroll. Henry's pace was not too fast, slow, involved, or distant.

A few minutes before closing time, Henry re-entered the *l'auberge de jeunesse*, where may have been only twenty souls in a large sleeping hall. At maximum capacity, it could accommodate perhaps five times as many people.

Two guys about his age were engaged in a conversation in French on the virtues of Gueuze Beer, which they were dying to try first thing in the morning. Henry was pleased that he was comprehending most of what they were talking about, but he wasn't pushed by his usual urge to try out his command of the local idiom or his usual delight in meeting people from different countries. So he just listened. *Wow*, he thought to himself, *I've never been such a typical tourist as I have been here in Brussels—and all by chance.*

Jean-Yves, the fellow in the bunk below his, was analyzing the composition of Gueuze. It was evidently brewed using a substance he called

Lambic that is composed of crude wheat, malt barley, and three-year-old hops. Jean-Paul, Jean-Yves' equally enthusiastic commentator on Gueuze, claimed that the brewers did not employ yeast to cause the beer to ferment. According to him, it just happened spontaneously in its barrels where two kinds of yeast grow naturally on its sides. However, Jean-Yves added that after it ferments for about three days, the Lambic is made and is left in the barrels several years. Gueuze, he insisted, is the product of combining several of these Lambics. At this point in their conversation, the master of the youth hostel shut off the lights for the evening.

CHAPTER 43

Although he was tempted to spend a few days in Louvain, Henry decided that he would go directly to England and, after finding out if he had any definite news on his draft case, would make his definitive decision about the U.S. Army and Vietnam. It was time to leave the continent this evening. There was a night crossing by ferry back to Dover.

During breakfast, Henry introduced himself to Jean-Yves and Jean-Paul and asked if he could follow them to the brewery this morning—explaining that he wanted to see Erasmus House and the *Musée d'Art Ancien* before he left the city.

Jean-Yves and Jean-Paul, students from Louvain, were two fellows who prided themselves on their sense of humor more than anyone else Henry had encountered all summer. They were constantly joking, laughing, or wryly correcting each other on some obscure detail of an obtuse subject in which both of them were interested. They accepted Henry as a hanger-on, but went on bantering to each other as though they had met a new acquaintance in school who would have to gradually fit in their self-entertaining comedy without taking precious time away from their weighty in-house jokes. The conversation about the details of the manufacture of beer lasted until they had reached the Grand Place where they found the *Maison des Brasseurs*—the Brewers' House—on the same side as City Hall. Upon entering this abode of the Knights of the Malt Shovel, the lads were overwhelmed by the oak paneling and the shining tile and parquet floors.

Once in the basement, they discovered a medieval brewing cellar decorated with wooden vats, *fourquets* (the wooden malt shovels), pan-strainers, ladles and skimmers. Next to the cellar was the place of Jean-Yves's and Jean-Paul's immediate craving, a medieval tavern with old brick walls, stained-glass windows touching the pavement, stone slab floors, hewn tables, benches and stools, and a large fireplace with logs in an iron basket. After they seated themselves, the heavy-set Jean-Yves, who resembled a Breughel peasant, offered the first round to the thin and princely-handsome Jean-Paul. In a few minutes the two Belgians had downed their first mug of Gueuze and were ordering a second just at the point Henry had sipped maybe an inch and a half of this champagne-like beer and was already beginning to feel somewhat relaxed. By the time they had chugged their fourth mug, Henry had managed to down his first, and all of them were approaching giddiness. While Jean-Yves and Jean-Paul were uproariously guffawing about a personal joke, Henry became decidedly drowsy from the beer. He remembered that if he were going to see the other sites, he would have to take his leave of the other two. Jean-Yves and Jean-Paul had shown an enormously greater tolerance of alcohol than had Henry.

"Il faut que je m'en aille toute suite. À votre santé," were his departing words as the merry duo sitting across from him was singing an old drinking song.

It was a short promenade from the Grand Place to the *Musée d'Art Ancien*, but the alcoholic merrymaking with the students from Louvain had consumed the better part of the morning. Upon entering the Neo-Classical structure from the end of the last century, Henry hurried through the central hall filled with the nineteenth and twentieth century masters. Spending somewhat longer in the next rooms on the Flemish Primitives, he lingered in the rooms with the works of Hieronymus Bosch, Pieter Brueghel the Elder and the renowned collection of Pieter Paul Rubens.

He chuckled imagining that the figures of the drunken Jean-Paul and Jean-Yves were thrust back as characters in these scenes of peasant life set in a landscape of nature where satire and cruelty existed side by side. And then he realized that all these masterpieces were suddenly swishing and dimming before his eyes as the mug of Gueuze he had imbibed was turning his impulses of gorging on high culture into a perfectly soporific dream in a haystack in an open green field.

Now was the time to move on to the neighborhood of Les Marolles. Down the rue de la Régence over to the Place Poelaert Henry raised his knees high as if practicing the good posture and rhythm of a military march. Soon he stood in front of the Law Courts—Henry preferred the pompous French designation of Palace of Justice. Over to their right was a stone balustrade overlooking the city's irregular rooftops and chimneys, occasionally interrupted by the green of the parks. Below, the city's division into two levels became strikingly apparent in the area. People bristled in barely visible narrow alleys. Henry could see dead-ends, and grimy, narrow byways. Their appearance of decaying history attracted Henry's curiosity. Down there were people, mobs of them, buying and selling at the street markets in closely packed stands. The red brick apartments were like slums in an American city but without their ever-present violence. Small boys ran about delivering goods on bicycles and on foot. Some adult men were cleaning windows, and tiny shops with cheap but useful commodities—like an American Woolworth's broken up into specialty shops—filled this quarter.

As he walked down into this section of the city, a whirlwind of thoughts blew through his mind. What was so special about this area? There was life! People were excited! They were moving all over just to do the essentials of everyday living. Some people were sitting and doing nothing, too. Old clothes, clocks, and furniture were trading hands, not only for money, but also for the joy of being with other people. *Was this what Tönnies meant by Gemeinschaft, by community? That's it!* it dawned on Henry. *That's what I liked about the medieval village scenes of Pieter Bruegel the Elder. People were together enjoying life in their own villages that were so close to nature. Sure there was the plague occasionally. Death, conformity, and persecution downgraded people's lives, but there must have been a lot of enjoyment and humor too. He knew how to poke fun at others with his brush.*

All of this sociability was so different from the poor neighborhood in America where he had lived with his mother for a short time before she fell ill. There people moved in and out frequently. You got to know them briefly. Often their values, customs, or beliefs were so different from your own. Rarely did the neighbors see one another after an initial flutter of borrowed butter or a shared dinner. Everybody from the spinster fundamentalist to the old landlady with her teenage-adopted son were so individualistic that they flung off other people when they realized their own special life pursuits made their short-time friends expendable to their new goals or reaffirmed values. Here in Marolles it appeared different on the surface. It seemed more trustworthy—maybe because they didn't have to worry that someone might shoot or harm them and because they had more social services. It seemed that their lives were more stable and that their way was more harmonious. But it was also more homogeneous. Either you were Walloon or Flemish. Most likely you were raised as a Catholic. There seemed to be many fewer African faces here compared to Holland. Henry wondered about this impression because the old Belgian Congo, now the Central African Republic, had been exploited for the material well-being of the Belgians. There had been less tolerance of his own people here in comparison to the neighboring Netherlands. Why? Were there different degrees in tolerance between Catholicism and Protestantism in general? Or had it been just Philip II of Spain's and the Inquisition's reaction against the Reformation in the Netherlands? Or had it been Napoleon's consistorial system? But even in modern times Belgium was said to be less welcoming of his kind than Holland—why? All these abstract questions he had pondered in college were divorced from the life he saw throbbing around him, but none of them were being solved by this visit. In the manner of a good tourist, he soaked in the scenes, the sculpture, the faces, the food, the places, and imbibed these inwardly to be stored in some kaleidoscopic area of the brain to be infrequently summoned in memory. Was not this being like a glob—a mushy, formless things that took in more and more and digested nothing? But then why didn't he feel this stuffing unpleasant? What was so delightful about standing in awe or finding disgusting the marvels of peoples and things which, while vaguely familiar, took on a more distinct admiration on closer regard? This trip was turning into Hieronymus Bosch's *The Temptation of St. Anthony* in which the place of the devil or the fearfulness of the demonic phantasmagoria were transformed into permissible activities whose significance was doomed to the passive recording of a general voyager.

It was nearing three in the afternoon. There would be little time to see the house of the great Renaissance humanist, Erasmus. *Too bad*, thought Henry. *Well, I never understood what he was about that well, anyway. Didn't he want to reconcile the spirit of inquiry, the new rationalism and classicism, with reforming the church from within? Oh yeah, he disliked Luther and others because he thought they were fanatics. He thought you could reform the church using your good old head. Oh, I remember, he was a good friend of Thomas More. More's Utopia was a terribly uptight and really oppressive place for the slaves and women—not to mention if you disagreed with his authorities. Now, I remember, I thought Erasmus sounded a lot like some of my profs who pointed out all the injustices in our country and in the world, and then left it up to us students to do most of the changing but didn't stick out their own necks.*

In spite of his hesitancy about Erasmus, Henry hopped on public transportation out to the suburb of Anderlecht, southwest of Brussels. The little town lay on both sides of the King Charles Canal. At 31 Chapter Street, on the eastern side of the square, he found the beautiful stone house with heavy dark glass laced with metal in the windows. The high ceiling and Dutch gables matched the trees with dense branches in the garden. It was strange peering back into the private life of a great early sixteenth century scholar. For such a roomy building, the interior was plain except for the simple elegance of Holbein's rendition of the great humanist. Even his wooden desk was down-to-earth. For a priest, Erasmus wasn't poor, but his books had sold well and he had good patrons. "Sucking up," observed Henry sarcastically, "Why do all of these big minds have to spend most of their time sucking up to the people with big money?"

The house was handsome and well worth the visit to understand how one of the great minds of the early 1500s had lived. By the time Henry had visited Erasmus's home, the nearby *Béguinage*, a convent for nuns who spend only part of their lives as sisters, was closed. In a few minutes there was a tram that connected back to downtown Brussels.

Back at the central station by six-thirty, he settled on a time of departure. He would take the night train back to London. There was a train leaving Brussels at one minute to eleven this evening—passing by Oostende and Dover—that would put him in Victoria Station in London at 7:09 in the morning. That would be the best way back to England. He could sleep on the train and boat and arrive relatively rested in the great capital. Meanwhile, he could grab a bite to eat and catch up on the news that he had missed over the last few days.

CHAPTER 44

Slowly sipping a mug of rich hot chocolate that was topped with a slab of whipped cream, he skimmed the newspapers of the last few days at a local sweets shop. Then something in his head snapped, *You have to rush to the Gare du Midi.* Just in the nick of time, he made the train. Tossing his backpack on the rack overhead, he stretched out. With his head on the thick cushion arm of the train seat of an unoccupied compartment, Henry, drowsy, fell into a deep sleep. He vaguely recalled paying ten dollars for his passage by boat from Oostende to Dover and from there by train to London's Victoria Station. This part of his journey was not included on his just-expired Eurailpass. As he walked through the large waiting room with a white ceiling laced with beams of steel, the cool damp air chilled him throughout his body.

Being back in London was more like being in a somewhat known, if not truly familiar, big city. His mind drifted back to Blake Nichols and Pierre Moreau with whom he had walked all about the city their first few days of the summer. How different had Henry's summer worked itself out than what he would have thought at its beginning. He would also have to check if there was any mail awaiting him at the American Express. *Come to think of it, Blake swore that he would write, and I haven't heard from him all summer. I should have some mail waiting about my draft case*, thought Henry to himself as he entered the Victoria Underground Station.

The colorful map of The London Underground was frightfully unfamiliar, even to an American lad who had never owned or had access to his own set of "wheels," as the current L.A. expression referred to automobiles. He liked the idea of a subway, but this map with black, green, red, purple, brown, gray, blue, yellow, and white-in-black lines was wholly undecipherable to him. In fact, Henry had never ridden a subway in his life before this summer.

As he stood there pointing his finger at a not-very-wide, sinuous light blue stripe that represented the River Thames, he finally mustered the courage to stop a passerby to inquire how to get from Victoria Station to St. Paul's Cathedral, in the neighborhood where the hostel was located.

"There are several ways to go. However, if I were you, I'd take a yellow, that's a Circle, line over to Liverpool Street and then transfer to a Central, that's a red line, going in the direction of Ealing, that's westward, and it's just two stops from where you transfer. On the other hand, it would probably be simpler just to stay on the yellow, Circle line, get off at Blackfriars and walk."

Without giving him the time of day to inquire if he had understood, the lanky, hippie in his twenties rushed off to his destination. With his right index finger, Henry then retraced what he thought the young man had just told him. *Well, here goes*, thought Henry to himself with trepidation as he wandered down the rounded corridors to the Tube. He glanced at the lines of advertising in the muted greenish light. As the train approached, its cars seemed very broad and low-lying—giving the impression that they would derail only with difficulty. There were crowds of people bustling here and there like little molecules floating and squeezing to the points of least resistance. *I must have hit the morning rush hour*, thought Henry, pleased by all the surrounding throngs of humanity. To simplify matters, he got off at Blackfriars and curved his way over to the centuries old decrepit building at 33 Carter Lane where he found accommodations in what had been for a long while a school for choir boys.

Anxious to catch up on personal news and already acquiring a taste for the underground over transit by car, Henry rushed back by the Tube to the Piccadilly Circus stop, where he chuckled at the "Way Out" sign—marking the exit right by Haymarket, where the American Express was housed at number 6. Unlike the rush hour traffic and lines he had encountered in Rome at this business, the London office was less crowded and the people were more polite. There was a letter from his mother in which was enclosed a letter from the government of the United States of America and a postcard from Blake Nichols. His heart began to beat so rapidly that he could barely swallow. Henry could not bear the thought of opening the governmental or personal letter before finding a quiet place where he could be all by himself. Suddenly the image of the small park by the side of Saint Paul's popped into his mind. Safely tucking these letters in his left shirt-pocket, he retraced his route and was back at the little spot of greenery and silence in the midst of this great city. He lay down on the bench and first read Blake's card in small print. As long as a letter, it had been written about ten days ago and post-marked Land's End, The United Kingdom.

Dear Henry,

It has been a great summer here in England, Scotland, and Wales. Yep, can you believe it? I've spent all summer walking around this 600-mile long, 300-mile wide island with almost 55,000,000 people—discovering the origins of at least a big part of my family. I'm leaving for France today and maybe I'll make it to Italy before we meet back on our flight. I've hiked all over this island, gotten soaked a few times, and fallen in love once. I'll fill you in on the details on the plane.

Take care, Blake

Then he opened the thick, long, white legal-sized envelope with his mother's distinctive penmanship. The large letters were slanting and rather closely bunched together as usual.

Dear Henry,

Enclosed you will find the letter that just arrived from Uncle Sam. I hope that it's good news for you. Things here down South are pretty much as usual. Aunt Violet took me out to lunch last Monday at The Place. She was looking good for her age and keeps herself real busy since Uncle Isaac's passing. I had roast beef and mashed potatoes with green peas and pecan pie for desert. It was real tasty. Your sister and family might plan a trip here late this summer, and will stay with her in-laws. Do you remember how her mother-in-law stepped on my foot and almost broke it last time? But I guess they are hard-working people. God, bless them! But I'm still hurt the way you-know-who called me such terrible names after I slightly scorched one of his collars. But I'll be civil—where there's a will, there's a way. We are all looking forward to hear more about your exciting trip. So far, four of your postcards have come. Don't forget that blood is thicker than water, and the Bible says to honor your mother and father. It would not hurt you to write more often.

Much love, Mother

With his heart pounding, he stuck his finger into the side of the governmental envelope and slowly pulled it along its adhesive seal so that not one piece tore irregularly. Pulling out the letter slowly from its envelope, he read, "Greetings...." His eyes speeded over the form letter and focused on the clincher, "You are due to report for induction into the Armed Forces of the United States of America on September 29, 1968." His heart stopped pounding and a cool, pensive mood overcame his whole body. *I lost my case. This is it*, reflected Henry. Without being overcome by self-pity, his exterior suddenly assumed an inordinately dejected state of down-turned mouth, watery eyes, and head that folded inwardly. Just as he was about to give in to an urge to cry, he heard a chorus of, "Eh, you, lying down so sad over there, the sky has not fallen. It's a beautiful day. Life is superb. Join us."

The loudest of the voices mingling among native and foreign accents was coming from a blond of medium stature with a largish forehead. Her skin was creamy white and her eyes soft blue. After his fantastic summer of open arms, houses, and hearts, such an encounter no longer exuded any air of disbelief. Yet this meeting was happening at a most opportune moment, when loneliness could only breed moping. A dashing young man with brown long hair and a goatee, dressed in a white jacket, and his friend in a green linen, old military coat chimed in a German accent, "Up, up, now! What's wrong?"

Next to them was a round-faced and chubby woman with dark black hair in her early twenties. Dressed in a gray blouse and a green sweater, she did not utter a word, but, instead, smiled in a narrow, timid, but genuine expression, aimed at soothing his anguish.

Henry pulled himself into a seated position with his large thighs trying, but never able, to feign a lotus position. His tightened lips attempted an upward lift of both of his cheeks, so as not to depress this small assembly of cheer.

"Would you like to accompany us on a walking tour of London, guided by a native English woman?" inquired the moderately buxom lass who was the leader of this crew. Momentarily uplifted from his own worries, this new piece of fodder for the military heaved the blue straps of his backpack over his shoulders and then extended his hand in a formal introduction to the woman in cotton pants. "Thanks for the invitation. I'm Henry Green, most recently of Los Angeles."

"I'm Ingwer, and this is my friend, Reinhard Schröder. We're from Hamburg and, of course, our championess, Jaq..."

"Jacqueline McIntyre, Jackie for short, of Reading," interrupted the comic but determined organizer.

"And I'm Safka Protic from Dubrovnik in Yugoslavia."

"So, why were you looking so forlorn, Mr. Green?"

"Just a minute or two before we met I was notified to report for induction into the armed forces of the United States of America. This means, no doubt, I will have to fight in my country's undeclared war in Vietnam, which I believe is very wrong."

"Are you going to go?"

"That's something I've got to decide in the next few days. It's the sixth of September today, and my plane takes off for New York on the ninth. At the moment, I think I am not going to go. I thought I definitely decided against going a few days ago, but I'm having some second thoughts."

"Good for you for not going. You know, we're planning a huge demonstration here for the twenty-seventh of October against the American war in Vietnam and at the Australian High Commissioner's and against the Soviets for their invasion of Czechoslovakia."

"That's great that people all over the world are putting their foot down on American imperialism."

"You got the right word for it," interjected Safka, "but don't forget that your country's not the only imperialist power, the Russians are too—look what they just did in Czechoslovakia."

Not wanting to spend this spectacular day reviewing the problems of the world, Ingwer jumped forth in a high flying leap and announced, "Let's get on with it! Isn't that what you say, Jackie?"

Ingwer's more sedate, shorter chum, Reinhard, with his pelican-like beak and small brown eyes, smiled in a gesture of sympathy for his enthusiastic fellow countryman. Reinhard, who knew the drudgery of spending from nine to five in a loud machinist shop outside of Hamburg, was more interested in discovering the intriguing world of this foreign metropolis than in deciphering the accuracy of this or that social issue. On the other hand, Jackie was able to use her charm, wit, cheer, and knowledge of London, to pull this motley group together and find out more about what she sensed to be Henry's better knowledge of what was happening in America and Vietnam.

"First, let's check our knapsacks over near Bank Underground Station and then we can get on with it," instructed Jackie as she sprung forward in an unpredicted leap and prance. The zestful Ingwer quickly pursued her, while the cautious Reinhard, Safka, and Henry were startled into a jog. They followed the game of chase of those two clowns who led them down Watting Street over to Queen Victoria Street, past the station and by the Bank of England. Gazing at Jackie's medium-length, bouncing, silky-blond hair and Ingwer's antics of crisscrossing the sidewalks and streets, Henry was uplifted by the playfulness of these energetic pranksters. In his usual amazement, Reinhard observed Ingwer's unpredictability while Safka's breath paced in and out trying to make sense of such bizarre foreign silliness. Jackie had already begun the orderly check-in of their equipment at the nearby baggage depot. Relieved of their heavy loads, the fivesome listened to Jackie's description of this area.

"You know, we could spend all day in the few miles around here. It's so full of history from Roman times onward."

"You're our guide, Jackie," they responded together. "You take us around."

Jackie led them by The Temple of Mithras in the neighborhood of Queen Victoria Street. As though she were just recalling the main points for a history exam without trying to over impress her audience, she pointed out, "This old religious shrine dates back to the second century A.D. when mainly the Roman soldiers used it to worship this Persian sun-god in great secret. Need I add that their cult was restricted to men?" she snipped and underscored by flapping her nostrils in and out in rapid succession.

During Jackie's little lecture, Ingwer hopped along the perimeter of the fence surrounding these low-lying ruins of the building from which the column feet were still visible in the base of large stone and mortar.

From the Temple, Jackie retraced their steps from the other side of St. Paul's Cathedral where they had met Henry lying in its gardens. She explained, "This is called Paternoster Row because pilgrims would recite the Lord's Prayer here during the Middle Ages. By the time they had finished, they were over here in 'Amen Court.'"

"Because they finished their prayer at this spot?" inquired Reinhard in his typical stern tone of concern.

"That's right! Come on this way," she said, waving forward down Warwick Lane over Newgate Street down Giltspur Street, curving around Smithfield Meat and Poultry Market to the gates and walls of St. Bartholomew's Hospital, where she halted her brisk march. At this point, Safka was panting heavily. She had to concentrate more on catching her breath than paying attention to Jackie's instructive talk. Then Jackie pointed over to the brown timbers and small windows set in white over the stone-arched gate. She noted, "We call this Barts. It was founded in the early twelfth century as a religious order. It is the oldest hospital in London, and the Elizabeth Gate house marks the entrance to a Norman church which is the oldest standing one in the city."

"Jackie, I just can't believe that so much history is squashed into such a little area," commented Henry.

"If you think this is old, just turn the corner," she exclaimed, jumping up with new enthusiasm, and in a few minutes, had taken her little group over to the Roman wall across the Museum of London.

"This wall and the bit of tower here were part of a Roman fort. If you'll look over to the right, you'll notice St. Giles Gipplegate. Oliver Cromwell was married there and our great poet Milton is buried there."

"There's just one more thing I'd like to show you in this part of London. It's called Cheapside," Jackie imparted as she resumed her brisk step down London Wall, turning left down Wood Street. Admiring her endless source of information packaged in crisp stories, the other four dashed after her and consumed more of her learning. "You know, in Anglo-Saxon 'cheap' doesn't mean what it does today. It meant 'to barter.' This place was a big open-air market that used to be named West Chepe. By the way," she continued, hiking up Cheapside and turning left on King Street, "There used to be a Jewish community in this section across from the Guildhall. That's why it's labeled St. Lawrence Jewry. The mayor's and city of London's courts are over there on the right."

Safka, impressed by Jackie's matter-of-fact knowledge without any pretense at being a show off, complimented her but suggested, "How about a lunch break soon?"

Across the street there was a small bakery, so Safka, without waiting for a reply from her companions, shouted, "I will return soon," as she stepped across the street to purchase a rectangular loaf of white bread with a thick light brown crust. Next to the bakery was a greengrocer where she picked up a long cucumber, and a few doors down from the vegetables she found a cheese store and a fruit stand. Inside, Safka bought a small block of cheese, butter, and a few apples. Back in less than ten minutes, Safka was rather proud to report that this lunch had cost a little over a pound. In proper socialist fashion, she immediately requested what amounted to fifty American cents from each of her fellow sightseers. Inspired by Safka's self-assertiveness, Reinhard finally made his real request known, "Let's eat lunch at St. Paul's Cathedral in the garden where we met Henry and then see the church before we move on. Either today or tomorrow, I would also like to see the War Museum."

Jackie glanced first at Henry, then at Ingwer and Safka. "Since it's so beautiful out today, let's take advantage of the weather and see as much as we can on the outside. You never know if it's going to rain. If it does, we can go indoors tomorrow."

With these words, she began to lead them back to Saint Paul's where they sat or gathered around the very bench from which they had plucked Henry a few hours before.

Reinhard took out his Swiss Army knife and started to cut the whole loaf into medium-sized slices while Safka buttered them. Then Reinhard began to slice the cucumbers into long strips onto which he placed thicker sections of cheese than he had wanted to cut. The five young people sat around each other and tossed their heads towards the sky. Interrupted by infrequent dense clouds, it was its clearest blue. They were grooving on one another, on nature, on the urban space of mankind, and on their sense of unity at this moment.

CHAPTER 45

Without any words, Jackie lifted herself upright. All the others followed her stretching, as though she were their gymnastics instructor. They got up and filed through the Great West Door of the cathedral as they peered upward at the innermost of its three domes and its circular Whispering Gallery. Besides reminding her guests that its style is late Renaissance to Baroque and rises 365 feet, Jackie pointed at the names and dates of the great ones buried here: John Donne; the cathedral's architect, Christopher Wren himself; Lord Nelson; General Gordon; and many military heroes. As they passed the center of the nave, she whispered, "*pax vobiscum sit*," which reverberated all the way to the other side.

From the cathedral, Jackie escorted her "foreigners" by foot, down Godliman Street, past the College of Arms. From there, they curved around the Salvation Army Headquarters and climbed up Lambeth Hill. Crossing a footbridge onto High Timber Street, they hurried by the warehouses until they reached the riverbank that led back to Blackfriars Railway Bridge and the Victoria Embankment.

Reinhard, who had habitual difficulty letting loose, sensed he was finally free to be accepted for who he was on his own terms. Safka, whose tendency to concentrate on the national peculiarities of the people she met in her travels, was overcome with a sensation that true union was possible now and forevermore with people of diverse backgrounds. Ingwer, who tended to wrap himself up with annoying tricks and dramatic exaggeration of real life events, imagined that he became a flannel band that encircled these new friends. Henry, who tended to be carried away by the intellectual details of a location, shifted his attention away from the dolphin-shaped iron bases of the lampposts along Victoria Embankment and experienced an enmeshed embrace of all of the arms of all of these friends. In her own way, Jackie dropped off sharing information to huddle in the aura of protective kindness and celebration in which her guests had enveloped themselves into one kindred spirit. Feeling this solidarity, they walked silently and slowly by the large granite slabs of the wall by the Thames. Occasionally the seats supported by kneeling camels caught their attention. This comradeship lasted until Jackie directed them rightward on Bouverie Street, passed the headquarters of the Knights Hospitallers of St. John and onward up to the Royal Courts of Justice up by Fleet Street. Very keen on relating how so many English newspapers were concentrated along and around Fleet Street, Jackie had now managed to push Henry from his state of solidarity back into his more typical mood of reflection.

These people are super, thought Henry, *but they're so different from my friends back home. What is it? I can't put my finger on it.* Henry didn't figure out the answer that summer, or for many years after that. He had grown up learning to respect and almost praise differences in people. This tolerant attitude muffled his critical sense of people and things. The more liberal aspects of his American education had inculcated into him an abhorrence of attributing differences to groups. This openness had blocked him from noticing that some of his friends in Los Angeles came from enormously, or at least, much more prosperous circumstances than his own. In contrast, these young people, with whom he was absorbing London, had worked during university and the summers as he had. This vacation had been earned. It was this reality of life that helped to fade their varying national characteristics into a special quality of mutual admiration of overcoming the hardship of life. True, they all rather boastfully saw their success in studies as more the result of their individual efforts than any genetic endowment of a sufficient intelligence. But they were acutely aware that their ability to study had been dependent on their respective governments' largess. Thus they all shared a thankfulness toward the state, to the collective will of all the people, as long as the state met the higher morality found through the contemplation of real world good. When the state failed to embody this ethics of equality, liberty, fraternity, and sorority, their own efforts had to be directed at changing it toward these goals.

If all these young people had been touched by the Summer of Love in 1966, it was not by the body changing accoutrements of drugs and their paraphernalia. Rather they knew that the real love had to be enacted by real laws protecting everyone's education, health, and welfare. If they were tolerant towards the wild experimentation of Haight Ashbury, it had been so through the joy of dance and song with their messages of peace and freedom—not the psychedelic dream that were its by-products. If they could learn to hate Simon and Garfunkle's "Neon God," they could be, nevertheless, warmed by "California Dreaming."

As the serious state of communion was passing, Jackie turned around, inquiring, "If you aren't yet sick of monuments by now, let's turn right by Charing Cross Station over into Trafalgar Square. St. Martin-in-the-Fields and The National Gallery are up that way. Then we'll take in a bit of nature by visiting the Mall over to St. James' Park, Buckingham Palace, Hyde Park and Kensington Gardens."

Henry retorted in proper Californian, "All right!"

The other three nodded their agreement with her. By this time Reinhard had gathered enough self-assurance to grab Safka by one arm. On her other side, Ingwer—partially playing a game of what he imagined a proper Eastern European promenade should be—inserted his own arm on her other side and skipped forward with gusto. Delighted at the sudden unaccustomed attention directed towards her, Safka skipped along to their jolly frolicking.

In his typical flightiness, Ingwer suddenly remembered he wanted to see the Houses of Parliament and turned to Jackie, "Are you going to show us Westminster Palace?"

"You know, we can see only the House of Lords, and, by the time we get tickets, we're going to loose a good deal of this beautiful afternoon."

Coming to Jackie's defense, Safka, Henry, and Reinhard almost simultaneously sighed, "But it's so beautiful out today. Let's stay outside."

"O.K., but tomorrow or the day after, we go back to the House of Lords."

"Good deal," commented Henry as he and Jackie proceeded somewhat ahead of the others.

Turning toward this tall American fellow whose hair had grown thick, longer, and curlier over the summer, Jackie noticed, "You look a bit preoccupied, Henry; you want to talk about it?"

"I see it this way, Jackie. If enough of us refuse to fight in the war in Vietnam, it will deprive the American military of its fighting force. It will provide an example to others that we don't have to follow unjust orders. It will show others that we think this is not a way to settle a civil war in the Third World."

"Listen, you don't have to convince me. I believe basically the same thing as you do. But are you willing to bear the burdens that this decision will put upon you?"

"Jackie, my whole life has been a heavy. I was born into a poor family but most of my relatives were upper middle-class or upper class, and, in the South where I was raised, family, not the government, was expected to help you out. There was never much of a welfare state back home. Although they all claimed to, my relatives didn't help us out to any extent. I wouldn't be surprised if they were all taking us as tax write-offs while my mother, my sister, and I would get altogether the equivalent of about fifty dollars a month from them beyond our social security money. One uncle was even illegally taking my social security money and giving it to my mother—telling everyone it was his money. When there were jobs available, we worked as soon as we could. What do I have to lose going abroad?"

"Well, you might have to face legal consequences."

"That's true, but America's allies, or nations which are friendly and have deep ties toward her, like Sweden, strongly object to the escalation of the war. That's why we resisters can go there in the first place. They want America to use her power and wealth to get the groups that are fighting to come to a reasonable, workable compromise."

"Do you have any money to live on to get started?"

"About seven hundred dollars, my life's savings; that's all. But I didn't have more than a few hundred bucks when I moved from the South to L.A., and I made it out there. I found jobs. I worked. I've always worked."

"You sound like a survivor. You'll manage then. Henry, I just hope that you people who are trying to stop this war will also have some influence on creating some kind of social welfare state too. When I see the conditions the people in your ghettoes are forced to bear, it makes me very angry. You don't even have the small medical services and family allowances that we do here. We have big problems here. But at least there's some security for all."

As Jackie and Henry's conversation deepened, they wandered without focusing on the side of Trafalgar Square by the Church of St. Martin-in-the-Fields. Reinhard pulled out his Pentax and light meter and began turning the dial for the appropriate film speed and shutter aperture. Safka sighed and stretched her head upward until she focused on the needle pinpoint of the progressively smaller steeple. Resuming her role of the informed native, Jackie pointed out, "There has been a church on this spot since the Middle Ages. This one was remodeled in the early eighteenth and nineteenth centuries. Besides its beautiful classical porticoes and tower, I like the openness of this place. Henry, this fits in with what you and I were just talking about. Even though there are royal boxes in this church, ever since World

War I, each night its doors are opened as a shelter for the homeless."

Just as Jackie was taking a native pride in certain policies of her country as compared to those of America, Reinhard had already leapt over to Nelson's Column with his left arm forming a V at this hip and his right arm bearing upward an imaginary sword at charge.

Even Reinhard's appreciation of military pomp and admiration of the defeater of Napoleon was enjoyed only briefly. Unexpectedly, the prankster, Ingwer, snuck up from behind and snatched his photobag to provoke his more sedate companion and their new friends on a sudden chase around the giant triangular quarter to their left. On the hypotheneuse, Reinhard almost seized back his possessions in front of Charing Cross Station, and Safka ran out of breath by the time they had reached the front of the first rounded white tower of the National Portrait Gallery. By this time Jackie had figured out that it would be prudent to wait for the two "boys" to tire themselves out, so she screamed to Henry to follow them and have them meet her and Safka by the spire in the courtyard. This run was more dramatic than the former ones and did not terminate before Ingwer broke out into an uncontrollable laugh slightly past the second tower on the left hand side of the gallery. Reinhard bellowed something beginning with *Dummkopf* in German, and then he found some ridiculousness in the absurdity of his friend's conduct that provoked laughter sounding more like a hiccup.

Henry found the unpredictability of Ingwer's chase more juvenile than fun but the high feeling of comradeship remained with him, leaving him to remark matter-of-factly, "Hey, the girls are back at the railway station on the other side of this building."

Reinhard put his arm over Ingwer's shoulder for a minute and they laughed together while Henry kept his pace a few steps ahead of them.

Back in front of the station, Henry said in a low voice to Jackie and Safka, "Well, Ingwer's silliness has taught me something. It just dawned on me how many different geometric shapes and patterns make up this city. Funny, it doesn't strike you so much when you're walking slowly, but when you're trying to catch up with Ingwer, it's more evident. To me the blocks designed as wholes and forming such different shapes are a lot more harmonious than the typical rectangular American grid."

"Yes, I rather like it too," answered Jackie, who made no comment on the stampede that had just occurred. Highstepping, she boldly marched back across Trafalgar Square and wound down a short street towards The Mall. Safka rather timidly requested, "Can we go into the park?"

Commanding, Jackie stepped backward toward the young men, "Forward across the street to St. James Park." She strutted as though leading a formal band across the tarmac but soon rejoined Henry and Safka.

"You know, most English people's lives weren't as comfortable as they are today at the height of our power. Henry, think about that when deliberating your decision. When we were at the height of our empire, the lot of the average person in England was rather brutish. It's really only after we gave up actively trying to control a fourth of the world that the lives of the average person improved and particularly after the Second World War when Labor came into power. That's when town planning became important and they cleaned up the big cities', like London's, air, and were able to control to at least a small degree the greed of the real estate developers. I'm not saying things are perfect, only that they're much better now than before for the common person."

As they strolled along the artificial lake by the willows, Safka asked Jackie, "What do you call those birds? How odd to see them in a big city."

"That one is a pelican, and the flock that's waddling on the other bank, they are geese."

Reinhard, equally delighted at the prospects of these water foul, began to photograph them and the ducks, before Ingwer persuaded him to take a group shot in front of the many colors of the formal flower bed laid out nearby.

Jackie added, "Don't ask me the details about this garden. The only thing I remember is that the French aristocrats used to look down upon our gentry mixing with ordinary English people here. This park was opened to the general public after the Restoration."

Jackie's cheer and competence were evident to the young travelers. She was pretty and cute without being strikingly beautiful. She was joyful and fun-loving but at the appropriate time and place sprinkled her knowledge of English history with juicy tidbits about this spot or that event. Somehow, and rather unconsciously, her meandering led them through streets crowded with people, cars, and buses or by the restful banks of the river or through the tranquility of the park. Safka, who along with Reinhard, had been the least talkative of the group, thought to herself that this Englishwoman has many admirable qualities. They walked quietly, not lingering long in front of the Victoria Memorial or Buckingham Palace, but rather continuing on to Green Park, past the elaborate gates of black and gold onto the wilder turf of roots and trees. When they stepped onto the wide path winding over to the silvery Serpentine Lake, Henry realized that he and Safka had barely chatted. Not wanting to seem aloof towards her, he struck up a conversation with Safka.

Because she spoke English understandably but with some difficulty, he spoke slowly and articulated each word, "It's beautiful here, isn't it?"

"Yes. Jackie made us a good tour," she responded matter-of-factly, not certain that she had employed the correct verbal idiom.

"What's it like living in a Communist country, Safka?"

"Our system has its good points and its bad points, like yours. And you know we're in the neutral, non-aligned camp, not tied up with the Soviet Union. In Yugoslavia, we have many national groups, but fewer than in your country. They don't always get along well, like the ethnic and racial groups in your country who don't always harmonize."

"Are you saying that all that diversity might be nice but would lead to conflict under any system?"

"Yes, you expressed it in better English than I. Many intellectuals in France, England and the Commonwealth, and Italy like our system of self-management."

"What's that?"

"What, you have never heard of self-management? It's the workers who choose their own bosses, and they are supposed to change those elected officials often. Nobody should keep the same position."

"Does it work?"

"Yes and no. Most of the time the same people are elected again and again by their fellow workers. Their products are usually good, though."

"So there's not all that much rotation of jobs?"

"Yes, you say it very well."

"Safka, why are all the students in Yugoslavia in revolt then?"

"For one reason, we have more freedom than in the Comintern countries, but it is still not enough. And there have been great injustices done by our security police, like your FBI and CIA."

"What do your parents do?" Henry asked.

"My mother is a doctor and my father manages a small construction factory for a long time. But their parents were peasants. What do your parents do?"

"My father died when I was two and my mother has been ill most of her life. She just started to work in a department store after many years of unemployment."

"What does 'unemployment' mean?"

"It means you don't have a job, even when you try hard and want to work."

"That is a very small problem in Communist countries. In fact, our

300

ideology says that there is none, although there is a very small amount. Henry, I must tell you; I feel I can talk to you because I heard what you were saying to Jackie. Yes, I come from a privileged family, and I assume you do not, and, in spite of all our system's problems, we live quite well. To be honest, after studying my country's history, I think that there must be a strong government or the different national groups would destroy the country. Some historians claim that our fighting among ourselves led to the First World War."

Walking on the banks by the waters of the Serpentine—set between the greenery of the park and the lake—the roughness of Safka's features blended in with the nature. She had a rounded head with wooly black hair, and her short stature was clad informally in worn blue jeans, probably acquired at an open-air market where used clothing was sold in London. Even though tuffs of her hair protruded outwardly, she had already come to accept the naturalness of this crop. There was something sisterly, or at least what Henry fancied as the qualities of a sister he would like to have, in Safka's being at ease with her own person. She was so unlike the hoards of bouffant-top teeny-boppers in miniskirts that mobbed the popular rock stars of the day. Henry found their fainting in public, adulation of passing fads, and simplistic humming of whatever was popular at the moment unattractive and irrational. Both Jackie and Safka were quite different, each in her own way, from those conformists. Was it peculiar that no one of this newly formed little group carried transistor radios or hummed the Beatles or Rolling Stones? In this silent interlude, Henry did not grasp the contradiction between his critique of music groupies and his singing to himself Dionne Warwick's, "Do You Know the Way to San Jose." *L.A. is a great big freeway. Put a hundred down and buy a car. In a week, maybe two, they'll make you a star. Weeks turn into years. How quick they pass. And all the stars that never were are parking cars and pumping gas.*

That's well deserved criticism, he thought to himself, *but how many fans that like that tune hear what it is saying? Most of them are mesmerized by the melody. That's all. London's 'Tube' is a much better way to get around the city than L.A. freeways are. That's for sure,* Henry observed to himself. Jackie dropped back to walk on Henry's right-hand side as they walked up The Ring to hazard upon the large Hudson Bird Sanctuary.

"What are you two talking about?" interceded Jackie.

Feeling more confident having practiced her English in a long conversation with Henry, Safka emerged from her timidity, "About my country, about how life is different under socialism and capitalism."

301

"Damn, I missed it! That's something that interests me, too."

"Excuse me for interrupting, ladies, but, Jackie, I was wondering if you were able to take in any of Bob Dylan's tour of England last year."

"Who, me? That was for people with pounds. Those tickets were very dear."

"I know what you mean. The only shows I could afford to see in L.A. were the ones I got cheap student tickets to a few times a year, for one to three dollars; these were usually a classical concert or a matinee or a play downtown. But there's lots happening on our campus that is top rate: plays, movies, lectures, dancers, art exhibitions, and sculpture. Would you believe that yours truly played in *Lysistrata* last year?"

"That's not too much different from what goes on in Yugoslavia, but if I can get tickets to something they're very affordable for nearly everybody. But for the very best entertainment, you have to be an important person to get the tickets. I am not so sophisticated that it hurts me."

"Have you heard any of Bob Dylan's songs? What do you think about him?"

"He's very irreverent to authorities," Jackie said thoughtfully. "I guess that's good in principle. His scratchy voice mocks all the smooth types from the fifties. It's satisfactory. I like the way he dresses. He's so thin and intense, not your strongman. I could do without all his chain-smoking cigarettes. He thinks he's so 'cool' criticizing the big companies, and he ends up giving free advertisements to one of their worst industries, the tobacco business. The lyrics to his songs tend to be quite nice; like 'The times, they're a changin',' but what are they changing to? You Americans make everybody feel high with your songs and your dance, but you leave people with fuzzy solutions to problems. Napalm is a change, but it's a sick torture."

"Have you heard Simon and Garfunkel?"

"Yes, and I've seen their pictures too. Now they are sweet. I think they describe the tension and boredom in many people's lives today. They're fluffy. If you go on one of your so-called head-trips or acid-trips or whatever your Professor-Guru Timothy O'Leary calls them, you make no connection between the companies and the leaders who got you into Vietnam."

In a low interrogative tone, Safka interrupted, "But, Jackie, are you not too hard on the American singers? They give the young people hope in beautiful melodies everyone can understand."

Not sure he totally comprehended Jackie's objections to these folksingers he thought he liked very much, Henry just listened to the two women.

Happy to see that Safka was becoming less passive, Jackie replied, "Yes, you have a good point. I wasn't objecting to singing anything you like, whether it be frivolous or not. I'm, just pointing out that, although these American folksingers are democratic, they're so much a part of their own culture that they don't even bother addressing the real solutions the British and European socialists have been proposing for most of this century. When did you hear them wailing about automobiles, big oil companies, and America's lack of social assurance and employment for all of its citizens? When did you hear them chanting 'Disarmament now? I never did."

"No. I understand what you mean now. Still, I like their music usually."

"I do, too. I could do with a bit more clarity of purpose, that's all!" Then pivoting in a 180-degree turn, Jackie went to see where Ingwer and Reinhard had meandered. Still in view, they were admiring the small spire of the Albert Memorial.

"Shall we run over there to catch them? What time is it, Safka?"

"16 hours."

"Hum. Then maybe we should leave Kensington Gardens the way out by Albert Hall and see if we can hop a bus back to Soho.

CHAPTER 46

"Jackie, can we take a double-decker? I still haven't ridden on one yet," Henry asked with the anticipation of a child.

"Yes, Mr. Tourist, if it's O.K. with Ingwer and Reinhard."

In a few minutes their international chums had fetched the lads from Germany, and they were as excited about boarding the two-level red bus as were their American and Yugoslav counterparts. After a short wait, they climbed aboard to the second floor of the vehicle and were fortunate to occupy the last seats by windows. Jackie was back to her happy role of their guide and was already explaining the general nature of the new part of London they would see.

"Henry, as an anthropologist, you will love it! There are people of many different ethnic groups. First came the French Huguenots after the Revocation of the Edict of Nantes. After them came Italians, Swiss, Greeks, Chinese, Indians, and many more. Safka, you might find something you'd like to take home along Carnaby Street. There are some very nice boutiques that aren't too dear. And Ingwer and Reinhard, you'll be surprised there's a pedestrian precinct similar to some of yours in Germany. There're also many good pubs, restaurants, and coffeehouses around there. We can eat out very reasonably this evening, if you'd like."

"Very good, *bier hier*," shouted Ingwer above the din of the rush hour traffic as he clinked an imaginary mug with Reinhard. As the bus squeezed its way in the automotive density, Henry and Safka watched below them the variety of people and stores along the passing streets. The constantly seemingly reshaken kaleidoscope beneath them melded into scenes construed from their knowledge of London's long history. The present meshed with the on-going past. Cruelty, kindness, and excitement were etched into nearly every corner.

The international fivesome descended the red bus near the Eros Statue by Piccadilly Circus and drifted down the sidestreets, eventually coming upon Carnaby. Despite Jackie's lauding the values to be discovered in this area, Safka, though amused by the short cuts of the skirts, confided to her hostess that the prices were above her budget. Realizing that this district had been upgraded since her last visit a few months before, Jackie turned off this pedestrian way and onto a side street where there was a short queue in front of a bar selling fish and chips. "Have you ol' blokes tried any of our national delicacy that they're selling here?"

"Can't say that I have," responded Henry in an attempted British accent.

"Well, ol' man, you better try a bit harder than that at the King's English. You sound more like a mid-western farm lad to my ear," taunted Jackie back in her attempt at American English—putting him in his place regarding his real abilities at perfect imitation of foreign idioms. Disappointed at the inappropriateness and perceived conceit at his try to go native, Henry cringed internally. Ingwer, Reinhard, and Safka eagerly expressed their desire to queue up for what must be a proper snack, given the joy of the patrons' standing up cheerfully to consume what they were all commenting upon as particularly delectable morsels. After a brief period of an orderly line-up, the visitors were able to indulge in the flaky fried white fish and golden fries, which, though adequate, elevated the Belgian ones to an even fonder memory in Henry's mind. With drooping eyes, Ingwer confessed, "I'm longing for a beer."

Safka added, "We have walked a very long distance!"

Jackie quickly picked up that everyone was tired of sightseeing on foot and brought to their attention the black-and-white sign hanging over a pub at the end of the block. After their snack, the friends stepped into the neighborhood pub with the simple brown wooden interior, probably no older than toward the end of Queen Victoria's reign. Jackie asked her team what they wanted, and she soon placed their order with the speedy waiter who was soon back with dark and light lagers and a cider. This was Henry's first time to imbibe dark ale, and all of them shared tastes of their beverages within their circle of companions. Several patrons were smoking but the air was not yet heavy with their blue fumigants. They stood looking at the varied clientele of this establishment. Old white haired men and a few elderly ladies in plain clothes, middle aged men who pretended to hide their paunches in order to seek the company of the women in their thirties, and lively, spiffy young people gave a bit of flair to this down-home neighborhood tavern. When the youthful patrons regarded one another, they marveled at their gleaming skin and exercised bodies.

With her usual combination of recall of facts and enthusiasm for discussing social problems, Jackie turned to Henry and said, "I just finished a course in current American history, and I am distressed by all the assassinations and causes behind the recent 'long hot summer.' Last year there were almost ninety deaths and hundreds of millions of dollars in property damage. You have had severe social upheaval in New York, Memphis, Chicago, Washington, D.C., Los Angeles, Miami, and many other small cities."

"Wow, Jackie, you have a better memory than I do. But don't forget the main point: social conflict may lead to social change, often in a better direction for the oppressed group, at least in the USA. For example, this July Congress passed a housing bill that aims at building housing for over a million poor and poor-to-moderate income people. The White House set up an Urban Institute to build fifty cities within cities on surplus government property. In 1967 the Air Quality Act curbed major pollution in four big cities. In L.A. private enterprise and foundations set up a new plant next to Watts. They would never have done that without the riots showing poor people in front of every TV set in America's living rooms."

"'Bullshit,' isn't that your 'in' word now. From what I've been reading most of those tax incentives went to build plants and equipment in your suburbs—leaving your poor and moderate income earners in the cities without more new jobs."

"I hadn't heard that before, but it doesn't surprise me. But a lot of poor young people of all backgrounds, including me, got our first paying job from those programs. And we did a lot of good for the city, too. We cleaned up its unkempt public places and parks," Henry noted.

Jackie inquired, "How much did you earn?"

"Thirty-six dollars a week. It was the first time Negroes and Caucasians of my generation had the chance to work together on an equal footing, although a serious fight did break out between the Negro and Caucasian teenage boys. Of course, the police arrested a few of the Negro kids. The Caucasian kids got off scot-free."

Emboldened by her new sense of having found her spot in this group, Safka questioned Henry, "But do not many of your internal problems result from the cost of the war in Vietnam to your government?"

"Yes, that's true. And many people in the peace movement are saying that

Johnson has hidden a lot of the costs of the war from public scrutiny. But I am not sure that even if the war in Vietnam ended if Americans would be willing to pay for the sorts of programs that would solve our major social ills. Gunnar Myrdal said it will cost a trillion dollars and a generation."

Ingwer and Reinhard were more absorbed in observing the quaint customs of this British pub than engaging in another political and social discourse. When a svelte young woman in her late-teens or early twenties began regarding Ingwer admiringly, he slipped away from the politicos over to the table of this welcoming office worker. His departure left the more timid and less attractive Reinhard to listen to more of this endless discussion about poverty, war, and injustice in which he was less genuinely interested than in the new details of the latest missile. Safka, who had now become relaxed in Reinhard's presence, asked him, "What do you think about this?"

Snapping his attention away from Ingwer's encounter at the far away table back to where he was seated, Reinhard inquired, "Do you mean all the trouble in the United States is caused by the war in Vietnam?"

"Well, for example, what do you think Henry should do? Should he serve in the war in Vietnam or not?"

"You know, I just did my service in the armed forces of the Federal Republic of Germany. It was not great, but I did it because I had to. I don't like the war in Vietnam, but Henry has to make up his own mind."

In the back of her mind, Safka was thinking to herself, *If the German young people had opposed their military before World War II, we in the Balkans would never have had to suffer the way we did. But, then, again, Reinhard's country reestablished relations with Yugoslavia, and their big army acts as a counterforce to the Russians.*

Jackie did not like lulls in conversation and was interested in what was happening in Germany, so she broke the pause and, to relieve all the pressure off Henry asked, "Hasn't your new chancellor, Kurt Georg Kiesinger, been much more liberal than Adenauer and Erhard?"

"Yes, that's true. He's trying to strengthen ties to everyone—east and west, and he's cut military spending and bought fewer American arms."

"But he hasn't gotten very far with the French, has he?"

"No, he hasn't because he doesn't like France trying to keep Great Britain outside the Common Market?"

Still not "coming out" as a Jew before his new friends, Henry, nevertheless, interjected to Reinhard a universal question of particular Jewish concern, "But I read your extremist right wing groups have grown since 1966."

"That's true. They've won in several state and local elections. They're the so-called National Democratic Party. But Chancellor Kiesinger has a Grand Coalition government made up of the Christian Democratic Union, the Christian Social Union, and the Social Democratic Party. Last year we had a recession, but his new policies are stimulating the economy. We're sound. No problem."

Jackie also picked up on Henry's concern but from the vantage of a student activist, "Reinhard, our student papers have reported that the Kiesinger government passed laws which entitled your government to suspend your constitution."

"We call it 'The Basic Law.' "

"Well, anyway, I read that they can take away this Basic Law in times of national emergency."

"Our students demonstrated strongly against it. And, anyway, it was passed as a result of your Allied forces surrendering their occupation rights this May. I am against it."

Safka jumped in the conversation which now had tilted away from Henry to Reinhard, "That's how Hitler got into power in the first place, yes? And I was upset that Bonn refused to sign the nuclear non-proliferation treaty which the Americans signed this June."

"Ladies, ladies, I thought that was wrong too, but you can't put the weight of the whole world on your shoulders."

All around him was an institution Henry had encountered for the first time this summer—a place where people of all ages came together to relax by drinking beer and many also by smoking tobacco. He could not recall ever having been to a bar in all of his twenty years in America. Drinking was an institution unfamiliar to those of his ethnic group and class, although smoking was prevalent in his family and region. Jackie was enjoying herself, although Henry suspected that she was not as accustomed to the world of the pub as she was letting on. Reinhard and Ingwer were more at home in this scene, but they suspected that it was much easier to meet and chat with the English maidens compared to young women in their own country. Indeed, Ingwer's appreciation of this cultural difference knew few bounds.

As Henry watched, he was irked at his awkwardness in the presence of WASPS. His clumsiness may have resulted from his days at prep school. He assumed a demeaning air of inferiority. Occasionally he could be impolite or burst forth in poorly-timed bits of anger addressed towards people of White, Anglo-Saxon, Protestant origin. Yet, every person he had met and every experience he had in England contradicted his deeply ingrained discomfort. This spunky Jackie had charmed him and the others to the core. It was hard to place his finger on why this was so, but Henry suspected that Jackie's strongly-shared beliefs and actions in an environmentally mindful, left-leaning social democracy gave them a similar outlook and almost a religious fervor toward enacting these goals in this life. Henry had never met an American WASP with these values and openness and interest in people of other backgrounds as he had in this young English woman whose wit, knowledge, and get-on-with-it-ness inspired everyone around her. Well, maybe Blake Nichols was an exception, but he was partly Jewish. Jackie loved people, fun, and travel, as did all these other young people, too.

Reinhard's self-confidence grew, as he kept up with these intellectuals in English, no less. His slouch changed into a more upright stance, and he was most contented with his response under cross-examination.

Jackie, who had unconsciously directed the conversation away from Henry to give him a few minutes to absorb what they had said, now focused in on the real issues that were bothering her.

"Damn it, Henry. I read that your government really hasn't done much to promote redistribution of the land in Vietnam. It is basically working with the landowners and the dependants they've created by a huge black market in South Vietnam. The U.S. has displaced the refugees from the land they've defoliated into a kind of concentration camp," observed Jackie. "Don't you think that shows a sign of contempt for the Vietnamese people?"

"I sure do. Besides, the American military personnel call them all the racist names they can dream up. I read someplace that our soldiers respect the Viet Cong, but they don't respect the Army of the so-called Republic of Vietnam."

"That's because one side believes in what its fighting for, while the South Vietnamese soldiers sense their force is rotten to the core."

"But what bothers me is that for all my years at college I've been studying about cultures all around the globe, and the message of cultural relativism is the major lesson that came out of all my undergraduate studies. But having grown up in the South, I know that the people on the street think that American culture is the best in the world, and they think that everybody else all around the world knows and wants the same thing as Americans. From what I've read in my two upper-division courses on Asia, I don't think that's right or true, except maybe on the surface. From what I've read about Saigon, American products and customs have overwhelmed it, and everybody's trying to get a cut of the action, including the Vietnamese. But everybody knows the huge extent of the corruption and black marketeering, and they sense the hollowness of all of that graft. Just because they do it and are wrapped up in it doesn't necessarily mean they like it or that it's good for them. They do it because it's the only way to make a living in their war-torn country."

"And I've read that their whole countryside has been bombed to hell with napalm and other chemicals that are poisoning the land for generations to come."

While Jackie, Henry, and Safka kept mulling over progressively more detailed accounts of the evils of the American intervention in Vietnam, Reinhard focused his attention on Ingwer. His friend had found the perfectly-formed specimen of womankind. Under the table in the distance, Reinhard detected the damsel and Ingwer's rubbing feet and holding hands. Worried that Ingwer would inadvertently drift off with the key to their rented bed-and-breakfast and miss their train departing the next evening back to northern Germany, Reinhold mustered the courage to interrupt the brewing passion across the room and introduce himself unexpectedly to Ingwer's new acquaintance.

"Hallo! I'm called Reinhard."

Startled by this sudden intrusion, Ingwer's head rose in a grimace indicating his annoyance at being disturbed in the middle of a conquest.

"Oh, excuse me, I don't believe we've met before," replied the large-eyed English woman politely, as she imagined herself the contested trophy of two bellicose German men.

Begrudgingly recognizing the ill-timed entry of Reinhard at their table, he surprised his new acquaintance by saying, "Please let me introduce you. Reinhard, this is Susan Berry, and Susan, this is my old friend, Reinhard."

"Sorry for interrupting you, but Jackie, Henry, and Safka kept talking about the war in Vietnam and all of the world's problems. It got to be too much for me."

"Oh, they're just too serious."

"Well, Henry does have a big decision to make. I guess it's bothering him, and Jackie's trying to help," Reinhard commented. Just as he was about to ask them the subject of their conversation, he stopped himself, realizing the stupidity of such an inquiry. The obvious answer had been inscribed in their body language that he had been recording for the last half-hour. Instead he implored, "Don't you think we better be getting back to our bed-and-breakfast, if we're going to go sightseeing with our friends tomorrow."

"Why don't you take our key, and I'll meet you back later on in the evening."

"But how will you get back if you don't have a key?"

Susan laughed at Reinhard's innocence, but, embarrassed that his motives had been so obviously detected by his compatriot, Ingwer added, "No problem."

"No problem?"

"No problem."

"Then I'll be leaving shortly. Nice to meet you, Susan."

"Good night, Reinhold."

Reinhold drifted back to his more political friends whom he alerted, "Don't you think it's getting quite late? If we don't get back to where we are staying, we will get up too late tomorrow and miss so many things before we leave."

"What about Ingwer?" asked the others in concert.

"Oh, he is occupied for the evening."

"Yes, I would say that it appears to be the case!"

"Well, let's be heading back to the hostel and our places."

"Cheerio," shouted Jackie over to Ingwer and his new acquaintance, and her enthusiastic good-bye was backed up by a high waving of hands in the air from all of Ingwer's other friends as they stepped out of the now smoky pub into the cool night air. As soon as they re-entered a main thoroughfare, they encountered the flashing neon lights and the obvious fleshpots in this part of town. Neither embarrassed nor excited by the vivid displays, the group of friends proceeded briskly back to the entrance of the subway at Piccadilly Circus.

The friends dispersed to their different lodgings and agreed to meet back at the park by St. Paul's at 9:30 the next morning.

CHAPTER 47

This was the last day the new friends would spend together in London, and everyone was determined to get Reinhard through the Imperial War Museum with the greatest dispatch. Jackie had been quick to point out that this was just one of five military museums in London, not to mention four naval ones. She interjected that no matter how intriguing it was, Henry had been promised at least two hours at The British Museum. Safka wanted to take in Bloomsbury and Holborn after that, and Ingwer hoped to "do" the area around Westminster and Millbank more thoroughly.

As they approached the two fifteen-inch two thousand ton guns in front, down the short entrance way, bordered on each side by two large bombs, the stately white Corinthian columns and frieze reminded Henry of the building of a state legislature in the United States. It also brought home to him the reality of war.

Although Reinhard had served in his military, it had been in peace time and his fascination with the large guns from HMS Ramillies and HMS Resolution stirred in him childhood memories of building models of battleships and playing war in children's games. Ingwer was more caught up in the technicalities of measurement and design, although he, too, was not overly anxious to "waste" his last few hours in London in this 1917 palace of war. Henry, Safka, and Jackie lagged behind Reinhard and Ingwer and watched Reinhard display his knowledge of the records of Britain and the Commonwealth's military operations since 1914. When Reinhard's attention began to dwell on one of the display cases on the former empire, Jackie commented to Henry, "See, America didn't invent pushing around smaller nations, fomenting strife of one faction against another, or distorting military lingo."

"I can't believe how the military corrupts language. Murdering kids is part of their 'clean up operation.'"

"That's just the surface. Your army has whole crews of public relations men trying to cover up slaughters. They make defoliation of large parts of Vietnam look like reforestation projects. Your language of war is a language of grotesque machines, not of people."

"How do you think they could get the public to buy their b.s. otherwise?"

"Henry, but was the Second World War different from what we are seeing now?"

"You better believe it was. World War II was fought for a good cause by the Allies. I would have enlisted the moment it broke out. I'm not a pacifist by any means. Hitlerism and fascism were absolute evils. The Russians were our allies then."

Watching his fiery streak when he spoke of fascism, Jackie asked softly, "You're Jewish, aren't you?"

There was silence. Henry's Adam's apple stuck in his throat.

Then before there had been too long a lull for any misunderstanding to develop, Jackie continued, "You know, Henry, I thought you were. I dated a Jewish fellow from Manchester. You're so much like him. When he took me home with him, I thought his mother would drop dead from the thought he was going to marry a gentile. We were just good friends then, nothing serious," she chuckled, then went on, "I've had a few courses on European Jewish history at university. I was very interested in them. Yes, the fascists' war was a war against democracy, racial equality, and your people were particularly targeted in Hitler's myth of race."

"As much as I hate the use of 'gook' and 'slope' by our soldiers, it pales in comparison to the Nazis' attitude toward groups that they thought of as *untermenschen*, doesn't it?"

"Yes."

Safka made no comment but listened closely and with acceptance as their conversation flowed from one thing to another. Finally she interrupted, "If we do not get Reinhard out of this place, we'll never reach the British Museum and Bloomsbury."

"You're right. Thanks for keeping a watch on our time," replied Henry, relieved for a pause in the discussion that touched so closely to home. Almost lunging towards the way out, Henry beat Jackie to stirring the group back to Lambeth North Station. By this time, Safka had begun to take pride in her new self-assurance on the underground. Pointing with her right index finger at the map, she explained, "Look, we get on here on at the brown Bakerloo line and get off at Piccadilly Circus. There we transfer to the purple Piccadilly line, going northeast and get off at Russell Square."

"Safka, you've caught on. Good for you," praised Jackie, who was satisfied at her own good teaching these newcomers the gentle art of faring on one's own.

"Finally! There are so many names. Sometimes it takes me a long time to locate exactly at which stop we should disembark."

But they did arrive with relative ease at the British Museum. Henry counted forty Ionic columns as they waited for Reinhard and Ingwer who were dragging somewhat behind. They were engaged in a conversation about the woman with whom Ingwer had passed the night.

Above the columns the light green color of the rounded library dome complimented the lush green of the puffy line of trees and grass in front of Montague Street. This was the first of the great national museums. Like a pictorial review of humankind's development, this place recapped much of what Jackie, Henry, and Safka had read about during the last few years of their studies. It was closest of all to Jackie's more classic training in the great civilizations. Soon they were, again, staring at well-designed maps explicating the layout of the ground and upper floors.

As they passed the collections of the Greek and Roman antiquities, Henry regarded the details of the relief in amber or gold more as curious beauties in an ephemeral moment of Homo sapiens' social and biological evolution. Most of these were products of post-Neolithic revolutionary cultures. These bits of treasure were less intriguing than the vastly varying social structures that the agricultural revolution accompanied by the domestication of animals had produced around 10,000 years ago. Such changes had lead to social hierarchies based on specialization of labor and extended families. This way of mankind's organizing itself had led to a surplus of food, larger populations, and war. Stopping in front of the frieze in the central room of the Duveen gallery, Safka fixated herself upon the scene representing the festival of Athene's investiture in a sacred violet robe. The horses and the chariot, followed by citizens and animals, appeared to thrust this festive procession in honor of the goddess Athene forward at a fast clip.

Meanwhile Ingwer and Reinhard shuffled along with the others in a nonchalant drift until they reached the Assyrian basement where Reinhard was suddenly overcome by the helmets, shields, arms, armor, and the relief of the Nineveh palaces depicting military campaigns.

Despite their different personal interests and styles, the friends enjoyably passed through the Egyptian galleries, by way of the entrance hall over to the manuscripts in the Grenville Library. The wealth of the collection and their limited time left all of them mesmerized by their hurried and passive sweep through this division. Jackie was always taken in by the Magna Carta Room and was stirred by the Lindisfarne Gospels and the unique copy of Beowulf. The exhibition explaining the granting of the Magna Carta by King John and two of the four extant copies of the Great Charter itself revived Ingwer's curiosity.

It did not dawn on them that their quick pace through the Oriental Antiquities expressed their removal from the increasingly popular preoccupations and conversation with the Californian and other Western varieties of Buddhism and Hinduism. They absorbed the bronze vessels, painted lacquer, and pottery tomb figures with admiration and respect. Appreciating the material creativity of other civilizations, the eyes of these young people interpreted them as products of specific temporal and material conditions. Although they were intrigued by the bronze statue of Siva Visha Pahavana and the carvings of Kashmir, the cut and enameled glass and engraved and inlaid metalwork from Islamic countries did not stir their spirits. For them it was a complement to their knowledge of a rich world where different beliefs and ways of life had led to specific patterns that were produced by particular influences.

The hunting scenes from Roman Britain came more alive to them than the Rosetta Stone. But from their comfort in their own traditions, from their fast view of an enormous collection of the material artifacts of human history, they moved onward to the third largest library in the world.

"Damn, I forgot to remind you to get a letter of recommendation two days in advance," apologized Jackie, "I don't think we'll be able to get in."

Confident of his persuasiveness, Ingwer walked up to the guard showing his German student identification. "Sorry, you'll need a letter from someone with a position," explained the middle-aged attendant courteously but formally to this brash young man. Ingwer, who was not one to take a put down lightly, nevertheless relegated his retort to an inward curse.

"Well, Safka, how about Bloomsbury now?"

"Is it true?" replied Safka excitedly—her heart beating at being so near a place whose literary greats had thrilled and frightened her. She wondered how much the others knew about the scandalous life of Lytton Strachey, Virginia Woolf, E. M. Forster, Roger Fry, G. M. Moore and the others. In her voyeuristic curiosity, she was too embarrassed to ask. Jackie, who was much more enthused about history and politics, had really not read any works of the writers of the circle except some of Maynard Keynes. She had heard that

Duncan Grant had been "that way," but it did not phase her one way or the other. It was simply another world and, deep down inside, she probably thought it a rather exploitive one at that.

Having briskly proceeded down Montague Street past Russell Square, they were soon at the main Bloomsbury hangout in Gordon Square. Safka, in her own dream world, sensed the freedom of purposefully slipping away conventionality, and, so plopped down on the grass, as if to absorb the intense emotion from Virginia Woolf's looming spirit. Ingwer, who was worried that the afternoon was slipping away from them, tickled Safka's fleshy hips and inquired jokingly, "Is this it?"

"Oh, no! We must walk over to Brunswick Square, number 38."

"Then let's be on with it. The Parliament will be closed by the time we get back there." So sooner than Safka had had a chance to fantasize being pulled through the time warp into the debauchery of Bloomsbury, they were off over to Tavistock Square down Woburn Place over to Brunswick Square. Here Safka related to the others, "Virginia Woolf lived here with Keynes, Duncan Grant, and Leonard Woolf." Although Safka knew the intimate details of the adulterous love affairs, she preferred withholding her understanding that Leonard had to live with Virginia's depression and Trekkie with her husband at war.

After the international constituency of young friends had indulged Safka's passion for the early part of the twentieth century's great English *literati,* it was now time to give Ingwer at least a glance of the House of Lords.

"We don't really have to go there now, if you don't want to," Ingwer conceded as he himself was beginning to lose his curiosity about the project. Jackie studied the faces of her crowd and added a bit of relevant information, "It is getting late, and I'm not sure if they are open to the public at this hour of the afternoon."

"I guess I will miss learning about your government this visit."

"Where would you like to go instead?"

"We have only a few hours left together. How about just going for a 'spot of tea' and chatting?" Ingwer suggested, pleased with himself for remembering the exact English phrase.

"Great!"

"*Wunderbar!*"

Everyone was pleased with the change of plans, for, although they had tapped the heart of this great metropolis, they could not seriously take in much more. Although none of them would have stated it so, they had all suddenly agreed to live what they had enjoyed most of all, just being with one another.

In a few blocks, they chanced upon an unadorned neighborhood restaurant where they sat down at a plain, clean table on wooden chairs, imbibing the warm afternoon sun and the relaxed features of one another's faces. While the waitress-owner with silver hair served them tea and crumpets, they wondered over the joy of truly liking each other. Each other's differences were thrilling. They could accept and marvel at this brief slice of time in their lives as though it would last forever. They were like children celebrating the fantasy of building a perfect, imaginary family castle, hewn out of pieces of junk, and plowed over land, on a vacant lot overgrown with quick-growing soft pines. While an intense beam of light cast itself into Ingwer's eyes, he closed them. It replenished his soul with the energy of this giant friendship. This unity equaled or surpassed in its own way his exciting orgasm of the night before that was heightened by his and her mastery of technique and the healthy functioning of their youthful bodies. This friendship was different. It did not shake one's back or thighs to the natural meeting of two attracted bodies. Instead, it absorbed a mellow radiance as one understood the words and actions of the superbly intricate others. The warmth flushed his forehead, and he wanted to remain in this pleasant half-sleep.

Henry interrupted this sublime silence. "I have something to announce."

"What is it?"

"I've definitely decided not to go. The war in Vietnam is wrong. It is not a just cause worth dying for."

"Good for you," commented Ingwer.

"Three cheers!" congratulated Jackie.

"Finally made the decision," Reinhard noted.

Safka, who agreed with his decision, still realized that this, the culmination of her summer vacation, would lead to the practicalities of everyday life, the busy schedule of work and family pressures that marked her real life back home.

Reinhard could not get over how pleasant it had all been, particularly how easy it felt to get outside of himself here in London in a way it was so difficult for him to do back home. If he had still depended on the exuberance of his chum to make everyday life more thrilling by meeting strangers, he had managed to assert himself and his interests while thoroughly immersing his being in the tastes and customs of others so foreign to his own personality.

Also basking in the sudden radiance of the afternoon, Jackie thought to herself, *How happy I am now. This is a special moment*. It was as though she and Henry had eloped in a union of secular social justice. This sharing would propel them back into the hard world of work. Although they had participated in this ordinary world with enthusiasm during their short lives as adults, they also recognized its boredom and fatigue. This short moment of play with others that shared their labors in ordinary life suddenly seemed real. Jackie had been like an elegant lady escorting her foreign guests around *her* home or like a well-paid tour guide working for a famous company in that she had demonstrated her knowledge of London's history while acknowledging the needs and limitations of the people she was leading. But she was totally different from a tour guide, too, for she was showing her friends London out of her appreciation of them and her capital. On her part there was pride and *noblesse oblige* with only an unacknowledged desire to be appreciated and possibly shown around their cities at some indefinite future date. With the grace of a noblewoman in the dress of a radical, Jackie delicately lifted her stoneware cup and saucer, sipped her tea, and bit a morsel of the marmalade-covered English muffin.

As the evening drew near, they had few words to utter. In the time still remaining, the very intensity of the proximity of their bodies carried on a deep discussion with one another. The tea ritual had been the instrument by which their rite of parting had assumed the elegance of English form coupled with the fact of being citizens of the world.

As she looked up at the old Victorian clock on the mantelpiece, Jackie realized it was time to bid Ingwer and Reinhard adieu. "*Meine Herren*, if we do not bid you farewell, you'll just stay longer."

Shaken from his comfortable torpor, Ingwer jumped up, hugged Jackie, and implanted a brief but firm kiss on her lips and then cheek. The more timid Reinhard extended his hand to her and then unexpectedly placed his other hand on top of her right one, warming her entire arm. Safka stood up and they repeated the same gestures toward her. Henry extended his right hand and the two young German men theirs, thinking it correct to mimic the American custom. Their grips exuded strength and coupling that must have signaled brotherhood.

"Safka, what time does your bus leave for Yugoslavia?"

"Early tomorrow morning. I will stay at the hostel another night."

"And I'm leaving for New York around midnight. We should land early tomorrow morning."

"Then I must be off back to Newbury, I suppose," declared Jackie in a sad voice.

Henry and Jackie met simultaneously in a big hug that lasted several minutes, and then he kissed Safka on both cheeks as he thought might he the custom in her country. She blushed but managed to implant a single peck on Henry's left cheek.

The three young men headed back to the parcel depot to collect their rucksacks and then onwards to Victoria Station from where they would embark upon their different paths.

CHAPTER 48

After Ingwer and Reinhard purchased their tickets back to Hamburg, they again shook Henry's hand with gusto. After they waved goodbye, Henry checked the schedules of the airline buses to Heathrow. It was almost four-thirty in the afternoon and he did not have to be at Heathrow until an hour before the take-off of his charter, although it would be fun to catch up on Blake Nichols' summer, if, indeed, Blake would get to the airport several hours early. So Henry decided to walk again in the area around Victoria. He saw a dimly lighted men's store with boxes stacked up to the ceiling and somewhat out-of-date clothing hanging on the rack. He still had about fifty dollars in his pocket which should cover his stay in New York, so when he saw a light beige-and-green tweed sports coat for two pounds, he purchased this closely-woven coat as a solid memento of London. It was, indeed, the only souvenir he was taking back besides the free pamphlets, a few postcards, and a few rolls of film he had taken all summer. It fitted perfectly and made him look somewhat older and more formal than the casual pants or jeans with a shirt that he customarily wore. With his new purchase, the first sports coat he had ever bought out of his own hard-earned money, he proudly put it on and heaved his loaded backpack over it. Within a few blocks, he was beginning to tire of the thickening mists and of walking aimlessly by himself, so he decided to risk his luck on returning to the airport in case some of his flight companions from the beginning of the summer might also be back early. There was a bus from Victoria Terminal that took about three-quarters of an hour to cover the fifteen-mile westward jaunt.

The walk inside the airport was more familiar now and Henry's mind focused on the large squares of what must be marble with patterns of many shapes of dark and light hue. The simple dress of the dark-suited businessmen with wide lapels and ties fit in with the straight-grained, shellacked counters which were topped by the various lighted signs of the airlines lifted above by black metal poles. In varied apparel, smiling blond lassies, hiding their breasts, passed them. So too did other young women under buttoned-downed coats, which suddenly stopped a full hand above their knees. Henry liked the relaxed style of the plumpish, round-faced twenty-year olds in cords and thongs with dark, high turtle-necked shirts and light wool sweaters that were pulled halfway down their thighs.

Withdrawing his ticket from the middle section of his money belt, he walked up to the British Airways section and deposited his backpack on the black conveyor belt. Then he stretched and began to explore the terminal for familiar faces.

At the British Airways' counter, a young American man in frayed jeans, threadbare, white at his knees, and hair down to his shoulders, placed a shredding, green duffel bag with sewn-on shoulder straps on the spot for the baggage check-in. A British woman, a few years his senior, clad in a dark navy uniform with polished metal badges identifying her airline, put on her white gloves and quickly pleaded with her male co-worker to take charge of the client's baggage. The passenger handed the BA clerk his ticket that she held by the tips of her gloved fingers. Seated a few feet away, within hearing and seeing range of this scene, Henry noted her sour, puckered-mouthed sign of disgust and disapproval of this fellow's style. When the guy with bushy-eyebrows politely asked if he could sit by the window, she snappily ran her finger down a chart depicting the seating arrangement and briskly informed him, "There are *no* more window seats available!"

After the receptionist's blunt statement, he asked her if he could sit near an exit and she responded, "There is only one aisle seat left—two rows in back of the way out."

"Fine. I'll take it," he smiled, hiding his anger at being treated like a piece of vermin. The airline employee nervously handed him his boarding card.

Henry guessed that the hippie, who had been treated with such contempt by the person whose salary he was supporting, must be a young Californian on his charter flight, although he did not remember him from the flight at the beginning of the summer. He also wondered why the lad had not protested. *Does loving your fellow man mean that you should accept such meanness? I surely don't think so!* Boiling over more and more as he recalled that he, too, was contributing to the upkeep of this prejudiced wretch, Henry got up and approached the now empty counter.

"Excuse me."

The woman kept peering at the chart organizing the flight's seating arrangements. Then he added more loudly, "I beg your pardon, ma'am."

"Yes, may I help you?"

"I must say as a disinterested on-looker that I found your conduct to the last passenger to be rude, to say the least."

"Rude?" asked the clerk. "I most certainly was *not* rude," she replied, raising her voice. "Who are you to tell me that I was rude?"

"R-U-D-E in plain English," he spelled it out, "means treating someone in a most impolite way."

"I was *not* impolite," the woman signaled to her male attendant, suggesting that this passenger was out-of-line and potentially violent.

"Excuse me, madam, but you did treat the last fellow with utter disdain. You acted as though he were a simple louse."

"Don't you think it would be better if you were to sit down, sir?" the male co-worker instructed affirmatively.

"Let's call a spade a spade. Your receptionist was plain nasty to the last guy. And I don't mind saying so because I am contributing to your salary and expect a modicum of human decency to be shown to my fellow passengers."

"But he provoked her. You should tell your friend to take a bath!"

"What do you mean? I overheard and watched their conversation. He did nothing of the kind. He is not my friend. I don't know the guy. But I can recognize harsh treatment. His body odor is certainly not more or less offensive than either of yours!"

The dark olive-skinned fellow who had suffered the indignation was now eavesdropping on Henry's defense of him. "Hey, man, cool it. They're just uptight. You seem like a nice guy. Come over and talk to me."

Just about this moment, Blake Nichols fell into Henry's peripheral vision. "Hey, Henry," Blake called out from several yards away.

"Blake!"

"See ya' on the plane," smiled Henry to the Middle-Eastern-looking Californian. "My buddy just got in."

"How're you doing?" questioned Henry, turning to Blake.

"Wow, do you look great!"

"You, too. Hitchhiking, hiking, camping—the rugged life—isn't so bad for you!"

"What a summer!"

"Yeah, a great, super one! Check in and we'll schmooze. But watch out for that testy bitch."

Even though it was obvious that Blake was a friend of her tormentor, the clerk, regarding the quality of his fine backpack, tent, and beautifully-woven Pendleton shirt, thick hiking pants, and Swiss boots covering his more Nordic facial lines and lightness of limb, treated Blake with the utmost correctness. Then she moved on to the next woman. She saw that the line for the feeder route to the charter was beginning to grow.

"Blake, so what's this business about falling in love once and finding your roots?"

"Well, it's certainly a lot deeper than your summer of bed hopping," he laughed.

"Is that the way you'd describe my summer?"

"It sure sounded that way."

"It certainly wasn't planned. And it wasn't all that frequent."

"So, who is this mystery woman? What's she like? How serious are you?"

"She's nice. She's beautiful. She's very British."

"Is she in love with you too?"

"I think so. She wants to finish her studies before we get together. Maybe I can convince my parents to bring her over for Christmas."

"Where's she from?"

"We met in the Lake District, but she grew up in London and goes to the London School of Economics here. I stayed with her family here."

"Where are they now?"

"Oh, her dad drove me to the airport. We said our good-byes at her home in the garden this morning."

There was an announcement in low but audible tones, "You may now board flight 822 for Prestwick with connections for New York. Departure is from Gate 2G."

"They're letting us get on really early."

"Yeah. Do you feel like staying here a bit longer or getting on?"

"I'd like to board now and avoid the rush. There're lots of kids behind us."

"O.K."

They walked down the ramp onto the rather small cabin. Across the aisle from them was the Mid-Eastern appearing hippie who smiled as they squeezed into the opposite seat.

"I guess that lady was thinking 'Birds of a feather flock together.'"

"Well, I'd say she was rather chuckling to herself, 'So do the geese and swine.'"

"Hey, man, that's pretty funny. You really got her number. Do you guys know how long we're going to be in this sardine can?"

"Just about an hour and then we change to a bigger plane in Scotland."

"Right on!"

A few minutes after the passengers had boarded, in front of them the stewardess began to explain the use of the oxygen masks and location of the ways out as they were glancing at the other passengers to see whom they would find from the beginning of the summer. Blake feigned inattention as he spotted the heavy plodder who was constantly complaining their first day together in London.

The airplane began to taxi down the runway and smoothly swish upward into a northerly sweep. Henry felt unexpectedly relieved to be airborne just as much as he dreaded leaving all the wonderful people he had met and the beautiful places he had visited.

"So, Blake, what's your new love's name? What does she do?"

"After being here only a summer, that sounds like such a strange question, so American. Why do we always measure a person by what he or she does to earn a living?"

"Come down off your high horse! What does she do?"

"A better question would be, 'What does she not do?' Jane is an incredibly gifted and well-rounded individual. She sings, dances, paints, writes, reads widely, has traveled all over, and speaks many languages. And she has a social conscience, too!"

"She sounds as refined as you."

"Thanks. And she's taught me to love Britain, to love England."

"But doesn't all of this hoity-toity stuff get to you after a while?"

"No, I love all the pomp and circumstance. Did you realize with all your progressive ideas that many scholars believe that constitutional monarchies, like the United Kingdom's, with all their inherited ranks, nevertheless, provide a social structure that better promotes egalitarian social legislation in the economic sphere where it really counts? It is thought that the aristocracy here feels a responsibility for the working-class. Whereas, in America. the *bourgeoisie* has cultivated the false belief that anyone who wants to make it can do it on his own."

"Hum, that's an interesting idea. I don't believe that I ever heard it before—'scuse me for eavesdropping," interjected the burly hippie across the aisle. "By the way, I'm Alvin from San Francisco, California."

"Hi, I'm Blake, and this is Henry."

"Where were you all summer?" inquired Henry.

"Not the summer—the whole year. I've been in Armenia, in the Soviet

Union, you know. I went over there to learn something about my people. And I'm coming back speaking the language. Knowing more customs than I ever did. 'Guess this beard turns off a lot of people; but I get off on it. You know, my whole family's so straight. They are all clean-shaven, well-dressed, and well-groomed. They're going to collapse when they see me. They'll think I've become a priest."

"Like those clerks back at the airport."

"Yep, just like them. It does 'em good to learn there's more to a person than his hair."

This comment struck Blake so offhanded that he was overcome by a chuckle.

As they were reacquainting themselves with each other and with the hippie with a sense of humor, the pilots instructed them to fasten their seatbelts again for landing in Prestwick, Scotland.

CHAPTER 49

The landing at Abbotscinch Airport in Glasglow and the trek across the hilly countryside to the international aerodrome in Prestwick were as beautiful as in their first few hours in Europe. Now the shock of its beauty was absorbed in a more eerie passing through the pitch of the night. The other young men whom they had met earlier in the summer hailed them with a high wave of the hand in the light-speckled darkness from a distance. Blake and Henry reciprocated with a not-so-enthusiastic acknowledgment. They had the urge to catch up on each other, to evaluate this splendid summer, and to see where they were going in their lives. Alvin's amusing company was accepted more out of courteousness to their chance encounter and their interest in his more exotic travels than any need to discover yet another intriguing human being. They showed their tickets again, were presented with assigned seats, and quickly boarded the charter flight that was waiting to deliver its passengers efficiently and economically to the New World. The hostess had seated Henry by the window, Blake in the middle, and Alvin by the aisle in a row of three seats slightly behind the left wing of the airplane. Many of the faces were vaguely familiar from the beginning of the summer, although more of the adults returning to the States seemed older. One of the last groups of people to board was a family-looking trio who had a strong resemblance to Mayor Richard Daley of Chicago, his wife, and one of his sons. As they squeezed in the small space—complaining out loud about the inadequate room of these second-rate accommodations—this family kept pace with the authoritative movements of the father's grimaces. The roly-poly man in a plain gray suit stared disapprovingly at the young man seated in front of them. This scowl was shared with his wife who, in turn, passed on this glum glance to her son.

If they're upset about being cramped, why don't they just get off and pay full-fare? wondered Henry, who rather enjoyed the propinquity of the other passengers.

Again the steward and stewardess demonstrated the use of the descending oxygen mask but added a visual display of the flotation device under the passenger seat. Just as she completed her ritualized reminder, Alvin felt a sudden kick in the middle of his back. Although he was a bit disconcerted at its occurrence just after the safety talk, he kept this mysterious dorsal jerk to himself. As the airplane rolled down the runway, the young men's eyes followed the lights in the pitch of the night. Soon thereafter, they were airborne. As they were climbing in altitude, Blake adjusted his seat one notch backward and Alvin one forward, thus creating a quick view of the knees and thighs of the Mayor Daley-look-alike.

"So what did you see all the time you spent in Britain, Blake?"

"Well, first I took the train and occasionally hitched all throughout the southeast. You know, it's where all the invaders left their traces. You can really see the Roman ruins incorporated into the medieval castles. After them came the Angles and Saxons, and then the Normans who built fortresses all over. There are ruins from the Stone Age, too. The Southeast is so beautiful with chalky hills covered by grassy slopes. In South Downs I saw the riding country. The brooks and valleys are so restful. Then I got a ride inland to the Weald. It used to be a forest, but today it is full of villages, mansions, farms, orchards and hop gardens. There are fields of bright barley, which are as beautiful as our 'amber waves of grain.'

"I visited so many castles. I found the beige, round towers of Arundel Castle incredibly well crafted. I got to see Richborough Fort where the Romans are supposed to have landed in 43 A.D. I also took in Deal Castle that was one of the twenty artillery forts Henry VIII built when he feared invasion from the continental Catholic powers. After that I saw some of the seventy-four Martello towers built to stave off invasion from Napoleon.

"I love the Pilgrim's Way with all of its neat, little Tudor houses—the ones with the exposed dark timber beams constructed in geometrical shapes with the white filling of wattle and daub in between. Sunset at Canterbury is one of the most exquisite sites I've ever seen. I went up to the South Midlands, which is called the 'Cockpit of England,' because the War of the Roses and the Civil War were fought there. Then I spent a few days in Stratford-upon-Avon and pretended that I had come to visit William Shakespeare—walking down with him beside the River Avon. Am I boring you? You want me to go on? I'm sure you and Alvin have had adventures as exciting or more exciting than mine."

Just as Blake had made his inquiry, Alvin was struck by a jolt so hard, that he thought his seat had been suddenly ejected from the airplane all by itself.

But Blake had seen the leg of the gray-suited blob behind him thrust all of his weight in a forward kick at the back of Alvin's seat. Blake made a signal with his covered thumb that the source of these disturbances was the man in back of him. Unbuckling his seatbelt, Alvin turned backward on his knees and jokingly asked the man in his fifties, "Sir, are you trying to kill a fly on the back of my seat or something?"

"No, just protecting myself and my family from certain germs in the vicinity."

"What kind of germs are you trying to clean off the seat?"

"A big, husky, olive-colored kind with lots of wooly covering."

"Yuck! It does sound bad! But would you mind calling the stewardess to see if she has some sort of disinfectant that might get it off more effectively?" pleaded Alvin, credulous of this Midwesterner's story.

Then Alvin turned to Blake, "Hey, man, I was just getting into your tale—go on."

"Me, too," added Henry, trying to get a clue of the people Blake encountered.

"I made it out to Stonehedge by June the twenty-first and saw the Companions of the Most Ancient Order of Druids keep their midnight vigil before midsummer sunrise. The place is fascinating. They worshipped the sun in ceremonies there as far back as around four thousand years ago. Holes around sixteen feet apart ring the whole circumference. And the two rings of sarsen stones are eerie. Southern England was the Saxon's capitol, and the English there have a really strong accent—like their Fs and Ss become Zs. Then I got a long ride all the way out to Land's End. It is weird to experience the difference between the Channel Shore and the Atlantic Coast out there. In the north the winds are super strong and the cliffs are black, but on the southern side you can see palm trees and camellias."

Impatient with Blake's wonderment with sites, geography, rites, accents and history, Henry implored, "But what about the great love of your life? Where and how did you meet her?"

"Oh, I'm getting to that in a while. It's strange, but I was so captivated with all the great works of history, literature, philosophy, and art finally finding places in real spots in my head, that for the first month, I basically forgot about the people around me unless they actively sought me out.

"It's a little embarrassing to admit, but when I was hiking in the south midlands, I got stuck late at night in the rain on a road with very few cars. A very nice middle-aged dentist picked me up and offered to put me up at his house. I thought, 'Great.' When we got there, there were pictures of his wife and kids all over. He said they were on a vacation. He had a very nicely kept two-story house. He served me a nice tea, crumpets, and orange marmalade, and said that there was only one big double bed made, and, being that it was so late, he hadn't had time to pick up the laundry, so, 'Would I mind sharing the bed?' So I said, 'Fine with me.' Well, I brushed my teeth and, after he shut out the light, he climbed on the other side of the bed shortly afterwards. All of a sudden, I feel somebody feeling me off, so I became frightened, ran into the bathroom, and locked myself in. I think he got as shook up as I, and, in a really civilized manner, he coaxed me out, saying that if I weren't interested, he would respect my wishes. Well, after I cooled down, I explained to him no one had ever done anything like that to me before, and that while I could understand that he might have an urge like that, it wasn't my bag. He was very understanding, and we both calmed down and went back to his bedroom and lay down again on opposite sides of the bed. I didn't sleep that night but the next morning he served me tea, crumpets, and jam, as if nothing had ever happened. That was about the only person I got to know at all the first month. Did anything like that ever happen to you guys this summer?"

"No, not even close," quietly answered Henry, rather overtaken by Blake's honesty about this event, and startled that it could have happened to him, but amazed that the thought of it had not even entered his mind.

Alvin's eyes rolled, and he chuckled in a deep baritone voice, "Man, I'm not sayin' stuff like that doesn't go on in Armenia, but I am sayin' that if the cops ever got ear of anything like that, or if they got their hands on somebody like that, woe is to the guy who got caught!"

"So maybe together with my being intrigued by jolly ol' England that experience kept me on the trains and cautious of people for a little while. I rode up through the rolling countryside of the south midlands and stayed in small country inns or youth hostels. There are so many towers all over, like Gloucester Cathedral and Tewkesbury Abbey. There are beautiful landmarks like one called the Devil's Chimney on a hill where there's a fifty-foot high column of limestone left after people had quarried around it for centuries. The Cotwold villages around there still look like they are right out of the fourteenth century when they were at the heart of the wood trade. I spent a night in Birmingham. It's still pretty dirty, but they're cleaning it up now. The canals themselves were worth the visit. From there I went up to Coventry and went through Warwick Castle, which is almost six centuries old.

"In late June I spent a week at Oxford and was tempted to spend the rest of my summer there. You asked about snobbery earlier, and I did feel it there, so I sort of stood by as a quiet outsider and watched things, even in the pubs. Nobody seemed interested in Berkeley, or me, so I just observed their way of doing things.

"Well, now I'm getting to the part you were interested in, Henry. I met Jane when I was camping in Cumbria, in the northwest, in the Lake District. In fact, on July the fourth I was on a footpath near Scafell, the highest mountain up there. It was a good day, the sky was thick with clouds and the grass was a lush green. I came upon a crystal clear lake with the mountain and clouds reflecting from its surface, when all of a sudden I see the still natural beauty joined by a human female one. All the classic signs happened! My heart started beating fast! I could barely get a word out of my mouth that didn't squeak, but the only thing she recognized was that I was an awkward American, and she was sort of turned on by my not having such glossy manners. The only thing I could do was to peer into her beautiful green eyes and red hair...."

Blake continued with his stories of romance and adventure all over the Lake District, from there on the trains to the Scottish lowlands and highlands and back down through York, the North Country and the Fens. The crew began to hand out a bedtime refreshment of milk or alcoholic beverages for purchase.

After the crew had served Alvin and had gone several rows past the Midwestern family, Alvin's seat received such a hard blow that the milk he was holding in his hand splashed onto his lap. His patience was reaching its limit. He turned around and lowered his voice, "Look, mister, I don't know what you got against me, but I can tell you one thing; if you keep on buggin' me, you're goina' feel it through that roll of lard around your belly. Ya' dig?"

At once the Major Daley look-alike hailed the stewardess who noted only Alvin's being turned backwards on his knees. The middle-aged- family man, short-of-breath, shouted, "This violent punk threatened me. I want him arrested at once!"

Before Alvin had a chance to explain his side of the story, the stewardess rushed back to the pilot's cockpit and signaled the other stewardesses to come to her assistance.

Staring accusingly into Alvin's eyes, the pilot asserted with absolute authority, "Any sign of violence on your part, young man, and we'll constrain you immediately. Do you understand?"

"But, sir..."

"Don't 'but sir' me; that's an order."

Both Blake and Henry interrupted almost simultaneously, "That's not fair. The man behind him has been kicking Alvin's seat and calling him nasty things practically since we got on this plane."

"You're damned liars, and you know it," the wife and the girlish-son of the heavy-set man screeched back in defense of their spouse and father.

"Listen, I don't know who started this, but I tell you guys, if I hear another complaint around here, you are going to be arrested the first thing when we get to New York. You get it?" the pilot—pretending to be evenhanded—instructed with a particular gaze at the innocent Alvin.

"Humph," snorted the father.

Alvin, who was about to begin recounting his year in Armenia, was so angered at the false accusations against him, he just turned his head to his age mates sitting to his left and moped, "This beard is not worth it. My people suffered enough from the Turkish massacres. Why should I bring down this horseshit on my head, man, just to be proud that I can be different in America? 'Sorry, guys, I'm goina' try to sack out. This has been a real heavy! See ya' in the morning."

"'Night."

"Goodnight, Alvin."

Speaking in whispered tones, Henry kept conversing with Blake about his summer and his decision not to serve in Vietnam. "It's strange, Blake, I can't really explain why, but I made such strong friendships in Europe this summer. I've never had such intense relationships with so many people I felt I shared so many basic beliefs with."

"Yeah, love and friendship. They're so different. But they must be a large part of what you and I appreciated about Europe this summer."

"For you it was a deep, passionate love, Blake. For me, it was a more intense friendship and a few really wonderful affairs that are going to take me a long time to sort out. They were great, but I don't really understand very much of what was going on."

"Who ever said life was simple? But isn't it great just to enjoy it to its fullest the way you and I were lucky enough to do this summer?"

"Considering we paid $120 round trip for a charter from New York, I'd say we got off rather reasonably."

"Do you mind my asking what this summer cost you?"

Rather taken aback by Henry's directness, Blake, nevertheless, responded, "I'd estimate $1200, if you don't count the round-trip airfare.

Actually, my parents gave me $1500. They'll be surprised I'm coming back with $300. The inns and the meals when I took Jane out are what boosted the bills; but Mr. and Mrs. Price, Jane's parents, really made it up to me. They wined and dined me, treated me to theater and museums when we got back to London. O.K., Mr. Nosy, how much did you get by with?"

"I know you won't believe me, but I spent exactly $120 all summer, excluding air fare."

"Incredible, how did you do it?"

"Well, I didn't have much of a choice, but I kept meeting these great people who would feed me and let me stay at their places for a while."

"Hey, it's almost 2:40 in the morning. If we don't get some sleep, we're going to be too tired to find where we're going tomorrow. By the way, what are your plans?"

"I'm supposed to meet my girlfriend from UCLA. We're going to go up to Canada together after seeing a bit of New York. She'll go back to California after I get settled."

"Good luck, and write me in care of my parents as soon as you know where you're going to be."

"Sure thing. What are you going to do tomorrow?"

"I've got to get back to the Bay area and reclaim my place in Berkeley before someone else grabs it. I have a three-hour layover, so I'll just hang around the airport.

"Goodnight."

"Sweet dreams of Jane."

CHAPTER 50

The landing at JFK was uneventful. Alvin's tormentors shoved their way past their proper place in line holding their heads with forward-cast eyes while their mouths and jowls were drooping downward in disdain as they passed the profane row.

Alvin and Blake decided to stick together for their westward flight, although Alvin was determined to get a haircut first thing. He justified his giving into the pressure from the majority by explaining his relationship to his parents: "Look, you guys don't understand. You don't come from a close-knit family like mine. We really love one another, and you know, I probably don't want to upset my parents. Even though they might be glad to think I was considering entering the priesthood, the minute they got the idea that I might share some of the philosophy of the hippies, I wouldn't hear the end of it."

"Hey, don't apologize to us. We're not exactly big on whiskers either, or at least we don't wear our hair all that long."

"Alvin, have a happy return to California."

"Henry, you take care, man. Stick to what you believe in," Alvin said, turning in the direction of a barbershop.

"Let's meet back half an hour before departure, O.K.?" Blake suggested to Alvin.

"See you there," Blake shouted as he and Henry walked to the coffee shop a few corridors away and sat down at a table.

"Blake, let me make a call to Penny. I'll be back soon. Order me a hot chocolate."

"O.K."

Henry stepped over to the open-air public telephones hung on stainless steel and dialed the number of Penny's cousin.

"Hello," ushered from the receiver a voice lowered several octaves from the tar of Turkish pipe tobacco.

"May I speak to Penny?"

There was a pause and then Henry imparted enthusiastically, "Hey, how was your summer?"

"Great, but I bet not as good as yours," Susan giggled.

"You're right. It was out-of-sight. But now we're going to have a great time here."

"Listen. I've got a letter from the Canadian Consulate for you and a cashier's check from your bank account in L.A. which your aunt had closed for you."

"Why don't you just stay at your cousins, and I'll get there as soon as possible?"

"It'll take you at least two hours if you come by subway."

"Don't worry. Just stay put."

"It's great to hear your voice."

"Yours too."

"Bye," quietly slipped off Penny's thin lips. Henry had not added, "Darling" or "I love you."

"See you in a while," Henry concluded as he hung up. Crossing the corridor, he walked at a quick pace back to the table where Blake was sitting. His hot chocolate and Blake's coffee were just being served.

"Well, Henry, I guess this is it; it's the last time we'll see each other for a long time."

"Hey, I'll keep you posted. But you have to keep my whereabouts absolutely secret. Promise?"

"Cross my heart and hope to die." Blake joked with a smile, then added more seriously, "At least I hope to keep the latter wish far from the shores of Southeast Asia. By the way, this summer in Oxford I came across a series of Mary McCarthy's articles against the war in Vietnam in the *New York Review of Books*. You should check them out."

"What does she have to say?"

"In a nutshell, she thinks we should get our ass out of there! We have no moral reason being there."

"I'll get around to reading them once I get my act together. There are so many things happening to me right now I hardly know what's happening next."

"Hey, take care of yourself. You have a good head on those shoulders; use it. Keep in touch. I'll keep my mouth shut one hundred percent."

"Blake, I feel I can really trust you. We've had some good times and shared a lot. I'll keep in touch. You too, you starry-eyed romantic."

After finishing their hot drinks, the two friends paid their bill, shook hands in a strong shake, and parted in different directions.

CHAPTER 51

Besides the twenty minutes it took to get his backpack and find the JFK Express, the sixteen-mile ride from the International Arrival Building at John Fitzgerald Kennedy Airport to Manhattan consumed another half-hour in morning rush hour traffic. Deposited at Avenue of the Americas and 42nd Street, Henry felt his heart beat heightened by the bustle and rush of the people on the street. The thrust of busy people hurrying off to their myriad of workplaces pushed him in their on-going throb. His excitement was anesthetized by the layers of yellowish-brown exhaust ascending from the onslaught of the automobiles, which he sought to avoid by descending the worn concrete stairs of the New York subway.

The American conception that it is an expression of freedom to destroy public property or underfund public projects like the subway is sick and ugly! thought Henry as he stared at the rusting graffiti and metal poles. *This must certainly contribute to all the tired looking-faces of the people standing around me.* He turned around and then paced along the long stretch of concrete before stopping to ask, "Can I catch a train to take me to 110th Street here?"

"Sure, stand right there," the short, heavy-set, middle-aged man in a soiled brown suit responded tersely but helpfully. Henry detected a note of muted amiability under the fifty-year-oldie's feigned toughness. Soon a train screeched to a halt as though to emphasize the touching of its metal wheels onto the metal rails. No sooner had he entered the car than it jolted promptly on its way. Henry anxiously watched each sign indicating the next station and dashed out from this moderately full vehicle, and climbed the staircase to the urban domesticity of the Riverside Park area.

As his eyes began to water from the burning sensation brought on by the air of the streets, he peered again at Penny's cousins' address. *It must be that plain, brick building near the corner*, he surmised, remembering that his professor of linguistics at UCLA had lived in the second story of a plain beach house in Venice. He hurried up to the small, black button buzzers and searched for apartment fourteen, which was not marked with a name plate. "Three rings are civilized," kept buzzing in his head. The door was promptly electrically opened to the same irritating sound. To the right of the small elevator, the faded, soiled poster on the wall indicated that the apartment was on the second floor. He decided to walk up the carpeted stairway over to the side of the elevator. It seemed so long since he had seen Penny.

When Henry reached the second floor, he noticed an exactly cropped, dyed-blond bangs and cereal-bowl, straight haircut peer out of the door. His stride hastened. "Penny, that's you?"

A wide smile curved toward her small blue eyes. Her ski-sloped nose, barely visible through the crack in the still-chained door, reminded him, *Why did she go along with doing that? Penny always gives into the things her family tells her to do.* But then he felt relieved at being in the presence of a perfectly dependable friend who really loved him. He could hear the chain being removed from the latch.

"Yes, it's really me here in New York. It's great to see you."

"Yeah, it's fantastic!"

"Henry, this is my cousin, Bernard, and his wife, Judy."

"Nice to meet you! I hear you're a professor of my favorite subject."

The saddened, downcast eyes of the man in his forties were visible by the bluish cloud of smoke from the pungent tobacco of his black-barreled pipe. He studied Henry and seemed displeased at his superficial exuberance. Judy, his equally dour wife, finally greeted him flatly, "Please come in." They were both dressed in ruffled dark suits that gave off the putrescent aroma of aged pipe tobacco. If they found him obnoxious, he wondered what they thought of Penny's totally polite, inoffensive, withdrawing character. "Excuse me, but I must begin work on my lecture for today. This is also Judy's painting day. So you will excuse us both, won't you?" asked the professor in more of a command that an interrogative utterance.

"Oh, sure, don't let us get in your way. I've got the key," smiled Penny, who was glad to have a free place to stay in Manhattan.

"Penny, before we go, may I call the people I'm staying with in Brooklyn?"

Proceeding down the plain corridor with an uncleaned tapestry of a hunting scene, Penny led Henry to a small cove in the wall where there was a black telephone with a thick black cord. Trying to leave this residence as soon as possible, he confirmed with the cousins of his cousins that he would arrive around eight in the evening.

While he was placing his call, Penny brewed two cups of tea from a Lipton bag and put a few butter cookies on the heavy oak table with the off-white place mats. When he sat down, she handed him a stack of letters in long, business envelopes and said, "Go ahead, take a look at them."

He immediately opened the official letter from the Canadian Government. It informed him that his request for landed immigrant status had been rejected but that he was granted a student visa. With moist eyes, he looked back towards Penny, "It's bad news; I didn't get the special immigrant status I had asked for. Instead, they gave me a student visa."

"Gee, Henry, I'm really sorry. What about the other letters?"

"Well, I shouldn't have any trouble with this. It's what's left of my life's savings: $700 dollars. If it's O.K. with you, I'd like to drop by a bank and cash it and put it in travelers' checks right away."

"Sure. It shouldn't take up much time."

"Here're a few letters from friends and family members. I can read them on the subway or bus. It's too loud to talk, anyway."

"So I've discovered."

"So you're about ready?"

"Just give me five minutes to make us a little lunch."

Penny delicately lifted her bag onto her shoulder, and Henry turned around to fold the large check into his money belt, the zipper of which he checked again before tucking the devise around his hips well down into his underpants. As Penny passed Judy's library, she waived silently so as not to disturb her serious relative. Henry checked the telephone book to jot down the addresses of the nearby banks.

"I'm so excited, Henry. This is the first time I've been away from home on my own, and with you it's even more fun."

"Pen, thanks so much for spending the bucks to come all the way east to get me settled."

"Would I treat my friend, Henry, in any other way? Of course not."

Penny's speech was always terse, accepting, uncritical, and full of self-doubt, which melted away when she was with Henry. He helped her shed her constant guard of social propriety, and, in turn, she eased his real insecurity by her willingness to be there whenever he needed her.

"These big buildings are so dirty."

"That's what visitors generally dislike about New York, but it's exciting, isn't it?"

"Hey, there's a bank on the other side of the street."

The couple dashed through traffic to the large building and was able to see immediately a teller. Henry reached inconspicuously into his pants to withdraw the check from his unobtrusive money belt. He laid out the cashier's check and his U.S. passport in front of the teller, who picked up the check and the piece of identification.

"Excuse me, sir, I'll have to check with my manager."

In a few minutes, a serious late-middle-aged, graying executive approached Henry. "I'm sorry, young man, but I am not able to cash your check."

"But, sir, it's a cashier's check. My aunt in Los Angeles was told that this would be the most reliable, safest way to insure absolutely that I wouldn't have any problems cashing it in New York."

"I'm sorry, there is really nothing we can do."

"May I see your superior?"

"I regret that I am the only officer in this division," the gentlemanly manager said, stepping back to his desk as Henry and Penny searched around the branch office for someone who appeared to have greater authority. Frustrated, they walked out of this bank and continued hiking toward Central Park.

Over the next two hours this scene repeated itself at least ten times in several variations. At some branches the employees were helpful enough to call their head offices. At others they were brushed aside with contempt or disdain as though they were petty thieves. At still others, they were gleefully informed, "This is New York—not the provinces."

"Hey, Pen, this isn't fair for you."

"Well, how are you going to live in Canada without that money?"

"I'll have to call Uncle Jonathan and Aunt Sally tonight to see what they can do. I know it's not her fault, but she wasn't given accurate, up-to-date information. Anyway let's take in Central Park and maybe the Metropolitan Museum of Art this afternoon."

"Wonderful!"

From the southern edge of Morningside Heights, the couple had wound in and out of the banks of the Upper West Side until they entered Central Park at Eighty-Sixth Street. Curving southeastward, they skimmed the green, tree-lined edge of the Receiving Reservoir until they came upon the Metropolitan

Museum of Art. By now in the early afternoon, the heat of the day had stacked the filth of the air in distinct layers.

"Are you hungry?" Henry asked Penny, who had retained a slight smile and cheer despite the fruitless effort to resolve Henry's monetary problem.

"Not yet. Do you want to tour the museum now?"

"Why not? We never went to the art museums together in L.A."

"No, I guess we never did."

Penny and Henry walked leisurely through the Egyptian, Greek, Roman, and Medieval art collections making small talk about how beautiful or unusual this or that object was. Penny thought to herself, *It feels really good to see all these beautiful things with someone you really care about.* While Henry began to worry, *I hope Penny isn't going for her MRS. Degree at my university. She's a great friend, but I'm not ready for that institution yet. If I tell her the true stories of what happened to me this summer, she probably won't believe them, and if she does, she'll hate me and think that I had betrayed her.*

They continued their leisurely stroll—not concentrating on any particular object for any length of time—through the branches of ancient Near Eastern, Islamic, Far Eastern, and Modern Galleries, "My head is just spinning with all these colors and shapes. This whole twentieth century period leaves me confused. How about having lunch someplace in the park?"

"Sounds great!"

They left the great museum by the Fifth Avenue entrance but quickly took a right turn back into Frederick Law Olmstead and Calvert Vaux's salvation of nature in the great metropolis. Climbing Cedar Hill, they swung back on the asphalt path that led them by Jose de Creeft's bronze "Alice in Wonderland" over to the Ice Cream Café and Deli on the East Side of the Conservatory Pond. Here they sat down overlooking model yachts and motorboats and ate the sandwiches Penny had prepared at her cousins.

"So you're going to dodge the draft?" inquired Penny matter-of-factly.

"I'd prefer to think of myself as going to be a war resister. It depends on whether you think there are higher laws that we must follow when our conscience tells us it's right instead of obeying the law on the books that our conscience tells us is wrong."

Not completely grasping Henry's point and disliking its self-righteous tone, Penny, nevertheless, shielded her true feelings and resolved, "I'm going to go up there with you."

Henry wondered to himself if Penny thought she wanted to stay with him, how she would get her legal status, but he was suddenly calmed by the thought that she had another year and a half before completing her degree. "Pen, are you sure you want to spend the money to go up there? You don't have to."

"Sure I 'don't have to,' but I want to."

"If you're sure you want to, I'd like the company."

They bit into the thin slices of kosher salami between the thick slices of a Russian rye smeared with a layer of mustard bedecked by the crunchy, light green Boston lettuce.

By later afternoon the heat was no longer unbearably oppressive, and their light fabrics absorbed their slight perspiration. Holding hands, they promenaded around the lake over the ramble across Bow Bridge and Cherry Hill through Sheep Meadow and by the zoo over to the bird sanctuary, and swinging back to the west side, out by the Merchants' Gate at Columbus Circle.

"Pen, to make it over to the Greenfields in Brooklyn, I'd better leave your cousins' place by six, six-thirty."

After dashing across Broadway in the nick of time before the pedestrian light had quickly changed, Penny's grin beamed toward Henry who was a few feet in front of her, "It's not only in Los Angeles you have to watch out for cars."

"Don't you feel like a little kid again? It's like crossing a street safely becomes a big part of your day."

"Who are the Greenfields by the way?"

"Oh, a few months before I left L.A., my uncle had a daughter of a cousin look him up. Well, he sort of dumped her on me. Don't you remember that weekend I had to show that high-school girl from New York around Los Angeles? She turned out to be really nice, though. She must have liked my tour because she told me that if I were ever in New York that I could stay at her parents' place. Well, I wrote that I'd be coming to New York for a few days when I got back from Europe. So since Rebecca's going to be out of town, I'll be staying with her parents and little brother, the Greenfields, in Brooklyn. It should be interesting. They're very Orthodox and keep strictly kosher. They know I'm Reform, but I'm still welcome. It should really be different."

"Well, it's just a few days, anyway. I hope you can get this money thing cleared up right away," Penny gasped while climbing the stairs onto the main mall of Lincoln Center.

"Too bad we don't have tickets for anything," Penny sighed.

"Ah, well, we'll come back for another visit."

"Do you think you'll ever come back, Henry?" Penny questioned half in puzzlement about the outcome of the unanalyzed state of their relationship.

"I really do think I will, Pen, I think the American people will come to their senses again. They can't continue supporting every half-bit dictator around the world forever. The Russians can't keep on putting down popular movements in the communist countries, like Czechoslovakia, either. Something's got to break, or we're going to blow ourselves up. Someday when things do change, the guys who put their feet down and said, 'No more; we're not marching to your b.s.' will be welcomed home."

"I hope so," Penny commented mournfully, not daring to express her doubts that she wasn't sure Henry was right about this matter.

"This place is a lot like the Ahmanson-Doolittle in Los Angeles," Penny remarked, changing the subject.

"Yeah. Both of them are awesome. They both create wind tunnels, too," Henry observed as they left the palace of the fine arts and continued to walk up Broadway until they caught a bus back to Morningside Heights where Henry escorted his devoted companion to her intellectual relatives.

"Listen, give me a call as soon as you get over to the Greenfields."

"Oh, don't worry about me. I'll make it fine over there. I think I can get back over to your cousins by ten in the morning unless you want to meet me in lower Manhattan."

"I'll take you up on meeting me here," Penny said, extending her face slightly forward.

Henry planted a warm kiss on her cheek and embraced her before letting go hastily.

"Tomorrow."

"*Bon voyage.*"

Penny's Gallic farewell was pleasant but worrisome. Their friendship had been one of talk and shared studies, not bodies. He wanted to discourage any signs in that direction but couldn't face the issue. He cringed slightly when he thought of his own dishonesty in not recounting his adventures of the summer, but he did not dare risk losing Penny's constancy now. To make matters worse, he was unable to articulate what was happening to them.

His slide down the painted metal banister sped Henry into the spotted, army-green of the subway cars which were dashing and jerking forward to Brooklyn almost as soon as he had entered the corridor of underground concrete and I-beams. It was seven in the evening and the rush-hour congestion had already thinned. Within minutes a tall, somewhat heavy man whose black pants were soiled with light-brown dirt and whose wrinkled white shirt was spotted with ashes, plopped down next to him and sized him up before asking in a rising lilt, "Y're headed for Brooklyn?"

"Yes, I believe the area is called Sheepshead Bay."

"Oh, dat's where I live, too," the fellow stated in a childlike phrase, each syllable of which was equally accented. And he continued, "Ya' Jewish? Me too, but my neighborhood's Italian and a little Greek and a little everything else, too," he chuckled.

Henry hated psychological classifications, but he was becoming overwhelmed by the sense that this guy's levels of thought and choppy speech were considerably below the mean on a normal distribution.

"Have you lived there long?"

"All my life. My aunt and uncle take good care of me. My mamma and daddy died. Where do ya' come from?"

"I've lived the last few years in California, but I was in Europe this summer. What do you do?"

"My uncle got me dis job. I'm a messenger boy. I carry t'ings around a few offices in a big buildin'. It's very interestin'," related with pride the friendly round-faced young man with eyes partially covered by a fold.

Henry, who constantly believed in taking people at their word, was, nevertheless, intrigued about what was interesting about the messenger business. "Do you mind if I ask what's so neat about delivering packages between business?"

"Well, it's de *schmate* business. People are nice to me in de *schmate* business."

"What's the *schmate* business?" asked Henry ignorantly—ashamed that he had questioned this fellow's mental capacity.

"De *schmate* business? Ya' dant know what de *schmate* business is?" the large fellow looked back at Henry, wondering if he shared his own problem of being a slow learner.

"No, I never heard of it before."

"Ya' know, it's like clothes and stuff like dat."

"Oh, I get it. You take mail and packages between the various firms?"

"Ya' got it. Excuse me for askin', but was it hard for ya' at school? Gee whiz, it was tough for me there. But I got special ed and it got better."

"No, it wasn't for me, but I can understand that it must be great working for nice people."

"Oh, yes, it's really nice. Dey treat me good. Dey pay me fair, too."

"Would you know how to get to this address?" Henry inquired, pulling out the slip of paper onto which he had written the Greenfields' address.

"Oh, wow, it's de same street I live on. I'll show ya' de house. What's y'r relatives called, anyhow?"

"They're not really my relatives, but sort of. Anyway, they're the Greenfield family. Do you know them?"

"Max Greenfield? Sure, everybody knows Max Greenfield. He sells de bagels to all de stores. Mrs. Greenfield, she's nice to me, too. And Danny, der boy, he don't let nobody boder me. His mamma told 'im to let nobody boder me. An' Danny's sister's real pretty, too."

"Yeah, I showed her around Los Angeles."

"Oh, yeah."

"Yeah," smiled Henry, getting a chuckle at this guy's sense of Jewish geography.

"Hey, we get off here."

"Here?" repeated Henry, searching to verify whether the name of the stop in the faded tiles corresponded to what he had written down on the piece of scratch paper.

Henry was struck by the ugliness of the houses in this neighborhood. The box houses in brick or wood were crowded in a row in defiance of any sense of wholeness. The individuality of each submerged its neighbor to conform to the baseline of acceptable building standards. In contrast, the southern poverty into which he had been born had individuality, being graced by some bit of God's nature that had been destroyed or neglected in these environs.

"Dat's it," the jovial, amiable messenger lad concluded his encounter with Henry, pointing to the two-story brown brick house with a tar-covered roof.

"Thanks, take care," responded Henry, realizing that he had not even exchanged first names with the fellow.

Noticing that this yard appeared to be the only one on the block where there had been some effort at gardening, Henry stared at a tall, clipped green hedge, somewhat browned by the dirt of the street, standing between this box and the next yard, which was covered with weeds. As he walked up the concrete stairs, he regarded the large white and yellow bushes of flowers lining the other side of the yard. In front of the light wood front door was an aluminum screen door that was slightly rusted by the proximity of the ocean humidity. Henry rang the small doorbell, painted over with an extra layer of white paint, also speckled with the brown particles of the street. A middle-age man of medium stature, dressed in suit pants and a sleeveless undershirt, his arms covered with very thick hair on his arms, came to the door.

"Hi, I'm Henry Green."

The man scanned Henry from his head down to his toes, and then nodded, "Max Greenfield. Please come in."

In the doorway to the living room stood erect an attractive woman of her husband's stature but somewhat younger in age. She wore a simple blue cotton dress, and her hair was thick and black. "This is my wife, Sarah. Sarah, this is the young man who showed Rebecca around Los Angeles. From what she tells me, Henry, you should open your own travel agency."

"Really?"

"Yes, she got so much out of your tour. She came back singing the praises of Los Angeles. She's trying to talk us into moving out there. Have you eaten?" Sarah added enthusiastically.

"Not yet, but it's so hot, I'm really not too, hungry."

"Yes, this sweltering heat does get to you."

"How about some cold seltzer water?"

"Sounds great," said Henry, smiling, not really knowing what seltzer water was.

Stretching his neck down the long corridor, Max Greenfield yelled, "Come on out, David, and meet our guest."

"Henry, would you like to put your things in Rebecca's room? That's where you'll been staying," Sarah Greenfield said, directing him to the middle room down the long corridor of shining wooden floors. He entered the small middle room which had the look of a teenage girl's homey quarters. Then, Mrs. Greenfield suggested that they all move to the kitchen.

Joined by the eleven-year-old, David, they entered the spotless square kitchen where a small rectangular table stood next to an ironing board closet. The floor was covered with yellowish linoleum with an artificial stone design. Their cabinets were roomy, their off-white finish yellowing, despite an obvious recent scrub.

Henry broke the ice, "Mr. Greenfield, I learned that you are a bagel wholesaler in these parts."

"Did Rebecca tell you that? I am a *treger* of bagels—that's it. It makes a living. I can't complain."

"Matter of fact, a young guy I met on the subway—who knew you— showed me here. He says everyone in the neighborhood knows Max Greenfield."

345

"Who could that have been?" inquired Sarah.

"He's about my age. I sort of got the impression he may have a learning difficulty."

"Loinin' difficulty," laughed David. "He's retarded. You're talkin' about Noah Becker."

"Ha. Ha," chuckled Mr. Greenfield, "So Noah Becker showed *you* how to get here. I guess they've been givin' him smart pills."

Henry, who was taken aback at the rather crude way Noah's intelligence had been so off-handedly categorized, nevertheless, held his opinion to himself, but modulated the mockery of their joke, "He's sure got more up there than I have when it comes to local geography."

Sarah, whose Brooklyn accent had been upgraded by a stint at Hunter College, had controlled her disapproval of her pre-teen's insensitive outburst and her husband's egging him on by thinking how lucky she had been to get through the last few weeks.

"Excuse me, Mrs. Greenfield, do you work outside your home as well?"

"I must; so I do; but if it keeps up like this, I don't know how much longer I will."

Henry seemed confused, and Max frowned at his wife that she would reveal her travail to a stranger. "My wife's a high school teacher of math. They've been on strike. Haven't you been readin' about it? Everybody's talkin' about it."

"I'm sorry, but I've had my own worries, so I haven't been following the story. But that reminds me, could I possibly make a collect call to my aunt and uncle in California and a call to Manhattan, to some people I met this summer? You see, when my aunt closed my bank account for me, the bank gave her a cashier's check for the remainder in my account and said it would be the surest way not to have any trouble cashing it here. Well, it turns out that no bank will touch it."

"Sure, sonny, it's in the nook right between David's and Rebecca's rooms."

Henry excused himself from the company of his hosts and withdrew to make the necessary call to Los Angeles. His aunt was shocked that he was having to waste so much time with this matter after she had been explicitly told that his money should be placed in this form of exchange. His uncle told him that he would call his friend who was a wealthy physician in Manhattan and he would ask him to countersign the check. If he agreed, he would call Henry back this evening. Relieved at his uncle's willingness to help him out,

Henry thanked them and hung up the telephone before dialing Drs. Helen and Joshua Meyer, whom he had met in Brussels earlier in the summer. After a warm welcome to their great city, Henry was delighted to receive their invitation to dinner the next evening. Having finished his calls, he walked back to the kitchen where Mr. and Mrs. Greenfield were bickering about something in quite loud voices. Henry picked up his glass of bubbly water he had left on the counter and began to sip it while listening to the husband and wife's heated discussion.

"Max, I tell you it's a few local *meshugana* preachers and hotheads that are being laughed at by the educational *makhers* who are manipulating them for their own anti-union ends," Sarah pronounced in a rising voice at her husband.

"Then how come all those *shvartses* were chasing all those *yidish* teachers out of the school? Tell me that, smartie," Max retorted in a veritable shout at his wife.

Henry could hardly believe his ears that a man of such respect in his neighborhood would employ such a crude slur as *shvartse*. The first time he had heard that prejudiced term used by a Jewish person was in South Carolina when he was visiting rich cousins of his cousins. *But what do you expect in the South?* thought Henry. *But this is supposed to be the region of tolerance and openness to racial and ethnic minorities.*

"How can you use such a word? Remember, 'we, too, were slaves in the land of Egypt'" Mrs. Greenfield, embarrassed that Henry had overheard Max's outburst, replied to her husband.

"Well, they are starting to call themselves 'Blacks,' now" grumbled Mr. Greenfield, who continued. "*Shvartse* means Black, doesn't it? Don't they like to be called that?"

"You know damn well that it is used in a pejorative way to imply many bad qualities," Sarah yelled back.

"I beg your pardon, doilin', look right here, right here in today's paper, it says, 'An Appeal to the Community from Black Trade Unionists.'"

"That's right; 'Black' is positive now. When you and your kind say *Shvartse*, you mean someone who does inferior work, who is lazy. I read that! What the Black Trade Unionists had to say," fumbled Sarah, searching for the copy of the *New York Times*." Look here," she continued, "it says '*Due Process* is the central issue. It is the right of every worker not to be transferred or fired at the whim of his employer. It is the right of every worker to be judged on his merits—not his color or creed....'"

"Alright, already, you made your point."

Baffled about the whole issue of the teachers' strike, Henry began to feel overwhelmed. He had the urge to turn away from this issue but reluctantly felt he at least better take a look at the paper tomorrow. In the nick of time the telephone rang. It was Henry's uncle from Los Angeles. Henry rushed out to the telephone.

"Henry, I called my friend, Isaac Hirsch. He is supposed to meet you tomorrow afternoon at one P.M. in front of St. Patrick's Cathedral. He'll be wearing a gray suit and a hat with a small red feather. He's fifty-eight years old and looks his age. He's stout and rather olive skinned in complexion. If some mix-up occurs, you can contact him at his telephone numbers. Take them down."

Henry thanked his uncle and wished a loving greeting to his aunt, hung up the receiver, and called Penny to schedule a ten-thirty meeting in Battery Park at the Statue of Verrazano. On the way back to the Greenfields' kitchen, he puzzled himself with the thought that he had never overheard such a quarrelsome duo who, nevertheless, seemed to deeply care about one another.

"Mr. and Mrs. Greenfield, if you'll excuse me, I'd like to get to bed now so I can meet a friend of mine early tomorrow. Could you get me up with you in the morning?"

"Max gets up at five every morning; I get up at seven and then wake up David. We usually leave by 7:30, but who knows with this strike? *Baruch HaShem*, we'll survive."

"Blessed be the Holy Name! Good night."

CHAPTER 52

Always trying to be the perfect guest, Henry arose at 6:30 after hearing Sarah Greenfield's first stirrings. He tucked in the corners of his sheets in military fashion and replaced Rebecca's pinkish bedspread with extra care, so that it would appear that no one had even lain on the bed in her absence. By the time his hostess was pouring herself a cup of coffee, he joined her and David at the breakfast table over bowls of cereal.

Having carefully surveyed Henry's character, he asked him, "Would you like to ride over to Coney Island after school?"

"Gee, David, I'd love to, but tonight I'm going to get in really late because I was invited to dinner by a couple I met in Brussels this summer. But how about this Sunday?"

"Great. I'll get some of my friends to help me show you around here."

Sarah glanced back at Henry, "So you won't be coming in for dinner this evening?"

"No, ma'am, I met two doctors this summer who want to have me over to dinner at their place tonight, if that'll be O.K. with you."

"Go, enjoy, we'll see you tomorrow night, and you won't have to worry about all my troubles."

They all walked out over to the dingy station where they caught the train. Henry was growing accustomed to the higher decibels and the urinal smell of the New York subway. But, in spite of one slow down, he made it to the designated meeting place with Penny in enough time to walk over to the Staten Island Ferry and back.

She was sitting on a park bench with her head tilted backwards towards the old buildings when Henry came upon her. Penny had dressed in a light blue and white cotton dress, going up almost as high as her neckline.

"Henry, am I glad to see you! You wouldn't believe my evening last night.

My cousins sat there over dinner fighting and practically pretended that I wasn't there. I don't think they spoke two words to me."

"What was going on between them?"

"They were at each other's throats about what happened at Columbia University."

"What happened?"

"Oh, some students disrupted the registration lines to get the students reinstated who had been expelled last spring. So while Bernard thinks he ought to get involved on their side, Judy keeps reminding him that he's only an assistant professor, and that'll be the end of his chances for advancement if he gets caught up in all the action. And between their 'bad vibes' toward each other, half of which weren't even spoken, there I sat, trying to be my innocuous self. What nerve! They act as though I don't have an idea in my head."

"Gee, Pen, that's too bad. Would you believe that last night I had to listen to a verbal fight between Max and Sarah about the public school strike? At least they screamed when they were angry with each other, and David and I got a few words in edgewise during the evening. By the way, I talked to my uncle and we're supposed to meet a friend of his at one in front of St. Pat's, if that's O.K. with you. Also this evening the two physicians I met in Brussels this summer are having me over to dinner. I would have liked to get you invited, but I couldn't."

"That's alright. I think my cousins feel guilty about neglecting me last night. So they're supposed to take me out this evening."

"That'll work out great! I'll get over my social obligation to the Meyers, and, then, tomorrow we'll have more time to be together!"

They got up from the bench and walked past the Whitney Museum then, turning right on Fulton Street, over to the New York Stock Exchange on Wall Street. Penny wanted to take the brief tour, and Henry agreed to watch the bustle and noise of Wall Street, the center of contemporary capitalism. The yells and ticker tape, the framed descriptions of its history all rushed past so fast that they were soon outside leisurely advancing up Broadway from the area of the small shops and galleries to Washington Square. Penny's mouth upturned in a grin as she absorbed the flock of hippies in the pastels of tie-dyed tee shirts singing Dylan to the tune of an amateur guitarist. She sat down on the concrete bench facing the large marble arch; Henry stretched out in the sun beside her and overheard the hippies' conversation about the astrological implications of being born under the sign of Leo.

In front of them a thin, pale woman in her twenties in a long sari of brown and red swirls stared intently at her audience. People sat around her in a circle. Her gaze fell upon the muscular young man with long, straight, light-brown hair down to his shoulders. He wore faded blue jeans with holes at his knees. In a serious declaration she taught, "The Zodiac reveals four types of basic substances: Fire-Air; Water-Earth. According to a triple rhythm these four cosmic elements will generate a scheme of operation." At this point she began to record on a hand-size blackboard which power is generated in which season by which sign:

"Thus, at the fall equinox Air-power is generated Libra then concentrated Scorpio lastly distributed Sagittarius."

First raising, then dropping her arms at her sides, she instructed them:

"Brothers and sisters, the Zodiacal signs of generation of power are cardinal. Those where power is concentrated are fixed. And those where power is distributed are mutable. In other words, here we have spirit, soul, and mind working in the total body."

Casting her glance at Henry, Penny's eyes met his as her mouth began to curl into a smirk. She got up and began to walk over to the New York University buildings surrounding the park. Henry caught up with her as she commented, "It's amazing how gullible people are. How do people fall for such junk?"

"Now, now, didn't we learn to be respectful of other people's subcultures? Haven't we been taught to figure out what makes people like that tick instead of jumping to conclusions?"

"But what would make obviously not-so-dumb people sit around and seek answers in what we have learned to be absolutely false by every scientific criterion."

"Well, I must admit my natural feelings want to jump to that conclusion, but there must be something else to that stuff to attract so many bright people."

"Maybe they're just plain dumb."

"Maybe, but then again, I've met quite a few who are really bright," Henry observed, not really wanting to defend their beliefs too strongly but not wanting to reject their mystical leanings out-of-hand.

From mid-morning to a little past noon, these first-time visitors to New York meandered through old skylines and new, by fishmongers and pizza parlors, alongside of art galleries and flea markets, through quarters of irregularly topped apartment complexes to the townhouses of the side streets of the affluent. Now a safe fifteen minutes before his scheduled meeting with the prominent surgeon who was to countersign his check, Henry and Penny sat down in the park in front of the two great spires of St. Patrick's Cathedral. They seemed to point toward a blue heaven away from the overwhelming modern Babylon, which surrounded them.

"Have you ever been inside a Catholic church before?"

"No, never. What would a nice Jewish girl like me be doing in a place like that?" Penny joked.

"Besides my sister's wedding, I had never been in one, either. But, believe me, if you ever go to Europe, you'll spend a good part of your time in them. So much of European history is told right inside its churches. It's funny, but this one looks a lot like the cathedral in Cologne I visited this summer."

"How about my taking a tour of the cathedral, then, while you are taking care of your check business?"

"Great! I'll meet you back inside near the pews toward the entrance when I've finished."

They walked over to the seat of the Archbishop of New York, and Penny entered while Henry remained on the stairs to the entrance. At exactly the designated time, Dr. Isaac Hirsch arrived. He was wearing a plain hat with a small red feather on its left side. His rotund body filled out his fashionable gray suit. This robust man in his fifties wasted no time in trivialities, "Henry Green, I presume."

"Dr. Isaac Hirsch?"

Keeping his dignified, large head in an erect forward gaze, Dr. Hirsch's demeanor let it be known without any pretenses that he was a busy man who had little time to engage a twenty-one year old in any meaningful conversation. Without any advance warning, the physician stepped down the stairs at a brisk pace, and they were soon at the branch of his bank, where the doctor requested Henry's check. "You know, young man, you can't trust anyone anymore, especially in this city. That's why you're having this problem. And it's going to be that way from now until the end of time."

Wanting to object to this man's dreary world view, Henry silenced his qualms, and responded, "I really appreciate this help, Dr. Hirsch, and I am sorry for the inconvenience I caused you."

Not a man to resist a sign of gratitude, Isaac cast a minor smile of *noblesse oblige* Henry's way and bid Henry "good-bye." For his part Henry was relieved to have his check cashed. Then he purchased, signed, and quickly stuffed travelers' checks safely into his money belt. Within an hour his nest egg was hidden in his underwear.

By now Penny had wandered around the high Gothic structure and was surprised at how the massive marble columns had done away with the need for flying buttresses. For her it was a strange world of side alters dedicated to people she had never heard of. "Who were Elizabeth Ann Seaton, St. Rose of Lima, St. Teresa of Infant Jesus, St. Anthony of Padua, St. Elizabeth, Michael Louis and Saints Brigid and Bernard? What are ambulatories and baptisteries?"

For Penny the color and statuary, this attempt at organic Gothic architecture in modern America, reminded her of a monograph on a different culture, which she had been required to read during her undergraduate studies. When, with head tilted backward over a pew, she was admiring the inner trusses, which supported the interior vaulting, Henry snuck up behind her and placed his head over hers.

He whispered into her ear, "You're planning to convert?"

With words tied up inside whenever someone caught her off her same mental track, Penny's cheeks tightened into small round pinkish circles and her grin puffed up controlling her entire face. She quickly pulled herself upright from her position and ran around to the other side of the heavy wooden seat.

"Thanks for bringing me here. I learned a lot I would have never known. Did you get your business taken care of?"

"Yep. There're seven hundred U.S. dollars worth of travelers' checks in my money belt."

"How about consuming the sandwiches I brought along?"

Inspired by their productive morning, the friends breathed deeply with relief at having the pressure taken off Henry's being without funds in a crucial situation. In turn, Henry felt so grateful to Penny for the unwavering solidarity she had displayed towards him since her arrival that his initial standoffishness began to fade away as they interlaced their fingers in the thickness of the busy pedestrian crowds.

Soon they were back in the serenity of the mulberry trees and hawthorns of the Shakespeare Garden in Central Park. As Californians, they seemed inevitably pulled to escape the density, people, and monumental buildings to retreat to the relative serenity of the greenery in the city. Penny sat with her back to the bark of a tree trunk while Henry sprawled out on the grass near her.

In an unusual moment of repose, Penny initiated a conversation, "L.A.

was a lot of fun this summer. It was super having time to go folkdancing at the International Student House. My job wasn't too bad—not that I lavish the thought of doing secretarial work for the rest of my life. How about you? You've hardly said a word about your trip outside the letters I got from you."

"Can you believe Dr. Senob didn't give us any maps or anything about how to get to his dig in the Périgord?"

"'Doesn't surprise me! I always took him for the absent-minded professor type."

"But I suppose it worked out for the best. Instead of digging, I ended up seeing every western European country except Portugal. I hitched or took the train everywhere. I was even in East Germany on my way to Prague the day the Russians invaded Czechoslovakia. But, best of all, I met people wherever I went, and I got to stay in people's homes all over."

"It sounds like a dream!"

"It was better than a dream. It was real!"

"I bet it made you think about a lot of things."

"Pen, like I learned so much I don't know where to begin. I feel that so many things I didn't learn in school fell into place or cleared up in my head. I made a decision about Vietnam. I guess I left the United States as a wish-washy liberal and am coming back pretty much convinced that Scandinavia's social democracy is a better way."

"You know, my sister-in-law's Swedish, and they prefer our kind of life in Southern California."

"But, Pen, her family is upper-middle class. What do you expect? They don't have to pay for the social welfare policies in California and the U.S. that they would have to support in Sweden. And they're the kind of people who prefer sitting around a concrete swimming pool to going camping on a nature trail."

"I guess you're right about that, Henry. But I still like our way of life. We're so easy going. The Svenssons are so formal and uptight."

"Pen, when you get to know them, they really warm up to you."

For the first time, Penny sensed that Henry had changed. There was something about his trip that had made him into a somewhat different person. He began to seem foreign to her. She couldn't exactly put her finger on it. Henry now seemed much more judgmental. His ideas seemed much more molded. He seemed so enthused by what he had experienced in Europe this summer that he was full of it. And she found his frequent criticisms of things American to her dislike. Nevertheless, she loved him and wanted him.

Penny's sandwiches of Velveeta cheese on Wonderbread covered with mayonnaise and Boston lettuce were not untasty or unfilling, reflected Henry to himself, *but they're as bland as the Cokes and Oreo cookies she brought along. Do not mention what they're probably doing to our insides. I guess she just likes to blend in and to grab what's convenient. She's so thoughtful, though. How many people would have even bothered to bring a lunch?*

"Pen, how'd you like to take in the American Museum of Natural History for the rest of the afternoon?"

"Sure! Isn't that *the place* for all the art we studied in Professor Finn's class?"

"You haven't forgotten all those footnotes, have you?"

Slowly standing upright, Penny whisked the crumbs from her lap as Henry picked up the brown-paper bag she left lying on the ground and deposited it in the trash basket at the edge of the garden. On the way toward 79th Street, Central Park West, they crossed at the pedestrian zone at the corner while glancing at the four high Doric columns on which large statues were standing in front of the enormous rounded porticoes cut into the huge rectangle of granite blocks. As they entered the first floor, the natural history of the plants and animals of North America and its indigenous inhabitants overwhelmed Penny less than her thoughts about Henry. She sounded these out only to her inner, silent voice. *He's lost his sense of humor; he's become so serious. He's so sure he's right. He's like a fiery prophet. He really believes what they taught us in Sunday school about social justice. But he may have gone a bit overboard. If I say anything to him, I'll lose him. So I better keep my mouth shut as usual.*

As they walked along silently peering into the perfectly-designed dioramas, the scenes of real stuffed animals set into models of their natural habitat humbled Henry, who commented, "Gee, we never learned how to design a good museum case. You know, even though these displays look like they were made in the 1920s, they were done with incredible precision."

Penny responded in a sarcastic chuckle, "Yeah, our classes at UCLA should have taught us to do something practical like that. It might help us get a job."

And then she managed to squeeze out a bit of what was really troubling her as best as she could, "Henry, isn't this museum the best of its kind in the world?"

"Yes, it's really terrific. It really shows the best of America. It displays our know-how, our popular crafts, and our ability to explain complicated things in simple, attractive ways. I'm not sure it's better than the British Musuem I saw this summer, but maybe its displays catch your eyes a bit better."

"Then why are you so down on America since you've come back?"

"I'm not down on America, Pen. It's just that some of our important policies are wrong! Vietnam is wrong! Our siding with rightwing dictators all over the world is wrong! The gross discrepancies between rich and poor are wrong; our treating nature with contempt is wrong!"

"That sounds pretty anti-American to me."

"Then you can't distinguish between objecting to certain policies and practices and objecting to the people in a country! We, who are protesting, we're Americans too! The haves, the conformists, and the bigots don't have exclusive rights to our national identity."

Penny was so taken aback by the emotional forwardness of Henry's blast that she immediately changed the subject, asking meekly, "Do you want to move on upstairs to see the exhibits on the dinosaurs?"

"Why not?" replied Henry—impervious to the fact that the impact of his booming voice and intensity had frightened Penny.

It became difficult for her to focus on the birds of North America, the primates, African mammals, reptiles or amphibians. It was vaguely interesting, but she began to feel that she could not absorb all this information. What was the purpose behind collecting all these objects, classifying them, and depicting their niches? Penny's values seemed to be under attack from all quarters, and the dreaded image of slaving away in that giant factory-office behind a typewriter like all the other typewriters on all the other desks under the unflickering, white fluorescent overhead lamps rose to her conscious mind again to torment her. Just as they were leaving the model of life among the Indians of the Northeast, she gasped for an extra breath.

"Pen, are you alright?"

"Sure. Let's walk up to the dinosaurs."

After climbing a flight of stairs, they watched the giant bones above them and to their sides. Biological evolution manifested itself in enormous remains and emphasized their own changing nature.

"I wonder if we'll end up becoming like them?" Penny worried aloud.

"No, no, we're becoming more and more differentiated. We're adapting to more and more varied environments, remember?" Henry objected optimistically.

"You're just saying that because you read it someplace," Penny objected.

356

"So what's wrong with reading it someplace? That means that somebody thought about it seriously and went places and gathered lots of evidence to prove or disprove what they wanted to find out."

"Don't believe everything you read, Henry," Penny wanted to say, but instead, she held it inside herself, and sluggishly suggested, "Let's get away from all these dead things. Let's start walking back to my cousins. It's getting late."

By the time they reached the exit, it was almost five o'clock, so they began to walk briskly north on Central Park West. Penny enjoyed watching the different exteriors of the elegant apartment buildings bordering the park. "Well, different strokes for different folks, I guess. I just prefer our one- or two-story homes in West Los Angeles. I like the land and gardens around them."

"I wouldn't judge until you have a chance to try out one of these apartments right by the park."

"There're just too many people here packed into too little a space. It makes me feel claustrophobic."

"I like having so many people around, but I could do without the noise and exhaust."

CHAPTER 53

The incessant roar of the street traffic, the screeching of cars halting at the last minute before red lights, the blurting of horns rumbled in Penny's and Henry's ears. All the way from the museum to her cousins' residence, this din rendered conversation uncomfortable at best and difficult at worst. It was agreed that they would meet early at the Guggenheim and would leave for Canada in the mid-afternoon. The young professors explained to Henry how he could reach the Meyers' by bus, and their directions proved accurate and efficient. He was in the neighborhood of the United Nations by six-thirty and found the flat-surfaced, darkened glass rectangle stretching upwards beyond the council of all the states of the world. "I wonder if this is a Mies van der Rohe building?" Henry inquired of himself. "Why, with all of its straight lines and use of the features of the industrial age in an attempt to beautify both, I bet it is, or I bet that one of his students did it."

There stood a heavy-set, man in late middle age of medium stature with a round face. His hanging pinkish jowls matched the bright turquoise valet-jacket that he was wearing. When he noticed Henry's simple polyester lime pants and tennis-style-striped shirt, he cast a suspicious eye at him and inquired in a bass voice, "Young man, may I ask where you are going?"

"Yes, sir, to the Meyer family's."

After he picked up his desk telephone and announced Henry's arrival to his hosts, the doorman added, "Welcome, just take the elevator to the right up to the fifty-sixth floor."

"Thanks," Henry responded nervously as he turned the corner and entered the box with a beige-carpeted interior and long strips of mirrors at the corners. Alone, he was pulled upwards in a gushing swoop that cracked his ears before winding down to a dangling, slightly swinging stop. He had barely had time to reflect, "I've never known anybody who's lived on the fifty-sixth floor before."

He pressed the doorbell which, nestled next to the ebony door, stood out in a simple, possible ivory, elegance.

Soon after he rang the door, Bea, their creamy brown-skinned maid in her late forties, greeted him with her large eyes and exquisite irises, and, then, escorted him into the enormous living room which was sunk a few feet below the level of the entrance-way corridor. Dr. Meyer was standing admiring the light-colored statue about a foot and a half in height, which struck Henry as being the head of a Meso-American Indian in headdress taken directly from one of the pages of his textbook of primitive art. Henry found Dr. Meyer's profile as engaging as that of the statue. Tonight Dr. Meyer again reminded Henry of the head of Franklin Delano Roosevelt. His hair was parted in a similar fashion to FDR's and his glasses resembled those of the president whom Henry had seen only in old photographs and film footage. His suit was as stately as the latest ad for elegant attire for men in *The New Yorker*, and, as before, Dr. Meyer was friendly and open to Henry while retaining a slight aura of merited authority, earned respect, and opulence.

Dr. Meyer stepped beside the statue to the cord of the drapes. He began to draw open the white linen curtains that served as a backdrop to the collection of the art work of the native peoples of the New World. These works of art were tastefully arrayed at several levels around the spacious room. Now instead of the plain white background, a huge panoramic view of the multicolored and many-shaped New York skyline bedazzled the onlookers' attention.

"Wow, Dr. Meyer, what can I say? It's *too* much!"

The gentleman, of humble origins himself, was amused at his guest's basic reaction on being introduced to the world of the affluent Manhattanite. Putting his hand on Henry's shoulder, he gently led him back to the figurine—even though he recognized that Henry had been shaken by the sense of power and magnificence that private access afforded to this view of America's capital of art, theater and finance.

"Henry, as an anthropologist, you can see that we are drawn to non-western art. All of these works are originals. This one was a lid of an incense burner. It is supposed to be a male figure that comes from Guatemala."

The rounded base of this head carried a face holding a kind of hatchet. On its head there appeared to be an upside down canoe at the base of which was a large hatchet decorated with rosettes. An inverted vase-like piece seemed to be pinching the face's nose.

"I'd say it comes from the Teotihuacan culture between 200 B.C. and 650 A.D."

"Close enough for my tastes."

Henry felt good he had impressed his host by identifying the origin of the piece.

"I really like that circular vessel with the brownish duck on the lid."

"Oh, it's from Guatemala too, but it's from the early Mayan civilization, I believe."

"Sir, did you know that your piece over on your marble table, the one that sort of looks like a bulldog, really is from the Olmec culture. It combines jaguar and human features. I'd date this piece between 1200 and 600 B.C. and say it comes from Veracruz. Some of my professors believe that the Olmecs were predecessors of the Mayas, but they're not sure."

"My Lord, Henry, you really know your stuff."

"To be honest, I just completed a course on primitive art the quarter before last. My prof was a knockout. She used to come to class in a mini-skirt almost up to her *tuchass* and low-cut blouses that displayed her plentiful endowment. On top of that, she used to brag about her male conquests, some of which she referred to rather vividly. Would you believe that her classes were as stacked as she was? I might add she wasn't typical of my archeology teachers."

Dr. Meyer bellowed a deep melodious guffaw, letting Henry know he appreciated turning that conversation from weightiness to the comic and human element embedded in searching for the past.

Just at this moment of laughter, Frau Dr. Meyer, attired in a creamy evening frock, floated across the marshmallow carpet into the living room, and with extended arms, grasped Henry's right hand between hers.

"How good to see you again."

"Great to see you, too!"

"Gentlemen, may we convene in the dining room? I believe *le dîner est servi.*"

They stepped upward a few steps, and over to the right was a long table that absorbed the surrounding light. Could it be black marble? There was a floral arrangement of red camelias in the centerpiece, and on top of each individually-weaved linen place mat was a large *Niçoise* salad.

"*Bon appétit.*"

Mrs. Dr. Meyer had retained the striking beauty of a Nordic goddess whose Weimarian elegance had been softened as she had aged. She had combined the demeanor of the best of *The New Yorker* wife and mother together with the competence and intelligence of a first-rate professional.

Forever admiring her good looks, her appreciative husband now turned his good laugh into a serious mood.

"Henry, did you win your draft case?"

"No, sir, I lost it."

"Then I have a perfect way to get you out. Tomorrow, you call up your draft board, and you tell them that you just met Jesus Christ Himself, who told you in person that this war is wrong, and He doesn't want you to fight in it."

"But, Dr. Meyer, first of all, I'm Jewish, so why would they believe that I had this vision about Jesus?"

"Listen, those southern holy rollers will eat it up. They'll think they got a convert, a Jew on the top of it all, and a crazy one at that. They'll classify you as being mentally unfit and that's that."

"But, sir, I didn't have any vision like that!"

"Listen, young man, if you believe that this war is wrong, then they're doing something wrong by drafting you. Here's a legal way for you to get out."

"Dr. Meyer, I decided that I'm going to Canada."

"Look, Henry, I don't know about you, but I can say that this country has been damned good to me. O.K., this war is a mistake, but, if you leave it now, you may never be able to come back."

"But I won't influence anybody if I get out this way. I'll only be selfish in getting out myself."

"That's one less person they're going to draft. In the meantime you can convince your fellow citizen that this war is wrong."

"But how am I going to convince anybody if I have been certified as being crazy?"

"To hell with them! You're going to be in California, and those rednecks are going to stay down south."

Mrs. Meyer interjected, "Henry, at least it's a way out."

Henry, who had so appreciated the Meyers' willingness to befriend him, now had no desire to alienate them. "O.K., it's a good idea. I'll think about it tonight."

"Meanwhile, let's enjoy our meal," Mrs. Meyer smiled soothingly, as she swung her hand in a tempting gesture toward the perfectly arranged vegetables in front of them. Just as he was about to follow her example, he noticed the grayish granular surface of volcanic stone that was carved with two large holes and a horizontal indenture giving the appearance of an Indian face. "Isn't that a *metate*?" Henry asked uncertainly.

"Yes, indeed; it had a practical purpose as well as a ceremonial one, you know," Mrs. Meyer replied. "They used it for grounding maize."

Then abruptly changing the subject, Dr. Meyer inquired in a muted tone of voice, "Henry, you know, our son, well, to tell you the truth, it hasn't been going so well between him and us for the last year or so. We've sought the best help money can buy, and he's become so distant, so rebellious, and not for any rational reason. Nothing seems to work."

Almost shocked that this successful psychiatrist and entrepreneur would seek his mere opinion, Henry sought further information, "What seems to be the problem?"

"For one thing, he is hanging out with a very bad lot at the moment. We think they're into drugs and God know what else."

"Have you seen your son actually using drugs?"

"Not really. We've found a few joints in his room."

"But, are you certain the group he hangs out with is into other, more potent drugs?"

"Not really. But we do get a feeling that they're into something that's not good."

"What specifically do you think his group of friends are into?"

"To be honest, we're not certain."

"Well, it seems to me that you have one of two options. One is that you have the means to hire a private detective to confirm your suspicions that he and his friends are dealing some illegal drugs, or, two, you can start trusting him, and make him feel that you trust him. If you find out he's into hard drugs, then you can act according to what you feel is right, but if you find out there's nothing behind your worries, then make him feel that he can be his own person. By the way, how much time do you spend together?"

"Basically he would come to meals, go to his room and do homework, and then see us at breakfast the next morning throughout his junior year in high school. He went to one of the best schools in the city. It's a virtual *Who's Who* of New York."

"Do you think he felt out of place there?"

"Well, we may be modestly well-off compared to some at that school, but, we're certainly not wanting for anything. No, he had as much to spend as the average kid there."

Mrs. Meyer offered, "It is true that we were gone on business a lot of the children's high school years. But there was always a responsible, well-trained adult sitting in for us. Most people who live the kind of lives we do also have to spend a great deal of time away from their families."

"But, ma'am, it sounds to me, like you've got to start spending more time together with your kids, or you're going to lose them, if you haven't already," Henry replied, enjoying giving sensitive advice more than receiving it.

"But they have to go to learn to be independent."

"That's true, ma'am, but do you want them to be totally independent from you and without you for the rest of their lives?"

"No, certainly, not."

After they had consumed the plentiful salad, Bea brought out a fluted plate of modernistic transparent glass edged by a gold-plated border onto which a moderately-sized, rather rare filet mignon had been placed by the side of rice pilaf and fresh *petits pois verts*. The tender, bloody steak was very tender, and the peas had been steamed so lightly that they almost had a crackling sensation. Thick husked wild rice had been blended with *herbes fines* to produce a filling and flavorful, but not overly spicy, grain.

"If you think he might want to, as soon as I get settled down in Canada, your son would be more than welcome to come up and visit me. We could try talking things out."

"That's a possibility, Henry. Thanks for offering. We might take you up on it," the father responded, looking into the distance at the wide wallhanging which hung in the entrance corridor. There were four young adult figures with orange faces and hands with small black rectangular mouths, which stared in dread at the beholder. Their bright clothing, the men's almost industrial blue overalls, and the women's more traditional purple, strapped dress, stood out on the white quilted background. Henry caught a glimpse of Dr. Meyer's trance-like gaze, and then leaned slightly to the left to get a view of the blanket which had captured the troubled man's attention. The faces, even those of the women, fashioned by the weaver, reminded Henry of the four sons at the Passover table: the evil, the foolish, and wise, and the simple ones. Was his host concerned that his own son might fall into one of the three negative types? Underlying their anxiety about their child was certainly an element of guilt, which they were reluctant to admit. Mrs. Meyer realized it was time to end all this brooding about their own woes, so she called to Bea in a bird-like crescendo, "B-e-a, is the cake ready?"

Shortly after, Bea rushed three generous portions of the dark brown desert, spotted throughout with orange specks and topped by fluffy white icing.

"I made it myself with the help of my natural food cookbook," interjected

Mrs. Meyer, wanting to let her husband and guest know that it was not below her dignity or time to enter a kitchen.

"Darling, it's thick, just the way I like it."

"Yes, ma'am, it's really tasty."

"Well, I am glad you two like it. It's very healthy for you too. It's quite high in vitamins A and D, you know."

"Then I shouldn't have to worry about finding my way home in the dark. I probably should leave pretty soon to make it back to Brooklyn by subway."

"Well, let's move back to the living room for an aperitif."

Henry, who was unaccustomed to being served alcoholic beverages, had been loosened up somewhat by having been embarrassed by being offered a strong drink by a "little ol' lady" earlier this summer. So without commenting on the adult offer, he walked between his hosts on their way to the large room with the spectacular night view. As they passed the corner to the living room, Henry caught sight of some small masks and statues, which he had missed before the automatic, focused lights from the ceiling cast a direct beam on their pedestal. He recognized the typical Olmec features in this jadeite, greenish-gray mask with its upward, slanting eyes and flared upper lip and downturned mouth. It had perforations in the earlobes and above the ears. This baldheaded piece looked as though it had died vomiting but was now happy in its deathly repose. From his position on the couch across from the entranceway, Henry's eye was torn between this bewitching talisman and the high concrete wall of the United Nations. Soaring into the night, the wall was lit by the thousands of blurry bright windows from the surrounding buildings.

The hostess poured three small, thick vase-like glasses with orange liqueur. Henry had never before imbibed this sweet, somewhat stringent beverage. He sipped it slowly. As the husband and wife peered at his persona, Dr. Meyer said, "Whatever decision you make—and I hope it will be the course that I suggested this evening—just make sure that it's the clearest, best thought-out decision you've ever made."

"Doctor, that I promise you."

"Henry, be true to yourself. Don't neglect how you feel. Do the right thing."

"Mrs. Meyer, I'll let you know what I decide and why tomorrow. Thanks for the splendid evening. You really have a magnificent home here."

"We've worked hard for it," Dr. Meyer reminded him. "It didn't come easily. It has been paid for with a high price."

After he finished his first after-dinner-drink, a sticky sweet almond-tasting concoction, Henry felt full and somewhat light-headed as he and the Meyers said their goodbyes.

When he stepped out of the hermetically sealed structure, the humid, warm air stroked his face like a soft flannel blanket on a late summer evening. The office workers, tourists, and diplomats had evacuated Turtle Bay, and the few remaining pedestrians in the area resembled straggling ants on the outskirts of an enormous hill. Henry took a bus across town and hopped down into the tunnel for the Brooklyn subway. His eyelids were like lead shutters that had to be propped up for safety against his strong urge to shut them.

An occasional image of a bedraggled alcoholic, a maintenance man in overalls, or a mini-skirted dancer accompanied by her companion in black jeans would fall into the corner of his eye before the train screeched into the station. He boarded a lightly-traveled dusty car headed for Brooklyn and gave in to his desire to doze. An unintentional nudge from the corpulent thigh of the immense cleaning woman carrying her metal pail and large wooden-handled mop and her odor of recently-smoked-cigarette-tobacco startled him from his deep sleep during which the car had filled up with a motley of ages, nationalities, and outfits. He asked the big woman how long it was to his stop and was informed to get off three exits from where they were at the moment.

CHAPTER 54

Stirred by Sarah Greenfield's morning preparation, Henry arose early the next morning. He was fresh from a profound slumber. His fatigue of the night before left him oblivious to his arrival at his hosts' home. It was as though he had been carried unconscious from the subway to the Greenfield's by the five hundred pound, muscular lady who had chosen to wrap her overflowing globules over his right leg. He chuckled at the silliness of his thought. He quickly showered, shaved, and tied his pack together before stepping in the kitchen.

"Thanks so much for putting me up, Mrs. Greenfield," Henry said enthusiastically upon entering her kitchen.

"But, Henry, I thought you'd be staying through Sunday," piped in David, who continued, "My buddies and me were goina' ride you out to Coney Island on our bikes."

"Gee, I'm sorry, David, but I'm worried about getting settled down for school for next year, so I think I'd better be leaving this afternoon. I'll take a rain-check, though."

"We've enjoyed having you. You're welcome back anytime."

"Same to you, Mrs. Greenfield. Please come up and visit me in Toronto next year. And thank Mr. Greenfield for me, too."

Both the young boy and the young man gobbled down their bowl of cream of wheat and milk as Sarah Greenfield finished her morning coffee. Soon they were on their respective paths, saying goodbyes with handshakes and "writes" and "sure you toos."

On the subway, Henry began folding a lined sheet of writing paper into four parts and began to calculate his expenses for the coming year. There seemed to be just enough to pay tuition, room, and board, if he could find a very cheap place to live. "Well, who knows, maybe something'll turn up, even if I don't have the working papers. I always meet people." He tucked the figures into his left back pocket and began to concentrate on the stops in Manhattan. This time he would try to transfer to a bus to get a different view. It looked as though the number five would deposit him near Penny's cousins' on the Upper West Side.

The morning was warm with a yellowish haze of particulates diffused throughout the air. Snuggled in this soupy atmosphere, Henry arrived to pick up Penny. She was floating with an unguarded excitement from anticipating her first trip to a foreign country with her closest friend who, perhaps, in the course of the excitement of the unknown and the adventure might evolve into her lover. It was a glorious morning, which was scheduled to be blessed by a visit to a shrine celebrating the beauty of twentieth century human art bestowed by the generosity of an American copper magnate, Solomon R. Guggenheim. Henry was relieved at Penny's letting down her shield of emotional defensiveness, which he experienced more as the blocking of a transparent wrap that could be easily pierced. They quickly arrived at Fifth and 89th Street by surface transportation.

On entering the inverted marshmallow, Penny purchased a brochure describing the building and its collection. As they wound their way from its top in a continuous, rounded sweep, Henry skimmed the booklet and read about its major features. The story recounted that the museum was the only one in New York, the architecture of which was considered as notable as its illustrious contents. It was the first Frank Lloyd Wright building in New York and had taken sixteen years to complete because the city officials had kept insisting on additional changes before accepting its design. Its benefactor had died and its architect was eighty-eight before the old museum for Non-Objective Art opened under its new name. To complicate matters, Solomon R. and Frank L. had quarreled bitterly during various periods of the museum's construction. This fact was disturbing to Penny's quiet world. "Why couldn't the greats get along?" she wondered. Only the abstractions of twentieth-century art and the renown of such frequently represented artists' names as Kandinsky, Chagall, Klee, and Picasso had been retained as valuable in Penny's memory from their required survey course in art history. Even such prominently displayed sculptors as Brancusi, Calder, and Yves Klein in the Guggenheim collection stood out as strange syllables somewhat humorously stored in the cute Finnish accent of their lecturer who had spoken from the podium of a vast functional university auditorium. However, they could not forget the name, Lipschitz, whose works adorned the recently laid-out sculpture garden of their alma mater.

Penny was not attracted to the earlier name of non-objective; nor did the contents of strongly cubist canvasses hold her attention. In front of Georges Braque's *Violin and Palette*, she commented in a flat, somewhat nasalized voice, "Why be non-objective? Isn't that just the opposite of what we've been trying to be?"

Henry tended to agree with her irritation at the chopping of the violin and music sheets which gave the impression of moving in so many different directions. He noted, "It says here that Braque was trying to get as close to the violin as he could through painting. This picture makes me feel that the violin was confusing to him and that he felt uncomfortable around the instruments he was painting. When he painted this piece, he was surrounded by musical instruments. Why does it make me feel so nervous and rushed then?"

"Maybe other people had the same reaction to it as you since he painted it in 1910."

They continued to walk down the ramps until they encountered Marc Chagall's work. They were both brought into the more human life forms and the Jewish *shtetl* themes for which their upbringing and identification had left them with more of an interest and enthusiasm. Although the portrait of Chagall's sister, Aniuta, with her dark oval eyes resembled Leah, their only Orthodox friend, they dwelled less on the similarity than the pity they recalled for their own friends' terrible acne, which distinguished the young woman they knew from the soft-skinned woman of the picture. Though Henry conjured that the wide, armed military man in *The Soldier Drinks* was probably up to no good—like eventually harming the small peasant lady who was dancing with another soldier by the samovar—Penny reminded him that the guide offered no support to his maligning all soldiers. Stuck in front of *The Flying Carriage*, Penny chuckled as she read the farfetched interpretations of the wooden house, the horse, and the cart. They seemed to be pulled upwards while the woman held her hand over her head. At the same time the hut looks as though it is burning. Penny just sighed, "I like the piece, especially the yellow orange in the sky, but I just don't understand why Chagall wants us to feel ecstasy on seeing it. I just can't."

"Oh, look at this one; it's great!"

"Which one?"

"It's called *Paris Through the Window*."

"It's pretty funny, isn't it? Look at the guy's head pointed in two directions—and his blue face and hand with a yellow heart. See that silly yellow cat with a human face and green bottom looking at the Eifel Tower lighted by that white band of light."

"Yeah. It's too much. There's everything in it. It makes me feel high like that man floating in space holding that white triangular parachute and passing through a red rectangle in the sky above the Paris roof tops."

"Oh, wow, that bowl of flowers is so pretty—the reds, the whites, the greens, the yellows, the brown vase, all those little leaves and petals. It's so delicate."

"You know, that one called *Peasant Life*, with the hunchbacked man with a whip in his hand and the sad-looking girl with her head bent together under the cows, has to be the opposite of the cheerful Paris scene. It makes me feel something for the peasantry I never did for them in all those non-judgmental courses in anthro."

"I think you mean that he makes their lives look harsh."

And so they continued to have fun commenting on the scenes depicted or the colors or shapes that Chagall had etched on their feelings when they viewed one of his works of art. Occasionally they stood in awe, as before the *Green Violinist*, and learned about how Chagall had been commissioned to design the sets and costumes for the State Jewish Kamerny Theater in Moscow. They absorbed that he had represented Jewish music by the violinist, drama by a wedding jester, dancing by a buxom woman, and literature by a copyist of the Torah.

Proceeding within this enclosure of beauty that had to shut out the noise, foul air, and the muggy sun to celebrate the lovely in this ugly century, they arrived at the works of Wassily Kandinsky.

Penny briefed them on the widely traveled Kandinsky He was of a Mongolian and Russian Orthodox background, had done a doctorate in law and economics before going to Munich to study painting. They marveled at the progression of his works while they grasped their significance in relation to their own studies and taste. From his *Landscape with Factory to the Sancta Francisca* to the *Painting with a White Border*, they began to understand and appreciate the art of this century.

"Finally, it's beginning to make sense to me—modern painting I mean—O.K., he is trying to get away from painting the colors, lines, and shapes we all can immediately identify, and, instead, to communicate abstract ideas and intense feeling."

"Henry, it's so fascinating to see how it fits into the whole course of his life. That's something I think we miss on those choppy little quarter courses we take. The ideas about the foreign societies and cultures that we're studying aren't being presented as the products of real people. It's as though they're like the salt that people need in a certain amount that can be bought at any supermarket. What's so funny about that is that our profs all have their little quirks which they pretend do not have any bearing on their ideas but really do. They pretend that iodized and sea salt taste alike, but they don't!"

"Yep, you're on to something. Look right here. It says Kandinsky wrote *Concerning the Spiritual in Art*. I didn't recognize that he was trying to depict St. George, a troika, a dragon or serpent. But does it make any difference? I think he would be glad that I feel the musical-like quality of his squiggly yellow or blue line. I don't think he'd care if I couldn't guess he meant one as a target, aggressive and round, and the other as the heavenly sound of a pipe organ. But I do sense something wonderful, and I think he'd be glad about that."

From the moment they had begun to get excited about Kandinsky, Penny's generally lightly-held distance from things began to wrest from her monotone voice. In front of the purples, blues, pink, orange, red, lavender, and yellow circles, superimposed on or outside of one another in a myriad of positions on a charcoal background, the couple entered into a meditative trance, just grunting "um, huh."

"It's strange how he ended up being so popular in Russia just after the Revolution and was permitted to set up museums all over the country, but then left for a position to teach at the Bauhaus in Germany's Weimar Republic. But it's no surprise that the Gestapo closed down the Bauhaus. That's why he had to spend his last years in Paris."

"No, it's not so strange. With his history, his innovations jive with the spirit of New York. It's not strange because whenever people become intolerant of new ideas and artists' freedom, the general society, and particularly its minorities, suffer. But, you know, New York is hated in most parts of the States for the very reason Kandinsky is proudly put on display in such style here. You think that down South where I grew up or in most of the middle of big America they'd understand or like his wild ideas or colors or even admit he's spiritual? Our suburban conformity is pretty damn oppressive too."

After Penny thought she had inspired Henry on a high lauding America's open-mindedness, there he went again, downgrading her untainted praise of the good ol' USA's freedom. Henry regretted his uncontrolled outburst because he sensed at once that he had made her clam up once more and this had not been his intent. So, his outburst spoiled their tour of the section on Paul Klee except for the *Contact of the Two Musicans*' almost cartoon childlike munchkins eliciting a crack of a smile on Penny's blank face. Neither the bright pastels of Frantisek Kupka's *Nude* nor Fernand Leger's contrasting shapes in *Woman Holding a Vase*; not the *Yellow Cow of Franz Marc*, almost like a painting from Mexico's anthropoligical museum; not Joan Miro's *Prades, the Village* moved her sullen hurt. Her openness to Kandinsky's abstractions was not displayed in front of Moholy-Nagy's work with its geometric play in plastic or in oil. She whisked by Mondrian's colorful compositions and showed only curt attention in the presence of Picasso's *Mandolin and Guitar*. Henri Rousseau she found silly and Egon Schiele depressive. Her quickly paced brushing aside the greats was slowed down only in front of George Pierre Seurat's soft impressionistic *Farm Women at Work*.

Penny's pique at Henry's new-found uncontained, unrestrained hypercriticalness found rest only in front of Amadeo Modigliani's *Portrait of a Student*. She stood enamoured by the long neck and nose, oblique ears, neatly-parted hair and oval head of this handsome young man. Henry could not help noting to himself, *You can't see his eyes. He has an almost feminine straight composure. She can admire him at a distance without risking to be shaken by unpredictable emotions. I bet that's why she likes him.*

After sitting quietly in the presence of this portrait, Penny read the short blurb on this Italian-Jewish artist's life of poor health, poverty, unhappy love affairs, and drug abuse. She didn't share the facts with Henry, who was looking at his other works. Instead, she recollected her cool and requested matter-of-factly, "Let's go."

CHAPTER 55

They rushed from the modernistic, concrete tent of meeting to pick up their belongings at Penny's cousins on the edge of Morningside Heights before descending upon the Port Authority Bus Terminal. In the transition from high culture to low the steel and concrete beams around them fixed their images like the geometric lines of the modernistic brush strokes on the canvasses of the Guggenheim's collection.

As they quickly purchased their tickets for Montreal, they were informed that there was a coach departing from downstairs in an hour. Anxious to absorb as much of the city as they could before leaving, they deposited their bag and backpack into the pay metal locker in the plain, functional space where everything was bolted to the floor. Suddenly, Henry remembered that he had promised the Meyers to call them, but, instead, to avoid a possible confrontation, he resolved to write them a note on the bus to inform them of his decision to go to Canada. With the onslaught of a busload of shoppers, Penny and he were caught up in the brisk flow that led out of the door onto 41st Street and 8th Avenue. From the corner they trotted over to the bright signs and history of the theater district, which captured their attention less than the not-so-muffled calls of "joints, real cheap, acid, speed, horse, smack or whatever you want." Penny felt assaulted by the outstretching of arms and the shrill whispers. The men and women whose trade was in their own flesh neither revolted nor shocked her usual proper self. Nonetheless, she wanted out of here quickly. The time was hurrying by, and she did not have enough of it to do a proper tour. The questions, *Should these characters be permitted to do their own thing as long as it doesn't hurt anybody else in an immediate way, or does society have to put its foot down at a certain point when it foresees that it will be harmed by their activity in the future?* rolled through Henry's mind more as spontaneous observations to-be-explored at a later date. Hastily, Penny looked up to Henry and shouted above the din, "How many minutes do we have left?"

"About a half hour."

"Let's get out of here, O.K.?"

He sensed her anxiety, and he wanted to move too. "Sure, Pen, it sort of gets to you."

They hurried back to the station. The tiles of the largest bus terminal in the world reflected an arc of a bubble-like rainbow. "At least they scrub the place," Penny remarked as they stooped downward to withdraw their luggage from the aluminum door just above the polished floor on which the cinders of a recently tossed butt had stained it a yellowish brown. Henry swung his own backpack over his shoulder and then picked up Penny's light green Samsonite bag in his right hand.

Wanting to poke some fun at Henry's contradictions, Penny found the courage to joke, "I thought you revolutionaries hated big museums and wanted all their money to go to those little store front places where 'the people' could display their art. You really managed to get off on the Guggenheim."

"First of all, I'm not necessarily a revolutionary. I think any system has to be constantly pressured to make for greater equality and a better life for all of its people. And secondly, just because I think neighborhood museums should get some money doesn't mean that I'm for tearing down the Guggenheim. You just got pissed off at my pointing out that liberalism isn't the in thing all over the good ol' USA. Truce, O.K.? You've been too nice to me to be on my case just when we are nearly ready to leave."

"Truce," she smiled as they trudged downstairs where people were congregating in a long line leading to a glass door in front of the underground loading places for the buses. There were several people with dark, almost shiny black hair and not a few deep carrot red-heads with yellow, creamy freckles. The screeches from outside blocked hearing their speech.

The glass door opened and the gas and honking diffused into the artificially lighted and maintained interior. Now it was Henry's turn to shove their luggage into the large, silvery container in the bowels of the vehicle. There was no more space for thought.

Printed in the United States
40031LVS00004B/1-78

9 781413 749144